# THE HASTENING WIND

# THE
# HASTENING
# WIND

BY

EDWARD GRIERSON

ALFRED A. KNOPF
1953
NEW YORK

*c. 2*

*L. C. catalog card number: 53–6843*

THIS IS A BORZOI BOOK
PUBLISHED BY ALFRED A. KNOPF, INC.

FIRST AMERICAN EDITION

*Published in Great Britain in 1953 as* THE LILIES AND THE BEES

B L

IS IT FAR TO GO?

*Ask the hastening wind,*
*The fainting star.*

C. DAY LEWIS, *Poems, 1943–1947*

THIS STORY IS NOT HISTORY: the only claim I make for it is that I have not consciously allowed any invented incidents of plot to distort characters or motives.

I would ask no more than that the sketches I have drawn here of the First Consul, of his stepdaughter, of Talleyrand, Fouché, and that prince of agents-provocateurs, Méhée de la Touche, should do them no more violence than Sir Arthur Conan Doyle offered to the Emperor, or Dumas to d'Artagnan. I would hope that, if my characters were to come to life and read this book, they would recognize—not themselves (for that would be asking too much of their tolerance)—but at least each other.

*Harrogate*

# The Characters

NAPOLEON BONAPARTE, *First Consul of France*

HORTENSE, *his stepdaughter*

LOUIS BONAPARTE, *brother of Napoleon and husband of*
*Hortense*

TALLEYRAND, *the Foreign Minister*

JOSEPH FOUCHÉ, *Senator and ex-Minister of Police*

COUNCILLOR RÉAL, *Fouché's successor*

DUROC ⎫
  ⎬ *Servants of the First Consul*
SAVARY ⎭

DIANE DE FLORIAN, *maid-of-honour to Hortense*

MORILLAC, *servant to Louis Bonaparte*

CADOUDAL, called Georges, *leader of the royalist conspiracy*

CHARLES, VICOMTE DE BELLAC ⎫
  ⎪
MÉHÉE DE LA TOUCHE  ⎬ *members of the royalist*
  ⎪  *conspiracy*
QUERELLE ⎭

1803–4    PARIS, NORMANDY

# THE HASTENING WIND

SECRETLY LANDING on the coast of France, young Charles de Bellac joins in a daring endeavor to overthrow Napoleon and restore the monarchy. It is the Year XII of the Republic. The fervors and frenzies of the Revolution have subsided, decorum has returned, and in the great salon at Saint-Cloud, under the watchful eyes of Napoleon, a new court is rehearsing quadrilles. In a Paris teeming with foreign agents and police spies, in boudoirs and dark country lanes, in desperate corners where a brave man can trust only in his sword, the Vicomte pursues his dangerous enterprise.

# *Chapter One*

T HE AUTUMN NIGHT HAD FALLEN AS the frigate *Vincejo* edged slowly in towards the coast of France; so thickly did the heavy banks of cloud obscure the moon that watchers on the cliffs would barely have caught the glimmer of her sails or the ripple of her wake through the dark and oily sea. It was remarkable with what silence and certainty she moved. There was no sound of her progress beyond the creaking of her masts and spars, the slap of the swell against her timbers, and an occasional voice calling the soundings from the bows, so muffled in the mist that it might have arisen from the bosom of the sea:

"Eight deep. Eight deep."

The *Vincejo* slid on her way into the darkness. There was no light anywhere to tell her crew that they were on their course, no glimmer out of the void to warn them of the sheer white cliffs, three hundred feet and more in height, that stretched before them from Le Tréport to Dieppe; the sea, dark as pitch except where the flank of some wave reflected a gleam of shrouded moonlight, might have stretched into infinity on every side.

"Eight deep. Quarter less eight. And a half seven now."

The Captain, standing among a group of officers on the quarterdeck, peered intently into the night. He knew this coast; he had made the trip a dozen times, ghosting his ship in to her anchorage in enemy waters close against the cliffs through perils that would have daunted the most courageous. It was natural that he should take a special pride in all that went to the perfecting of this adventure—his own skill in navigation; the crew that translated his commands into instant action; the ship herself that answered with the sympathy of a living thing to every order, to every breath of wind or touch of helm.

"And a half seven. And a quarter seven. By the mark seven."

This was the shelf; beyond it a gentler slope would lead them in to shore, broken only to the west of Biville cliff by an outcrop of rock not marked on the Admiralty charts, but of the presence of which he was aware from personal experience. Soon they would see the cliff lights that his friends had set. Yes, there they were: small pinpoints winking at him out of the darkness, mysteriously suspended in space above his head like truant stars. He shook his head, rebuking himself by his own immaculate standard for the fact that they were not directly in line ahead.

"Mr. Armstrong, get those lights in line."

"Aye, aye, sir."

The *Vincejo* ghosted on. Now the coast could be seen as a more solid wall of darkness towering up towards the sky; a paler edge showed where the moon, penetrating the film of the cloudbank, touched with a fugitive silver gleam the knife-crest of the cliffs themselves.

"Deep six," the voice of the leadsman called. There seemed to be a sharper edge to it, the words rebounding from the land mass instead of losing their resonance in the wastes of sea.

Another light was showing now—from shore level—a light that winked its message to the waiting officers on the frigate's decks.

"Signals all's well, sir."

"Good. Prepare to heave to, Mr. Hawkins. Mr. Armstrong, bring her round."

For the surf along the beach could now be seen, a listless surf that cast only the faintest line of spume. It was child's play coming in on the ebb on such a night, but there had been other nights when his heart had almost failed him, when faith in his charts had dimmed, as he had seen the wave-crests tumbling shoreward and heard the thunder of their breaking on that lonely coast.

"Round. Steady, steady. Let her ride now, Mr. Hawkins, let her ride."

So silently was it all done that hardly a murmur would have reached the shore, where only the continual flickering of the beach light told of human activity in that pall of darkness.

"Lower the longboat, Mr. Hawkins."

"Aye, aye, sir."

Captain Wright glanced round, checking his position with the cliff lights, seemingly so close now that they might have been hoisted at his masthead, and as he did so the tension on his face relaxed and he nodded approvingly to himself. A good, neat job of seamanship. He would do it again, how many times?

Perhaps one day the wind or currents would defeat him and the *Vincejo* would be ripped to pieces on the rocks; perhaps his anchorage would be discovered or betrayed, and he would find himself under a battery of guns. It was all in the fortune of war, and he could do no more than lay his ship where he was ordered, trusting in his skill and his good fortune, the loneliness of the coast and the darkness of the night.

"Bring the French gentlemen on deck," he said.

When they joined him a few moments later, he looked them over with the same careful scrutiny he would have given the sweepings of a press gang—two men who matched the conspiracy of which they were a part, not only in their resolute manner but in the long black cloaks they wore, clothes so well suited to romance and so ill suited to the physical task ahead that for all his many anxieties he could not help but smile.

That side of them appealed to the Captain's ironic sense of humour, but there was another side that called to his admiration and to that sense of adventure, strong within him, which was one day to lead him to his death. Provided nothing untoward occurred he would be under way within the hour, and next day, if the wind held fair, would be home on English soil. But these royalist agents of the exiled Bourbons were going into the throat of danger—up a perilous cliff path, through a countryside swarming with Bonapartist police and troops, into isolated farmhouses where their hosts would start at every knock at the door, and so to the great city, the stronghold of their enemies. Only brave men would venture there, and he saluted them—in intention only, for it got no further than a stiff inclination of the head.

"M. Touch."

Méhée de la Touche returned the bow more formally. A travelled man, with the appearance of the professional adventurer, he knew the English well and was used to Anglicized versions of his name.

"Well, sir," Captain Wright continued, "this is not your first landing, and I need say no more. Arrangements, I understand, will be exactly as before. Troché is to meet you at the cliff face; he signals that all is well. Beyond that is no concern of mine, so I wish you good-day and a pleasant journey. And to you, sir"—turning to the Vicomte de Bellac, the younger of the two men, whose name he did not attempt, for he was sparing with his courtesies.

Both the Frenchmen bowed. It was their dismissal, a typical dismissal from a member of this laconic island race that greeted them on arrival and sped them on departure with unfailing politeness and a complete absence of enthusiasm. But that it was kindly meant was obvious from the look in the Captain's eye; approval and comradeship shone there, with—yes—just a suspicion of the look of the undertaker as he covers up the corpse.

Mr. Hawkins, now in charge of them, was courtesy itself, but even less articulate. He spoke no French, and disbelieved, in spite of evidence to the contrary, that his guests could speak his language; so he sat them in the place of honour in the longboat—in a rather dedicatory manner as to men about to die—and smiled at them, even while he swore under his breath at his oarsmen as they lumbered the heavy craft laboriously through the sea.

Straight towards that flickering light they went; it grew suddenly out at them, held by a dim outline of a figure on the beach, and next instant, with a crunching and a grinding, they had made their landfall and were being handed out by Mr. Hawkins, who gripped them in the process as though he feared that they were so unhandy as to fall flat on their faces in the sea. Even at the last he spoke no coherent word, but grunted, a companionable sound that left an unaccountable warm feeling in their hearts when the plash of the longboat's oars had faded into the silence of the night.

"M. de la Touche."

The man with the lamp had advanced, holding it above his head so that it cast its beams on the two cloaked figures at the water's edge.

"Yes, Troché."

"And M. le Vicomte de Bellac, is it not?"

"It is."

"Good. Then follow me, messieurs. All is quiet; there is no alarm. Nevertheless, it is best that we move quietly. There are soldiers in Tréport, ladies in Dieppe, and though it is a cold, uninviting night—who knows?"

"Where do we go now?" the young Vicomte asked.

The man with the lantern pointed up the cliffs.

"Along a path."

"A path up there?"

"Yes, you will see. To call it a path is perhaps an exaggeration. A track for goats is better. Monsieur will have the assistance of a rope."

All the time he had been talking, Troché had been guiding them towards the cliffs, which could now be seen quite clearly, a white wall rising sheer from the narrow beach.

"If you will follow me, messieurs, with this gentleman who is new to the path immediately behind me. M. de la Touche has some experience and will not mind bringing up the rear."

"I shall regard it as an honour."

"Monsieur has not left his wit behind," Troché replied, passing a length of rope into the Vicomte's hands and testing it with a sudden vigorous pull. "This is anchored at the crest. It is a long climb—and a long fall. I recommend short steps, calmness, and not too great a reliance on the rope. M. le Vicomte has a head for heights?" And having asked his question, Troché began to move cautiously forward along what appeared to be a narrow ledge cut into the cliff, keeping his body pressed well forward and his eyes fixed on the ground ahead.

Steadily, without uttering a word, they climbed; there was no noise but their laboured breathing, the murmur of the sea, and the rattle of stones dislodged by them in passing to fall with a muffled clatter on to the beach beneath. It was very disconcerting to hear that rustling and that fall, and to count the time between them; it conjured up the most unpleasant picture of their position—flies without wings on a gigantic wall. Perhaps it was fortunate for them that it was very dark and that there was no temptation to look downwards to see how much progress they had made, to where a grey arc of surf alone would have met their gaze, expanding and contracting with the motion of the waves like a figure in a dream. But, following Troché's lead, the newcomers did not glance down. They could gain some idea of progress by the dying whisper of the sea, and, taking encouragement from this they moved slowly on, their vision bounded by the bulk of the man in front, all the efforts of their will concentrated on the action of putting one foot before the other on the narrow, uneven ledge.

Troché, being the soul of the expedition and its eyes and ears as well, had to find time for other things. He could see dimly above him the sharp hill-crest where it was etched against the sky, and the topmost signal lantern, shining out at him from the hollow where it was hidden so that its beam was only visible from the direction of the sea; he was on the point of congratulating himself on the ascent when that sixth sense of the countryman gave him warning, so that he stopped in his tracks and flattened his body against the cliff. His companions, brought suddenly to the halt, imitated him as best they could; they were sensible enough to ask no questions, but waited silently with that calmness that comes to those who are held in the vice of danger without the power of influencing their fate.

At first they heard nothing except the distant scraping of water on the shingle, a sound infinitely remote, then a padding, rustling noise arose above them, and a voice spoke quite distinctly, springing on them with paralysing suddenness out of the darkness of the night:

"There's a ship, I tell you."

Another voice replied: "A ship! What nonsense, Raoul! What would a ship be doing here?"

"Smuggling goods or émigrés or damned English spies. Use your eyes, man. There!"

A pause ensued during which it could be imagined that the two men on the cliff top were straining their eyes into the void. It was all the party on the path could do to keep from imitating them in peering downwards to catch the glint of the *Vincejo*'s sails. But they lay still.

"Where? Just show me where," the second voice was asking; and it was easy to catch the disappointment in the tones of Raoul as he replied: "It's gone now. I can't see it either. It *was* there."

"So now it's gone! A queer kind of ship to sheer away like that! One bottle too many, if you ask me."

Raoul laughed—rather a puzzled sound. It was clear enough from both their voices that the diagnosis had been a just one—soldiers in Le Tréport, women in Dieppe, as Troché had remarked, and a tavern somewhere between the two.

"Well, come on, then; we'd best be going. Don't go so

near the edge, man. D'you want to swim and look for it?"

The voices ceased, the padding sound of feet was heard again—and then a sudden exclamation. De la Touche and de Bellac felt the guide in front of them stiffen with a sharp involuntary motion.

"What are you doing now?"

"I've tripped over something," Raoul said.

"What the devil, he's tripping now! It's a marvel you didn't trip yourself into the sea."

"Well, there was something there."

"The ground, you blockhead."

"Why not a rope?"

"First a ship and now a rope!" said the second voice with a fine display of irony. "It'll be fairies next."

"I've a good mind to go back and look for it."

"And if I wasn't a good friend, I'd let you do it. Good food for the gulls you'd make. Come on, now. Wine and women don't agree with you. Come on before you break your neck and that poor slut Françoise's heart."

Tensely clinging to the cliff face, the three men listened to the argument; heard the hesitating feet, the slap of a friendly hand, and then the rustling, padding noise again as Raoul, still protesting, was led away. It was some time before they found the strength or courage to raise themselves from the positions into which they had fallen at the sound of danger, or to begin the last steep ascent towards the crest, which disclosed itself without warning in a sudden lightening of their horizon.

But when at last they had left the cliff face and were standing on the bare plateau that crowned its brow the darkness seemed to close in on them once more, and they followed blindly behind their guide, moving now in a silence so profound that they half expected to hear the voice of the *Vincejo* as she wafted out to sea. They could distinguish no landmarks in the darkness, but Troché led on unhesitatingly over the featureless expanse of down, a stoical certainty in every line of him and in his flat-footed peasant's gait, so that it seemed no more than a materialization of his will when a darker shadow loomed across their path and they saw before them an old dark house tucked in a fold of ground—a secretive house around whose eaves and in the surrounding belt of trees the wind was whispering, a sound as stealthy as a warning to those who travelled from the sea.

# Chapter Two

A S SOON AS THEY HAD ENTERED THE
farm the three men reacted, each in his individual way, to the night's adventure: Troché began
methodically to trim the lamps, the young
Vicomte looked around him at the doors and windows with
a tactician's eye, while Méhée de la Touche, who knew the
security of the house, asked questions, for his exertions had
made him talkative.

"Well, Troché, how is it since I left? How is it at Paris?"
Their host murmured a noncommittal answer.

"No, but you must tell me. Remember, I've been away
and have no news. Things change rapidly nowadays, and for
all I know Bonaparte may have turned into a Robespierre or
an Emperor. No? Still First Consul? And Cadoudal and our
other good friends are still at large?" He said this with a
smile, conjuring up the strange union of these two names,
to cover both of which Paris itself did not seem quite large
enough.

"They're safe enough," Troché replied, shielding the
young flame of the lamp, which began to throw long pulsing
shadows along the walls. He was perhaps the only man in
France who was not surprised by the continued presence of

his leader in the capital. That Cadoudal—Georges, as he was popularly called—the almost legendary hero of royalist resistance, should have been in Paris would have struck the First Consul and the numerous agents of his police as fanciful in the extreme. It was hard enough for anyone to escape official notice in a town that had become hag-ridden with secret services, and Georges was unmistakable—a huge bulllike figure with pendulous, enormous jowls. Bonaparte himself—little 'Boney,' with his cocked hat and green Guards' coat—could as reasonably have been hidden in some leafy London suburb, where his presence would not have been more dangerous to established government.

Méhée, for his part, understood this irony very well.

"And he's been there for three months. He must have a talisman. What about the others? Is Querelle still with him? Devotion incarnate"—this as an aside for the benefit of the Vicomte, who was not acquainted with the minor figures in the plot. "Devotion so incarnate that it'll end by selling him."

"Yes, Querelle's there," Troché replied, a trifle more warmly, for in this matter he agreed. "And Picot and Le Bourgeois, and Bouvet de Lozier."

"And where do they live now, this circus?"

"At Chaillot. Except for de Lozier, who has a rich mistress."

"Oho! So we make ourselves comfortable! It's quite clear that this conspiracy improves. You will tell me next that we've achieved something; that General Pichegru's arrived and General Moreau's joined us."

The Vicomte, who had not taken too kindly to this badinage, pricked up his ears. These were names he knew: Pichegru, the exiled conqueror of Holland; Moreau, Bonaparte's only possible rival in the affection of the armies, Moreau the disaffected, living in sullen retirement from the Consular Court.

But Troché, turning from the lamp, slowly shook his head.

"Nothing's done. Moreau won't stir. He distrusts Georges. It might have been different if the Comte d'Artois himself had come."

"Yes," Méhée agreed. "These generals, however Jacobin, are susceptible to princes of the blood. We can't expect the King, with *his* flesh and gout, to hoist himself up Biville cliff, but Artois would do it splendidly. One day—perhaps next time—he will come."

"I hoped tonight," Troché said.

"Ah, my friend, but don't imagine that you worked in vain. Tonight has been a very special night. Tonight, Troché, you have brought back to France someone of the highest importance, someone close to the First Consul, or rather to his wife and to his stepdaughter, Hortense, someone with the entrée to his family." And Méhée looked at the young Vicomte with an expression that showed that he was restrained only by sensibility from adding that the entrée was also to their beds.

"They were my friends," the young man said in tones that conveyed a warning. "They were my benefactors."

But Troché, who was of a practical turn of mind, had been impressed by these credentials.

"Close to Bonaparte, that's where we want to be. Georges got near him once—do you remember?—during the truce after the campaign in Morbihan. Bonaparte sent for him and tried to charm him, all sweet reason and republicanism, but he could have saved his breath. Georges saw the tyrant in him. D'you know what he said—but later, unfortunately, after his chance was gone? 'I should have strangled him with my bare hands.' He could have done it too."

There was a pause, during which it could be seen that the Vicomte had quite failed to react with favour to this program, and Méhée put the matter into words:

"I think you're suggesting a barbarism, Troché."

"A barbarism! To kill him! He would certainly kill us."

Méhée bowed his head at this reminder—no very comforting one. But, as he explained, Bonaparte was a usurper and a man of blood. "Whereas legitimacy, like ours," he went on, embroidering his words in a way that was hardly suited to his company, "does well to be legitimate."

"It's certain," the Vicomte said, pointing the text in his forthright way, "that I've not come to France to assassinate the man."

But Troché's work induced a certain cynicism: "The last time I heard those words, monsieur, was from someone who about a month later was guillotined for an attempt. Let us go into the kitchen. The food will be ready now."

That night and the following day the royalists spent in the farm, which even in the autumn sunshine kept its secretive, forbidding character; an old house in the Norman style, first cousin to the timbered barns that hemmed it in, and making only this concession to human vanity, that its occupants lived in rooms instead of stalls. No strangers approached, and the two young men were able to exercise themselves in the stockyard and the orchard, a sad little orchard, its trees so buffeted by the Channel gales that their fruitfulness seemed less a gift of nature than a defiance of it. "Note the ground," Méhée said. "We may have to return here to meet other travellers from the sea." And the Vicomte did as he was advised, memorizing the landmarks of the barns and massive well-shaft, and marking the direction of the farm tracks that led inland towards the long meadow and the sunken ribbon of a road.

That night, as soon as darkness had fallen, they received from Troché directions for the next stage of their journey to the capital, a ride of some forty miles across the meadows and cornlands of the Norman countryside to the first *maison de confiance* on the royalist secret route—also a reminder of realities that their quiet day of rest might have been in danger of dispelling: "It's not the same house that M. de la Touche remembers from an earlier time. That's a house of confidence no longer: it's a ruin—all that the police left of it."

At ten o'clock the horses were brought from the stable, and Troché, whose optimism seemed notably to have diminished now that he was no longer to be in charge, was ready with much daunting but excellent advice. "Avoid towns and villages, you know that. But avoid roads and fords and bridges too. They're guarded. Swim the horses over rivers. If you lose your way, lie up in woods till nightfall. There! May God be with you." And he turned abruptly from them with the air of a man who has added the last refinement to his labour, not bothering to watch the figures of the horsemen merge into the shadows of the night.

They rode silently for a while; indeed, they had reached the crest of the downs and were entering the woods before Méhée gave his valediction in return:

"That Troché! An original!"

"I trust so," the Vicomte said. "I trust very much that he's original and alone in his beliefs."

Méhée was puzzled.

"What beliefs? Oh! his ethics? The ethics of assassination?"

"Yes."

"You can take my word for it, he is."

"I've Artois' word for it too," the Vicomte said, pursuing his train of thought. "I've his word that nothing dishonourable will be attempted. Rebellion's one thing—assassination is another. Well, I can be frank with you. You know my business; you know I carry letters—appeals, if you like—from the King and Artois to Bonaparte. If Bonaparte rejects them, then, within limits, I'm at Cadoudal's disposal. But to begin with mine is a kind of embassy, and I don't think Troché for one agrees the protocol."

Méhée laughed softly and reining in his horse, pressed closer to the Vicomte's side.

"As to Troché, don't concern yourself—an invaluable man but a subordinate. But as for your embassy, my friend . . ."

He paused.

"Yes?" the Vicomte said.

"You *should* concern yourself. You should take care to proceed through diplomatic channels—through the most diplomatic channels, your friends, the womenfolk of Bonaparte. Anything more direct might have its disadvantages, for since the conspiracy of St. Régent the police—and Bonaparte himself—have shown the most regrettable alacrity in recognizing spies."

"And the ladies?" asked the Vicomte with a smile.

"Ah! If it were not for the delicate matter of your friendship for them, Charles, I would tell you that alacrity in women always takes a kinder form." He waited to see how this pleasantry was received; then asked: "You've known them long?"

"Since I was sixteen. I knew Hortense when she was a schoolgirl in Mme Campan's academy at Saint-Germain.

Her mother was then in Paris." He added in a voice so low that Méhée scarcely heard him: "They saved my life. I would have been guillotined. You understand now why Troché's words disturbed me."

"They saved you! It's true, then, as people say, that they're secret royalists? They have at least royalist leanings?"

"And Bonapartist inclinations," replied the Vicomte, urging his horse into a canter. "They're good souls, they want the best for everyone—the King at Versailles, Bonaparte at the Tuileries, and a refuge for themselves at Malmaison. All they will get in the end is probably a grave for me."

On the second night of the journey Méhée expounded on the state of things in Paris, a necessary lesson, for the Vicomte had been absent from the city for five years and knew little of events there beyond the mere fact of the First Consul's rise. It was not easy for a man so placed to appreciate the success of the regime, its chauvinism, its formidable power; nor were the personalities of the courtiers surrounding Bonaparte much clearer. Indeed, it came as a considerable shock to Méhée, a political being to the bottom of his soul, to discover that in his friend's eyes M. de Talleyrand was no more than a renegade bishop and Joseph Fouché just a man who had been dismissed from the portfolio of the Police. "He will climb back, that one," was the opinion he confidently expressed. "The police have degenerated sadly under his successor; omniscient no longer, merely ubiquitous." Which brought him by gentle stages to the chances of the royalist conspiracy, and to the dominating, restless character of Georges.

"Describe him to me," the Vicomte said.

"I'll try. He's rather too solid for description. The body of an ox—imagine it—a barrel of a chest, monumental arms and hams. And then his face—a huge, bloated face with overhanging chops and a little pig's snout of a chin between them, frizzy hair like a St. Domingan's, and sidewhiskers that curl inwards in two arcs across his face. A caricature of a face, but then look at his fine forehead and eyes. An original. Half priest, half brutal peasant who's picked up manners in England from the milords and a taste for fancy millinery. He dislikes privilege, he hates the nobles almost as badly as he hates Bonaparte; but for all that he's the best royalist of the lot."

In such talk the second and third nights were passed. They were now well clear of the dangerous region of the coast, travelling through a sparsely populated countryside of plains and meadows and low wooded hills. The *Vincejo* and their hour of peril on the cliff seemed very far away during these rides under the stars, these conversational hours when it seemed hard to credit that there was a city out ahead that they must enter, the capital of Bonaparte and the secret police. It all seemed a game, hardly to be dispelled when with the morning they would come upon the homesteads on the route, simple houses with their wells and meadows, and orchards on which the late fruit hung, utterly remote from the stir and violence of the world.

In such stir and violence Georges had lived from his youth up. For the first time the Vicomte heard the full tale of his leader's exploits: the early struggles, the gallant, hopeless duel in Morbihan with the overwhelming forces of the Revolution, the brief truce during which the two great antagonists had met. Now the battle was being joined again, a more secret battle that aimed at stirring up a new rebellion, a new Vendée in the very heart of France. "It will succeed too," Méhée said. "We have many assets: a group of dedicated men, a vast royalist tide that's running under the soil of the Consulate, disappointed generals like Moreau who have armies at their disposal, the support of England—and twenty million francs in gold."

These were pleasant reassurances. Refreshed by them, the Vicomte felt only the spur of adventure and no sensations of uneasiness as the dawn broke on the fifth morning of their journey, disclosing to them the spires and towers of Paris, the great shape of Notre-Dame riding like a ship above the Île de la Cité and the brown stubble of the plain.

## Chapter Three

TWO PHALANXES OF COURTIERS FACED each other across the great salon of the palace of Saint-Cloud. To the older men it must have seemed that 1780 had come again; there were the same tights and silk stockings, the same buckled shoes and dress swords that had graced the last years of the old regime; only a few incorrigibles in field uniform and boots, trailing long sabres in defiance of the new wind of fashion, reminded them that this was the year XII of the Republic One and Indivisible. It was amusing to see where this new democracy had led—to rows of courtiers lining the state apartments of the palace, a trifle clumsily perhaps (for sansculottism had been buried yesterday), a little at a loss in this finery, but recognizably courtiers, all the same, with their anxious, obsequious expressions.

Shortly the doors would open and the Revolution incarnate would walk in—a general turned politician, who would be an emperor within a year. Those who could remember the great days of monarchy might smile at this—even M. de Rémusat, now engaged in teaching this raw court its manners—but at Bonaparte himself no one would smile, even when he committed the solecism—an appalling one—of wearing a black cravat with his consular coat of purple velvet embroidered with cloth of gold. Towards him all eyes would turn humbly, obediently, imploringly, signalling their devotion—which was in some cases questionable—and their dependence—which was absolute. The ladies in their classical Greek gowns, the Jacobin soldiers flaunting their tricolour cockades, the diplomats and senators, the savants and the ministers, all would bow down as low as the chivalry of an earlier and more polished age had bowed before the Roi Soleil, for theirs was a true court, even though its members had just graduated from cellars and attics and the sergeants' mess; they were the court of the Revolution—the generals who had saved it, the politicians who had sold it, and Senator Fouché who would sell anything, including its successor, if he could.

This man stood apart from the throng of courtiers at the far end of the room. He regarded himself as in a class apart —and his fellows would have agreed with him, for in their eyes he was in that last hell peopled by fallen favourites. While he had been the all-powerful Minister of Police, he had been courted like a king; but now that he had fallen to the empty dignity of a senator, there was nothing to admire in this thin, ghostlike figure with the hooded lids and lacklustre, pale green eyes. Bonaparte had seen through him and had dispensed with him, that was the general opinion, and there was very little sympathy for Joseph Fouché, ex-Oratorian, ex-regicide, ex-terrorist, and ex-Minister. He could wait there as humbly as the rest, but if any crumbs fell from the consular table to this Lazarus of the Jacobins they, the courtiers, who had their ears close to the ground and their noses to the scent of favour, would be surprised.

Fouché knew what they were thinking and was glad to stand apart. He had his own ideas about preferment, which could not be judged from his impassive face; he waited, wrapped in that dignity peculiar to him, which triumphed over his bony figure, ill-fitting clothes, and unkempt hair. He was there to be seen, a reminder to the ruler of the land that the cleverest man in France was waiting in his ante-rooms for employment.

And now the doors at the far end of the apartment were opening. Two footmen appeared—less uneasy in their livery than many of the courtiers—and flung them wide. All eyes turned in their direction. It was the moment for which the servants of the old regime had waited each day at Versailles to be charmed by the grand entry of the king, an event never dulled by repetitions, for with all their faults the Bour-bons had known how to carry themselves like royalty.

The first part of the procession that now entered was sat-isfactory enough—M. de Talleyrand limping into the salon with that grand contemptuous manner that was one of his chief assets in the stucco world surrounding him. If there was a faintly apologetic air about him, only those trained in the nuances of irony would have noticed it; a raised eyebrow might tell M. de Rémusat that he found this court of clods entrancing, but the vast majority would only recognize the indomitable spirit of the old France in the body of this subtle servant of the new. Such was his grace that he made the transition seem natural, and it was no fault of his that the effect was spoilt as his master strode into the room.

Bonaparte was thirty-four. It required a real feat of imagi-nation to remember that the victor of Arcola and Lodi, Marengo and the Pyramids, the architect of the Concordat and First Consul of France for life, was so young a man; it was hard to see below the aura of the demigod the face, sharp and ascetic still, of olive colour, the thin body not yet filled out into its imperial maturity, the short legs, the abrupt, nervous movements of the man.

Bonaparte was not at his best in drawing-rooms. He wore his brilliant court dress, but he wore it with a very bad grace, as though regretting that he was not in his uniform of Colonel of the Light Infantry of the Guard; his cravat, in spite of the efforts of his valet, was already disarranged, and there were traces of snuff on his sleeve and collar. He looked thoroughly irritable and unhappy, for he was too adult a person to take pleasure in a mummery that he suffered because he believed it necessary to his status, and would have given almost every courtier in the room, and certainly all the ladies, for a company of grenadiers.

But the court was here for some purpose, and he must do his duty. He advanced in the wake of his Foreign Minister down the lane of lowered heads, stopping occasionally to speak to a man of his own choice—soldiers and savants—or of Talleyrand's ambassadors and diplomats. He rarely stopped opposite a woman, and when he did could find nothing affable to say, while for their part his ladies dreaded him, for he would be sure to find some gaucherie, some comment on the faults of a dress or the redness of a complexion. That they had minds to appeal to never occurred to him for a moment, for he had been brought up in the Corsican tradition, almost Oriental in its attitude to women, and believed that they had no place outside the drawing-room or the bed. Since at this time he was not recruiting mistresses, they sometimes wondered why he felt the need for speaking to them at all, not appreciating quite how low his opinions were, not only of the morality of women but of the sense of the entire human race. Mankind was led by toys, such was his belief; this court was his response to it, and his anger at this degradation peeped out through every word he spoke.

Behind him in impressive cavalcade came Cambacérès and Lebrun, Second and Third Consuls, each in his purple coat, two Lepiduses, the one bland and pompous with a cheerful, hedonistic face, the other like a dried-up attorney worrying over his bill of costs. It was sufficiently remarkable that these men should have worn the distinguishing costume that put them on a level with a man so overwhelmingly superior. It was just another illustration of Napoleon's guiding rule—the coats were toys, something for two incompetents to play with and imagine that they shared the power; though in fact Cambacérès and Lebrun were more realistic than he supposed, knowing their places and keeping them—at their master's heels as he moved slowly down the room. It so happened that the one enjoyed the glory of the uniform, the other the pleasure of the pay, and each was perfectly suited in his station.

Looking down the room from the entrance doors, it was possible to see the order of the procession reflected in the faces of the courtiers: excitement as Talleyrand approached, fulfilment as the First Consul spoke, reaction as his colleagues added their humble quota, and then, when all these had passed, something quite unexpected—smiles. For Mme Bonaparte was making the tour also.

Josephine was dressed in white; her slim, supple figure seemed to glide down the salon in contrast with her husband's nervous steps. She had spent hours in her dressing-room arranging the folds of her skirt, the ringlets of her hair, the set of the diamonds that glittered around her neck. The finished product could not be faulted by any standard; she was the perfection of elegance. Yet there was something more. All this glory, arranged with so much care, was carried with so easy a grace that everyone was charmed; her smile was sweet and unaffected, her manner gracious; she gave a meaning to all this ridiculous display, and made this company of self-seekers tolerable, since they were the setting for her grace and beauty.

So, forgetting for the moment to watch where the breath of favour was lighting in other quarters of the room, the courtiers smiled. The older men were seeing the royalist in her, Marie Rose Tascher de la Pagerie, born of an impoverished but noble family; the younger men, the woman, still beautiful with that languorous Creole charm that had attracted the lechery of Barras and the passion of young General Bonaparte, as well as of many others of whom one did not hear much nowadays; and if the ladies of the court were a little envious as they looked at the arbitress of fashion, that envy was more admiring than malicious and was the greatest of all tributes to the talents and character of Josephine.

Even Fouché smiled when she reached him in his corner of the salon, though it was not easy to read enthusiasms from any expression in those dull, glazed eyes. Talleyrand, the barometer of favour, had not even glanced at his old rival and brother beneath the skin—the First Consul had ignored him and Cambacérès had passed without a word. From all this it could be seen that his disgrace was absolute, and that being so, the attentions of a pretty woman would go no way to compensate a man who was as constant in his family life as he was fickle in his public one. Nevertheless, he did smile at Josephine, an old ally whom he had not yet found it expedient, or possible, to betray, and spared a second smile—rather a weaker edition—for the next lady in the suite, Josephine's daughter by her first marriage, Hortense de Beauharnais, now the wife of Louis Bonaparte, a young woman of small influence and less character, who had been much in his mind of late.

The Senator read her very well. Unhappy wives in general were of no interest, but when they were married to the great there might be profit in them. Rumours had surrounded this woman from the first—rumours of her shrinking from her husband, of Louis' jealousy and unkindness, even rumours of an incestuous attachment between her and Napoleon, her stepfather. Though almost devoid of salacious imagination, the Senator smacked his lips over the thought of that, for he had no cause to love the Bonapartes, and appreciated that scandal and rifts in the ruling family might be useful levers in his hands. Personally he did not believe a word of the grave charge they made. The girl was innocent, a pretty, affectionate creature who had been sacrificed on the altar of policy to one of the more odious of the Bonapartes. Looking at her, the Senator almost felt it in his heart to pity her, for he was not naturally a vicious man; but beyond the charms of the woman he could not for the life of him help seeing the future dupe—a distracting thought that did not add to her attractions.

Scandal, that was the way of it. Scandal had brought down the Bourbons, for they could say what they liked but the Affair of the Diamond Necklace had ruined Marie Antoinette and had been one of the major causes of the events of '89. And if a monarchy that had lasted close on a thousand years was so susceptible, how much the more so was the regime of this upstart, surrounded as he was by grasping relatives and light women. Morality, thought Fouché, was the weapon; it should certainly be added to the Liberty, Equality, and Fraternity that had been the watchwords of the Revolution and which this Corsican had turned into a mockery. Well, they would see. Perhaps one day in the shape of the young Hortense it might prove to be a stick to beat the Bonapartes, just as a Queen's weakness and extravagance had helped to drive poor Louis XVI from Versailles to the Place Louis Quinze beneath the guillotine.

They were going now. Bowing with his best grace, he watched them move from him up the room. How many lovers had that charming Creole taken in her life? No one would ever know. The voluptuous Barras had been one of the many with the entry to her bed, and then there had been that young officer, Captain Charles, with whom she had amused herself at the time of her husband's victories in Italy. She had lived wantonly in a dangerous time when promiscuity had seemed natural, but it was over now. And in spite of a background that would have disgraced a dozen Antoinettes, there was no denying that Josephine had come to be beloved; people had forgiven her; she was unassailable in virtue, Cæsar's wife who *was* above suspicion.

But Hortense was different. There was something defeated about the girl; one could see it in her eyes, in the droop of her head, even in the set of her back, which lacked the erect confidence of Josephine. Yet she was passionate enough, they said, and beautiful. Such a woman would inspire love and would yield to it, not experience it as her full-blooded mother had done throughout her life. Scandal or the appearance of scandal, either would do. For times had changed. Already there was the breath of a new Spartan strictness in the air, and the women, always the more sensitive, were beginning to cover up their bodies, a retreat from the fashions of that harlot Cabarrus and the other "*Sans Chemises*" of the Directory. Yes, the day of moral judgments was being reborn, and in its noon there would be no place for fallen women—or tripped ones—or for the men, no matter how high their place, who sheltered them. Perhaps even Bonaparte might be sorry then that he had left his ex-Minister of Police cooling his heels in unemployment.

For he, Fouché, had a plan, one that he could savour as he waited, head bowed, watching the parade of royalty as it moved back through the doors of the salon—first Talley-rand, whom he hated, then Napoleon, whom he envied, Cambacérès, Lebrun, pitiable shadows, and the women, un-witting allies in his plot.

# Chapter Four

JOSEPH FOUCHÉ DROVE BACK TO PARIS IN his coach, alone. Like Bonaparte, he was a fully adult individual, but he could not help recalling, as he lolled back among the cushions, the long road that he had come from the cells of the Oratorians to the possession of this magnificent equipage at which the people of the faubourgs stared in envy as it passed.

It was no empty show. This man, whose origins were obscure, who had slaved for a schoolmaster's pittance before graduating to be the butcher of the Revolution, was now one of the richest men in France. It was rumoured that on the occasion of his retirement from the Ministry he had received as a gift from Bonaparte the sum of 1,200,000 francs taken from the coffers of the police, and though the malicious excluded Bonaparte and his gift from the story, the total was generally agreed. And this was the disgrace that the Senator resented! He resented it sincerely. To do him justice, he would have given every sou for a return to office, for though he loved money and had a talent for amassing it, he loved power more—power, moreover, which he did not misuse but devoted, on the whole, to the welfare of his country and only secondarily to the welfare of himself. An interesting person, this Senator Joseph Fouché, now driving home to his wife and four young children whom he loved devotedly: a man kind by instinct though hideously cruel to order, a faithful family man who had betrayed every master he had served, a generous miser, a politician of supreme talents who was distrusted by the rulers he had helped to raise and idolized by the police agents he had robbed.

The day was fine, the autumn sun shone down from a cloudless sky on Paris, bathing with a gentle radiance her streets and churches, quays and bridges, and the grey waters of the Seine. The Senator, who loved it, sat forward in his coach to gaze out at the city. Changes could be seen everywhere around him, for the hand that had seized the State was directed by a brain that hated chaos and the sanguinary shambles of the Revolution and was busily engaged on sweeping every trace away. Order and security were returning after the mad, wasteful years—new streets, new buildings, a new way of life that could be seen reflected even in the clothes the people wore. Everywhere one saw uniforms —not those of the Republic, those grimy uniforms that had been in the smoke of Valmy and Fleurus and Jemappes, but colourful, romantic ones, plumes and faced jackets and braided epaulettes that might figure in a greater story.

The Senator, essentially a civilian, shook his head at sight of them, for he could trace the course the new master of the land was steering, and found in it one more reason in favour of his own return to influence. He was not afraid of Bonaparte. He had opposed him openly in the past, and had fallen as a result of it; next time he must be more circumspect, but he would continue to oppose. These new streets and this new air of prosperity were good and could probably be given only by a Bonaparte; but the uniforms were bad, the pledges of a war that France could not afford. A pity that only a soldier should have the power to bridle the Revolution and consolidate its work, for it was a civilian task that only a civilian mind could understand. Perhaps all this new order along with the old disorder would be put into the melting-pot again. What would emerge? A new Directory or Consulate, perhaps, with Joseph Fouché at the head of it. Odder things had happened, thought the Senator, watching his carriage turn into the familiar street; it was by no means so momentous a progression as the one he had made already from scrivener to millionaire.

The carriage clattered to a standstill, and he descended and entered his unpretentious house. Saint-Cloud and the Tuileries would be a change from it, but no greater than the difference between it and the garret where he had begun. In these surroundings he was at his best, a family man returning home to simple comforts embodied in his children and his plain, plebeian wife. There was a smile on his lips as he crossed the threshold between his public and his private life —speedily shed when they told him that he had a visitor. In that instant all traces of animation left his face; his manner became secret and he was once more the Fouché familiar to his contemporaries—a creature without substance or emotions.

The Senator took off his coat, which he handed to his valet. As he crossed the hallway to the study he was seen now in his handsome uniform, too handsome for the house and too handsome for the wearer, hanging loosely on his emaciated figure so that it did not look to be his own. Nevertheless, there were things about him that prevented him from being ridiculous: his height, an air of watchfulness, the thin scholar's face—the face of Marat, one enemy had said; of Robespierre, was the verdict of another; while the world of fashion awaited the *mot* of M. de Talleyrand, who would be sure to think of something more unflattering still.

One man could have been counted on to refrain from these comparisons—at all events in doubtful company—and that was Méhée de la Touche, who now sprang rapidly to his feet from his chair by the unlit fire; the reverence he made would have satisfied Bonaparte himself, it was so deep and abject. Such an attitude towards a fallen Minister, not treated considerately nowadays, must have been dictated by some subtle insight, but Fouché, for his part, did not seem to be the least bit gratified; he may have had foreknowledge of his visitor's news, and grunted, "Ah, so you're here, then?" in a tone of voice that suggested he would much have preferred the sight of someone else.

Méhée bowed.

"Sit down," the Senator continued. "There's no need to tire yourself after the exertions of your arrival; though from the fact that you arrived in Paris yesterday and present yourself alone today I deduce that the exertions were unprofitable."

"Say disappointing, Excellency." It was not for Méhée to use the salutation "Citizen," still in official use but on the wane.

"Disappointing, certainly. It's provoking that Artois is still shy of Biville cliff."

"He will come one day. He has promised."

"No doubt. But this time, it seems, you made the climb alone?"

Méhée's expression in itself would have told him that things were not as bad as that.

"No, not alone. I made it with a gentleman whose name is not unknown to you."

Fouché waited. It was beneath his dignity to guess.

"With the Vicomte de Bellac. I told you, if you remember, that he would make the journey soon."

"Ah, Bellac! The young man with the attachments?"

"In high places, yes."

"Did he talk of them?"

"Only by inference. The Vicomte is discreet." And Méhée smiled an ironic smile for a virtue not abundantly possessed by the romantic or the young.

"He will be seeing his friends, of course?"

"He was ordered to do so; so much I know. He is not as discreet as all that nor so intelligent."

"But is he resolute?"

"To see the ladies, Your Excellency means?"

Fouché nodded at this proof of his agent's understanding.

"Yes."

"Well, if you ask me, I should say that the young man is already repenting of the adventure."

"Repenting?"

"Yes, he is afraid of harming his friends, you see. The Vicomte is a man of sensibility. We must also reckon with the ladies in the case, who may have objections of their own."

"Impossible. You forget that we are dealing with old friendships, M. de la Touche, and that these are the most compromising of relationships."

"Or can be made to appear so," agreed his agent, with a smile.

Fouché nodded, conscious of the fact that he had unwittingly uncovered part of his design. That was unwise.

De la Touche was an invaluable agent, but perhaps too well acquainted with his intimate affairs. There was always the danger when dealing with a man primed with priceless information that he might discover a little too much and try to value it.

"We shall see," he said in the most noncommittal manner possible. "Your part will be to ensure he makes an approach—a discreet approach—to Hortense and Josephine. Where is he, by the way?"

"At a house on the river near Chaillot."

"At a house near Chaillot," repeated the Senator, who had taken account of the reticence of this reply. "Is he alone there?"

"No; there are others, Cadoudal among them. It is a *maison de confiance*, you see."

Fouché had a wintry smile for the confidence of these conspirators.

"We could take them all tomorrow," he said. "Do you know what that would mean?"

"It would mean a triumph for Your Excellency."

"I can think of greater ones—the taking of Artois in that house, for one. But I will repeat my question."

"I can see Your Excellency does not wish me to repeat my answer."

"It is not the answer I was wanting, citizen. You will appreciate as well as I that by going to the police today you could win golden opinions for yourself."

"What would I do with opinions?" asked Méhée with a smile.

The Senator gave a sigh of relief, so well controlled that it escaped even this most watchful of antagonists.

"I see you are a realist. You have not forgotten that you

plotted against the First Consul, that you were arrested, condemned, and that I saved your life."

"I have not forgotten, either, that Your Excellency has paid for such small information as I have brought."

"And I shall continue to pay. I think we understand each other. When I am restored to my post of Minister of Police —and I shall be restored, don't doubt that for a moment— I will repay you even more handsomely than you deserve. Keep my confidence and do not play too many games."

"Now I fail to understand Your Excellency."

Fouché, looking into his agent's dissembling face, might have been pardoned for doubting it very much.

"Very well," he said. "I will make myself clear. I know that you have approached Bonaparte himself and informed him that certain émigrés are in Paris plotting against him. You have even given names."

A self-righteous, protesting tone was very marked in Méhée's voice as he replied:

"Not Cadoudal's; not Bellac's."

"Perhaps not. But you *are* giving the First Consul information. Why?"

"Because I needed a pardon from him. Naturally I cannot run up and down Biville cliff at the risk of being captured by the police and shot."

"So you're a police agent too?"

Méhée drew himself up, and an expression of devotion— by no means entirely false—shone in his eyes.

"I am serving you," he said.

"And Bonaparte. That does not suit me, sir."

Méhée saw that he must explain. He was tied to the Senator by bonds of gratitude and gold.

"The information I am giving him is valueless," he said,

"or rather, just valuable enough to enable me to move about France without fear of the police. I have told the First Consul that there is a royalist plot against him. He suspected as much himself—pure intuition. I have named one or two—small men who know nothing. He has no idea how formidable that plot is becoming. He has no idea that Cadoudal, for instance, is in Paris, that General Pichegru is due, and that Artois will shortly be on his way. I am saving these delicacies for Your Excellency. I hope that you are not complaining of the fare."

"It is very appetizing, Méhée. But one thing occurs to me."

"What is that?"

"It would also suit the taste of the police."

"Your Excellency should believe me when I express my devotion to your interests."

The Senator accepted this with one half of his mind. But he knew something of gratitude and greed, and interest always meant self-interest to him.

"I think you underestimate Bonaparte," he said, "though I think you overestimate the police. Really my successors are quite miserly; they have no idea how to reward a man. Now that has never been a fault of mine."

"No, you have been the soul of generosity."

"And you have been the soul of service. Here is a personal equation, Méhée, and I have confidence in your ability to solve it and remember it."

De la Touche bowed in answer to the compliment, while the expression of cupidity in his eyes showed that the Senator's faith in his intelligence was not misplaced.

"You see, the game is becoming interesting," Fouché said. "We have important conspirators here already, and even more important ones may come. But, for the time

being, don't despise Bellac. Don't be tempted to give *his*
name to Bonaparte. In one sense he is the most important
of them all."

"Through his friendships, yes."

"Ah, you understand me perfectly. Minister of Police, did
I say? Who knows, my friend, whether that may not have
been an underestimate—of me!"

# Chapter Five

"I WILL SEE THE VICOMTE HERE."

Hortense, with her companion Diane de Florian, was in the round salon of her house in the rue Victoire. The two beautiful young women matched to perfection the elegance of this masterpiece in the style of Louis XVI —the perfect proportions, the slender columns worked in arabesques, the medallions and bas-reliefs of a room opening on to a garden as formal as the house, the product of an age that had become too civilized and had been struck down in the first moment of self-doubt.

It was a fatality that it should have been the scene of some very uncivilized emotions; built for the notorious Julie Carraud as a framework for her frailties, and now occupied by a wife who did not love her husband and a husband who was insanely jealous of his wife. Two people worse matched than Hortense and Louis Bonaparte would have been hard to find; they were united only in regretting a marriage forced on them by obscure fears and ambitions operating in the minds of the First Consul and of Josephine.

"Here? But, madame, do you think it safe?"

It was plain from the speaker's voice what she thought

about the matter. Louis might be absent in Montpellier—on a health cure which had become a hobby—but he had left his eyes and ears behind in the person of the major-domo, Morillac, and Diane had been long enough in her mistress' service to know this elegant house to be a cage.

"Safe? Nowhere is safe. Better here than in my room."

"For you, madame. But did you not tell me that the young man is an émigré illegally in France?"

Hortense coloured deeply; it suited her, for the pallor of her face, flawless in first youth, was already beginning to show the tinge of sickness.

"What if he is?" she cried. "*He* will not know." "He" being Morillac, who always appeared in her thoughts in this disembodied form.

"Is it fair to the Vicomte to take the risk?"

"You are reproaching me, Diane," said Hortense, laying her hand on her friend's arm. The two women made a charming picture as they stood there side by side, the one of delicate blonde colouring, the other small and lively with traces of Provençal blood in her eyes and jet black hair.

"I am not reproaching you."

"What, then?"

"Advising you, that's all."

Advice was always a soothing matter to Hortense. From her earliest childhood she had leaned on others—on her mother, on Mme Campan, at whose school she had spent the carefree years, on the First Consul, and now on this attendant, this young woman of her own age who seemed to have no shrinking from the world, no hesitations, no fear of it.

"Tell me, Diane."

"Very well then. I should suggest even for the first, as certainly for future meetings—somewhere out of this house."

"Future meetings? What future meetings? I think you have strange ideas of my feelings for this man."

"I have no ideas, madame. I just believed him to be a friend."

A deeper flush had settled on Hortense's face.

"You believe much more. Confcss it." Shc laughcd—almost a gay sound, an echo from the past. "You believe he is my lover."

Diane, with the appearance of being shocked at the suggestion, denied it utterly, even while there was shining in her eyes that light that comes to women as they skirmish round the defences of a love affair.

"But, Diane, you do. I can see it. My lover! You believe it, and it is ridiculous. Think of this: when last we met I was sixteen."

"A charming age."

"We were children, just children at school. Oh, I know that one is romantic then. We would admire the young men—such soldierly young men—at the Irish College and the officers that we peeped at in the street. But lovers! We were not so bold—even in our thoughts." She sighed, and suddenly with the memory of her youth the look of youth was gone. "I have not seen the Vicomte since that time."

"And now you are no longer children."

"Not even in inclination. I know what you are thinking, but you shouldn't tease me. You know how I am placed. I am no longer romantic; I no longer feel young. No, I mean it. I am not interested in gallantries. I am not interested in the Vicomte any more."

"No?"

"But that's true. Why are you smiling?"

"At your memory, madame."

"My memory?"

"Yes. You are remembering the Vicomte as he was—as a boy at school. Is it to be wondered at that you find the picture lacking in attraction? Let me substitute another: a tall figure, mature, well dressed, a foreign star or two, a silk cravat, a sword."

It was an attractive picture, but it did not seem to interest Hortense; and Diane, looking at her mistress in surprise, was suddenly aware that what had seemed a lighthearted evasion was the truth. It was hard for her to realize that such an abdication was possible in a young and lovely woman; it seemed unnatural, but now that she remembered, there had been a listlessness in her friend's manner for some time, a weariness with a world which she, for her part, found enchanting.

"It does not amuse you, I can see," she said.

"No, I prefer the Vicomte as he was."

In the light of her new knowledge Diane accepted this, though it sounded like the denial of common sense to her. She was remembering the picture she had painted, and was wondering with a smile how closely it would match reality. It was unlikely that a supporter of the old regime would be a coarse-grained soldier, all spur and sabre and cavalry moustache; the chances were that he would be that rare thing in Consular France, a man of manners, elegance, distinction—she knew already that he was young.

"What sort of man is he?" she enquired.

"You ask me that! And you have just described him!"

"The real de Bellac, madame."

"The real de Bellac is a schoolboy. What interest can he have for you?"

"All your preferences interest me."

Hortense was not deceived; she knew her friend, but did not bear her any grudge for trespassing. She had no feeling for the Vicomte except as part of a fabric of youthful happiness that had vanished from her life, and when Diane, not attempting to hide her inquisitiveness, persisted, "Describe him to me," she tried her best to do so.

"He was tall—tall for a boy, that is; dark hair; rather a high colour; small hands"—her companion smiled at the detail of this description—"dark eyes, very dark, darker than yours, if that's possible; rather a slim figure, but there! as I say, he was a child."

"You have a vivid memory."

"Yes, I remember those days. Believe me, I could describe a dozen personable men of that time to you, to say nothing of all the young ladies at Mme Campan's."

"You should do so. I would like to hear it."

"It would not interest you so much," replied Hortense, smiling at her friend. "Shall I tell you instead about his voice? A pleasant voice with just the trace of an Auvergnat accent. He had never been near the Court, you see. Don't think, though, that his manners were coarse in any way. They were masterful, perhaps, the manners of a boy who was certain of himself, who believed that he would do great things." The sad tone in her voice that was becoming habitual to her returned as she said: "And now he is an émigré and proscribed."

"You could obtain his removal from the emigrant lists."

"Perhaps."

"You *could* do so. The First Consul wants such men."

"But do you think such men want the First Consul, Diane? The Vicomte is a royalist, you must remember. His father is exiled, his mother and his brother died under the guillotine, his sister and her child were killed in Vendée. There's much here to forgive."

"To forgive the Revolution, madame. But the First Consul has not harmed him. He cannot hate Bonaparte, else why is he in Paris?"

"Ah! And why is he in Paris? You may well ask that."

"To obtain his erasure from the lists through you, of course."

A troubled frown had appeared on Hortense's face—lines on the forehead and at the corners of the mouth that were too deeply marked for so young a woman.

"Do you think so?"

"Naturally. Why else? What could bring the Vicomte here but the wish to be restored to his home, to be reconciled with the government, and to see you again?"

"Another thought occurs to me. Suppose he has come as part of an intrigue?"

"Of the heart? Most probably. The Vicomte must share your excellent memory of Saint-Germain and happier days."

"Not of the heart. Of politics."

"Of politics!" And it could be seen from her expression what Diane de Florian thought of this motive for the actions of a man.

"Why not? Others have come for that reason. You will not have forgotten the conspiracy of St. Régent. The bomb that was to have killed my stepfather was the work of royalists."

"You cannot suspect the Vicomte!"

It was strange how loyalties and imagination had changed the positions of both women; the young man seemed to have acquired a new opponent and a new defender.

"No; he would have had no part in that, he is a man of honour. But there is more than one way of conspiring, Diane."

"Suppose the worst, then. Suppose the Vicomte is a spy?"

"I could not help him, naturally."

"But would you betray him, madame?"

The expression now in Hortense's face told the story of her life. The anxious lines, the startled eyes, were those of a young girl suddenly faced with a realization of the world's baffling complexity.

"Would I betray him? What a question!"

"It is one you should ask yourself, I think."

"I love my stepfather," Hortense replied—it was the first article in a creed. "He has been good to me. My mother, my brother and I owe everything to him."

"Of course."

"And I do not love the Vicomte; you should believe that, for it's true."

"So you've answered me."

The answer came, reluctantly and low:

"No, I have not. The Vicomte is my friend and my mother's friend. He has suffered, and I could never betray him, never." Her voice dropped to a whisper as she betrayed herself. "He has suffered for my beliefs, you see."

"Royalism, madame?" and Diane's voice now matched her mistress', for the shadow of Louis and his creature Morillac seemed to have fallen on the room. "All the more reason for finding, as I urged, another rendezvous."

Hortense threw up her hands.

"So you will make me see the Vicomte! You will compromise me! You have even the place of meeting ready, I can see it from the look of you."

Indeed, there was a knowing expression in the dark young lady's eyes; she enjoyed planning assignations—particularly her own.

"Yes," she admitted, "yes, I have."

"And where?"

"In the house of a friend of mine."

"And you are so discreet that you will not say his name?"

"His name? Why, certainly, and believe me there's need for much discretion. It is the house of M. de la Touche, to whom I have the honour to be related—in a cousinly sort of way."

It was there, next day, they met, old friends long parted, discovering the disenchantment that travels in the lap of time, the fruit, as Hortense told him, of "years that have worked their change in me."

"Yes, and it's a change on which you should congratulate yourself, madame."

But even as he spoke the Vicomte felt the hollowness of the words. His brain could think of compliments and his tongue could utter them, but in his heart he knew that Hortense had told the truth. He felt the weight of sadness and oppression as he looked at her. She was still beautiful, with her elegant figure, her pallor, her lovely hands and arms, her hair—*blond cendré,* as one admirer had described it—but she was no longer the young woman he had remembered; her gaiety had deserted her and, absurd though it might be in the presence of flesh so uncorrupted, she seemed already old. All that was romantic in his nature tried to put such thoughts aside, but there was no escaping them. The truth was that to his horror he had almost failed to recognize her; his hesitation, his disappointment, had showed clearly in his eyes and had carried their message to Hortense.

"If I congratulate myself," she said, "it's in the rediscovery of a friend."

He could respond to that, for gratitude for her help in years past and affection for her were two of the strongest emotions in his heart. It sounded from the tone of her voice as though she too had revalued their relationship, and he gave an inward sigh of relief as he saw that he would not have to act the lover.

A little bolder in the possession of this knowledge, he looked for the first time into her eyes, and as he did so her words acquired a deeper meaning. How lonely she looked, how defeated and afraid! Youth and high spirits had been of little use to her; greatness had not helped her; this woman whom so many envied was friendless and unhappy: and as the Vicomte appreciated this, a wave of tenderness for her rose into his heart.

"I was rejoicing in that too," he said.

He was glad he had spoken as he saw the pleasure in her eyes; it was touching to see such transparent emotions in a woman bred to courts. She must need a friend. She must need him. It was only then that the Vicomte remembered how much he needed her.

"Truly?"

"Can you doubt it? I have so many pleasant memories." He saw the danger of lingering on this ground and hurried on: "And I have so much cause for gratitude. I know I could never have escaped the Revolution but for you."

"A Revolution, Charles, which I must remind you still exists." He must have looked incredulous, for she hurried on: "You've seen Paris; you've seen how quiet it is, the new uniforms, the new streets and buildings; a return to order, it must seem to you."

"Yes."

"But it's not a return. Believe me, the Revolution is still very much alive; it has become respectable, that's all. Why do you think I met you here in a stranger's house rather than in my own? Because I am part of the Revolution also."

"You were part of it, physically, the last time we met."

Her face softened as she replied:

"The last time you saw me I was free."

He could not reply to that, but watched her compassionately till she explained.

"I am altered now—don't misunderstand me—not only in the possession of a husband. There are other things. My stepfather . . . has risen since that time. There are loyalties that one can't explain, that I feel I needn't explain to you. I don't express myself well, but you understand my meaning."

"And that meaning is that we're in opposite camps?"

It had been said, and ironically enough, as they appreciated their division an expression of increased comradeship showed in both their faces.

"Yes, in opposite camps. That should not affect our friendship."

"But it might affect our meeting; is that what you're telling me, Hortense?"

"Do you wish to meet me?"

How he would have laughed at such a question an hour before! But now that he had seen her he could consider it on its merits, and knew the answer that honesty would give. He had met a stranger in this room, someone for whom he could feel pity and affection, but whose personality was marred by the death of an illusion he had carried in his heart. Artois' orders were poor substitutes for love, and his voice may have missed the right note of eagerness as he replied:

"Of course I want to meet you. There's so much that we can say to one another."

"About our conflicting ties, no doubt?"

The tone of bitterness did not escape him. He had deserved and accepted a reproach that made it easier for him to turn the conversation into the business channels that he had looked for from the outset. And the words themselves determined him, against his better judgment, to try a daring blow right to the heart of her defences.

"I suspect they are not conflicting at all," he said.

"What are you saying?"

"That you helped an enemy of the Revolution once."

"I helped a victim."

"Call me what you like. The facts remain that you saved me, that I am still opposed to the Revolution and that your sympathies are on my side."

"My sympathies have nothing to do with it."

"Loyalties, then."

"Loyalties! Just because you serve the King—"

"There!" he interrupted her. "Your tongue betrays you. He is the King to you still."

She turned from him, and for a moment he thought that she was about to leave the room.

"Why punish me with denials of what is true, Hortense?"

"I have told you that I've changed."

"Not in your heart."

"And you must come to Paris to tell me that!" she cried. The recurrence of an old suspicion struck her. "If you've not come for something worse."

"What are you thinking now?"

"That you're a conspirator. You behave like one."

"Conspiracy! A new name for loyalty, I suppose?"

"Then why are you here? Tell me. Tell me."

The Vicomte looked at her with sorrow in his heart. He would never have credited a relationship with this woman that had fallen to the level of an intrigue.

"I am here with proposals," he began.

"Proposals!"

"Honourable ones."

"And what am I to do with these honourable proposals?"

"Consider them. Weigh them. Pass them on."

"To whom?"

"To your mother. To General Bonaparte."

"From who do they come?"

"From the Count of Artois. From the King."

"And they suggest a restoration, I suppose?"

"In substance, yes."

"Do you imagine they are the first proposals the First Consul has received?" He shook his head. "Complaints and begging letters. That is what my stepfather has got for saving France."

"I carry something better."

"Something better than his Consulship?" An expression, the nearest to pride he had ever seen reflected there, shone in her eyes. "You would have to raise your offer high, Vicomte."

"The office of Constable of France."

It was an echo of her own words to her attendant, and though the young man did not appreciate the reason, he could not mistake the effect his words had had.

"It means security," he said, pressing his advantage home. "The First Consulship is very magnificent, no doubt, but it's built on instability—on the blood of the Revolution. Only the King can give peace to France. To say that is not to suggest limitations in your stepfather; the limitations are in his office. As long as he remains a revolutionary, he must act as a revolutionary. You know what that will mean. As his partisan, quite apart from your loyalty to His Majesty, you should welcome what I bring."

She looked at him as he stood there, his manner so earnest, so much at odds with his romantic appearance and her memories. At this moment she truly pitied him, for she knew the strength of the forces arrayed against him, the power of the current that was sweeping them along.

"What I welcome is of no importance, Charles. I have no influence with the First Consul, nor has my mother." The trace of a smile showed in her eyes. "It's a man's world we are living in, my friend; there are no more Pompadours in France."

"He can't be indifferent to your opinions."

"Oh, my opinions! He smiles at them."

"But would he smile at the offer of the King?"

"He would ignore it. You see events only in royalist colours, and so he seems like a usurper. But in his eyes it is different. He sees himself as the heir of the Revolution. Oh, I will be frank with you. I don't have these beliefs myself; I wish with all my heart that he would accept your offer. But we're friends? I can be frank with you?"

She paused and he saw these were questions.

"I want frankness," he replied.

"Well then, leave Paris. Go back to the King. Tell him to be patient. Tell him, above all things, not to compromise himself by conspiracies that can only fail. My stepfather is strong. There is no hope for the King or the Count of Artois —for their successors, perhaps, after we are gone."

"Then we wouldn't meet again."

She turned, and he was looking into her eyes of deep gentian blue.

"No, we wouldn't meet again."

"Do you want that? Am I such an embarrassment to you?"

The moment he had spoken the Vicomte realized how effective his words had been, and in that same instant he reproached himself for so working on the loyalties of a friend.

A flush of colour had spread in her cheeks.

"I shall meet you whenever you ask, Charles. If you stay, you will need friends in France . . . and I need them also. I ask only one thing of you."

"Yes?"

"That you're not plotting against the First Consul's life."

The Vicomte drew himself up. He was becoming used to half-truths which he had not foreseen when starting on this mission, but on this point he could speak with honesty. His was no dishonourable commission: he had the word of Artois for that, the word of Cadoudal, and the certainty of his own chivalrous, upright mind.

"I give my word," he said.

There was a reproachful quality in his voice that matched all these assurances and carried the ring of sincerity to her; but somehow, in spite of this, he had not found it in his heart to be surprised that she should have taken him for an assassin.

# Chapter Six

BONAPARTE WAS SITTING AT HIS WRIT-
ing-table in the small drawing-room of the palace of
the Tuileries. It was a modest room, lit only by a
three-branched flambeau that cast its light on to
the table, and furnished with a bookcase, a roll-top desk,
bronze ornaments, and chairs covered in the First Consul's
favourite shade of green. Upstairs a wealth of gilt and
tapestry and mirrors surrounded Josephine, but the small
salon and the adjoining study from which France was ruled
faithfully reflected the personality of a man who liked display in others but preferred a Spartan simplicity for himself.

M. de Talleyrand, an habitué of these apartments, de-
plored them; he found the décor plebeian and regrettable
and said so frequently, though never in the presence of
Napoleon or of the third person in the room—Councillor
Réal, who had a policeman's acute hearing and a habit of
repeating confidences. These two made an arresting com-
bination: the aristocrat whose manners were as easy as his
morals, and the official with the rigid instincts of an administrator, both servants of a man who seemed capable
of driving the whole world in harness.

This dynamic quality was the thing one first noticed about Bonaparte. He was very plainly dressed in the uniform of colonel of his Guard, his figure was small, his face sallow, his movements awkward and abrupt, but there gleamed through this outward shell an extraordinary impression of power. There was something elemental about him: his personality was not shrouded, his spirit did not appear to be shut in by the flesh, so that it struck with the force of lightning at those with whom he came in contact, and he gave the impression, even with his most banal words, that thought had somehow got itself a voice. As a result, even M. de Talleyrand, insulated from the world by his own cynical, resilient mind, was overborne and looked a servant as he stood there, leaning on his stick with an appearance of languor that was certainly assumed; he was a little less than himself in Napoleon's presence, in contrast with Réal who, in a state of blind obedience, was absorbing his master's magnetism.

"Réal."

"Yes, General."

"Do you remember a man called Méhée de la Touche?"

Réal's mind, a filing cabinet of misdemeanours, went to work and sorted out a card.

"Yes. He was one of the conspirators of Nivôse."

"Arrested, condemned to be deported, and escaped?"

"That is so."

"And now returned to France. He was in this room yesterday."

Réal was not to be drawn into any comment. An experienced official, he was not in the habit of anticipating blame.

"For he has changed sides, you see, and might be said to have qualified for your department. He gave some interesting information too. Are you aware, for instance, that a group of royalist conspirators has made its way to Paris?"

"No, General."

"That at least is honest. Have you any comments on the blindness of my police?"

"None, General."

"M. de Talleyrand?"

The Foreign Minister shrugged his shoulders. It was plain to see that he took no responsibility for blunders of any kind, particularly when they were the concern of a department beneath his notice.

"When Fouché was at the Police, such lapses did not occur," continued Bonaparte. "But since I have suppressed the Ministry and left the Grand Judge, Regnier, in charge of police matters, no one seems to be interested in security any more. This cannot continue, even if I have to restore Fouché. What do you say, Talleyrand?"

"That it is not in my department, Citizen First Consul."

"So it is like that! You do not share the general feeling of the indispensability of our friend?"

The Minister, who would have dispensed with Fouché on a scaffold if he could, leaned more heavily on his cane and looked inscrutable, for he knew the futility of advising Bonaparte.

"Even M. Fouché would not claim so much for himself," he said. "He did great service at the Police. He had his finger on the pulse of France; he knew everything and controlled everything—within his department, of course. You could find no more efficient, all-seeing Minister"—and rival, his manner seemed to say.

"So you recommend that I restore him?" enquired Bonaparte, who could read between these words, and knew that they had expressed the exact opposite of what was meant.

"It might add to your security."

Napoleon smiled; he thought this nicely put, a delicate hint of the Senator's ambitions.

"I have something rather different in mind." He turned with an abrupt movement toward Réal. "You are to replace Regnier," he said.

"I, General? As Minister?"

"No, not yet, for I do not want to reconstitute the Ministry. But you will be in charge of all police matters and directly responsible to me."

"I see."

"Don't look so stolid and unimaginative," cried Bonaparte, driven by a spasm of irritation at the sight of his servant's face. "It's no easy task I am giving you. It's not a matter only of arresting a handful of small conspirators."

"No?" replied Réal in tones that suggested that this had been the limit of his ambitions in the matter.

"Certainly not. I have believed for some time that something important was in the air, a plot of substance. You, M. de Talleyrand, have felt this too."

"Information from London leads me to suppose it."

"And if the English government is involved, as appears to be the case, then we can be sure that good gold sovereigns are not being spent in keeping a few small émigrés in Paris. The English want value for their money; they will insist on it, like the merchants that they are."

"You think that they have important agents in Paris, General?"

"I don't know it, Réal, but I suspect it. I suspect that Artois and General Moreau are mixed up in the affair. Méhée could not tell me; he only knows of minnows—but even minnows have their uses."

At this hint of police process Réal began to look relieved; the conversation was coming to a point where he excelled, for he was a man of ability in his sphere and had a way with witnesses.

"We arrest them and they talk?" he said.

Talleyrand looked grieved at this. He was bored with the topic of a barbarous department, and believed in the value of showing emotions that gave him an ascendancy over the uncivilized.

"That was in my mind," said Bonaparte.

"Have you their names?"

"Yes, and addresses, for Méhée was exact. There are three men he knows of—Picot, Le Bourgeois, and a Breton surgeon called Querelle. Have you heard of them before?"

Réal thought methodically, then shook his head.

"M. de la Touche was more informative. All are émigrés, veterans of the war in Vendée, small men, it appears. How did they get here? How did they come from England? How did they reach Paris? How, in spite of our system, are they able to support themselves and remain unseen?"

"Does the informative M. de la Touche not know that?" demanded Talleyrand with a smile.

"No, regrettably."

"And yet the informative M. de la Touche, also a conspirator—though resigned now, it appears—has himself arrived here and has contrived to support himself among us."

"He is a man of resource."

"Evidently. He is a man of so many resources that if it were my department I should feel impelled to question him about them."

Réal nodded his approval of so admirable a suggestion.

"You think his answers would be interesting?" he enquired.

"At least as interesting as the replies of this Picot, and Bourgeois, and the Breton—what was his name?"

"Querelle."

"Yes, and Querelle. M. de la Touche, if approached in the proper way, might give the same answers earlier and far more entertainingly, I feel sure."

"You are thinking he is really one of them and is being used?" asked Bonaparte.

"By someone, most probably, Citizen First Consul. I remember the man and I know the type: a conspirator by nature, an agent-provocateur by inclination, and a servant by economic need. He is utterly untrustworthy."

"You mean," cried Réal, "that his information should be disregarded?"

Talleyrand, with an elegant gesture of his hands expressed his opinion of this intervention.

"My dear Réal, I should treasure his information like a pearl. Additionally I should open up the oyster."

"And end its usefulness in the process," the First Consul said. "That is not sensible. I have other uses for M. de la Touche."

The thought that de la Touche might have uses for General Bonaparte flashed into the mind of Talleyrand and lingered there agreeably. A perfect master of his emotions, he retained his bland demeanour even while he was imagining the discomfiture of a man whom he feared as much as he disliked.

"But I have seen the implication of what you said," the First Consul continued with a sour look at Réal, who patently had not. "There was much truth in it. I, too, recall his part in the affair of Nivôse."

"Of which charge," said his Foreign Minister, "he actually had the duplicity to be innocent, I believe."

Bonaparte was not responsive.

"So de la Touche alleges," he replied. "There were

mysteries and misunderstandings connected with that affair that no one, except M. Fouché, who was in charge of the investigation, will ever be able to explain."

A rather wintry smile had spread across the face of the Foreign Minister.

"Then I should certainly ask M. Fouché to explain them —two matters in particular. I should ask him how a man who was condemned—justly or unjustly, it makes no matter —was able to escape. And—not now but at a later date—I should want to know how that man was able to return. Embarrassing questions, I flatter myself to hope."

"And sensible ones. They shall be asked. But for the moment Réal here will confine himself to the arrest of the three men denounced. They should be questioned—or approached, as Talleyrand puts it—in the proper way. Later it may be necessary to approach others, even more properly, in a way that will surprise them."

# *Chapter Seven*

DAWN WAS BREAKING AS RÉAL EN-
tered the cell where the surgeon Querelle lay, a
cold grey dawn, whose light glowed dully
through the grille, low-set in the bare stone wall.
Until the beam of the candle in his hand had steadied, he
could scarcely see the form of the prisoner on the trestle, an
amorphous bundle sprawled out there as though already
dead. That consummation did not seem likely to be long
delayed, bearing in mind the refusal of the prisoner to talk,
a refusal persisted in equally by Picot and Le Bourgeois, his
friends, condemned like him to die this morning by the
firing squad. For all three the Councillor felt the irritation
of a prosaic man who cannot distinguish obstinacy from
heroism, for he was not cruel by nature, and resented killing men he could much more profitably examine.

"Querelle."

His bewilderment had sounded plainly in his voice. But
the prisoner, woken suddenly to consciousness, naturally
heard only the accents of the executioner. He stumbled to
his feet.

In the soft glow of the candlelight the two men stared at
one another, though from the look of anxiety and enquiry

in each face it was hard to tell which was guard and which was prisoner. And if Réal with his mild manner failed to look the part of jailer, it was certain that Querelle did not seem a hero; there was a strained look about him, natural perhaps to one in his position, which gave point to the generally held belief of the police that here was the weak link in the conspiracy, a man less resolute than Picot or Le Bourgeois, a man who might oblige.

Appearances were deceptive, the Councillor thought, looking his man directly in the eye. Querelle had persisted in his denials on arrest, during interrogation, and at the trial; he had betrayed no one, even though his own case, as one of the Vendéan rebels, was hopeless; the promise of a pardon had not drawn him—the most unreasonable stupidity of all. There must be a way. It must be possible to prove to this man that death was a senseless thing by an appeal to reason; to prove that it was a painful thing by an appeal to that fear that clutches at the heart.

"You have heard the sentence," he said in a formal voice. "They will have told you yesterday that you are to be shot this morning."

"Yes," the prisoner said.

"That sentence will be carried out."

"I know."

"Are you prepared?"

Querelle looked slowly round the cell. He was dressed in the clothes in which he had been tried. His sole possession was a small silver crucifix lying on the table by the bed.

"Yes, I am prepared."

"You have just ten minutes."

"So little time."

The Councillor glanced at the grille towards the grey light of the day. Speed had been the watchword throughout the case. He had wasted no time over the arrests, the criminal court none over the conviction, the firing squad would not be dilatory. Such was the way of Bonaparte. There was a merciful side to it, the Councillor thought, even as he prepared, in obedience to his orders, to extract the last refinement of cruelty from a delay.

"Ten minutes, that is all. You are to be the last to die."

An appearance of distress showed in the surgeon's face.

"They're going now? Can't I see them?"

Réal shook his head at this absurdity. The worst of this romantic heroism, he reflected, was that it expected romantics from its enemies. A community of suffering had given power and courage to the victims of the Revolution beneath the guillotine—a very undesirable state, looked at from the point of view of a policeman who still hoped for information, even at the end.

"I regret not. You can hardly expect any relaxation in the rules," he said. "You have not earned it in any way."

"You mean I have not betrayed my friends."

"That's your way of putting it. I would say that you have been intractable."

"And I shall certainly continue so."

"Yes, I believe you," replied Réal, forcing down his irritation, which might spoil the part he had to play. "You have been a hero in your opinion. I could also find another word for that."

"You dishonour yourself," the prisoner said, drawing himself up proudly. There was something in his manner at this moment that impressed the Councillor, though it had the effect of destroying most of the small stock of optimism he had left.

"I regret that," he said. "I admire your courage; I admire it as much as I deplore your lack of common sense. You are part of a conspiracy—only a small part, I suspect. Where are the principals? Where are your friends? They have come to Paris full of great plans to overthrow this man and over-turn that institution, but they have not moved to save you. You have deserved loyalty and received none; they have not deserved it, and three men are dying for them. Where is the sense in it, Querelle?"

The Councillor had stopped in some embarrassment, startled by his own eloquence, which had been called out by a conviction of the justice of his words. For a moment he felt an acute sense of comradeship with the man before him, a victim of a code of honour that seemed an anachro-nism in his tidy modern world. He knew the force of the argument he had used and believed that it must convince the most fanatical; but he was disillusioned the moment he saw the surgeon's face, set in an expression much firmer than at the interrogation and trial.

"You are wasting your time, Councillor."

Réal sighed.

"I am offering you your life," he said.

"And I am greatly obliged to you."

The bantering tone of this reply impressed itself strongly on Réal; it seemed so divorced from the realities, an echo of the victims of the Terror, herded in the tumbrils, who had gone jesting to their death. But this man was alone. No friends were with him, no jeering crowd surrounded him to stir pugnacity or courage in his heart; there was just a prison cell and, outside, a yard backed by a high stone wall.

"You should be obliged to me for the offer of your life," he said. "You would be if you understood the meaning of life and death."

The voice of the prisoner was full and ironical as he re-plied:

"But you understand it! And you are greatly to be congratulated on the solution of mysteries that have baffled the philosophers."

"It is no mystery that I'm referring to," replied Réal; "it is a simple matter of feelings and emotions. You can talk glibly of life because you are alive, because, as I much fear, you have not appreciated that in ten minutes—five now—you will have ceased to live. Death has no meaning for you —yet—for you have not understood that you will die. You *will* understand it. There will be a moment when you are standing by the wall when you will know how unrealistic you have been, when you would tell me the names of all your friends for one hour of life. But you will not cry out; you will be too late; death will have overtaken you."

"But this *is* philosophy, Réal."

The Councillor sadly shook his head.

"I see that I have not moved you, nor did I expect to. Words are of no use. The tragedy is that only actions can convince people in a case like this, though the actions in themselves end everything. I feel truly sorry for you. To die in the knowledge that one has been a fool is the saddest thing of all."

"You are right," the prisoner said. "Your words are useless. Life is a small thing compared with honour."

"That is your mistake. You will find that life is everything. Honour is a word, and a very unimportant word. It is really a pity that we shall be unable to discuss this later, in the light of your experience. We should be quite agreed."

"Ah, you are dishonourable! They have sent you here to torture me."

"With good reason," replied Réal, encouraged by the sight of the prisoner's face, drawn and haggard in the increasing light of dawn. "To be frank, I need your confession.

It will avoid bloodshed in the end, for if we take your friends before they have compromised themselves in crime, it may be possible to spare their lives. That is one reason why I am telling you the truth about your misplaced courage. But there is another reason: I am not indifferent to you; I would like to spare you. Neither is the First Consul cruel. Speak now and save yourself."

Before the prisoner could reply the noise of a door opening was heard from far off and a muffled sound that gradually grew into footsteps approaching along the stone-flagged corridor: slow, reluctant steps echoing hollowly in that dark and secret place. The two men in the cell remained silent as the sound grew louder and more distinct, passing the threshold of the door. It was possible now to distinguish the regular footsteps of the guards and the dragging movements of the man who marched with them.

"Picot," Réal explained, watching the hand of Querelle, which had fastened on the crucifix so tightly that the whites of the knuckles showed. "He is the first."

"It is infamous."

"But it is happening, and that is the important point. Give me the names now and you will save him. But you must be quick. It will not take above two minutes for him to reach the wall, and after that the whole procedure becomes rather less predictable. He has reached the end of the corridor now; he is nearly at the entrance to the yard."

For the sound of footsteps was dying away into the distance—a dull murmurous noise so low and indistinct that the prisoner could scarcely hear it above the beating of his heart.

"You won't speak? You have very hardened emotions. Tell me the names. It's not yet too late."

The surgeon's face, grey with the unearthly tinge of the

winter morning's light, could be seen to be working uncontrollably; his hands were clasped in an attitude of prayer, his whole appearance so pitiable that the Councillor could hardly bear to look at him. But he had been trained in a hard school of duty.

"Tell me the names. Why are you silent? To save your friends? And yet one of your friends is about to die because of you. Where is the reason in it?" He raised his voice. "Tell me the names. You still have time."

But no sooner had he spoken than he was contradicted by events: a fusillade of shots rang out, harsh and vibrant within the circle of the walls, echoing with unbearable clamour in the narrow cell.

Querelle had flung himself on his knees.

"You have kept faith," said the Councillor, looking down at him, and there was a ring of contempt and bitterness in his voice. "Let us hope that it will be some satisfaction to you when your turn comes."

"My turn. Pray God it may come soon!"

Réal seized on this with a lightning dart.

"Why do you say that? Ask yourself the question. It is a confession of guilt. You cannot bear your guilt for these men's deaths, so you cry out. It's yourself that you are sorry for, not that body by the wall."

Querelle did not reply. His eyes stared right through his torturer as though following some vision of the mind. He did not move when another cell door clanged to far off down the corridor and the movements of feet were once more heard—brisker movements as of men moving gladly to a rendezvous.

The Councillor was relieved to hear them. His distasteful task was coming to an end, and, though he dreaded the First Consul's anger and had not wavered in his disgust at a useless sacrifice, he felt he could not support much longer this assault on the emotions of a man.

"Won't you speak?" he said. "Will nothing move you? Don't you realize at last where your obstinacy has led?" He added softly: "Look out of the window. You will see. It is so much lighter now."

He moved towards the prisoner and drew him unresisting to his feet; half supporting him he turned towards the grille. The dull, sullen light lit for them a view of the prison wall, but to the left, beyond the wilderness of an untended garden, a rectangular courtyard could be seen and figures muffled in greatcoats drawn up in uneven line.

"This is the reality," he said. "It's not very heroic at this hour. See, they are coming now. That one walks like a soldier. Won't you speak for him? Give me the names."

Querelle was gazing at the scene, as it unrolled, like a figure in a trance. He made no movement as Le Bourgeois was led towards the wall; no sound escaped him as a handkerchief was placed over the condemned man's eyes or as the officer in charge stepped back towards the firing-line.

"The names! Quickly! You have only this moment."

The surgeon made a convulsive movement, but he did not speak. As the rattle of musketry sounded in the yard he stepped back from the window and sat down on the trestle bed; he made no further movement, but the crucifix he had been clutching slipped from his hands, falling with a clatter on to the floor beside his feet.

Réal, for his part, had turned away, sickened with the part he had to play, appalled at this butchery of brave men. His only wish now was that the guards would speedily arrive, and that this unfortunate would die as fast and as painlessly as possible. He made no further attempt to get his answer, but remained like a sentinel by the door, listening for the firm tread of approaching feet and the end of the unhappy story. He had not long to wait. While the surgeon still sat motionless on the bed the sound of marching could be heard, and a hand was fumbling with the heavy latch.

"It is over now," he said, and behind him the door swung open to reveal the officer and four soldiers of the guard. "Be courageous. It is nothing. You will feel nothing. Remember the way your friends have died."

But the prisoner did not stir; he did not seem to have heard the Councillor's well-meant words or seen the guards; the light from the grille, shining directly on him, showed a mask of apathy, secret and withdrawn.

The captain of the escort stepped forward. He had no understanding of the springs of men's emotions, but he did have a practical knowledge of their results and recognized in the prisoner's silence the prelude to a storm. That would be regrettable; it was always regrettable when prisoners wept and raved instead of standing quietly, as they should, where the soldiers—the rather inept, half-trained marksmen of these days—could shoot them reasonably neatly near the heart. It was better for everyone that way: better for the soldiers, better for the victim, a relief to him personally, for though war had made it hard for him to be impressed by death, it had not brutalized him or made him rejoice in suffering. Co-operation from the condemned, that was what he liked, that was what he expected, and what he most often got. He did wonder about it sometimes, marvelling that of the participants at an execution the victim was so often the most composed, the most efficient of the lot.

"Come," he said, and he went forward towards the bed, the clatter of his boots sounding loud in that confined and narrow space.

Suddenly Querelle looked up at him. He saw the heavy bulk of the man, the impassive, official face, the hands, one resting on the hilt of a sabre, the other holding—unobtrusively—the length of cord. And as he saw these things he started to his feet.

"Come. It is time. Come now," the captain said, soothingly, as he would have spoken to a child. It was strange to hear the delicacy in that voice, and to know that it was not due to any sensitivity, but to the demands of the task in hand.

"No," the prisoner said.

One word, but it spoke volumes to the officer who sighed under his breath at this confirmation of his fears. He beckoned over his shoulder at the escort and advanced the rope significantly towards the victim—a warning and a reproach.

"You must do as you are told and fall in with the guard. This is unnecessary; you are wasting time."

"And injuring yourself," added the voice of Réal from the doorway of the cell.

The captain did not turn, but a slight movement of his shoulders reproved civilian interference at such a time.

"Fall in, as I said. You surely will not wish me to call my men?"

Querelle did not reply, but backed slowly from them, his hands held out in front of him as though pushing away some unseen presence that was grasping at his throat.

"It's disgraceful," the captain said in slow grumbling tones that revealed how greatly he was affected by this breach of the decencies of death. "For the last time, are you going to obey me?"

There was no reply from the prisoner, who was now standing braced against the wall.

"Very well. Roche, Clairmont, help me to secure him."

Two guardsmen advanced into the cell. They seemed less assured than their commander, young conscripts, the merest boys, but bulky in their greatcoats so that they towered over the shrinking figure of the surgeon.

"Go on, take him. We shall have to carry him, I can see."

As the rough hands grasped at him, the prisoner cried out—a loud cry of intolerable anguish and despair. It was small wonder that he was roughly handled as he was dragged towards the door, still crying out spasmodically through the barrier of hands reaching out to smother words degrading to them all:

"No, no, I don't want to die! Spare me! Spare me for the love of God!"

Dishevelled, eyes bloodshot and staring so that the corners of the whites showed, his coat in rags, the prisoner was a terrible sight as he reached the door. But when he saw the two other guardsmen in the corridor his strength revived, he tore himself free and cried out in a strident voice:

"Réal, Réal, I will tell you. Spare me and I will tell you everything."

Immediately the Councillor stepped forward. He had no pleasure in a triumph which he had not won and was shocked by this degradation of a man, but there was his duty to be done. As for the captain, who had become incensed in the violence of the struggle, he looked at his victim with the expression of an animal cheated of its prey.

"You won't listen to him, surely?"

"Yes. Yes. Speak, Querelle."

"But will you spare me?" the prisoner cried.

"Yes, I will spare you."

Querelle sank down on the bed. He sat there limply, his head in his hands, while the captain, standing over him, muttered his hatred of a man whom he now wanted actively to die, and the guardsmen rearranged their clothing and stared wide-eyed.

"Time is passing. Will you speak?" the Councillor said.

"Yes."

"Then do so. Be accurate. Be truthful. You won't want a repetition."

A spasm shook the prisoner.

"I'll be truthful. I'll tell you all I know."

"You had better," said the captain, whose resentment boiled over into matters that were no longer his concern. "You had better, or I will carry you out there personally and strap you to the stake."

Réal rebuked him with a gesture. But the outburst had had its effect on the prisoner, and the words came suddenly with a rush.

"There are a few of us in Paris. I don't know all the names. There's a man called Bouver de Lozier I know well. He's living at a house in the rue St. Sauveur that belongs to Mme St. Légier, his mistress. There's another, a carpenter called Spein, living in the rue Carême-Prenant. Two men arrived recently. I've not met them. I'll think of their names presently. I'll try to. I've not met them, you know. They only came in recently."

"Small men," said the Councillor, shaking his head in a disappointment that boded the prisoner no good. "Who sent you?"

"A royalist committee. The order came from the Count of Artois, I believe."

"In England?"

"Yes."

"And the Count of Artois, who wants presumably to return to Versailles and his privileges, sends to Paris to arrange for his return Picot and Le Bourgeois, yourself"—the contemptuous tone was marked—"a Bouvet de Lozier who seems to be engaged with mistresses, two unknowns that we shall remember presently, and a carpenter who lives in the rue Carême-Prenant, wherever that may be! Distinguished conspirators, you'll agree!"

"They are all I know."

"Then you know the wrong people, regrettably, monsieur. You are giving me nonentities, not names. It is not good enough. You must do better or I will be forced to turn matters over to the captain here."

"But I know no others," cried the prisoner, his face deathly white. "God knows I fear death. But if you gave me to this man and he took me out there to that yard, I still couldn't give you names; I could only invent them and lie to save my life."

There was a ring of sincerity in this, and in spite of his suspicions the Councillor was impressed.

"You receive orders in Paris, I presume?" he said. "Who gives you them?"

"De Lozier."

"He shall confirm that. Is he the head of the conspiracy?"

"I suspect not. There is someone bigger."

"Have you an idea of who that man might be?"

The prisoner replied unhesitatingly: "No."

"What were the orders you received?"

"To lie low and wait. We were no more than an advance guard. Later others will come."

"What others?"

"Bigger men. I have heard it said that even Artois himself is on the way."

"And when they are all here? What is to be the object of this distinguished gathering?"

The prisoner, who had been speaking in a tone of increasing confidence and looking his interrogator in the eye, dropped his gaze.

"Bonaparte," he said.

The captain of the escort, relegated to the background, took a threatening step nearer to the bed; nor was the Councillor less moved.

"A congress of assassins!"

"Not of assassins. We would do nothing dishonourable. We respect Bonaparte. But we serve the King."

"What form would this respect take, do you imagine?"

"A deposition. We would not harm him. If you suppose otherwise, you do not know us."

It was not a fortunate choice of words, for it reminded Réal how little he did know about these conspirators with such conveniently little knowledge of themselves. His face hardened till he looked blood brother to the captain at his side.

"Is this all you are telling me?" he said.

"What else can I say? I have given you the names I know. I have told you that others are on their way to France."

"How are they coming?"

The prisoner hesitated.

"You had better tell me," the Councillor said, and he did not need to refer by so much as a look to the executioners in the room.

"They are coming from England," Querelle replied.

"And that is illuminating too. Do you suppose I imagine the Grand Turk is sending them! How are they coming? You had better speak very fast. In this case, you had better know."

Querelle understood this. But the memory of his friends

whose bodies still lay below the wall was in his mind, and his voice was very low as he replied:

"They come in an English ship. They land at Biville cliff between Le Tréport and Dieppe. There is a path cut in the cliff. There is a farmhouse near the sea and a man called Troché who is a guide." He paused, and added so indistinctly that they scarcely heard him: "Another ship is due. Artois, perhaps. There will be a landing four days from now."

# Chapter Eight

LATE IN THE EVENING OF THAT SAME DAY
Charles de Bellac arrived for his third meeting with
Hortense at the house near the Palais Royal, where
Méhée de la Touche had rented an apartment. It
was in a district traditionally associated with the pursuit
of pleasure: the gardens had been the rendezvous of lovers,
the arcades the pitches of the prostitutes, while even the
houses on the outskirts of the palace had the look of dow-
agers with a lot to hide. The Vicomte, too young to have
sampled the Paris of Egalité and the amorists and agitators
who had surrounded him, knew its reputation, and would
have been glad to taste the flavour of a vanished age. He
was a man of ardent and imaginative nature, who had carried the memories of Saint-Germain constantly in his heart,
so that they had survived the knowledge of Hortense's rising
star and her marriage into the circle of the Bonapartes,
reaching out for some such dream as this—a house in a
quiet street, a mistress, words and passionate embraces, a
secluded room. He had found the setting; but the dream
had faded, and he was left with an intrigue. It was typical
of him that the danger of the course he was pursuing never
occurred to him for an instant; his thoughts as he knocked

softly at the door were concerned only with self-disgust at his deception and pity for the woman he had loved—a strange mixture in the mind of a man calling late in this street of assignations.

The night was cold and dark, and few lights showed in the old quarter where on that July day the Revolution had had its birth; the houses with their shuttered eyes seemed to be set in disapproval of the foster-child that for the time impaired their gay prosperity; not so much as a woman of the streets was abroad to hear that gentle rapping sound or to see the figure of the caller slip past the opening door.

De Bellac was familiar with the house and with the arrangements for his reception; he needed no guide to lead him down the dark corridor; he waited for no introduction but entered the lighted room beyond. But no one was there to greet him. Turning in surprise, he saw that the lady who had admitted him had followed and was standing just inside the door.

At that moment a very strange sensation assailed the Vicomte, a quickening of the senses which he did not recognize as part of the fabric of his dream. He felt this even before he saw her clearly for the first time in the candlelight, the breath of an emotion which his mind, not understanding, translated into a warning so that his hand moved towards his sword. He withdrew it slowly as he saw that she was alone—a very beautiful young woman, a fine young woman with the eyes of a Provençal and a white skin that glowed warmly, alluringly in that kindly light.

Unconsciously he drew himself up. All the lethargy with which he had approached his rendezvous had vanished, and in its place was the pleasurable excitement of one who stands on the threshold of an adventure. A man of experience, he recognized at once the active quality that distinguished her from Hortense more clearly than their difference in colouring, the lively, independent spirit of a woman who did not fear the world or set great store by its opinion. All this could be plainly read, but the Vicomte in the excitement of the discovery thought that he could see a great deal more—so much, in fact, that he forgot the reason for his coming, the absence of the woman he had arranged to meet, and felt when he was reminded of these things a sense of grievance at the interruption.

Reality was slow to return, but when at last it did he began to see significance in Hortense's absence, remembering his own frank words, his self-betrayal, the avowal of his royalism that had met with so guarded a response. It looked very much as though he had lost an ally, though he might have found a mistress in exchange.

"But why is she not here?" he said. "I don't understand. Is it possible I have offended?"

At that he saw a smile tremble on her mouth. He was not to know that Diane was aware of the substance of the earlier meetings, and that by every canon of gallantry in her eyes he *had* offended. She herself would never have tolerated such a lack of ardour—would not tolerate it, indeed, when her turn came, as she felt certain that it would.

"There must surely be a message?" he went on.

"Yes. I am to tell you that my mistress cannot come. She is detained."

"By some engagement?"

"By her husband, who has returned unexpectedly from Montpellier."

A frown had appeared above the Vicomte's eyes. It would have been easy to mistake it for the reaction of a lover, but Diane was not deceived.

"You are grieved at this, monsieur?" she said.

"Naturally. Devil take it, do you expect me to be pleased?"

"At a husband's return! Monsieur is laughing at me."

But the Vicomte was not laughing. As he looked at this young and lovely woman, he was regretting the corrupting power of courts.

"Ah! So they have taught you that?"

"It is an elementary lesson—a necessary lesson in this case."

De Bellac drew himself up. He did not propose to begin one love affair by accepting advice about another.

"I can hardly believe that you were sent to tell me that," he said.

"But then you wouldn't believe the circumstances of this case, no matter who told you them, Vicomte. You would accept a jealous husband, but would you accept an insane jealousy such as Louis', a hatred that feeds on the idea of infidelities? Would you accept a man who employs others to spy on his wife?"

"It's an unpleasant picture."

"It is certainly a dangerous one."

The young man shrugged his shoulders and airily replied:

"Jealousy is jealousy and no more than that. Love finds a way."

"Ah yes, love. You love madame?"

He stared at her, unable to understand this intrusion into his affairs, and as he looked into her eyes the very question seemed absurd. With such feelings for her stirring in his heart, it was impossible to give the reply he had intended.

"You are a very strange messenger," he said.

"But you do love her? Love for her has brought you here?"

"Does it surprise you?"

"Very much. I should have put it down to politics."

Immediately the Vicomte became watchful. It was all very well to fence with this lady and desire her, but it had to be remembered that she was a servant of the Bonapartes and that there was a great deal to be explained—the mistress' absence, the evasive words. He did not know her, he had taken her on trust, but how would it be if she were herself one of the spies she had talked of as set upon Hortense? It was an unpleasant thought, and the expression on his face was troubled as he looked at the woman for whom, an instant before, he had had the liveliest emotions.

"Politics? What politics? I don't understand you."

"Royalist politics, to make myself quite plain."

De Bellac glanced round the room. At this moment he feared and expected an arrest. All his senses were alert for signs of danger, he had weighed his chances of escape, discarded them, and chosen a position in the angle of the wall; but his voice sounded lighthearted and ironic as he replied:

"Royalist politics! In Paris! You have an amusing fancy. And who told you this?"

"My mistress."

It might be a lie, he had no means of knowing. But if it was the truth, then a new complexion was put on the matter, not necessarily a reassuring one, for even an old friendship might not save him from betrayal. It seemed the likeliest explanation, for Hortense would naturally have shrunk from witnessing such a scene; indeed, for an instant the Vicomte accepted this, till the complete silence of the house restored his confidence. The trap, if trap it was, may have been baited, but it had not closed.

"What are you telling me?" he said.

"Nothing that need surprise you. That you are a royalist and an émigré. You won't deny that?"

The Vicomte did not reply, but continued to look at her, watchfully, admiringly.

"What is more, you are illegally in Paris. You might have come to gratify an old romance. I asked you if you loved her. You did not answer. Why?"

"You should appreciate that," said the Vicomte with a bow.

"'The delicacy of a gentleman, no doubt," replied Diane, who thought she knew the real reason very well, and was pleased by it as she was pleased with everything about this new adventure. "This visit to an old friend has all the ingredients of an affair of tenderness—except the tenderness itself."

"You deceive yourself, mademoiselle."

"No. Believe me, it is impossible for a woman to be deceived in matters of the heart. You are fond of my mistress, you admire her, she is a dream you dreamed once. But you do not love her. When a man is asked whether he loves, he either admits it, if he does, or evades the question. Ah, you were evasive, M. le Vicomte, so evasive. And since you do not love her, why do you arrange these meetings—dangerous meetings, as I have told you, meetings at which you risk her reputation and your life?"

"Don't you understand friendship?"

Diane's lips parted in a gentle smile. The Vicomte, watching her, saw their ripe fullness and felt a strange constriction in his heart.

"Oh, friendship! Don't talk to me of that. Don't tell me that these meetings were arranged so that you could exchange tales of Saint-Germain. One meeting, perhaps, no more. You either arranged them as a lover—and you are not a lover—or as a conspirator of sorts."

"So now you have defined me. I am a royalist conspirator, and I meet your mistress to enlist her in the plot!"

"That is what I believe."

"You really think that's the truth! Does no other reason for my meeting her occur to you?"

"What other reason could there be?"

"Well, suppose I am an émigré illegally in Paris, as you say. But suppose also that I am anxious to return to France. I must have my name removed from the emigrant list. To whom should I turn but to my old childhood friend?"

She stared at him.

"Is that the reason?"

"My dear young lady," said the Vicomte with the almost avuncular aplomb of one who has explained the unexplainable, "that is the truth."

"Then in that case you won't be interested in my news."

"What news?"

"That Querelle has given information to the police."

The blow was so shrewdly given, so completely unexpected, that she could have laughed at the consternation on the Vicomte's face; it was delightful to think that he would soon realize what had moved her to give this warning —a feeling for him which she was sure was ardently returned. At this moment she was filled with a sense of elation, of amusement, of pleasure in her cleverness; while he received a blow more terrible than any threat of danger to himself, a blow at the heart of the conspiracy and at the safety of every émigré in Paris.

"Querelle! Informed! It's not possible."

She saw the strained whiteness of his face and began to understand.

"But it's true."

"How do you know? How can I tell that you've not been sent to trap me?"

"Just because I *have* told you. I needn't have done so. It's common knowledge at the Tuileries; everyone is talking of it. They're saying that a conspiracy has been unearthed. Names have been mentioned, places too. They say that the Count of Artois is involved, that he will be landing soon at some smugglers' beach in Normandy."

"They say that!"

"And more. He will be arrested when he lands."

The Vicomte was breathing heavily, one hand on the hilt of his sword as though impelled to action. Facts that she had mentioned proved her knowledge, and he accepted this, though in the turmoil of his mind he could not guess whether she was royalist or Bonapartist, friend or foe. One thought alone came clearly to him through his bewilderment and fear:

"Why have you told me? I don't understand it. Why?"

"To save you, naturally."

"But why should you connect me with Querelle? How should you know that his confession is dangerous to me?"

Her expression softened and her voice was very gentle as she replied:

"Because you are among those he has denounced."

# Chapter Nine

CHARLES DE BELLAC HAD LITTLE SUBtlety, but he possessed the virtues of a man of action, being calm in adversity and knowing the value of time. Bad news acted as a form of challenge with him; he was not unbalanced by it, but stimulated towards quick decisions—sound ones, for his military training had taught him to be logical; bold ones, for he was by nature resourceful and adventurous.

The news he had just received would have disconcerted most men, for the transition from romance to ruin had been made almost in a breath, but after the first shock was over the Vicomte accepted them both and made his plans to match. The lady had given information that might save his life; it was possible, of course, that she was lying or working to trap him in some way; but this seemed fanciful, and since in any case she was beautiful the Vicomte was determined that they should meet again. There would have to be a pause in view of the betrayal by Querelle. No one of importance seemed to have been denounced, but new arrests might lead to new betrayals in an ever widening ring. He must see Cadoudal at once, Méhée too, for this house belonging to his friend must now be suspect; above all, there was the knowledge that Artois was expected and, unless warned in time, might find unfriendly watchers on the shore.

A few questions, a few brief tender words, and the Vicomte left the room. He was not altogether easy in his mind as he went down the long corridor towards the door; his hand was on his sword as he stepped out into the street —a narrow, sombre street of shadows cast by the tall houses of the quarter in which human shadows could so easily wait unseen; and as he moved away, walking in the centre of the road, the noise of his soft footsteps seemed to be accompanied by other sounds, some late homecomer, probably, stumbling on the uneven flagstones.

Unconsciously the Vicomte quickened his pace. He was a man of proved courage, but he had no wish to die obscurely in this warren. The footsteps in the road had halted now, not far, he estimated, from the house he had just left. The police? Or some loiterer? Suppose it were someone who knew the reputation of the quarter and had seen the door open and the shaft of beckoning light—someone with hopes and inclinations? It was not a pleasant thought, no pleasanter than the one that had come to him when he had first heard the steps behind him in the darkness like echoes of his own. For a wild moment he thought of turning back. He would have done so if any further noise had followed, but as he halted in indecision the deep silence of the night enveloped him, a silence that he read as a kind of invitation, and one which he was sufficiently prudent to refuse.

Walking more slowly, he moved on. The house was secure, the doors were barred, the place was a little fortress in its way; the danger lay ahead at Chaillot, where Georges and Méhée slept oblivious of their danger, and on the roads stretching northwards to the coast. A realist, he scarcely thought of Bouvet de Lozier, of Mme St. Légier, and Spein the carpenter, except in so far as their strength or weakness affected the conspiracy. He knew that they were lost and that by now they would be in the clutches of Réal, subject to police interrogation, which did not have the reputation of being gentle. Nevertheless, it was reasonable to hope that they would hold out for a while, long enough to give their friends the chance to disperse and reorganize, for even Querelle, it seemed, had been resolute till near the end. For one day—which surely must be the minimum of resistance in men and women pledged to loyalty—Georges and Méhée could be considered safe; it was only at this point that the Vicomte, lost in his plans and reflections, remembered that he was among those who had been denounced, and was far from safe himself.

At first he felt inclined to smile at the remoteness of the threat in this vast city even now stirring in its uneasy sleep, but the laughter died as he sensed around him the evidence of his enemies' power, the barracks of the gendarmerie and soldiers, the palace of the Tuileries directly across his path, a darker looming shadow in the false dawn. Suddenly the conspiracy that had been so substantial in London and on the ride from Biville seemed very small, the house at Chaillot a mere dot in the immensity of Paris, dwarfed by the knowledge that the resources of a State of thirty millions were at the disposal of one man lying in that palace set among the chestnut trees.

It was growing light when de Bellac came down to the quays beside the Seine, and grey leaden clouds hung low over the rooftops, ominously tinged on the eastern horizon by a garish orange glow. A wind had risen with the dawn, a mournful wind sighing in the branches that overhung the riverbank, a cold wind, a breath of the northern winter already beating up against the Channel coast. On such a morning Paris was not herself; her luminous quality was lost, and the smoke from her chimneys, rising to meet the lowering clouds, made of her a second London, a chillier London, without defences, inviting the cold to enter down the avenues to her heart.

The young officer, as sensitive to the spirit of the city as he was to the vileness of the weather, drew his cloak closer around him as he walked. He felt conspicuous, for the world seemed to be waking slowly to this inhospitable day; few lights showed in windows, and the people who were abroad seemed to creep along, huddled in the shelter of the houses in a way that looked too ridiculous to imitate. Crowds were his allies, but he was not so confident in these sparsely populated places, where too many were now paid to be inquisitive; it might be noticed that he had the appearance of a soldier without the uniform—a deserter, perhaps, for there were many of that kind in France, youths who had tired of one illusion and had not yet been fattened on another.

Such were the Vicomte's fears as he made his way through the windswept streets, but characteristically, as he approached the point of action, his doubts faded and he grew resolute. A day's grace had been his estimate, and he saw no reason to alter that, even though one of the prisoners was a woman. Mme St. Légier, taken in her house in the rue Saint-Sauveur, would be no less constant than her lover, for like Bouvet de Lozier she was a devoted servant of the King, and would not betray his agents; certainly not at the outset and under a form of questioning which would probably only proceed by degrees towards its brutal end.

The house was quiet, it seemed as though its inmates

were still asleep, and there was no response to the young man's discreet knocking at the door. For good measure he knocked again, a little louder, so that the noise could be heard echoing hollowly in the barely furnished rooms. It was then that he remembered something that had escaped his memory—the property registers that would disclose Mme St. Légier's ownership of this house also, so that her confession might in police eyes be considered almost as a luxury. In that moment of silence, as the sound of his knocking died away, he knew that they might have discovered this hiding-place by the riverside, and he glanced around him at the streets and gardens and at the windows that reflected the glow of the sunrise, calculating the chances of their concealing enemies who waited patiently for him to walk into the net.

No one was visible, the path was open, there might still be time for a retreat: all these thoughts flashed through his mind, conflicting with that stubborn streak in him that had determined to warn his friends; an instant later and he had stepped back a pace, his sword gleaming in his hand.

For he had heard the sound of footsteps inside the house; the door was opening.

Georges? Or some agent of the police? So deep was his concentration that the movement of the door, swift enough in reality, seemed to him to be held in a void of time, and it was with an absurd slowness that he recognized the face of Méhée de la Touche peering out at him from the threshold.

A wave of relief flooded over the Vicomte at the sight of him, so intense that he could not trust himself to speak, for he had not appreciated how much he had been moved by that sudden sense of the imminence of danger, the feeling that he was helpless in a trap. Still carrying his sword unsheathed, he followed Méhée into the house, but not until the door had closed behind them did he find his voice with the abrupt words: "Fetch Georges at once."

De la Touche was looking at him queerly.

"Fetch Georges! But, my friend, I must tell you that he is not here to fetch."

"Not here?"

"No, he has left for the north, you see, for Biville. He has gone to meet Artois. We have heard that in three days the ship is due."

If Méhée had known of Querelle's confession, he could not have delivered this barbed news to more effect; for an instant even the Vicomte's audacity was quelled by the sudden menace that had surrounded the conspiracy and by the absence of the man whom he relied on as his leader. Three days. Cadoudal riding north would be in time, but so would the agents of the police. It was easy to imagine the scene on that lonely coast—the guards in the farmhouse and at the cliff face, the signals carrying their false message out to sea. From his own experience he remembered the confidence placed in these pinpoints of welcoming light which the English seamen on the *Vincejo* would no more think of doubting than their charts. Why should they doubt? The arrangements had stood the test of time, and it would not so much be negligence as plain misfortune if Artois stepped ashore beyond the reach of the longboat to find that it was not Troché who stood with the lantern at the water's edge, nor royalists who waited there to greet him in the shadows below the cliffs.

"Three days," he said, and the sequence of his thoughts could be plainly seen in his face, which had recovered all its old alertness.

"Three days? Three days for what?"

The Vicomte suddenly realized that in the shock of hearing de la Touche's news he had forgotten to tell his own.

"For reaching Biville and preventing the landing of the Count. For warning Georges that we're betrayed."

"Betrayed!" cried Méhée, looking in horror at his guest. This air of great affairs, the dawn arrival, might have no concern with him, but as a specialist in betrayals he was never very comfortable with the word. The Vicomte had not behaved as though he suspected him, dropping his mysterious words almost as an afterthought, but this might be merely subtlety, a quality which Méhée, arguing from the experience of his own slippery mind, was prepared to see in everyone he met. Suppose his visits to Fouché and Bonaparte were known! As he looked at his unpredictable visitor and that blade of steel he felt, perhaps for the first time in his life, a sense of inadequacy, speedily removed as de Bellac answered him.

Querelle! So that was the way of it! He sighed, not in tribute to the man he had destroyed, but in relief at the passing of an unpleasant dream. He was surprised by the news, for he expected a high standard of fortitude in his victims; but the possibility had always existed, and his mind lost no time in weighing the new situation that had arisen, relating it to his own hopes and those of Fouché and Bonaparte.

Two points stood out from the Vicomte's story.

"He has denounced Troché and indirectly Artois, is that what you're telling me?"

"Yes."

"And he has denounced you too, Vicomte?"

It could be seen that de Bellac regarded this as an irrelevance, but Méhée did not share this view, for at Fouché's request he was engaged in fattening his cattle and deprecated any premature attempts at slaughtering them. It was evident that in trying to humour Bonaparte he had overreached himself through using inefficient instruments— men like Querelle who could not be trusted in a little matter like a martyrdom. The probable results of this miscalculation, the arrests of Artois and Cadoudal, would not amuse the ex-Minister, who had hoped to profit by taking them himself; they must be saved if possible for a better day. And here, providentially, in front of him was the means of doing it.

"You spoke of three days," he said.

"Yes."

"Will you ride to save them?"

"Yes."

"Méhée looked keenly into the Vicomte's eyes. He never ceased to marvel at the self-abnegation of the men with whom he came in contact. Bouvet de Lozier, Cadoudal, this young man, asked nothing for themselves; they were prepared to take the gravest risks for an exiled King who half disapproved their actions and a Count of Artois who would conveniently forget them the moment he returned to France. Such conduct seemed incomprehensible to a man who believed he was pursuing selfish aims even at those very moments when he was risking his own life to further Fouché's ends.

"When will you set out?"

"At once."

"What are your plans?"

"You must advise me."

And after a moment's reflection the resourceful de la Touche complied. The Vicomte must make his way to the first *maison de confiance* on the northern road; there he would find a horse. Using relays, he could be on the Chan-

nel coast a clear day ahead of the *Vincejo*, and with luck
might overtake Cadoudal and the police agents on the way.
On the night of the landing he must lie up near the cliffs.
It was possible by using a path through the woods to the
eastward of the farm to approach to within a short distance
of the crest, from where, using a hooded lantern, he could
signal out to sea. If this warning was disregarded he must
take the risk of firing shots; but he must do this only as a
last resort. The Vicomte—and here the thoughts of Fouché
spoke through the mouth of his faithful agent—the Vicomte was valuable to the conspiracy and must not sacrifice
himself. All should go well; the nights would be dark, for
it was the last quarter of the moon.

All this was sound advice, the clarity of which de Bellac
admired as he set off on his journey, so wrapped up in his
adventure that it never occurred to him to wonder why his
friend had not claimed a share in it. If he had been reminded of this he might have been surprised, but would
certainly have said that he preferred things as they were—
the freedom, the sense of self-reliance, the long solitary
rides over the plains.

On the second evening, just before dusk, he reached the
edge of the downland country that stretched towards the
coast, a sparsely wooded country of rolling hills affording
little cover. With his soldier's eye for ground he studied it,
looking for the copses and re-entrants and sunken lanes
along which he might move in the friendly shadows without fear of being seen in silhouette.

The night would certainly be dark. Heavy banks of cloud
hung in the northern sky, against which the sculptured folds
of the downs shone up with startling clarity; with the approach of evening a rather sombre and steely light crept
across the landscape, and in the oppressive silence a few

flakes of snow came drifting down, the fat, lazy outriders of the storm.

Watching them from his cover in the woods, the Vicomte considered his position. He had seen no trace of Cadoudal or of the police agents, whom he might conceivably have outridden in his dash towards the coast. A careful reconnaissance might be the prudent thing, but against that must be set the dangers of delay. If he pressed on he could reach the farmhouse early in the night, protected by the storm which would hide him even more effectively than he could have hoped. The quicker he made his junction with Cadoudal and lay up in the woods near the coast, the better for them both; for there was the danger that the fall would be followed, as so often, by brilliant days and nights when every movement could be seen against the crystal background of the snow.

The thought decided him, and as soon as the last light was gone he set out from his hiding-place, surrounded already by the whirl of falling flakes, mysteriously unlike themselves in the darkness, fluttering against his face like moths towards a flame. It was not easy to find the way, for a moving curtain shut off the small glow of light on the horizon to the west, and he went blindly forward over the coarse tufted grass in the gullies and re-entrants and the carpets of pine needles in the woods, guided by his instinct and that feeling for the contours of ground bred in him by experience of night patrols. It was a long approach—so long and arduous that in its last stages his tiredness and irritation overcame him and he pressed forward imprudently through the storm that slackened as he neared the coast, stumbling on the rough surfaces in hollows half filled with snow. In such a mood he might, for all he knew, have fallen into the arms of some patrol, he might have found himself on the treacherous ground at the summit of the cliff, and it was the merest chance that took him into the orchard that lay between the farmhouse and the sea, freezing his heart momentarily with a sudden indistinct vision of ghostly lime-washed figures on parade.

The snow no longer fell; a faint breeze was stirring in the trees—small, squat trees that seemed to be aware of their exposure and the strength of the Channel gales, so that the night that had been so silent became full of tiny sounds, rustlings and scrapings, the soft fall from the branches, in whose motions and thousand voices it was easy to imagine the presence of enemies abroad.

The orchard lay immediately behind the house covering the main entrance to it on the north—an obvious place for a sentry, the Vicomte thought, remembering his earlier visit and appreciation of the ground. His caution fully restored now that he had identified his position and recognized his danger, he turned about and moved with infinite care at right angles to the way that he had come, making for the angle of the long meadow and the covered approach past the outbuildings of the farm, where the shadows were deepest and the escape route lay inland towards the open country of the downs. Half an hour had passed before he had worked his way into the lee of his objective, which he could see rising before him, shadowy and indeterminate under its snow-white mantle.

The windows on the ground floor were bolted and barred and not a chink of light showed through them, but a faint glow, masked till now by the outbuildings, shone through an upstairs window in the room that he himself had occupied on his earlier visit. The Vicomte, who had an enterprising spirit, studied the problem of reaching it. The timbering would give him a foothold of a sort, and he might be able to make use of the pear tree trepanned against the wall; he had not had time to be intimidated by these diffi-culties—insuperable, if only he had known—before he re-membered the loft across the way, from where it would be possible to see directly into the room.

But how was he to reach this point of vantage? It could only be entered from the barn below, the door of which was locked—these being Norman farmers, among the most prudent of mankind. Fortunately there was a window that gave air and light, and this could be reached without undue difficulty from the ground. Without a moment's hesitation the Vicomte obeyed his impulse; he swung himself up, found the catch—a very old and rusty one—and squeezing through the small space available, dropped to the floor among the stalls.

It was not the least intrepid thing that he had done in the course of an adventurous life, and even he felt a mo-mentary qualm at the sudden stir in the pitch darkness that surrounded him, the sinister rustling and breathing of the beasts. Stooping and with his hands held defensively in front of him, he began to grope his way around the walls, feeling for the ladder by which he could climb out of this perilous and uncertain ark, touching now and again, in spite of his precautions, a hairy flank or mass of horn spring ing with a most unpleasant solidity from the limbo of the night. He breathed a profound sigh of relief as he found what he was seeking in the far corner of the byre, a rough wooden ladder, the rungs chipped and worn with constant use; gratefully his fingers closed on it and he began to climb, forcing up the trapdoor and emerging into a small storeroom, its floor deep in straw and redolent with the musty odour of the stackyard.

With rapid strides he crossed it and, lying down by the

low-set window, gazed out towards the house. There, not thirty yards from him and on the same level, was the room in which he had slept on the night of the landing on the coast. He recognized it clearly: the bed, rustic beyond belief, the stained white plaster between the massive beams, the steep pitch of the roof, the table with its oil lamp—he had thought it at the time to be a fitting room to appear in the adventure, perfectly in key with Troché and the *Vincejo* and the path cut in the cliff, a strange barrack of a room in a house of mystery.

But of occupants there was no sign. Perhaps no one was to be expected there; perhaps the light was a signal, a warning, for the place had been in darkness when he had approached with his companions from the sea. He had begun to accept this, when he was suddenly aware that a shadow was moving in the room, a long shadow that slid along the walls as though in the steps of some macabre and stealthy dance. Backwards and forwards, along the ceiling, into the angle by the door it went, then with a sudden leap swung over towards the bed; an instant later and its slower-moving body came into view—the figure of a man.

De Bellac's heart gave a leap as he recognized the face of Troché turned to gaze out into the night. Up to this moment he had not realized how exposed and lonely he had felt in these last hours in the storm and darkness, but now, as he looked at this colleague who knew the secrets of the cliff, this invaluable colleague who would know the means of sending the warning message out to sea, a feeling of overwhelming gratitude filled him, so that he rose to a kneeling position by the window and reached out a hand, as though trying to declare himself across the gulf that divided him from his friend—and from that other figure that at this moment appeared behind Troché in the room.

At once the Vicomte drew back from the window and dropped down among the straw. He had not known the face of Colonel Savary, but he had recognized the uniform of the special gendarmerie, and with wildly beating heart watched these two shadows that danced in the lamplight with the jerkiness of marionettes—to the window, and away again, and so out of his sight—two shadows in partnership, proofs of a betrayal more deadly than Querelle's. The possibility had been in his mind from the beginning, and he wasted no time in recrimination or regrets. Only the fact of Troché's capture was important, and as soon as the first shock was past the Vicomte began to consider the courses open to him in the light of this new discovery, judging them on their merits with a most admirable coolness.

What should he do? Should he lie there in his hiding-place till the following night and then make his way towards the cliffs? It would have been a test of courage for a man who had no way of knowing whether or not he had been enticed into a trap, but he would certainly have been equal to it if it had not been for the knowledge that Cadoudal was on his way and must be saved if possible from making a trio of shadows in that upstairs room. He must leave, then. He must leave his cover, pass through the ring of sentries, using the stackyard path and the well-shaft as his guide, and hope to waylay his leader at the most likely point of approach—where the sunken road he had noticed on his first reconnaissance met the main track leading inland from the farm. There were obvious dangers in this also, but the worst of them was removed as he saw from the window a flurry of snowflakes pass between him and the lamp in the distant room—grey, hurrying flakes, no longer billowing through the air, but driven purposefully groundwards, where they would soon cover up all tracks.

Having made his plan, de Bellac put it into immediate execution: he turned from the window, opened the trapdoor and climbed down the rickety ladder into the body of the barn. A rather grim smile was on his lips as he found himself once more among the beasts; he was remembering the uneasy feeling with which he had passed by them before, a nervousness that had its humorous side in the light of the reality he had encountered from his window, the knowledge that he had other enemies more formidable than these patient creatures whose shufflings and stampings had created so sinister an impression on his mind.

Climbing rapidly from the barn, he began to move forward in the shelter of the wall, testing each foothold and stopping at frequent intervals to listen and to search the ground ahead, his steps making only the slightest sound in the drifted snow. Yard by yard he crept on, all his senses alert to the spell of danger that he could feel around him in the darkness; though he had seen or heard nothing, he felt that it was a very narrow track of safety down which he moved, running the gauntlet of invisible enemies hovering just beyond his range of vision. He was telling himself of the absurdity of these fancies when, just at the limit of the stackyard and directly in his path, he heard an irregular thudding sound, so soft and muffled by the storm that for a moment he believed it might be another creature of his anxieties.

Imagination? Or falling snow—snow tumbling from the stack above his head? At such a moment the Vicomte showed a discretion worthy of an older and less sanguine man: he dropped on his face where he had more chance of seeing the ground ahead in silhouette. It was as well he did so. From this position, not many yards away a shadow

could be seen projecting from the angle of the barn, a
shadow that moved in a rhythmic movement that he recognized at once. Of course! That muffled, thudding sound—a
sentry warming himself by swinging his arms across his
chest. The man's back was to him; he knew this, for otherwise at such a range the white of the face must infallibly
have shown.

Backwards and forwards swung the arms in the heavy
greatcoat, backwards and forwards like the wings of a huge
bird preening itself in the dust; there was something inhuman and terrifying about the faceless figure gesticulating in
the night. A sentry here at the southern exit; there would
be others, of course, at strategic points around the farm;
and even at this moment of acute peril the young man
found cause to wonder that he had succeeded in creeping
past them in reconnaissance—an uncomfortable pointer to
his theory that he had been invited to slip into a trap.

The man still had his back towards him, he still swayed
in that undisciplined motion to which the Vicomte knew
he owed his life. There was no time to lose. Silently he rose
and darted back the way that he had come. When next he
lay down to take stock of his position the sentry's figure
could no longer be distinguished from the surrounding
gloom, and only the faint noise of his movement still persisted.

A detour to the east seemed the best plan now. Another
sentry could be expected between the orchard and his landmark of the well-shaft, but with good fortune he might
hope to pass between him and his careless colleague, still
playing the part of beacon with a vigour that would have
distressed his commanding officer very much. To the east,
that was the way; and moving with a caution that had been
increased still further by this last adventure, de Bellac began

to pick his way down the small tracks that led between the barns.

As he approached the limits of the yard, the silence of the night was reasserted and his own steps began to sound again quite loudly in his ears—the crunch of loose flakes as they packed beneath his weight, the occasional scraping of stones against his feet. He knew that such sounds would not carry far through falling snow, but it was with a beating heart that he felt his way forward towards his landmark, the well-shaft that lay, he judged, equidistant from the likely sentry posts at the main southern exits from the farm. There it was! He could see its superstructure rising up, a more solid shadow in the darkness, almost in the shape of a man, with its central wheel for a head and its beams branching out into shoulders around the bore.

It *was* a man. The horrid realization came to the Vicomte just as he was satisfied with his position and was moving forward freely. There could be no mistake. Now he could see his enemy—not clearly, for the snow still fell—but sufficiently distinctly to know the full extent of his mistake—the second sentry, posted much closer to the first than he had imagined, and still within the circle of the yard. There was no chance of evasion. He remained motionless, only a few yards away, numbed for an instant by this danger that had struck so suddenly from the shadows of the night.

His footsteps had betrayed him. The man, whose back had been to him, turned, and he could see the glimmer of his face; a voice spoke out of the darkness in a throaty whisper:

"Who's there? André, is that you?"

The question gave him back his courage. André would be the first sentry by the barn; it was not hard to make such a deduction, and the Vicomte, who may have been fortunate in the quality of his opponents, replied immediately in a whisper even more indeterminate:

"Yes, it's me."

"Well, devil take it, man, you're off your beat."

"I know. I'm taking a stroll. I'm cold." And the Vicomte's tone was so convincing that it struck a chord in his fellow sufferer.

"Cold! You're right there. English weather for that damned English ship. Seen anything?"

"No."

"Nor me. Not so much as a cat stirring. Stands to reason that no one—not even these émigré swine we're expecting —would travel on a night like this."

De Bellac was now able to understand the sentry's simplicity: the man was on guard against possible arrivals from outside the perimeter, and naturally would not suspect someone who came from the direction of the farm. Good fortune of this sort amounted almost to an omen, and he was relaxing in the sun of rising hope when he heard the sentry—apparently a man of a strictly subordinate turn of mind—say to him quite sharply:

"But all the same you're off your beat."

"I know."

"You were told to patrol only to the limit of the barn."

"You're right. I'd best get back."

So saying, and with a confidence he certainly did not feel, the Vicomte turned his back on his supposed colleague and slouched off down the way that he had come. He had not gone many yards before he heard a movement behind him and the sentry's voice, raised for the first time above a whisper:

"André, it is André, isn't it? Here, come back!"

He continued to retreat.

"I said, come back. I want to talk to you."

The Vicomte did not look round; he had caught the tones of awakened suspicion in that voice. Not hopefully, but with some sort of fidelity to the part of André, he called back in a loud and not unimpressive whisper:

"Shut up! D'you want our officer or those cursed émigrés to hear?"

This had at least the effect of stopping the sentry's voice —no small advantage, for there was the danger that noise would bring reinforcements to the scene. But deprived of words, the man had fallen back on action, and the Vicomte, as he stumbled forward, became painfully aware that steps now followed him, purposeful steps that seemed to gain with every stride.

There was only one thing to do. By a fortunate chance he was aware of his position—he had caught sight of the well-shaft close at hand, startlingly similar to the vision that had so recently deceived him, so that for one terrible second he imagined that he had run back into the true André's arms. Beyond the well lay a gap in the hedge leading from the stackyard out into the meadow. As he reached it he half turned, catching a glimpse of his enemy looming dimly through the curtain of the storm; next instant he had dived through it and taken to his heels, not running outwards towards the down but doubling sharply on his tracks to bring him back to a position opposite the second sentry post. He had bargained on the stupidity of his antagonist— and with reason, for when, after a short burst at top speed, he stopped to listen, he heard the sound of feet stumbling out at a tangent from his course, and a moment later heard that guttural voice calling out a belated warning to the guards.

So far, so good. He had every reason to suppose that he

was clear of the line of pickets. Admittedly the enemy was now alert and he must expect the appearance of a patrol, but the Vicomte was not disposed to worry over dangers in the offing; he was too greatly relieved at having escaped the trap. Moreover, he knew his precise position, and soon found the sunken road at its junction with the farm track, the objective that he had had in mind from the moment of leaving the shelter of the loft.

Here he paused for breath and gave rapid thought to his future plans. He could not, as he had intended, lie up in this place in the hope of intercepting Cadoudal; to do this was to invite capture and to deny Artois the last chances of escape. No, he must move farther back into the wooded country through which he had passed on his way down to the farm. There he could hope to lie up in safety during the day, and from there he could come at dusk to make his way to the cliffs. This meant the abandonment of Georges, but he was too much the realist to fail to see the necessity for this. There was always the chance, too, that his leader would be warned by the patrol activity, manœuvres which would not be carried out in a silence likely to commend itself to the writers of manuals of war; indeed, a confused shouting could already be heard in the vicinity of the farm, a babel that had a not unpleasing quality, muffled as it was by distance and the falling snow.

So far they were well off the scent and he had ample time to do what he had to do—move back to his hideout in the forest. It was a straightforward journey and, to make assurance doubly sure, there was plenty of cover near at hand: the road itself beneath its steep bush-covered banks, and beyond it a small wood that lay in the mouth of a re-entrant, one of the landmarks that he had unaccountably missed on his way down from the hills.

The little wood, when he reached it, seemed bowed under too heavy a burden of snow, its individual branches sensitive to the slightest touch to release their load, so that the Vicomte was accompanied in his progress by a score of miniature avalanches softly cascading down. How dark it was there in spite of the fall of purest white! Next morning when the storm had lifted the place would glisten like a fairy palace under the crystal candelabra hanging from the trees, but tonight it was more like a cave—a cave far from the seashore, where only the murmur of the breakers was echoed by the soft, languorous patter of the snow.

In the hollows of the wood it was already drifting deep. He must pick his way carefully, keeping to the narrow ride where the foothold would be firmest; indeed, as it was he could see behind him the scars of his passage—deep tracks, too deep for comfort, marks that would betray him if the weather eased. Ahead, a grey carpet was spread out, level to the eye, unmarked.

And suddenly the Vicomte stood very still. Peering into the darkness, he had caught a break in that virgin smoothness—a line of footsteps cutting at right angles across his path.

# Chapter Ten

IN ALMOST THE SAME MOMENT THAT HE
recognized the footmarks the Vicomte saw the man
himself, an indistinct shape not ten feet from him and
to his left. So sudden was the discovery that he had no
time for thought; he was hardly aware that he had tried to
draw his sword when his right arm was pinioned across his
chest, the wrist forced painfully down against the guard,
and it was with a sensation of the utmost unreality that he
found himself lying clasped against his enemy in the snow.
For a second while this tide of action flowed he had no
plan; his actions were responses that had no more effect
than the movements of a twig drifting on the surface of a
stream. In that time he came very near to death. The sudden force of the attack had flung him to the ground; a knee
was on his chest; a hand grasped his throat, found it and
forced him downwards so that most of the upper part of
his face was covered in the drift.

With returning consciousness came the most acute perception of what his body suffered. He seemed to be aware
of the exact force exerted by each finger of that hand, till,
after a time that seemed interminable, but which must in
fact have been extremely short, each individual pressure

merged into a whole, a slow, dreadful weight bearing down on him like the closing of a vice. Down, down. With a sense of wonderment existing outside of himself, an intense disembodied curiosity, he felt the mounting constriction and measured his own capacity to bear it. His breath was very laboured, so loud in his ears that he no longer heard the movements of his enemy, a soundless force as anonymous as it was powerful.

After the first vain struggle the Vicomte had lain quite still. Already some traitor instinct was telling him that he need stay so only a little longer and the pain would be gone for ever; it would be so easy, so effortless; the way back would be long and arduous, and this present agony had a strange fascination of its own. But there was more to the Vicomte than the resignation and defeatism that lurks in every human soul: with a sudden effort, doubly surprising after his long yielding, he flung himself sideways, striking out at the same time with all the strength of his left arm. He heard a muttered exclamation as his blow went home, felt an easing of the tension, and with another desperate lunge flung himself loose and rolled from under his antagonist.

Almost in the same motion he was on his feet, ready to grapple with an enemy who rose to a kneeling position in front of him from the drift. The Vicomte's right hand was free and he had drawn his sword, but even as he measured his distance for the stroke—a regretful necessity to a chivalrous man faced with an enemy who used no arms—he caught sight for the first time of his rival's face, and, with an exclamation of surprise, lowered the point towards the ground.

"Georges!"

He might have guessed as much from that giant strength.

The man's figure now towered up before him, the oxlike body, with its great arms held out defensively in front of it.

"Georges, don't you recognize me? De Bellac. Do you have to kill your friends by way of greeting them?"

Cadoudal took a step forward, tentatively, as though fearful of a trap. His eyes, less sharp than de Bellac's, peered into the night.

"It's you, Charles! What a scare you gave me!" At which the Vicomte began to laugh, softly but in a way that suggested the presence in his heart of very unhumorous emotions, before replying: "And what effect do you suppose you had on me?"

By way of answer the leader reached out an arm so that it fell with all the friendliness imaginable around the Vicomte's neck. A slight spasm passed through the young man's body at that touch, and he could not prevent himself from drawing back.

"Yes, I thought you'd done for me. Do you always fight like that?"

"Like what?"

"Blindly, like an ox."

Cadoudal's grip, which he had not allowed to be disengaged, tightened on his friend. He was not remarkable for sensibility.

"Ah, *mordieu*, how was I to know! I believed you in Paris. I know there are enemies at the farm, I see a man tracking in the wood; what should I think? At such times one doesn't ask questions, one just acts."

"You acted. But afterwards? When I was lying under you? Didn't you even look to see whom you had the honour to be strangling?"

It was Georges' turn to laugh—a soft but uninhibited sound.

"But, my poor friend, you had the misfortune to be half buried in the snow. You were unrecognizable."

"It's certain that in a few more moments of that grip I should have been."

Georges expressed his professional agreement. From his tone of relish it might have been imagined that he was speaking of a game; de Bellac, however, was to be pardoned for failing to share these enthusiasms.

"So we nearly killed one another, that's what it amounts to. We nearly saved the police the trouble."

It was enough to recall Cadoudal to his responsibilities. He listened quietly while the Vicomte told him of Querelle's confession and its results.

"So that's why the sentries are there!" he said at last. "And they've got Troché, you say? He'll betray the landing lights. Since they know of your arrival, we must expect patrol activity as soon as it gets light. These fellows can't see beyond their noses in the dark—not that you or I were very noticing just now, though we'd some excuse."

It was plain that de Bellac, still bruised and shaken by his experience, would take rather longer in accepting explanations of it; the fact that he had escaped from a ring of enemies to be nearly dispatched by a friend could not be expected to strike him as quite so humorous as it did his leader. He gently disengaged himself from Georges' arm, which still lay around him, rather too solid a reminder, and moved a few paces down the ride.

Cadoudal was not sensitive to atmosphere, but he was to the call of action.

"You want to be going, Charles? Well, it would be wise. We'll get back into the hills."

And without another word he took the lead. He marched almost with the certainty of Troché on that earlier night, de Bellac thought as he followed silently in his tracks. It was interesting to see that Georges had made the same appreciation of the ground as he had himself—a route out of the wood into a re-entrant, along the low ground beneath a hill of pines, and rising towards that spot where he had made his reconnaissance at dusk.

There, in that hollow on the edge of the wood, they halted, stripped some branches from the trees to form a hide, and lay down to snatch in turn a brief hour of sleep before the dawn. Both were awake when the first flush glowed in the eastern sky, and they looked down from their shelter across the plain that lay between them and the sea, a landscape that seemed featureless till the increasing light picked out the farm and its outbuildings, the ravines and copses, so many irregularities standing out from the level mantle of the snow.

The storm was easing; the flakes were beginning to drift as though uncertain of their ending, whisked here and there by the air currents around the barrier of the woods, so that they resembled in their motion the play of gnats on a summer night. Even as the two men watched, the last drops fell, wrung from the cloudbank, ragged in its emptiness, that was being broken up and driven inland by the wind. With delicate subtlety the scene was changing: the grey carpet seemed to be charged with some secret internal glow, moving by gradual progression till the whole was a dull metallic white; so it persisted till the sun, breaking through the film of cloud, revealed the myriad crystals that glittered from every twig and blade of grass.

The sun had done more than wake this hidden spring of nature that had lain dormant through the night; below them in the valley, from the distant farm, two files of ant-like figures could be seen emerging—the police patrols. On they came, extending into open order as they reached the down, one striking away in the direction of Dieppe, the other advancing directly inland, breasting the rising ground in an untidy arc.

From their hollow at the forest's edge the two fugitives had almost a bird's-eye view; they could look down on their enemies who advanced with the slow, ragged air of men who had not breakfasted—a sight not without its humour, though the unpalatable fact remained that the line seemed to be directed on that distant screen of woods. After half an hour of mountaineering in the snows, this fact was all too clear. Whether the troops were following a definite set of tracks or were merely blessed with a fortunate eye for ground, there could be no doubt that they were moving in a direction that would bring them to the hill-crest in the region of the hide.

As soon as this became clear, Cadoudal and de Bellac took stock of their position.

Two alternatives were open: to retreat inland at once; or to lie low in their hollow under the tracery of boughs. Both courses had their dangers. If they followed the first they would be laying a fresh spoor, a cord that would attach them to their pursuers and make their secret arrival at the cliff face an impossibility. On the other hand, to stay where they were seemed to court disaster; for though they could detect no flaw in the surrounding snowfield, no mark of their passage that could betray them, there was always the chance that farther down in the plain the fall had been less heavy and had failed to cover up their tracks.

Less than a mile separated the parties when the choice was made at last—the bold choice, the one that gave them the best chance of carrying out their mission. It was no easy decision to take—to lie like rabbits in a warren while their enemies passed by above their heads. They had no means of knowing how their shelter would look from the outside—a few branches spread over a hollow thinly covered with a film of white. In the short time left to them they did their best to make it impenetrable, packing the gaps between the boughs with snow and bracken and dead leaves from the pit bottom, so that they left themselves only a small peephole out into the plain, a viewpoint empty now as the patrol climbed in the dead ground between valley and escarpment; in compensation men's voices came to them, sharp and exclamatory on the brilliant frosty air.

Huddled together in their burrow, the fugitives watched and waited. Such words as they could distinguish gave them no answer to the question whether or not their tracks were seen. They found a dozen reasons for hope that they were not; the route followed by the patrol was, after all, the obvious one, the line of least resistance along the valley, avoiding the slopes and ridges, the toilsome ground. There could be no doubt that the field around the hide was undisturbed, a comforting thought, as was the knowledge they had obtained during the night of the clumsiness of their enemies.

As they reasoned in this way, each to himself, they became aware that silence had fallen in the world beyond: the voices that had grumbled and called to one another ceased. Perhaps the patrol was moving on another line; perhaps—it seemed a reasonable explanation—it had turned back. They were gazing through their peephole, focusing on the point on the down where it first became visible beyond the dead ground at the foot of the escarpment to catch the sight of men's retreating backs, when the first figure of the patrol loomed suddenly into view above the crest a hundred yards in front of them, an officer of gendarmerie, a gigantic figure silhouetted against the sky, followed an instant later by others who seemed to spring out of the ground on either side.

As he gazed in horror at these apparitions, the Vicomte heard a rustle and felt the barrel of Cadoudal's pistol, withdrawn from the holster, pass close to his body to slide forward into a position of readiness at the pit mouth. Georges had been armed, then; that meeting in the depths of the wood might have had another ending; and de Bellac, moved by the memories of the night, felt with his hand to where his own pistol and sword lay in readiness, pitiful weapons, he knew, seeing that line of men advancing on the hill-crest.

They were very close now, so close that the watchers in the hollow could see the pale unshaven faces of the men and their lieutenant, an eagle of a man with a mane of hair and predatory nose so that he looked like one of the swashbucklers of Murat's cavalry. He was the nearest to their hide: his fierce bright eyes seemed to peer into its depths, so that the fugitives, obeying a natural impulse, looked out no longer but flattened themselves as low as possible in the snow.

Now they could only listen, placing their enemies by some muttered exclamation, the jingle of equipment, the noise of footsteps—one set in particular, coming closer, closer, so that it seemed to them that the ground itself was trembling about their ears.

Would they never pass? In these seconds, so great was their concentration that individual movements were taken from their pattern; footsteps were prolonged so that they imagined they could distinguish the sharp crackle of the boot against the freezing top surface of the drifts, the packing noise of flakes compressed, the lighter dragging note as the step was carried through the powdery centre of the field.

Heads down between their arms, they lay there listening, waiting for the end. By what fantastic ill chance had their most dangerous foe been brought to the very entry to their refuge? They could not know that below them in the valley two lines of half-filled tracks had pointed the way towards the hills. They had not led directly to the hollow, ending well away below the pine wood, wiped out by the heavy fall that had swept the escarpment in the last hour before dawn, but even so they had been of help to a man who had an eye for country. The slowness of his steps was not only a fantasy of the imagination of two men whose hearing had been sharpened by their danger; it was a fact, for, with every sense alert on this hill-crest that seemed to him an ideal point of vantage for his quarry, he was moving forward step by step, searching the ground with his penetrating eyes.

Lying as they were, the fugitives were spared the sight of his shadow as it fell across the entrance to their burrow, cutting off most of the thin, filtered light; a second later they were jerked into a realization still more terrible as a sharp crash sounded immediately above them—the lieutenant had struck out at the canopy of branches with his sword.

A cascade of snow fell into the pit, and if they had looked up they would have seen clearly, through the rift the blow had made, the black surfaces of the soldier's boots towering up like monstrous snakes with hood and body raised. At this instant any sudden movement would have destroyed them: they must have been seen and dug like foxes out of an earth. But something of the instinct of all hunted creatures had entered these two brave men: they lay there, silent after that sudden stir of terror, in a kind of paralysis of the will that did not know its danger—or its salvation.

For the blow had been a random one, an act of routine

suspicion marking not their discovery but their release. After a moment there came again the sound of footsteps, as slow as before, but now gifted with the flying quality of time, merging into the perspective of the pursuit—the muttering voices, the jingling equipment of the patrol. The men were past, though it was not till the sounds were falling very faintly on the morning air that de Bellac and Cadoudal dared to peep through an opening in the hide to see the line of figures moving on their way, menacing no longer but dwarfed by the immensity of the forest, so that even their leader seemed only a stunted and faintly comic figure as he peered and searched among the trees.

All that day the patrols were active in the ground between the hill-crest and the farm. The results of their dawn search seemed to have had a depressing effect on them, as could be seen from the forlorn way in which they straggled back, and the work of the afternoon hardly pretended to be more than a formality, a routine check on the terrain near the mouth of the re-entrant.

Free from the menace that had threatened them that morning, the watchers in the hollow were able to take an Olympian view. The dots that crawled over the brilliant surface of the fields had an unreal air; it was hard to imagine anything more than an insect intelligence behind these forays over the empty ground. But towards nightfall there was a change: the lines drew in, merged into a swarm, parted, and formed a series of geometrical patterns in the long meadow behind the farm—none the less sinister because of the evening light that shone on them so that they seemed to be anchored in a pool of blood.

This was the concentration for the main business of the night. It was at hand, for the sun was setting in the western haze, so fat and swollen that his retreat seemed only com-

mon prudence, leaving the sky to less robust luminaries—
the planet Venus and the moon, the one poised almost in
the crescent of the other to form a constellation of their
own. Dusk came and the afterglow, shading into a brilliant
night—one of those nights that start immodestly and are
soon censored by the clouds. They were already on the horizon, large snow-laden ones advancing on a north wind from
the sea—the same wind that would bring the *Vincejo*
speeding to her rendezvous.

As soon as darkness had fallen Cadoudal and de Bellac
had begun their march, keeping below the hill-crest to avoid
the danger of silhouette. Their plan was simple. They
would make a detour to the east, come down to the coast
beyond the probable defence perimeter of their enemies and
work their way back to Biville along the summit of the
cliffs. From that point onwards they must depend on the
good fortune that had been with them from the beginning,
enabling them to survive not only the patrols and sentries,
but each other—a rather sterner test. They had no means
of signalling, and must therefore hope in some way to inter-
fere with the lamps arranged by the police.

The two men, tired and hungry though they were,
marched at a fair speed along the ridge. Action of any kind
was pleasant after the long hours in the hollow, and they
welcomed it joyously, stretching their cramped limbs and
breathing in the crisp night air. Here in the hills they had
no fear of enemies, for they had seen enough before dusk
to guess the plan of Savary—a tight perimeter sealing off
the landing beach.

To creep inside it would be no easy matter, but they did
not concern themselves unduly; a more pressing fear was
that they might be late at the rendezvous, forestalled by a
wind that was freshening with every moment, so that those

stars lowest on the northern horizon were already masked by cloud. This might bring advantage later, the cloak of darkness at the cliff face, but for the moment it was a threat, hurrying them forward along the smooth, deceptive carpet into which they floundered sometimes to their knees.

The going was easier once they had left the ridge, against which the morning snow had driven, and were descending towards the sea; they even found a kind of path whose course could be traced by its raised banks humped protectively on either side. They followed this for close on a mile, they left it and veered slightly to the east in case their enemies had marked this feature of the ground; it had done its work for them, for before the cloudbank had passed across the moon a faint murmurous sound came to them, the noise of breakers beating in against the rocks.

Moving more cautiously, the two men completed the short distance to the cliffs and, reaching it, flung themselves down full length. Below them the arc of surf shone dully, so much less white than the snowfield that had glittered in the starlight, and beyond it the Channel waves merged into a sky as dark and sullen as themselves. The mood was one of emptiness like that of a darkened ballroom before the arrival of the guests; there was no sign of the *Vincejo* or of the lights to guide her, no sign of her hosts or of the precautions taken to guard against the uninvited. The first sentry, Cadoudal guessed, would be less than half a mile away, part of a ring stretched around the farm. One way of penetrating it was obvious: descend the cliff and attack the lights from the direction that the defenders would never dream of—up the path itself. But one look at the ground showed the impossibility of this, for below them the cliff sheered away as though cut by some gigantic knife.

There was no alternative, and the two men, accepting

their destiny without question, rose to their feet and began
their cautious approach towards their enemies. They were
fortunate in the darkness that was deepening around them
as the storm gradually crossed the coast, rolling its immense
snow-laden pillow in front of it and smothering the starlight as it came. Visibility was still moderate, but already
the ridge where they had lain that afternoon and the wood
between the re-entrant and the farm were ceasing to be
landmarks, so that they were glad to have as guide at their
right hand the dull booming of the sea.

With the utmost caution the two men moved forward,
pausing at almost every other step to listen and search the
ground ahead. They were nearing the summit of the cliff
path, but still they could hear no sound nor see a light—
not even a glow from the concealed lanterns that must
now be in position in hollows in the rocks. Such discipline
on their enemies' part called for special precautions of their
own, and they dropped to a crawling position in the snow. It
was slow and painful progress, but in the rising tide of excitement they hardly felt the effort or the cutting edge of
the frozen crystals against their hands; all their thoughts
were directed outwards from themselves towards the inno-
cent-looking country that stretched before them and the sea
beyond, both so empty that it might have occurred to them
that they were responding to the menace of a dream.

The sight of the first picket was the proof of the reality.
The royalists caught a glimpse of his shadow, heard the
rustle of his movement, and lay still. The man was inland
from them at a distance of about fifty yards, apparently lying in a hollow that he had scooped out for himself so that
the rim showed clearly from ground level, a small crater
banked with walls of slush. At a touch from Cadoudal the
Vicomte began to edge closer to the verge, and soon the

two men were lying there side by side, looking down once more on Biville beach. If they had hoped to find some ledge in the chalk, a covered approach to the heart of their enemies' position, they were quickly disillusioned, for the cliff could be seen stretching down from them, slightly concave near the crest and providing not the semblance of foothold for a man. The thought of continuing along the summit past the picket might be a daunting one, but it was even more unpleasant to dream of venturing on that wall, grey and ghostlike where it first sheered away below them, disappearing into a void of darkness slashed by the line of breakers of the ebbing tide.

The beach itself could only be guessed at—an indeterminate space between the grey suggestions of chalk and surf, but even as they watched a sudden pinpoint of light flashed out from it, was dimmed, flared out, and burned with a steady flame—the beach light, the last in the galaxy of signals to the sea.

The sight of the lamp by itself was a call to action, and the knowledge of who held it added the spur of anger to the watchers on the cliff. They turned inland and crawled, one behind the other, westward into the defence perimeter, aided by a slight depression in the ground, from the trough of which they could not see the sentry or the glacis he had built up around his hide. They must, they reckoned, be within pistol shot of the summit of the cliff path, though even now they could see no trace of the higher guide lights, presumably set by Troché in their usual positions where they would be screened from the landward side.

They might be out in their calculations, and therefore the only thing to do was to continue to advance. They did so, yard by yard, wriggling like lizards along the surface of the ground, till Cadoudal, who was leading, stopped suddenly and with a thrust of the foot signalled to his friend.

The Vicomte came up alongside his leader, and both men peered into the night, judging the quality of the darkness, the suggestion of more solid shadows that seemed to move in it. A second later and their fears were realized as a whispering was borne downwind to them, punctuated by the sound of stealthy movement and the clink of steel. They had reached their objective and were lying within a few yards of the path they had climbed so painfully on their journey to France—a path guarded, as they could see now, by at least a dozen men.

It was a grim discovery after great and sustained efforts—the ruin of their hopes. For two men, very indifferently armed, to assault twelve was unpromising enough, but the chances of bursting through the cordon to the lights on the cliff were slighter still. They were weighing the odds with that detachment that is part of the stuff of courage when suddenly, as a terrible spur to their decision, a flicker of light shone to the northward from the void of sea—twice repeated, then answered from below them, where the beach light began to move in a frenzied dance. For a few seconds the two men on the cliff top could see no more; then gradually a pale glow began to part the darkness, revealing the phantom of a ship running under the lightest canvas towards the shore. So soft and purposeful was her movement, so strong the suggestion of a remorselesss power at work to cast her on the rocks, that it seemed almost a departure from the natural when, a cable's length offshore, she luffed into the wind.

At sight of her de Bellac had drawn his pistols from their holster, but Cadoudal held out a restraining hand. At this

moment they could have talked out loud or made any movement they chose, for all attention on the cliff was concentrated on this guest coming from the sea.

The *Vincejo* lay close offshore opposite the beach light,
her small spread of canvas drawing in the breeze and holding her against the tide with such delicacy that she might
have been at anchor. Of human agency there was no sign;
she had manœuvred herself close to shore and had then
turned her stern to it as if by whim; so that it came as no
surprise when she performed another independent action,
spawning a shadow into the sea. It seemed a lengthy process,
and for a while the details were not clear: umbilical cords
of ropes and oars seemed to hold it to her side; then they
were severed and it emerged as a creature of its own—a
small, pugnacious-looking body rustling through the waves.

And suddenly the creaking of rowlocks could be heard.
The noise, so touchingly familiar in that silence that had
seemed to belong to an alien world, broke the spell that had
held the royalists on the cliff. Now was the time. There was
no chance—there never had been a chance—of altering the
cliff lights, and their only hope lay in the weapons in their
hands. They were in the presence of their enemies, but then,
as their ears and eyes reminded them, they were also in the
presence of their friends.

Next instant they were on their feet, pistols in hand, and
the warning shots, springing with paralysing suddenness out
of the darkness and silence, were volleying from the cliffs.
In the wild confusion of that moment, the two men turned
and raced inland through the line of pickets. But they had
seen the swirl of waters round the longboat's stern, and
could guess the passage of her darkening shadow back towards the *Vincejo* and the open sea.

# Chapter Eleven

A S SOON AS FOUCHÉ HEARD THE FIRST
whisper of Querelle's confession, he set off hot-
foot for the Tuileries. This dastardly plot affected
him profoundly, he told Méneval, the First Consul's secretary; furthermore, as ex-Minister of Police, he
believed that his assistance might be welcome.

The Secretary seemed to doubt it. His long, thin face and
nose, which would have equipped a setter very well, were
trained on the visitor as though testing the wind of favour
—not blowing very hard in this direction—and though he
showed the utmost deference to the Senator, it was clear
that he had a poor opinion of the man.

It was most unfortunate, he explained, but the First Consul was engaged, very heavily engaged. Certain matters had
arisen affecting the security of the State; he was in conference and could not be disturbed.

"But I require to see him," Fouché said.

An interview? That could be arranged. It would certainly
be arranged for the Senator with the greatest possible dis-
patch. Tomorrow, probably. Or the day after. M. de Talleyrand was with the First Consul now, also Réal, charged with

the affairs of the police—all of which went to prove that Claude François de Méneval, recently appointed in succession to Secretary Bourrienne, was settling down very nicely in his place.

The Senator had to bear it. Not a flicker in those dull green eyes showed how affronted he was by this impertinence, the renewed proof of how low he had sunk in the hierarchy. Everything in Méneval's manner seemed to be saying that when junior officials can indulge in pleasantries of this kind it was time their butts thought seriously of retirement, though Joseph Fouché, who had been insulted by more men than he could remember—including Robespierre —was the last person to be impressed by such manœuvres. He would wait, if that would not incommode the Citizen Secretary; he would wait there in the office on the off chance that Bonaparte—separated from him only by a single door —might spare a moment, some time, for important news.

The Citizen Secretary pricked up his ears at that. "News?"

Well, naturally. Dignitaries of the Consulate, ex-ministers who knew the strict business routine of Bonaparte, would hardly pay courtesy calls in office hours.

And what sort of news was it that brought the Senator at this time?

News of the gravest moment. But he, the Senator, would wait. He was always prepared to wait. Time was no object to him. It might be to the First Consul who was rather more intimately concerned. And in his rather graceless way Fouché sat down in one of the green leather chairs, his face as impassive when dealing blows as when receiving them.

The operative word was time. Méneval knew his master, he knew his maxim that it was the one thing that could not be spared; he remembered also the order given to his predecessor, Bourrienne, never to wake Napoleon with good news but to communicate bad even in the middle of the night. It was one thing to protect him from unwelcome visitors and to score off so detestable a public figure in the course of it, but it was quite another to risk his own employment; and he rose from his desk, rather a worried expression in his pale young face, creased already by that almost intolerably burdened look that is part of the camouflage of small officials.

He would see. He would enquire. Perhaps the conference with the Foreign Minister and the police would be ending soon—but even this salvo failed to penetrate the defences of the most inscrutable of men, who watched his antagonist's lame retreat with those hooded eyes at whose secrets a whole generation of politicians had guessed without finding out anything to their advantage.

Left to himself, the Senator looked round the room approvingly. A functional room like this, a workroom, appealed to him, and he had created something similar during the days of his power at police headquarters on the Quai Voltaire. There was much that he admired about Bonaparte, the only fully adult individual—Talleyrand apart—that he had met; they had a great deal in common and were divided only by ambition—which would have divided Fouché from the devil himself if that functionary had been in politics. A great man, Bonaparte, an inevitable man who had been called to office, if not even into existence, by France's need. But very soon his work would have been done. After the soldier and administrator, the statesman; and Fouché, who believed himself to be every bit as inevitable as his master, was waiting for the turning of the wheels of fate in the intervals of giving them a surreptitious push or two to roll them on their way.

This conspiracy of the émigrés had shown every sign of helping the juggernaut along; he had had the greatest hopes. And now, thanks to the duplicity of de la Touche and the weakness of Querelle, all his plans were compromised and his dupes forewarned. He had had to come hurrying to the Tuileries to scramble some advantage from the wreck, sacrificing his dignity and putting himself at the mercy of officials like this cockerel of a Secretary. That was the sort of man springing up under the Consulate—loyalty without intellect, routine without experience, creeping into the ministries and the armies, the new automata—and he, Fouché, was unemployed. Soon there would be no one left with initiative or the capacity for intrigue—excepting Talleyrand; he was always excepting Talleyrand, and for a moment a gleam of an expression not entirely hostile shone in the Senator's eyes as he thought of the man who had been his bane and brother all his adult life.

That trace of humanity promptly vanished with the returne of Méneval—rather a subdued return, he thought, reading his own triumph in the Secretary's face. The First Consul was agreeable. The First Consul was free and would see him. The First Consul was greatly pressed for time, but if the Senator would follow, please—and Fouché, smiling inwardly, was led into the salon where Bonaparte sat working in the candlelight. He could have foretold his reception in perfect detail: the silence, the abstraction of Bonaparte who, though a genius, was a badly brought-up person, as Talleyrand remarked, given to these senseless displays of power that could hardly hope to impress a Fouché and, in fact, only succeeded in amusing him still further, so that it was almost with benevolence that he stood waiting for its end.

"Ah, Senator."

It was over. Bonaparte was looking up at him with that direct, penetrating gaze that seemed to reach into men's hearts. Fouché alone was perfectly equipped to meet it, being so little overawed that he was capable of analysis. Blue-grey eyes and sallow skin; the eyes of a Nordic and the complexion of the south: there lay the fascination of this complex man with a Cæsar's will and intellect, and the instincts of a brigand; two personalities not fully integrated struggled in one brain and body, a source of weakness that would mar the Consul's life. Armed with such knowledge, the Senator was able to meet his master's stare as calmly as he had borne his silence—also the abrupt words that followed.

"I am busy. What brings you here? Méneval says that you have news."

Fouché inclined his head.

"What news?"

"Of police matters, General."

At that Bonaparte sat back in his chair and laughed his harsh and mirthless laugh.

"Police matters! You're always concerned with them. You think of nothing but the police."

"That was my trade."

"And is now the concern of others"—for it was part of the contradiction that Napoleon's great qualities should be matched by petty meannesses.

The Senator remained unruffled, for he never expected generosity or delicacy from Bonaparte.

"It's their concern," he said. "But are they concerning themselves, do you suppose?"

"The police? You are criticizing it, that matchless organization that you built up! You have told me a thousand times that not a dog barks in France but it's known of at the Quai Voltaire."

"I must remind you, General, that I'm no longer there these days to hear it."

"But you've heard something. You still have your contacts, it appears?"

Only an impassivity not acquired but bred in his nature prevented the Senator from smiling at these words. His master would have been astonished to know how many contacts he had retained, how many police agents still reported to him, more faithfully than they ever did to their nominal superiors. Through those long bony hands there still passed the threads that led into the clubs and salons and the most remote provincial hamlets, connecting him as intimately as in the days of his power with the life of France.

"I do manage to hear things," he replied.

"And they have made you critical of your successors? Come now, speak openly. You accuse them?"

"Say that I reproach them, General."

"With what?"

"With permitting a conspiracy to grow under their noses."

"A conspiracy," repeated Bonaparte, feeling with a sense of elation that he was about to triumph over one of the two men of whom he was secretly afraid. "What sort of conspiracy, may I ask?"

"A royalist conspiracy, Citizen First Consul."

"Ah, a royalist conspiracy! Here in France?"

"In Paris."

"And at Biville, possibly."

"You know that, General!"

Napoleon's face was pitted in a smile—not a natural expression, for his eyes and mouth seemed to have been fashioned only to show the play of intellect. In rather an unguarded moment he had assumed that what was common knowledge at the Tuileries had not yet percolated to those frontiers where this fallen favourite lived, and he could not resist taking the advantage that he believed he had obtained.

"Perhaps you will be giving me names?" he said. "Querelle, for instance, who was tried a week ago?"

"And Bouvet de Lozier."

"And Bouvet de Lozier, Senator, your information is exact. Perhaps you would add the man's mistress to the list, and Spein, and Troché, and a young hothead called de Bellac?"

Even the mention of that last name, a special delicacy that he had been waiting to serve up in his own good time, did not shake Fouché's calm, though he did contrive to look a little surprised and wounded—a reaction which he thought would be expected of him.

"You are the one who is exactly informed, General," he said.

"By the police, Senator. By the police whom you accused."

"I can see I was in error."

"Greatly in error. How much so you may appreciate when I tell you that Savary is at this moment at Biville waiting to arrest Artois when he lands."

"Artois landing!"

"But this is news to you!" cried Bonaparte with deepest irony, well pleased that he had spared the time to see this troublesome ex-Minister.

"Of course."

"Though it has become—through some lapse in security which is certainly a matter for reproach—almost common gossip here."

The Senator slowly shook his head, as though in amazement at his own defective information.

"One must admit," the First Consul added, "that you are a trifle out of date."

"Oh, I agree."

"Querelle, Bouvet de Lozier, Troché, Bellac, Spein. Vieux jeux. Have you anything to add?"

"Nothing, except that you have omitted Cadoudal from the list."

Not for the first time in his dealings with the Senator, Bonaparte suffered the awareness—intolerable to one with his military turn of mind—of being outmanœuvred and dropped into a pit. The patronizing smile was wiped from his face, and he leaned forward suddenly in his chair.

"What's that you're saying?"

"Cadoudal, General—Georges, if you prefer. He has been in Paris for three months."

It was some satisfaction to the Senator, who had had a disagreeable afternoon, to see the outburst of rage that followed this news that he had delivered with such artistry; he watched, contempt curving his lips, this deplorable lapse in self-control, the reversion to the barbarian. That Regnier and Réal should be threatened with court-martial seemed no better than their due; that the entire police force should be remodelled, an amusing fancy; but even in his ungovernable fury against his officials and "*ces bougres d'émigrés*" the First Consul did not fail to find one comment that came nearer home:

"That assassin in Paris for three months! And you have known of it."

The ex-Minister speedily disclaimed so great a knowledge, but to no avail.

"I suppose you will tell me that you discovered this today."

"Yes, General."

"You expect me to believe that when you have known it for some time! This is some intrigue that you are playing."

"With what object, may I ask?"

"With the object of discrediting your successors and succeeding them. But you won't be Minister, don't dare imagine it. I would rather be incompetently than treacherously served."

The Senator had listened with complete calm to this abuse, so divorced from the normal emotions that he was even able to admire the sharpness of Bonaparte in recognizing the motive behind his visit and in using anger as a means of policy. But he knew the value of firmness, and said in his colourless, icy voice:

"You put a premium on incompetence by rewarding truth this way."

"Rewarding truth! What does it matter how I reward it? At the best you have only done your duty. And you have been well repaid: you are a Senator; you did not leave the Ministry exactly in a state of penury."

How typical that was of Bonaparte, who believed that he could attach people to himself through the medium of rewards. Fouché, who knew rather more of human gratitude, could have foretold that the only people who would not desert this Cæsar in his hour of need were the N.C.O.s and subalterns of his armies, the men whom he had loved the most and helped the least.

"I was not referring to material rewards."

"No?"

Some men might have become heated at the implications of that question—if only they had dared—but the Senator was proof against such impulses; he may also have shared his master's ironical surprise.

"No, I meant something more intangible. Permit me to

say, General, that you are ensuring the suppression of the truth. People will be afraid. They will tell you what they think will please you, and you will be the sufferer."

"Then when that time comes," said Bonaparte, rapidly recovering his good temper, "I shall call on more candid advisers—men like you."

"I must wait, then?"

"Yes, my dear Senator. To return you from the Senate to a mere Ministry would be demotion—the time is hardly ripe for it. But we digress. Cadoudal, now. Where can he be found?"

It had been a miscalculation, to say the least, for as Fouché showed in his expression of blandest ignorance, the time was hardly ripe for telling that.

# Chapter Twelve

EARLY IN THE MORNING DIANE DE FLO-
rian had presented herself in her mistress' room
with her report on her meeting with the Vicomte—
full and accurate and only less than candid when it
came to the matter of the reporter's state of mind. Here she
felt herself to be on uncertain ground, for she could not be
sure that Hortense was as disinterested as she appeared; indeed, it seemed unreasonable when one considered the
young man's looks and thrustful manner, and compared
him with this husband who had crept home from Montpellier like the bloodless invalid he was.

Her mistress was afraid of Louis, that was clear, but that
did not mean that she was any the less aware of the attractions of de Bellac or that she would be pleased to find a
rival in her maid-of-honour. Discretion was desirable in sub-
ordinates, and this young woman, once so very liberal with
the gossip of the Tuileries, was now so guarded in everything
she said that Hortense, who understood her well, could not
help being amused.

"I suppose you compromised us both, Diane," she said.

"Compromised us? It's certainly compromising politically
to meet a man who is proscribed."

"And that is what I meant, of course," replied Hortense, reaching out her hand along the coverlet towards her friend. "Politically." And she smiled that sad smile of hers that contained only a hint of mockery.

Diane was alarmed by it; it seemed to confirm her fears.

"He was proscribed from the beginning, madame. The case has changed only in degree."

"Of course."

"And it was your wish that I should meet him."

"Against your inclination, naturally?"

Diane gave an uneasy laugh. In court circles she had a reputation for discretion—only it was called intrigue—but she found it hard to keep countenance with her mistress, a woman who seemed unworldly but who in some strange way was perceptive, with an instinct for the truth.

"I don't think my inclinations enter into it," she said. "I do as I'm told, even when the orders are dangerous—or treasonable."

"So you were afraid?"

"A little. There is the police to think of. It is not easy to forget that the Vicomte is an enemy of the State."

Hortense, who had been lying back against the pillows of her bed, suddenly raised herself.

"But did you forget he was, Diane? Did you forget to the extent of telling him that he had been denounced?"

It was a dangerous question. Diane knew the strong ties of affection that bound her mistress to the Bonapartes, an interest that might, for all she knew, far outweigh any sentimental attachment to de Bellac or the King; nevertheless, she did not hesitate but replied at once:

"I did."

"You warned him?"

"Naturally. I knew that you would wish it."

"Were those my orders?"

"They were the commands of your heart, madame, and I read them perfectly."

The young lady had lowered her lashes over this sententious answer; looking up, she saw that it had had an excellent effect—her mistress had sunk back among the pillows, lips parted in an agreeably ironic smile.

"Perhaps they were the commands of *your* heart, Diane?"

"Can you believe that?"

"Without the smallest difficulty," replied Hortense, looking into her friend's dissembling face. "It's natural, it's reasonable. Why do you look so shocked?"

"That you should think such things of me."

"But they are pleasant things that I am thinking. Yes, they are, believe me—love, tenderness, the quickening of the senses. I know. I have felt them. I have been fortunate in my time."

"You have a habit of speaking in the past."

"Because it suits my present mind. I told you that I am no longer amused by gallantries of my own. But I am a woman, and I have kept my interest for them at second-hand."

And what could that mean? Was it a warning? Or an invitation? That was the worst of people whom the world judged transparent, thought Diane, looking down in perplexity at her mistress, and feeling that simplicity was an enigma of its own.

"So you amuse yourself with fantasies?" she said.

"Nothing so bloodless or uninteresting. Nor is it right to use the word amuse. I am not amused by your romance, Diane."

She paused and her attendant waited breathlessly and with a tug of fear stirring in her heart for words which might end her new love affair for ever.

"No, I am touched by it. Young love is always sad. I know I wept my heart out over the star-crossed course of mine. Now you are gayer, stronger, but even you are not immune."

"From love?"

"No, that's the infection. From heartache and disaster, the results of the disease."

"First you must catch it," said Diane, with a shrug of her elegant shoulders that would have convinced most people that she was as heartless as she seemed.

"Yes, that's the first stage, the most painless one, as can be seen in you. No, don't look so offended or surprised. I can read you well; it's easy for me; I had very much the same—would it be wounding if I said quite the same experience myself?"

The maid-of-honour looked away from her mistress towards the wall. She did not know how to take this last comment, whether to regard it as an admission of past failure or as a thrust at her defences. While she was still making up her mind she heard Hortense's gentle voice continue:

"It was not a happy experience, you know. The Revolution didn't concern itself with trifles; it rode roughshod over life, so what were the hopes for one small tremulous love affair? You know the rest. I stayed behind; he went away. He has returned, but I have changed. It's ironical that the story should repeat itself with half of the same cast—and you."

"You really believe this, madame?"

Hortense raised herself again from the pillows and her voice was full of assurance as she replied:

"I do. I know it. You love him. You are attracted, certainly. And that is why I am warning you."

Warning, an ominous word. But whatever the outcome—and it seemed likely to be unpleasant—there was the one advantage that her mistress was revealing the secrets of her heart.

"Warning me? Of what?"

"Of the consequences when love gets at odds with politics. It gets crushed or caught up with the stream, and either way the results are most unpleasant."

"Yes, I can see that. You are telling me such lovers die of broken hearts or broken necks."

"Really you're quick, Diane!" exclaimed Hortense. "You're quick to see the consequences. Whether you'll apply your knowledge is quite another matter."

"Naturally I shall attend to what you say."

"So dutiful! And yet you have already stretched my instructions. I send you to meet the Vicomte and make my excuses, to remain neutral, as it were, and what do you do? You warn him. You did right of course; you read my heart. But see the way yours runs on ahead. You have sided with an outlaw. Politically that is bad enough, but politics are the smallest part of it. How will you feel when this poor young man is put before a firing squad?"

Diane drew in her breath sharply, half fearful that these words had formed a threat. If Hortense had been in any doubt at all of the feelings of her friend, it was resolved by that small, revealing sound.

"It could end like that?"

"Yes, it could end like that," replied Hortense, repeating words that had hardly been spoken above a whisper. "We must face the possibility, for all the elements are there: his treason, the knowledge of the police. Now he is on the run.

Where will he go? What will he do? You know, for he has told you."

"He told me nothing."

"Nothing that you will repeat, at least," said her mistress, with a wry smile for this fidelity and this distrust. "Perhaps you are right. Secrets are best . . ."

She broke off and, as a commentary to her words, laid her finger to her lips. For a soft footstep had sounded in the corridor outside the room.

It was no new thing in this house, where even the servants had the look of diligent agents of the police, nor was the rather forced nonchalance adopted by both women changed when the door opened and Louis Bonaparte appeared. This was the paymaster and husband, a sickly young man with the First Consul's features, blurred and coarsened by the sedentary habits of an invalid. But there was something common to all the Bonapartes, from the smooth-faced Joseph to the lively Messalina called Pauline—an imperious set to the mouth and eyes, noticeable here even in this the most bookish of the clan. He was a man of virtue—feigned virtue, Napoleon said, complaining that it gave almost as much trouble as brother Lucien's vice—and its assumption gave him in his own eyes the right to enter his wife's room with the air of one who suspects there is a lover underneath the bed.

Summarily dismissed to her other duties, Diane had time to ponder on this miserable marriage, and if for a moment, in defence of her new adventure, she had felt out of sympathy with her mistress, this feeling had been removed by the sight of the man whom she despised more than any other, with the possible exception of his shadow, Morillac. That a husband so newly married should be insanely jealous without reason was only carrying a natural feeling too far, but that in spite of this jealousy he should not desire his wife seemed to her the height of lunacy.

In the indulgence of this anger against the master of the house, pleasurably mixed with comparisons between him and the Vicomte, Diane descended to the salon that looked out over the garden. She wanted very much to be alone with her many problems, and it was with a disagreeable sensation that she became aware of the major-domo, Morillac, standing by one of the pillars at the far end of the room. She was turning away towards the door when she heard the light tread of his feet on the parquet of the salon, and saw him glide towards her with that sinuous motion that she found so repellent.

"Mademoiselle."

There he was in front of her. It had to be admitted that he was a handsome fellow of a type common to her country on the southern spurs of the Cevennes, a neat, dark man, active in his movements and with eyes as black and sparkling as her own. Perhaps it was the resemblance between them that made him so odious in her eyes; it made the slyness of his movements more personal in some way.

"Mademoiselle. A moment, please."

"Yes, citizen."

"You've been released early from your duties."

"I am not released."

"Relieved, then, shall I say? It was hardly tactful attending so early on my lady. After all, it was only yesterday that M. Louis returned after a long absence."

Such bait was a severe test of discretion in the maid-of-honour: she could have expressed herself on the value of a husband who waited till the morning to pay his call. But she kept her head and did not speak.

"Perhaps you didn't expect my master," continued

Morillac, in that soft voice of his which matched his movements, the evasive quality of everything he did. "Or perhaps you believed he wouldn't be admitted."

Diane made a movement towards the door, only to find that he had somehow insinuated himself into the way.

"Was that it? Did you believe your mistress wouldn't fancy him?"

That called for no answer but a look of scorn, which Morillac bore with fortitude.

"But why did you believe that?" he went on. "That's what I want to know. They're husband and wife. Your mistress is a woman, with the instincts of a woman, and we know what they are. Why should you imagine she didn't want him?" He waited, head on one side, as though he really thought it possible that he would get an answer, then added with evident enjoyment: "Unless you know of other interests she has."

"Do you find this entertaining, citizen?"

"Don't you?" replied Morillac, who was impervious to sarcasms of this sort and only sharpened his own malice on them. "You should. It concerns your mistress intimately— almost as intimately as it concerns my master."

That cried out for a riposte, and she was foolish enough to make it.

"As though they had anything in common!"

He pounced on this at once.

"A divided household! And who divided it? Who is responsible for this feud that exists even down to the level of the servants? Not us. My master has the best intentions, and in my humble way I echo him."

"You have good intentions towards my mistress?"

"I don't raise myself so high," Morillac replied. "My intentions are towards you, Diane."

What they were could be seen clearly enough in his little darting eyes that lingered on her with all the familiarity of a lover, and seeing this and watching his lithe, restless hands moving as though in the course of a caress, she felt a wave of nausea sweep over her, partly physical, partly fear that he should dare to be so bold.

"What's the matter? Are you ill?"

In an instant she had recovered. She must show no sign of weakness or he would touch her, but by the same token she was prevented from leaving him, for that would mean brushing past him where he stood between her and the door—a contact of bodies that she did not feel she could endure.

"I wouldn't want you to be ill," he continued, with a lingering gentleness in his voice that was almost more intolerable than his presence. "I have such an interest in your welfare."

"Then you show it most offensively."

"Offensively?" repeated Morillac, with a convulsive movement as though he were trying to look inwards at himself to verify his spotless purity.

"Yes. You accost me. You insult me. And you are standing in my way."

He made as though to draw aside. But there was about him that same elusive quality that one sees in the most expert matadors, the mastery of movement and of the appearance of movement, and as she turned towards the door she saw that he had anticipated her.

"Is it wise to be so candid to a friend?" he said.

"A friend!"

"Or to anyone, for that matter? You are taking risks, Diane."

"May I remind you that *you* are. You are detaining me. I

am not quite without rights, as you will find when I report you to my mistress."

Morillac leaned back and a smile, the nearest to good humour possible, showed in his face.

"Oh, if it's a case of making reports," he said, "then we'll see who makes the best ones."

"What do you mean?"

Her tormentor nodded his head as though finding some sanity in her at last.

"Well, that shows some interest, Diane. What do I mean? That you may take your complaints straight up to your mistress. You have my permission; indeed, you have my blessing." And he stepped aside with a gesture of the theatre, leaving the path to the door open to her if she cared to take it.

He had read her well; he knew that she would choose this moment to be inquisitive.

"You think my mistress has no power over you, I suppose?"

"Oh no."

"You think M. Louis will always support you and go against his wife?"

"After the tender scene now going on upstairs!" said Morillac with a suggestive laugh. "I have more knowledge of human nature. After all, these young people have been apart for months. At such moments you and I, Diane, count for so little that we would be best employed in imitating them."

"You think I would with you?"

"I think you will, which is perhaps another matter."

At that, impelled by a feeling of disgust so acute that it overpowered all other instincts, even that of policy, she did try to move past him to the door; she had not gone far before she felt the grip of his hand on the fleshy part of her arm, a moist grip backed, as she knew, by a most deceptive strength.

"I said, you will."

"Then you'll believe anything."

"There's one thing I believe in," he said reflectively, "and that's your fidelity to your mistress."

"Let me go!"

"Fidelity to your mistress," repeated Morillac, baring his teeth slightly and moved by a sudden fierce sensation at the feel of that soft flesh beneath his hand. "You love her. You wouldn't see her come to harm."

"What harm?" For even at such a moment the inquisitive strain in her was still responsive.

"Well, that's where *my* report comes in, you see—my report of your mistress' visits to a certain house down by the Palais Royal and of her friendship for a man who is proscribed."

# Chapter Thirteen

THE NEWS OF THE HAPPENINGS AT BIville cliff came rapidly to Paris in a variety of forms. It was as natural that street rumour should accept the capture of a prince of the blood as that Bonaparte should be favoured by Colonel Savary with a soldierly report, which—no doubt for soldierly reasons—omitted nearly everything except the *Vincejo's* nonarrival. Only a very few were in the way to being perfectly informed, among them Joseph Fouché, who had the unique advantage of knowing Méhée de la Touche.

"What exactly happened?" he inquired, having paid for this privilege with rather less than his usual generosity. "You say that Cadoudal and de Bellac were at Biville?"

"Yes."

"And actually broke inside the cordon?"

"Yes. They fired their pistols as a warning signal, and in the confusion that followed they escaped."

"Escaped! From a company of gendarmerie! Now, that shows enterprise, Méhée. We must watch these men or they'll be too much for us."

His agent smiled, being perfectly able to distinguish between the talents of a Savary and a Fouché. In addition, he had the lowest opinion of the conspirators, as was natural in a man who was making dupes of them.

"You can rely on my vigilance," he said.

"Oh, I know. You are all-seeing, or all-hearing, as is proved by the way you are ready with the news so soon after the event. Of course the men themselves were your informants?"

"Naturally, Excellency."

"So they're back in Paris?"

"Yes."

"And where?"

"In the rue Langrais."

"Quite an unfashionable address," said the Senator, with the abstracted air of a man who is ticketing information elsewhere in his brain. "One must admit that this is a regression after Chaillot; in fact, one might say that the whole enterprise is getting rather down-at-heel. Now, Artois would have given tone to it. It's really the greatest pity that that barbarous reception was prepared for him on shore; he would have made a distinguished conspirator in Paris, and a model corpse."

De la Touche, listening carefully, as he always did to every word that Fouché spoke, was not deceived by this tone of irony; he knew it to be the prelude to some attack. It came.

"You, Méhée, I regret to say, were the original cause of this decline. You denounced Querelle, who betrayed Biville, and as a result the police and Cadoudal have interfered in a game that was my own. I wanted Artois in Paris, and now it's certain he's in London or Edinburgh or somewhere equally unapproachable."

"It was a fatality," Méhée said.

"It was not a fatality," the cold, level voice replied. "It was an inanity on your part, or worse."

"But I explained to Your Excellency why it was necessary for me to give some service to Bonaparte."

"Yes, you explained, and I thought the explanation a bad one at the time. That was before Querelle's confession. Now I find it execrable."

There could be no reply to this. Méhée knew his own worth—none better—but he also had the misfortune to know the Senator's. The disparity between them in wealth, in genius, in ruthlessness and cunning, constantly depressed him and made him a servant where his information should have been worth a partnership.

"Yes," the Senator continued, "you have blundered badly. It is really peculiar that in this one action of denouncing Querelle you should have done a disservice to me, to the conspirators, and to yourself. The whole affair shows the danger of divided loyalties."

Méhée was immediately up, protesting. In his own way he was faithful to the Senator, and liked, for a variety of reasons of which a belief in the power of flattery was the first, to give effect to one of the true emotions of his life.

"Excellency, you wrong me there. I have always tried to serve you. I am devoted to your interest. If I hadn't been I could have denounced Cadoudal to Bonaparte long since."

"And received what?" replied the Senator, refusing to be impressed by this most impressive of arguments—one that had the appearance of verging on a threat. "A meagre reward, a small pension, a brilliant career as a police spy. You're a man of intelligence and ambition. You know Bonaparte will never trust you as I do; that he has the parsimony of a peasant. You would be a fool to betray me."

"I should be a knave," cried de la Touche, who believed

that his master had a conceit to appeal to, if not a conscience. "It would be an act of gross ingratitude."

"And you think that's an argument! If you believe in what you're saying you won't last long in politics. Now, I prefer to avoid gratitude and such fine emotions which are so much less stable than self-interest. No, don't protest, it's quite unnecessary. Continue to be grateful to me to satisfy yourself, and interested in your own advancement to please me. The result should be a most harmonious relationship."

"Oh yes."

"With no discordant notes—like Querelle or Artois, for example."

"Certainly not."

"And played on a single instrument. No more visits to the Tuileries, I mean."

Méhée shook his head vigorously as though he had a horror of the place.

"Then I'm happy to announce that we're in agreement. It only remains to decide on a line of policy."

At this word de la Touche sat extremely still. He was of too independent a mind to be an ideal subordinate, but he had two of the attributes, concentration and pleasure in his work.

"That policy," the Senator continued, "depends in some measure on the answer to some questions I shall put you. First of all, what are the chances of a second attempt by Artois?"

Méhée replied unhesitatingly:

"None. It would be too costly. It would take too long to organize now that the Biville route is sealed. It's certain that the royalist leaders are no longer considering the possibility."

"That seems sensible of them. Perhaps, after all, Artois

will be more at home with a court than a conspiracy. But
without him what will they do? Time is running out. They
can't hope to lie safe in their holes for ever."

"That's true."

"You agree there, Méhée? The time of waiting—waiting
for Pichegru, waiting for Moreau, waiting for Artois—is
over?"

"You're right. Now they'll act—or try to."

What Méhée thought of the chances of the attempt
could be deduced from his voice, but the Senator had been
impressed with the news from Biville and reproved him:

"Don't be too contemptuous. There are twenty or so of
these émigrés, and we've seen what two of them can do.
They certainly overreached the police. Don't belittle that,
or I shall be tempted to see some reflection on myself."

Méhée was anxious he should not. He sensed the feelings
of Fouché for the instrument he had created—a sort of pa-
ternalism not untouched by jealousy and pride. The removal
of this man from the Ministry had been more than a dismissal, it had been a bereavement; and Méhée, who had
sometimes wondered at his master's policy, thought he
understood the springs of it at last.

"Oh, I mean no reflection," he said. "These men had the
devil's luck."

"Don't belittle that, either; it means they showed the
devil's calculation. All that you've told me of their actions
convinces me that these men are as capable as they are bold.
They'll try some daring stroke, we can be sure of that."

"Against Bonaparte, perhaps."

"Yes, against Bonaparte," repeated Fouché, and in his
eyes there shone for an instant the suspicion of a smile.
"These men are no respecters of persons, I'm afraid."

"You think they could possibly succeed?"

"My dear Méhée, if we weren't in the field the consequences would be unpredictable. As it is, I feel they'll fail. It's a matter of timing. It would be no bad thing, for instance, if the First Consul were to have cause to be seriously alarmed. For in the moment of release from fear the strongest emotions are generated—of revenge, and gratitude. One thing's certain: he is not sufficiently grateful yet."

Méhée's eyes opened wide, for it was not often that he was let so deeply into his master's confidence. His quick brain had already grasped what he had been told. Evidently Fouché had sold Cadoudal, or part of him, and had made a bad bargain in the process.

"Suppose these men are even abler than you think?" he said. "Suppose their boldness actually succeeds, and Bonaparte is killed or taken?"

"Then that *would* be a fatality, to use a word of yours. And for this reason: since I would not have participated, it's hard to see how I could hope to benefit. From Bonaparte I have the chance of wringing favours; from a royalist restoration I would, at present, have very little to hope for except an early death. In other words—and in order to answer the question that is all too obviously stirring in your mind—I am not a member of this conspiracy in fact or spirit. To think otherwise is to credit me with treasonable motives. Oh, and I suppose you'd add ingratitude as well!"

It was a comprehensive statement on a subject that had troubled de la Touche at times, and he nodded his relief. There were moments in the complicated game of triple-dealing he was playing when he began to fear that he would get finally committed to one party—the losing one; that was the worst moment of the dream.

"I understand," he said. "We're on the side of Bonaparte"—a free translation of the central position he occupied physically, though morally, if he could be said to have morals, he was in Fouché's camp.

"Yes, that's the position," the Senator replied, not troubling to correct so obvious a misstatement, for he had never been on anyone's side but his own. "These men are facing a dangerous game, and we must stir them to action or they won't live long enough to play it. That will be your task. Encourage them. Push them along. Keep them moving. Feed their optimism."

These classic precepts for agents-provocateurs were dutifully accepted by de la Touche, who hardly needed coaching in his profession. But they were only general precepts, as the sequel showed, for the Senator moved on to the particular.

"And then there's the matter of de Bellac. In the absence of Artois, it's my opinion that this young man is our most promising prospect. He has only to show the same alacrity in love as he has done in war, and he will afford me the greatest satisfaction."

Almost a pleased, anticipatory expression was in the Senator's face and voice, for in such small matters he could give rein to his emotions. But Méhée, by contrast, did not look hopeful.

"All is not smooth there," he replied.

"Not smooth? You mean that the Vicomte has his limitations?"

"Or the Bonaparte women their loyalties, Excellency. I have no progress to report."

"But they've met?"

"Oh yes, they've met. But I'm having the greatest difficulty in arranging through my intermediary for another meeting with Hortense."

"Another result of your ill-timed denunciation of Querelle," commented Fouché sternly. "The young man is on the run, and naturally the women are afraid. I won't disguise from you that this setback ranks in my mind with the loss of Artois. It's essential that these women compromise themselves with de Bellac—or have the appearance of doing so."

"I will do my best," Méhée replied, as though adding another and less respectable profession to his role of spy.

"Do so. And on no account fail. I'm being frank with you today. When that young man is arrested—as he will be in my own time—he's to be taken in the house, and preferably in the bedroom, of Hortense."

"But if she won't see him?" protested the agent, who may have found this rather a tall order for a beginner.

"She must be made to see him."

"Most difficult."

"Or he must be made to see her."

"And there again there's a difficulty," Méhée said.

"Oh? And why?"

"Because, by some unfortunate chance, the Vicomte's affections are being directed elsewhere."

"Then redirect them."

"It won't be easy. The young woman concerned has the disadvantage of being beautiful. There's the greater disadvantage—one that is insuperable to my mind—that she shares the Vicomte's inclinations. Such being the case, I cannot disguise from Your Excellency the probability that the young man will end up in the wrong bed—from our point of view, of course."

"Ah," said the Senator, whose interest in the matter remained political. "And who is this complaisant lady? Not your cousin Florian?"

"I regret so, yes."

"Then I can see possibilities in the case."

Méhée looked at his master with a rather disillusioned expression. He respected him for his almost superhuman understanding and ability, and was shocked by what he took to be a lapse to mediocrity.

"You're surely not imagining, Excellency, that I can influence Diane de Florian in this matter?"

"Perhaps not."

"Or that I can exercise the rights of a kinsman in an affair of honour?"

He had shown a needless concern for the Senator's abilities, for Fouché met this catechism with the prompt reply:

"I should hope not. The lady would laugh at you and the young man would probably run you through."

"So you agree, Excellency? There's no arguing with love."

"Oh, quite."

"What can one do, then?"

The Senator was happily married and a devoted father of a family, but in spite of this he regarded the emotions of the heart with the same disenchantment with which he viewed all human conduct and was ready with maxims to express it.

"The best way to bridle love is to promote it. Passion is an affair of diminishing returns. Let these young people meet; let them go to bed together. They're both political beings—the one by instinct, the other by profession—and after indulging the flesh they will be bound to turn to an intrigue."

Méhée, who was never parted from this instinct even for

a moment, nodded his agreement. His momentary doubts of his master had passed, and he recognized that even in the matter of heart the Senator was capable of filling in a deficiency of nature by sheer force of intellect.

"But here's the interesting part," the Senator continued. "After the consummation—provided, as I think we may assume in this case, that it's a happy one—after the consummation, as I say, the bent of intrigue in a person's nature tends to change, for submission of the body encourages submission of the mind."

"You are thinking that the Vicomte will be dominant?"

"For a while," replied the Senator, weighing up love and desire, the refinement of the spirit and the abandon of the body, with the accuracy of a pharmacist. "Just for a little while. It's natural; it's the result of the way nature has fashioned us. Woman is the recipient of love, and her life is devoted to using the gift for her own ends and changing it. She is a perpetual contradiction, because her mind can be ambitious, her body only satisfied. Need I say which part of her has the ascendancy in the early days!"

Méhée had listened intently to these words, which had deviated further from the practical than he considered necessary; but he saw their application and replied:

"You believe we can use this love affair?"

"To bring the Vicomte to Hortense. Yes. That is what I meant when I said I saw possibilities in the affair. If the Vicomte had been attracted elsewhere it would have been deplorable. But where is he attracted? Into the household of Hortense, where he will forget his disillusionment and remember Artois' orders. You look incredulous. But he should do so. He's a soldier. He wasn't sent to France for pleasure but for politics. That being so, he'll progress from one bedroom to another, and by easy stages to a prison cell. One can almost feel sorry for the young man."

He paused and added reflectively:

"But—although it may not be entirely delicate to say so in a kinsman's presence, Méhée—he will have had the compensation of a great deal of happiness on the way."

# Chapter Fourteen

IN THE SMALL HOURS OF THE MORNING
Diane de Florian awoke. She had no idea what had disturbed her, she only knew that she was lying tensely in her bed, filled with an expectancy so acute yet so unreasonable that she fancied it was part of the fabric of a dream.

The room was full of shadows—the small bulk of the dressing-table and inlaid cabinet, the chairs, the guardian pillars at the foot of the ornate four-poster bed. These were her familiars, and as her gaze travelled slowly round the room, identifying them one by one, the inquisitive faculty was alert in her, demanding the reason for this sudden wakefulness and the pounding of her heart.

The silence was absolute, for the noise in the streets outside had long since ceased, and it was not possible from behind those tightly shuttered windows to hear the mournful sighing of the wind. Nevertheless, she felt sure that she had been awakened by some sound, and her quick mind was in the process of imagining it when she was overtaken by the reality—a sharp rapping from beyond the casement like the sweep of branches against the windowpanes.

At that she sat up in bed, no longer afraid now that she

had proved the sound's existence, but consumed with curiosity. Branches in the wind? There was a tree in the garden that could be the cause, though surely only in a gale. A bird tapping at the window, a small, lost creature of the night? Gravel, perhaps, thrown by some hand from the terrace? Or the hand itself? There it was again, firm, deliberate; it was no wonder that the sound of it had dragged her back from sleep.

None of the possibilities racing through her mind disconcerted her in the least. She had a clear understanding of the strength of her position, for the windows were closed, the shutters barred, her mistress was sleeping on the same floor and there were servants in the house. In the circumstances, she was even prepared to lower the defences, and moving on tiptoe to the window, she reached for the heavy shutter and with a forceful gesture drew it back.

Curiosity had prepared her for some sudden revelation, for she had forgotten in her excitement that the darkness of her room would be matched outside by a darkness equally profound, so that a few seconds, almost of disillusionment, had passed before her eyes detected the greying edge of sky against which a blacker shadow could be seen crouched down near the cornice of the balustrade. That sight did disconcert her, perhaps because the shape was indeterminate and she could not be certain that the sprawling figure was a man; there was a suggestion of the monstrous about it, not entirely removed by the sudden way it rose to its full height and pressed its face against the panes.

Diane took a quick step backwards, a nervous reaction to a movement that seemed to threaten her, but in an instant fear was merged in other less definable emotions as she recognized de Bellac—intuitively, for the features were blurred and impersonal in the gloom. The two figures, separated by only a few yards and a rectangle of glass, stood motionless, watching one another, the one expectant, the other obsessed with a sense of unreality at the place and the hour, so that she seemed to doubt her visitor's existence. The man, who had the more pressing reasons for advancing, was the first to move, tapping with his hand against the pane, a much softer version of the sound that had awakened her. He had to repeat it more insistently before she unlatched the window and, with a reluctance that surprised him, stood aside to let him in.

De Bellac stepped into the room. He was used to his own gasconades, and never paused to think how they might appear to others: the result not so much of callousness as of too direct and adventurous a nature. He had made attempts through Méhée to see the lady and had failed. He needed to see her, and he accepted without question that this lonely room would be a good place for business—he could hardly be blamed, young and active as he was, for suspecting that it would be an even better place for love.

Entering in this unquestioning spirit, he found himself strangely greeted:

"Well? What does it mean? What do you want?"

Presented in this way, the answer was not easy. He was not without experience in such affairs, and could not recall one with quite so unpromising a beginning.

"I've tried to meet you," he began.

"Yes."

"I've made several attempts. It's not been easy, for we can't move openly. There's the danger now of compromising you."

"So you avoid it by climbing through my window! Evidently you are a man of tact."

"You say so," replied the Vicomte, encouraged by this

sarcasm and by the trace of amusement that he had caught in the lady's voice. It was still there, he thought, as she continued:

"Half the police in Paris are looking for you, and you must enter the house of the First Consul's brother!"

"There's a virtue in going where one's least expected."

"Virtue! Absurdity, you mean, climbing into Bonapartist houses under the noses of the police. Well, I will allow myself some absurdities of my own."

And before he could reply she had pulled the shutter to and was busy with the lamp on the table by the bed. The flame, springing out of the darkness, suddenly revealed her, a purposeful little ghost in a white nightgown that reached down to her feet.

"There!" she said, looking up at him as the light steadied and shone with a gentle glow. "Don't be alarmed. I sleep badly, so no one will wonder at the lamp. Our voices are the danger."

The Vicomte had appreciated this, and was already moving nearer, certainly not alarmed, and alive to the possibilities of whispered conversation. But it was not with an easy mind that he approached her. Like so many of his race, he regarded love as a kind of duty, and he was startled to find in himself emotions that he could not recognize, scruples that seemed irrelevant, and a sense of his own inadequacy— the most disastrous accompaniment of an affair. The woman was here, and the place, so quiet and secret, and there seemed to be an inclination on her part that promised the best results. He knew love with the certainty of an expert, but it must be confessed that this was not helping him to recognize its stirrings in his heart.

"Why did you light the lamp?" he said.

"Why? To see you. I don't like talking in the dark; it's like dealing with a shadow."

But even in the lamplight the Vicomte was conscious of this insubstantial quality that made it hard for him to treat her as he felt she should be treated. It baffled him. By reaching out a hand he could touch her—the raven hair charmingly disordered by contact with the pillows, the firm flesh, as white as her gown. It would have been impossible to find a more human and perfect instrument of love, vital, glowingly alive. But for the life of him he could not move to put her to the test; not all the promptings of desire and the self-reproaches of the amorist could make him perform that one simple action. He stood beside her, not more than a yard away, so that their shadows, one behind the other, were projected on the farther wall to make a mocking commentary on his hopes.

The silence and inaction impressed themselves on Diane, who had a shrewd idea of their cause. The Vicomte was not a puzzle to her as he was to himself, though he was certainly a problem, and one that she would have to solve when the time came. But she would not anticipate, and so, as much an opportunist in mind as he was in action, she waited for developments which she believed—not without some pleasurable doubts—she could control.

"Have you forgiven me, Diane?" he said at last.

"Yes, I think so."

"I didn't mean to frighten you. Do you know, it never occurred to me. I suppose I was too taken up with the railings and the parapet and the police."

"The police!"

"Some police spy or other. I didn't see him. But I heard someone nosing around in the street just below me: backwards and forwards, backwards and forwards, like an animal on the prowl. Well, I must have satisfied him. I lay very still and after a while he went away."

"So you continued your climb!"

The Vicomte remarked the note of wonderment, but ignored it. In certain matters he had no vanity, and was equally surprised by praise of his courage and exasperation at his rashness.

"Yes, it was easier to go up than down, you see. There was always a chance that my friend might be waiting round the corner."

"And it hasn't occurred to you, I suppose, that he might still be waiting round the corner—with about a battalion of assistants?"

"Then in that case," said the Vicomte, "I shall have to go out another way."

"Which way?"

"The most direct one—by the front door into the rue Victoire."

"I believe you'd do it," she said.

"Naturally. It would be much the easier way. I don't think you realize, Diane, how uncomfortable these cornices are. Nothing but the desire for your society would have made me climb them—oh, and the wish to thank you."

"For what?"

"For saving my life. No, I'm serious now. By warning me you did save my life, and you did more than that—you were the means of saving Artois' life as well."

It was true that the Vicomte had become serious; he was remembering his obligations with a deep sense of gratitude, and was surprised by the tone of her voice and the light of amusement in the eyes now turned to his.

"So you were responsible for that!"

"For what, Diane?"

"For the Biville incident, for making an idiot of Savary. Believe me, you've become quite a sensation at the Tuileries —anonymously, of course. The impudence of it! To take the fish right off the line! It was even more impudent than your arrival here."

"For which you've already forgiven me, I must remind you."

"Whether Savary, to say nothing of the First Consul and Réal, will be as forgiving is another matter. They'll find out eventually who you are. It's inevitable. Bouvet de Lozier is bound to talk: it's rumoured already that he has. They will move from one of you to the other in a sequence of betrayals, and in the end they will come to you. In the circumstances, Charles, I have some advice for you: get out of that window, or of the door, if you like; get out of Paris; get out of France."

From the expression in her eyes he may have had his doubts as to how sincerely this advice was meant; certainly he found enough encouragement to sit down close beside her as he replied:

"But that would make my efforts pointless. I came here for a reason."

"Yes, and what it is is just beginning to occur to me."

The Vicomte, who knew enough about women to appreciate the speed of their reactions, smiled.

"My purpose was to see your mistress. You'll remember that in spite of all my efforts I have only seen her three times."

"That surprises you?"

"Yes, it surprises me. I expected more of an old friendship." And he looked at Diane in so hurt and troubled a way that it seemed as though for the moment he had forgotten what he expected of the new.

"You believed she'd compromise herself for you! I don't think you realize, Charles, how you appear from the ante-rooms of the Tuileries—a brigand, an assassin, a friend of Cadoudal's."

He shrugged off these excuses with easy confidence.

"Hortense knows better. In any case, there was no danger. We had a system. We had a meeting-place."

"An excellent one! It was under observation by one of Louis' spies."

This time she had moved him. He half rose as he cried out:

"A spy of Louis' on that house!"

"And in this house too. You see into what sort of hornet's nest you've climbed."

The Vicomte did see, and his reaction was a forthright one:

"The man should certainly be killed."

"No doubt. And it would be a very useful field for your activities, Charles. No," she continued, as he showed signs of taking her at her word, "no, I really won't be compromised to that extent. But you see the difficulties of our position. My mistress wants to meet you; she'll do anything in reason. But she won't meet you at my cousin's house, or here, or anywhere where she can be spied on by Morillac."

"You're refusing me all hope," the Vicomte said, and he could not keep reproach out of his voice.

"By no means. Even this Morillac is not as ubiquitous as you. Louis has taken up an appointment as Colonel of the Third Regiment of Cavalry at Compiègne. His wife follows soon; his spy does not. Now, there's the opportunity. It may

even be possible to arrange a daylight meeting." She added
with a sidelong glance towards the balcony through which
he had come: "It would be a relief to me."

How much of a relief the news had been to de Bellac was
seen in the way he reached out a hand and clasped hers—an
act of pure gratitude which underwent rather a sudden
transformation.

"Then I should see you again, Diane."

"No doubt. Though I thought your object was to see my
mistress."

This seemed like coquetry to Charles, who began to feel
himself on familiar ground. He looked slowly round the
room. The lamplight shone with charming effect on walls
whose bareness, broken only by shallow fluted columns, was
a support for one of those ceilings in the Italian style in
which nymphs and knowing cherubs, each one an Œdipus
untouched by fate, combined to provide the worst possible
example. Outside, the night was very still. Not a stir in the
house nor a rustle of wind in the trees reminded them that
there were people or things existing in the world beyond this
cloistered room, where the rich glow of the lamp shone on
Diane and on the sculptured beauty of her arms, as creamy
white as the skin of the Venuses who disrobed above
her.

Such hints were not wasted on a man who had enjoyed
experiences—though never before in quite so artistic a setting. Every refinement of seduction was present—the
woman, the hypnotic effect of the lamplight, and the suggestive silence of the night. He had only to touch her. He
felt sure of her response, and imagined with a fierce glow
in his heart the feel of her body in his arms, unbelievably
warm and supple, her mouth open to his kisses, the nectar
of her tongue. Love! How small and quiet a word for pas-

sionate actions, the pricked touch, the intimacies of an embrace!

But when he turned towards her all these imaginings of an ardent nature died; a feeling of humility overcame him, ill suited to his nature and to a room not designed for very rarefied emotions, so that in place of the outpourings of his spirit he managed just one word—"Diane."

He had chosen well, so well that it is certain that the practised man of the world would have done no better. Diane was less moved by her surroundings; she had lived a great deal longer with them and could have judged her cherubs and Venuses—unkindly—as works of art; furthermore, she was no woman of easy virtue. These were formidable objections, but one thing alone outweighed them: she loved the Vicomte; she had loved him from the first with that swift reaction of a woman that is so fallible, and so lasting; and the moment she saw the expression in his eyes and heard his voice she gave no further thought to her defences but moved towards him—a very slight movement to have settled a relationship that engrossed the deepest and most passionate feelings of their hearts.

Next instant he had seized her in his arms, swept by desire and tenderness such as he had never dreamed of. The touch of her body against his own was the promise of possession, but in the moment of their kiss he knew a feeling of poignant and unbearable sadness at man's loneliness—a knowledge echoed in the words he used, "Diane, I love you; I love you," as though love were the cure and not one of the badges of mortality.

At such moments women are often more realistic than their men; more resigned, perhaps. She lay in the circle of his arms; her nightdress had slipped half off her shoulder and he could see below it the firm moulding of her breasts.

She might have said in words, "Well, love me, then," for this was the message of her eyes and lips, parted in ecstasy under the touch of his hands. She adored him; she would have made any sacrifice for him; and now to this feeling that she had had from the outset—love that had hoped for but had not expected satisfaction—there was added the almost uncontrollable emotion that his kisses had aroused—a feeling so wild and elemental that she hardly understood herself. "Yes, love me," and her arms reached out for him, drawing him down towards herself.

But even now, when every emotion and feeling of his mind and body was concerned with the approaching moment, the soldierly instinct of the Vicomte was still awake. Suddenly he raised himself from the bed, oblivious for a moment of her hand that moved to follow him. To Diane it was an interruption—not wholly unpleasant, for it tantalized and she could approve of this play on her emotions. But when he did not even respond to the touch of her lips, her body felt aggrieved and she whispered:

"What is it, Charles? Are you afraid?"

He did appear to be afraid, though certainly not in the way she was intending. He remained silent, so withdrawn from her that she asked again, "What is it?" repeating this more loudly with a trace of impatience.

He whispered back:

"I heard a noise."

At that she sat up in bed beside him where the lamplight shone full upon her. She appeared to be listening, but the point of this reminder was not lost on her companion, who saw how far she had moved in mind and body after the few moments in his arms. He repeated, almost as though she had used words of actual invitation:

"There *was* a noise, I tell you."

"Do you hear it now?" And when he shook his head she turned towards him, her face so dedicated, so serious and intent on her surrender, that the Vicomte did not know whether to be the more moved by desire or pity.

Unconsciously his concentration was relaxing as a profound silence once more descended on the house. The sound that his keen ear had detected had been a very slight one, the click of wood or metal—a door opening, perhaps, far off down the corridor, the sort of sound that was to be expected in a place where many people slept. He recalled the risks he had already taken, the climb, the entry through the window, the conversation, the lighting of the lamp: all these were reassurances; indeed, it was remarkable with what ease that alert sentry in his mind was satisfied.

"I don't hear anything now," he said.

"Of course not. There never was anything. Just the wind."

"Not the wind, Diane."

"Well, someone, then, someone far away; very, very far away." And in the dying whisper of her voice he caught the suggestion of endless distances stretching out, leaving just the two of them alone, forgotten, in the silent room.

Even the light seemed more subdued now, shining with gentle invitation. She had sunk back among the pillows, and, looking down at her, he was struck with a sense of wonder at her beauty. It was hard to see in her the young woman of the house near the Palais Royal whose confidence and cleverness had first attracted him, or the demure figure in the white nightdress on which the lamplight had first shone; in their place was someone he hardly recognized, though she was the creature of his making, warm and desirable and passionately alive.

Like an artist who finds that unwittingly and from ques-

tionable motives he has made a masterpiece, the Vicomte
was abashed in face of his own handiwork; his self-confi-
dence had vanished, and in its place was a feeling that was
almost fear. He had not known that he was in the presence
of a problem; he had approached it almost without thought,
for he was not a man of very introspective mind; and it was
with bewilderment that he began to recognize the presence
of that enigma that sooner or later faces everyone, the mysterious knowledge that lurks, sensed but never perceived, beyond the boundaries of the flesh to spiritualize one of the
most carnal of the body's actions—the truth was, of course,
that while he had been concerned with more definable emotions love had overtaken him, as usual without the least
warning or apology.

In its two facets, love is equally ambitious and the object
of ambitions. More than anything else in his whole existence Charles wanted to express this, to explain the mystery,
not only to himself but to Diane; he felt the limitations of
the body and knew that not by touch, nor kisses, nor in their
most secret intimacy, could he disclose to her the depths of
this new revelation that had come to him and transformed
him—violently, as is the way with converts to a faith.

He turned to words. How much he had to say! He could
tell her of her beauty, the natural grace that so delighted
him, the perfection of her flesh and figure, the wonderful
softness of her lips. He told her how he had always longed
for her, always dreamed of this moment, always known that
they were destined for one another. And he told her that he
loved her, again and again, as though each repetition could
explain the unexplainable and prove the reality behind a
word.

He was very eloquent. Into the silent, lamplit room his
whispers came with the relentless flow of a mountain stream

set on just such another journey through the pointless pattern of the world. And with the passivity of nature she lay and listened to his words, moved by their passion, touched by their humility. Did she understand him and the thoughts he struggled to express? She knew both less and more. Love was not so great a mystery to her; she loved; she knew the truth of that in the weakness of her body and the beating of her heart.

Suddenly, in the midst of his most passionate words, she reached out for him and laid a finger on his lips. In surprise he stopped, and remained very still, looking down at her as she lay against him, one of her bare arms thrown back in a way that contrasted touchingly with the look of irresolution and enquiry that had come suddenly to her eyes. For an instant they stared at one another in the knowledge of that conflict that lies at the heart of love.

But even as they moved into each other's arms the sound of a soft and furtive step came to them from beyond the door.

# Chapter Fifteen

E VEN BEFORE THE VICOMTE COULD FLING himself off the bed and reach his arms which lay at the foot of it, the door was opened and the figure of a man glided across the threshold and into the lamplight of the room with the haste of an actor making a late entry on a stage. It was certain that part of the scene had taken place without him, and at the evidence of this he nodded to himself as though he had justified his fears. There was the man whose presence he had detected from the street, and there was the woman, the magnet that had drawn him—a very powerful magnet, it was clear from the sight of her, caught in that fleeting moment of abandon. Intent on his plan, which promised vengeance as a prelude to more tender aftermaths, it was still both tantalizing and inexpressibly painful to Morillac to see such proofs of her accommodating nature, and his voice as he spoke to them perhaps lacked that urbanity that he prized.

"So you're here, then!"

De Bellac, who had created *his* effects, and was therefore less intent on making them, wasted no time on words; he had drawn his sword—the only weapon for this sort of work—and advanced on his opponent with his usual resolution, somewhat impeded by Diane, who flung herself between them.

"Now this is an embarrassment," said Morillac, looking past her at the man he meant to kill. "This isn't your place, Diane; you're not suited to it." And where he believed her place to be was hardly open to a doubt. The Vicomte caught the implication and was enraged by it. He moved to thrust her aside, so blind to his own interest that she cried out:

"You can't fight him. You don't know him. He's one of the best swordsmen in the country."

The newcomer had brought a duelling pistol, too, though the best parts of his armoury were words, which he had found to be excellent aids, capable of softening up the strongest opposition.

"What am I to do with him, Diane?" he said.

"Do with him! Why, nothing. What is he to you?"

"My predecessor," answered Morillac, levelling his weapon as he saw a sudden furious movement of his enemy. "My fortunate predecessor."

"It's untrue."

"Why, you're denying the undeniable! Do you think I didn't see! I called him fortunate advisedly. Any man is fortunate—no matter what his end—who has enjoyed such a mistress."

"I was never his mistress. Let him go. I won't see him again."

"Or lie with him again; we must include that, I suppose?"

Even this insult went unanswered.

"I promise. I'll do anything."

"You'll certainly say anything, Diane. You'll say, no

doubt, that I may succeed; that you'll be my mistress by reversion. Is that your offer?"

"Don't answer him. Stand back," the Vicomte said.

"But he'll kill you."

"I shall certainly kill him," Morillac agreed. "And *you* will be accommodating. Let me tell you why."

And covering his victim with the pistol, he proceeded with the greatest composure in the world:

"I know that you, M. le Vicomte, came here to see one woman—with what fortunate results we're all aware. But my master will believe you came to see another—his wife. Do you see now why I'm so certain of enjoying favours which, I assure you, will not be spoilt for me by any memories of you? After your death it will be for Diane to say whether to accept you as a corpse that can be hushed up —with my assistance—or as the most compromising visitor I can possibly imagine—a proscribed royalist, a man engaged on a plot to assassinate the First Consul and debauch his stepdaughter: lese-majesty, in itself. Picture her choice, Vicomte. She might sacrifice herself. Would she sacrifice her mistress too? For these reasons—apart from other trifling ones that concern the pleasure you have enjoyed with her—it's now my intention to blow your head off." And he stepped back a pace with the serious look of a man who retains, in spite of familiarity, a certain sense of the gravity of death.

She cried out:

"You'd be murdering him."

"An outlaw! My dear Diane!"

"Consider yourself, then. Do you think that fear or conscience or anything will count with me once he's dead?"

He seemed to weigh this for an instant, moved perhaps by

the expression on her face. Then his resolution hardened, for the fact was that the trifling reasons he had mentioned were not trifles, but represented the fiercest promptings of his heart.

The Vicomte, looking steadily into his enemy's eyes, read their message. He said suddenly:

"Let her leave the room."

She protested, straining back against him.

"Let her leave the room," repeated the Vicomte, thrusting her away, for he saw that in the madness of jealousy the man might kill them both. And in the urgent need of saving her, he advanced the one argument that could influence his enemy. "It will be better for you. You love her. What will be your chances if you kill me in her arms?"

"That's true," said Morillac, looking from one to the other. To kill his victim in the way he had intended would be an indulgence of the spirit that might be fatal to a later indulgence of the flesh; he saw that and repeated: "That's true, that's very true. Diane, you'd better leave us now," in the voice of a man who appreciates reason himself and expects that others will appreciate it also.

But Diane did not move. She remained close to her lover, shielding his body with her own, an invitation to that lurking idea of Morillac's brain, the execution of which would have a terrible appositeness of its own.

"She had better leave," said Morillac, and though the words were the same there was a thickness in his voice that showed the imminence of danger.

The Vicomte had been in the presence of death too often to misread the signs. "Go now," he said, and with his left arm he pushed her away from his body. "You must go." Blindly she resisted him, till, with a violent movement that stirred in his heart the most acute emotions of remembrance, he grasped her and flung her sideways to the wall.

In the same moment he struck out at his enemy with his sword.

The blow, so rapidly delivered that the eye could hardly follow it, took the pistol at the butt and dashed it to the ground. Only with a frenzied parry with the weapon carried in his left hand was Morillac able to save himself from the lunge that followed, a thrust that penetrated high up in the fleshy part of the shoulder and forced him back against the bed. A second thrust of the same quality would have been enough. But the Vicomte's self-control was not proof against the elemental feeling of conflict raging in his heart: he strained towards the body of his enemy, using his sword more as a lever than a weapon, forgetting all his science, the poise and balance of the fencing school.

This rashness gave Morillac his chance. Though not the stronger, he was the quicker of the two, and as the Vicomte thrust forward he slid from under him, transferring his sword from his left to his right hand, and faced about, calm, collected, the perfect master of his emotions now that these emotions were solely concerned with the killing of a man. De Bellac, recovering from the pit that his hatred had dug for him, found himself in the presence of a very different adversary, as could be told even from the ring of their blades as they crossed; he was driven at once on the defensive, maintaining his ground with difficulty against an enemy who fully justified the warnings of Diane—the product of the best fencing schools and the bloodiest practical experience.

No one was ever in less of a hurry than this man who now advanced to the attack with the easy familiarity of the expert, measuring his opponent in thrust and parry, and so conscious of his mastery that he would probably not have bothered to regain his pistol, even if he could have done so. The resistance now being offered him was just good enough to add the final pleasure to the encounter, the spice of achievement that he could relish even before the final blow went home. The Vicomte was a good swordsman, Morillac recognized as he tested the defences, a gifted amateur whom he could admire with a truly professional detachment. But there were weaknesses: a lack of balance, a tendency to clumsiness in the footwork, above all, an optimism that pointed to the very worst results.

Slowly, savouring each moment with a pleasure that made him almost grateful to the Vicomte for providing the opportunity, he began to drive him across the room, turning him, when they reached the wall, with the ease of a puppet master, as the thought occurred to him that he would kill him on her bed. It was a prospect, the fitting nature of which appealed to him, so that his eye kindled and he himself began to display in his fencing some of that enthusiasm that he had censured in his enemy, till reminded by a thrust that went close to passing underneath his guard. At that, he drew himself in and ceased for the moment to press his man, even giving ground a little, so that he in his turn was forced against the wall. His enemy could fence; and Morillac, feeling for the first time the need—or at least the desirability—of allies, began to talk.

"Where did you learn your trade, citizen? In London? Or do you émigrés keep schools for bravoes here in Paris— schools for assassins, shall I say?" At this moment he caught sight of Diane's face over the shoulder of de Bellac, and struck by her expression, added: "That's what he's come for, of course. Do you imagine his only aim's to sleep with you?"

The Vicomte's reply was a thrust that Morillac parried

with contemptuous ease, refusing the riposte that would have destroyed his enemy—prematurely, for they were still at the far end of the room.

"You don't believe me," he said, stealing another quick glance at her. "You can't believe he's come here to destroy."

"Destroy! Destroy what? You, I hope."

"Bonaparte, I mean."

Here he slipped under the Vicomte's guard and forced him several rapid paces towards the bed.

"Yes, my dear Diane," he continued, falling back on the defensive. "He's here to assassinate the Chief of State."

If his object had been to distract his enemy he had failed. Not a word escaped the Vicomte, who fenced on, more watchful now, for he too had measured his antagonist. But Diane had been moved by these suggestions.

"Assassination! *You* are the assassin."

"I! In fair fight! Why! come to that, the man has wounded me." And with his left hand Morillac pointed to his shoulder, where a patch of blood showed dully against the black fabric of his coat.

"There never was a fairer fight," he added, supplying a commentary on these words with a sudden fierce assault that all but beat down the Vicomte's guard. "The man can fight. You're learning of his accomplishments. And, believe me, if I didn't kill him now, you'd learn some more—less pleasant ones. Do I notice traces of belief in you?" And, indeed, he may have done so, for his words had awoken echoes in her heart.

"Keep away and don't talk, Diane," the Vicomte said.

"You distract him, you see," Morillac continued pleasantly. "He doesn't like to know that you can see him for what he is—a royalist bully sent here to kill the man who's committed the crime of saving France. There! Do you see how he's moved by that?" For the Vicomte had been goaded to a furious onslaught that would have tested the powers of a less skilful enemy. "There now!" he added as the attack failed and he recovered mastery. "Isn't that evidence? You don't answer. Are you afraid of harming him? You couldn't do worse than by just looking at him the way you're doing now. He knows, you see, he knows."

By now, Morillac had worked his rival to the spot he had marked out beforehand for the *coup de grâce*. The truth was, however, that he was no longer quite easy in his mind, for the Vicomte had profited from his lessons, and there was now a watchful caution in everything he did. Morillac, who could have killed him at least a dozen times, began to regret his own too great sense of artistry, faced with an enemy who, constantly defeated, still retained his equanimity and —what was a great deal worse—his guard. But this unwelcome discovery did not daunt him. He had taught the Vicomte too many lessons but not the whole of the curriculum; there remained the tricks that he had learnt in a hundred sword fights, many of them against men of far greater ability. He had had his failures and carried the scars of them on his body, but the successes had given him a reserve of confidence that was never allowed to degenerate into carelessness in his ice-cold brain. He would play no longer. He would fight to kill.

The Vicomte. watching his enemy with unwavering concentration, recognized the difference at once. The climax was approaching: he could read it in Morillac's glance and in the increased tempo of his swordplay, the snakelike dartings of his blade. In spite of all his efforts he was pressed back towards the bed till his left hand, extended behind him, touched against one of the ornately carved pillars that stood guard above it. He tried to move aside, but found himself held as though in a vice by a swordpoint that gleamed against his breast; he tried to advance, but at the moment of his lunge sensed the trap, the quick parry and riposte to come—sensed it, and at the last moment checked and flung his sword outwards to turn away the plunging steel. Desperately he fought off an enemy who seemed to be always present but never within his reach, a will-o'-the-wisp that danced before him, companion of the shadows on the wall, yet could materialize with terrifying suddenness and force.

Stubbornly he fought on. At one moment he was doubled back against the bed; at another he stumbled and heard the rip of the blade as it tore through the cloth below his arm. He could not spare a glance or a word for his mistress, who stood in anguished indecision against the wall; but though his breath was laboured and his wrist ached with the intensity of effort he continued to hold his enemy at bay, drawing from Morillac himself a grunt of approval, the tribute to endurance that can be wrung from even the most unchivalrous of souls.

In fact, the master was becoming tired by his mastery and by the knowledge that even his most skilful play could be frustrated—it seemed like diabolism to him. Insensibly he relaxed, the speed and ferocity of his attack died down, and the Vicomte, with the sense of wonder of a man who survives some cataclysm of nature, recognized that a respite had been granted him—his natural buoyancy had been so much chastened by his experience that he no longer thought of it as more than that.

Morillac, foiled in action, turned to words.

"You're still there, Diane! What are you waiting for? To

see me killed. It's a possibility. But notice that he won't attack. No, he'll keep on the defensive till the whole house wakes and the servants are about his ears."

No noise of any person stirring could yet be heard, though it would have been easy for a man in the Vicomte's position to imagine it. But he was now alert to his opponent's ways, and he accepted this invitation to impale himself in the same spirit as he had borne the fencing lesson—with an unruffled coolness.

"He's cautious, you see," Morillac went on, not with quite the same fluency, for he was tiring under his exertions. "He takes no risks. He's safe behind that guard—or nearly so." For, taking advantage of a parry executed with less than the Vicomte's usual firmness, he had sprung forward, and his sword, moving obliquely through the narrow gap, had pierced his enemy's left side below the arm.

A cry of horror came from Diane. But the Vicomte made no sound; he did not even glance down to where the steel had made a slanting wound in the soft flesh; his face was deathly white and drawn with pain, but though he had been forced back by the impact till his body was pressed against the pillar of the bed, he continued to fence with resolution, and the ring of his blade against his enemy's was as true as though he had just begun the fight.

Morillac had felt the thrust of the sword into de Bellac's body, and as he saw the stain of blood spreading in response to it he was filled with exaltation so passionate and ungoverned that it even amazed this specialist in savagery; he had killed many men in his time and had believed himself beyond enthusiasms, but this one wounding could make him forget the discipline of years. With a cry of triumph he flung himself on his antagonist, who could retreat no longer; he had him there against the bed and he would drive the sword through and through again, pressing forward till he was covered in his victim's blood. An insane strength was pitted against the Vicomte in this last assault, a mad fury that beat up against him till he was submerged beneath its weight and power, forced down on the bed, from where he looked up into the eyes of Morillac, half closed in an ecstasy of hate and passion.

Three blows he parried; the fourth took him in almost the same place beneath the arm; then, with an effort more of the will than of the flesh, he forced himself up, thrusting at his enemy with his hands. Miraculously the pressure eased, and as though in a trance the Vicomte stumbled forward, his sword extended like a blind man's stick in the surroundings of an unfamiliar room. He hardly saw the blow, swift as an arrow, launched at him from space. Wildly he flung up his left hand, felt the sharp bite of steel along his wrist and the weight that flung him backwards, and in that instant he felt with an unbearable poignancy the sense of failure. Moments had passed before he realized that his sword, still grasped firmly in his hand, had driven deeply into the body of his enemy.

# Chapter Sixteen

A S THE VICOMTE ROSE FROM THE BED the body of Morillac slid from above him to the floor, where it lay, moving convulsively in the pitiful way of a wounded beast; it made only the lightest sound, a scraping of nails and a sword-hilt on the highly polished surface.

Diane and the Vicomte dropped on their knees beside him. But he would not have felt the gentle pressure of their hands as they withdrew the blade and raised his head; only his body responded to their touch in sharp, jerky movements that pumped out the blood from his wounded side. Neither of them had any cause to wish him well, but it was with a feeling of compassion that they held him and felt for the beating of his heart—astonishingly loud and steady, as though this part of the living organism had an existence apart from the writhing limbs and rough, uneven breath.

There was little they could do; there was no light of intelligence in the eyes, only the whites showing and staring up at them with a dreadful blankness; but in spite of their danger they could not bring themselves to leave him. They remained there on their knees, while below them the house stirred into life in the noise of footsteps from far off and the murmur of voices in the night.

"Charles."

"Yes?"

"He's dying, isn't he?"

The Vicomte looked down at his enemy, seeing himself lying there with that sword-thrust in his body—a quicker and more merciful one, perhaps. A slight tremor passed through him as he replied:

"I think so. I can't tell. It may have missed the lung. I've known men to survive as bad." And at these words and their implications they turned and looked at one another, seeing in each other's faces the conflicting hopes and fears that they had not wanted to recognize in themselves.

"We must try to save him," she said, as though answering some argument that he had used. And with sudden energy they set to work to wrap the wounded man in the coverings from the bed, raising him and placing the pillows beneath his head. The slight and wiry body felt heavy in their arms. When they had done, they rose to their feet and stood for a moment looking down at it, avoiding each other's eyes.

"That's all we can do for him," he said. "You had better get a doctor. I think he's done for."

"He would have killed you. I was afraid."

The noise of voices swelled out below them, but neither heard them, so engrossed were they with one another and with the gentle touch of hands.

"Are you afraid now?"

"Only for you. You must go."

"And leave you here to be accused!"

"Of killing him?" And she glanced towards the amorphous bundle of Morillac's body, from beneath which there peeped the point of a sword-blade dull with the Vicomte's blood. "Or of harbouring you?"

"Either way you'll be disgraced. Come with me."

She withdrew her hand and moved towards the shutters through which he had come, telling him:

"You must go. You must really go."

"But we'll meet again?"

"Yes, at Compiègne, perhaps. That's if my mistress keeps me and by some miracle this matter is hushed up."

"If he doesn't denounce us?" said the Vicomte with a quick glance at Morillac. "If he dies, you mean?"

"I suppose I do mean that."

De Bellac looked across at his enemy, and now, in response to her peril, the harsher side of his nature rose uppermost.

"I should have settled him for good and all. I should have made sure of him. It's a pity I didn't get him in the heart."

She protested, so warmly, with so much feminine charity, that he burst out:

"You'd say that even though he's a danger to you! Do you think he'd be grateful for what you've done for him! If he lives, you'll see."

If he lives—and their eyes returned to the figure swathed in bedclothes whose breath rose harshly into the silence of the room.

"I should have done it," the Vicomte repeated. "I should have finished him. It would have saved a lot of explanations."

They looked at one another and, neither speaking, moved into each other's arms. They stood very close together while the sound of voices rose in the corridors, no longer a murmurous background to their actions, but sharp and distinct. Then softly she drew away.

"Charles, you must go."

"But I love you."

"I know, and I love you. All the more reason why you mustn't be taken. I think I can manage my mistress and the servants, but if you were caught here, it would be too much."

He moved to the window and stepped out on the balustrade. As she saw him swing his legs over the parapet the sense of his danger, lost since the moment of Morillac's fall, revived, and she ran to him and put her hand in his.

"Be careful, Charles."

"I shall certainly be careful," replied the Vicomte in the buoyant tones that came to him with the breath of action. "One needs to. This façade's the devil." He was already testing his purchase with his hands. "I must find another way when I come tonight."

She began to laugh softly.

"Tonight! You're mad. You'd say anything."

"I'd certainly do anything to be with you."

"And you mustn't. No, listen. Listen. It would be too dangerous. You don't realize the danger everywhere."

Dimly behind them they were aware of voices on the threshold beyond the door.

"I don't care. I must see you." As he spoke he swung himself outwards so that to her horrified eyes he seemed to be clinging like a spider to a wall.

"But not here," she said.

"Where, then?"

"At Méhée's house. Yes, it will be safest now. And if I don't come . . . you'll know—"

"I'll know I must come and fetch you, wherever you may be."

She did not reply. Leaning from the casement, she could just see the dark shape of his body touched by the faint grey light of dawn, and she heard the whisper of his voice:

"Tonight."

She turned back into the room. A small figure, white in the lamplight, was standing just inside the door.

There was little to be said. The shutters were still open, and from where she stood Hortense could plainly hear the stertorous breathing of Morillac and see the bulk of his body stretched out on the floor. She came over to him at once and stood looking down into his face; unlike the others, she did not stoop to touch him, but remained motionless, even when the maid-of-honour in her agitation pressed close to her.

"Madame, you'll have guessed."

The ghost of a smile passed across Hortense's face as she answered:

"Yes, I have guessed."

"Charles came to arrange a meeting with you: and to see me, too, I can't deceive you. Morillac broke in. They fought. And regrettably this happened."

"You regret it?" said her mistress, still looking down at the face of the wounded man. "Why should you? He spied on us and did us harm. We often wished him dead. We'd be foolish to be sorry when our wish comes true."

Diane said sharply:

"He's not yet dead, madame."

"So I can see." And she looked away from the struggling figure with a gesture of disgust. "Well, we must get a doctor, I suppose. Tell Renard to fetch one. And bring me a nightgown from my room."

She was still in the same place when Diane returned. She took the flimsy gown without a word, and with a gesture to the maid-of-honour knelt down beside Morillac.

Diane had watched her in surprise.

"You'd save him?"

Hortense's lips were pursed, and there was an expression on her face that her companion had never seen before.

"He may be dying. I can do little. See here." She paused to master herself. "See the blood. Listen to his breathing. He has richly deserved it. He will be better dead."

"You feel like that and still help him!"

"Just as you helped him. Thoughts are one thing, but actions are another."

All this while she had been tearing the gown to strips, and now, leaning over the body of her enemy, she began to apply them, swabbing the blood that still welled from the wound.

"I have often longed to do it myself," she said. "Strange isn't it? Such a worthless man! So terribly strong! Listen how regular those heartbeats are. He could live through it. He's the sort that could."

Diane, on her knees beside her mistress, deftly seconded her, conscious all the time of a sense of awe at the discovery of the strength that hatred had given to this gentle woman and at the use to which the power was put—the saving of a man they both wished dead.

"It's a clean wound, you see," Hortense went on, fixing one of the swabs in place, strangely white against the dark stains that had spilled on to his clothing and the floor. "A flesh wound, possibly. But deep—so deep!"

"Yes, he ran right on the sword."

"Ah, I wondered how it happened. He was such a good swordsman."

Diane shuddered, remembering with terrible clarity the sight of the man's face as he plunged forward, the cry of triumph, the ferocity of that last attack.

"I thought Morillac would kill him, madame."

"No doubt Morillac thought so himself. The wretch, the vile wretch!" And tenderly she placed the second swab in position above the wound, smoothing it down with a caressing motion of the hand. "He provoked it, of course?"

"Yes, he provoked it. He had a pistol."

"And Charles had climbed in, I suppose? By arrangement?"

"No, not by arrangement."

"I believe you," said her mistress, returning to her task. "I believe you. But you let him in?"

"Yes."

"And he made love to you?"

"He came to arrange a meeting—with you. But afterwards . . . yes, we did make love."

"He loves you?"

"He has said so."

"And you feel for him?"

"Madame!"

"Never mind. I can see it was a foolish question. Well, then, you're agreed."

Diane was watching her friend with mingled alarm and tenderness. At last she said humbly, in a very gentle voice:

"This has hurt you."

"Hurt me? Why should it hurt me? I've told you that the Vicomte is nothing to me. But you should know that you are fortunate."

"Oh, I know it."

"He's a good man, a courageous man; too courageous,

I'm afraid. You should check him. Another time he would not get the better of Morillac."

Moved by the same thought, both women looked down at the body in their arms, a light brown body, almost hairless, so compactly built that only when the limbs moved in their sharp convulsive movement could they see the powerful muscles of the neck and chest.

"Another time! Is it possible?"

Hortense leant forward suddenly, for it had seemed to her that the man had answered for himself.

"There! Did you see that?"

"What?"

"A change in expression. The eyes moved."

"I didn't see."

"It was very slight, just a tremor, a glimpse of the iris. I thought for a moment he was coming round."

Diane was struck by a sudden chill. But as she looked into Morillac's face she saw only the features of the wounded man, flesh and blood made more inhuman than any mask by the blank white cavities of the eyes.

She repeated:

"No, I didn't see. A tremor, did you say? He must be dying."

"Then it's happening very quietly," replied her mistress, whose head was now bent down over the body. "The congestion's easier."

In profound stillness both women listened, catching the changing rhythm of his breath.

"There, Diane! Do you hear now? The rasping sound's gone." She added in a flat voice: "It would be like him to recover."

"Impossible."

"No, not impossible. He's that sort of animal. It happened once before." She was pointing to the scar of an old sword wound high up beneath the shoulder, a discolouration much whiter than the surrounding skin.

Diane's fingers, moving above the wound, traced the course of it towards the heart, and with a strange idea that it had significance for her she asked:

"When did it happen?"

"About four years ago. It was in a duel. He should have died then; but he's indestructible, I think."

"And the man who wounded him?"

Her mistress understood what lay behind the question, and answered with reluctance, though it had been her intention to convey a warning:

"He was killed at the next attempt. The whole incident impressed Louis very much, and not long afterwards he took Morillac into service."

Till then, in the conflict of their feelings for the servant, they had not thought of the master or the other dangers that surrounded them; but mention of the name was sufficient, and Diane started to her feet.

"I'd forgotten your husband. It's a bad turn that we've done you."

There was a suspicion of a smile on her mistress' face as she replied:

"It's certainly a bad turn that you've done him."

"And he'll revenge himself. I shall be dismissed."

"Dismissed! But you're in *my* service. And I shall certainly not dismiss you."

"You'll be forced to."

"Forced to part with you! Never, never!" And with an impulsive gesture she put her arms out to her friend and tenderly embraced her.

As the two women clung together they heard a movement close at hand. The body of Morillac had changed position, so violently that it seemed as though he had tried to struggle to his feet. But it was at the eyes they looked—at the pupils now wide and staring. Before he lapsed back into unconsciousness they recognized there the spark of a feeling more sinister and malignant than they had ever dreamed of.

# *Chapter Seventeen*

D E BELLAC SWUNG HIMSELF OUT FROM
the balustrade to reach the narrow ledge of
moulding above the windows of the *rez de
chaussée*, and using this as a foothold he worked
his way along the face of the house till he came to the guttering in the angle of the wall. This was the way that he
had come an hour before, and he approached it in a familiar spirit, undaunted by its smoothness and by the sight
of the ground uncomfortably far below. The house was
roused, lights were showing in windows, and there was no
knowing whether or not there would be enemies to deal
with in the garden or the street, but he gave little thought
to it, for he had lived so long with emergencies that he had
begun to treat them as inseparable companions. He was
ready for the worst, and approached it with optimism, lowering himself down the glacis of the house, with his face
to the wall and an imperturbable back turned on all other
dangers—irrelevancies till he reached the ground.

It was a slow and painful descent, more dangerous than
the climb. Friction rubbed the skin off his palms and knees,
an aching cramp seized hold of him, and once his foothold

slipped and he found himself clinging with his fingers as though trepanned against the wall.

He struggled gamely on, till at last, sensing the nearness of the ground, he relaxed his grip and tumbled softly to earth. He was up in a bound, sword in hand, but there was no threat to him in the formal garden that stretched before him, dim and ghostly in the light of early dawn; nothing stirred there except the bare trees and shrubs, familiar shadows rustling in the wind.

The Vicomte, identifying them, knew that for the moment he was safe. But was his mistress? The light still shone in the windows of her room, and in the stillness he could catch the murmur of voices. What was happening? Who was with her? Was Morillac dead? And suddenly the room that he had left became a place of mystery, so that for one wild instant he thought of climbing to her balcony again.

It was a momentary impulse, a flash of curiosity submerged at once in the harsh realities of his position, for it was obvious from the lights that he had no time to lose; he must get out of the grounds before the chase began and he was cornered like an animal in a trap. A high wall appeared in front of him dividing the garden from the street, and running at it, he drew himself almost in one motion to its crest and down into the street below, along which he hurried with steps so buoyant as to match his hopes for the evening that she had promised, the lively fancies of his dreams.

As he reached the open spaces of the city he could see how much lighter it had become. Around him the pattern of Paris was unrolled as though materializing under some magician's hand: the shapes of gardens, houses, churches, palaces, rising out of the grey limbo of dawn in a thousand jumbled outlines of branch and roof and steeple like the stage properties of fairyland. As the light increased, so did the perspective deepen: the flat lines of streets, as anonymous as the night through which he had made his way, were pushed to the forefront of the view; behind them others shouldered their way towards him like bystanders at a parade, till the whole scene was given solidity and depth, part of the living city that stretched its vast, majestic size from the Porte d'Orléans to the hill of Montmartre, and from the Revolutionary quarter of Saint-Antoine to the western faubourgs on the Seine.

Through this charming scene he went with a light and eager heart, seeing no danger, but the brush of the artist, in the light that was spreading beyond the rooftops, that soft, luminous glow of Paris that seemed an emanation from the pearl-grey stone and pearl-grey river that wound between her quays. His coat was in tatters, his left shoulder caked with blood, a strange figure to be seen on the streets of a city where respectability was back in vogue. Already there were folk abroad. As he marched along he could see the lights start up in a thousand windows and hear the clatter of feet in the avenues—men going to what employment of the day? returning under the cloak of darkness from what pleasures of the night?

His own objective was the house where he lodged with Cadoudal in the rue Langrais. The morning sky was touched with rose as the sun climbed towards the rim of the horizon, banked in strata of puffy clouds, and in this gentle radiance the vista of the street disclosed itself to him as he turned the corner from the rue Saint-Force. He had been three months in France; de Rivière and the Polignacs two months; Pichegru two also; their leader more than half a year. Their funds had amounted to forty thousand pounds sterling. There had been such hopes: of Artois, of Moreau, of all the disaffected. As he came up the street he saw the place that was his home—the mean house where the leader of the conspiracy now lived, the heir of great expectations that had vanished with the rising sun of the reality—Artois still in Edinburgh, Moreau returning to inactivity at Grosbois, the royalists in the anterooms of the Tuileries and Saint-Cloud.

At sight of it the Vicomte, who had been so filled with the joy of his own personal memories, was suddenly struck with a feeling of sadness and oppression, the consciousness of the weakness of his friends and the power of the giant that they had challenged—this city waking into life in the bodies of hundreds of thousands of its citizens, an entity with a terrible inertia of its own.

Unconsciously his pace quickened as he neared the door, passing up that side of the street that still lay in the shadows. They were early risers in the rue Langrais. There was a figure standing in a doorway; two more were huddled in the angle of a wall. The Vicomte, a man of no Puritanical mind, spared a smile for them—rather a melancholy one for so much discomfort at such a time. He averted his head as he passed, catching a glimpse as he did so of two others directly facing them across the street. It was strange. He had not expected so much from the quarter, whose drab façades would not have hinted at even this poor measure of romance.

At the end of the street near the junction with the rue des Fossayeurs a group had formed, and as he stood on the threshold, key in hand, he counted them idly—four men, no, five; the light was still imperfect, and at this distance the small, huddled figures seemed to merge into one another and their shadowy background. Who would have guessed that there could be so much activity in the quarter at this hour?

As the question formed in his mind he frowned at an intruding thought. Activity! But there was no activity. For some time now he had been walking through the awakening city filled with the sound of footsteps and movement on every side, but here in the rue Langrais there were only shadows to be seen and silence reigned.

It was at this moment that the first promptings of danger came to him. The scene looked innocent enough—a small group of men at a street corner, a figure in a doorway, lovers in one another's arms. It might have been the uneasiness caused by his experiences of the night or Diane's words about de Lozier and a sequence of betrayals that made him see significance in them, something intensely menacing and personal to himself.

Once this feeling had taken possession of him the Vicomte was even proof against the call of curiosity, and without a backward glance opened the door and, passing inside, ran quickly up the stairs. The house was in darkness, the shutters were half closed in Georges' room, and it was only in the thin filtered light that he could see the body of his leader sprawled out on the bed, a vast shadow, formless, indeterminate. He called out:

"Georges!"

He had spoken softly, hardly above a whisper, but he knew at once that Cadoudal was awake. There had been no sudden movement, no definite sound, but he could read the message of the altered rhythm of the breath. He knew this uncanny ability of his leader to wake silently from sleep; he could feel his eyes peering up at him through lowered lids; and he said, still in the same quiet tone:

"There are men in the street. The house is watched."

There was a sudden movement and next instant the looming shadow rose almost noiselessly from the bed till it towered over him, seeming to fill the narrow room. The man's voice came out of the darkness, harsh and vibrant but free of any trace of fear.

"Watching us? You're sure?"

The Vicomte moved towards the shutters and gently drew up one of the slats so that a narrow angle of vision was disclosed on to the street. There, immediately opposite them in the angle of the wall, two figures were clasped together in an embrace. At sight of them Cadoudal gave a muttered exclamation, partly of anger, partly of relief, but the Vicomte was less impressed with this masquerade of love. He said coldly:

"There are two more on this side. One must admit that the police show sensibility. But it's not all so romantic, you will see."

"See? From where?"

"From the attic. There's a wider view."

For an instant it seemed as though Cadoudal might be going to refuse; suddenly he noticed the Vicomte's pale, drawn face and the bloodstains on his coat. Without a word he followed as the young man led the way out of the room, and up the stairs and to the attic window festooned with dirt and cobwebs. From this vantage point they could see the junction of the rue Langrais and the rue des Fossayeurs, but a moment passed before the little group of figures that had gathered moved into their view—five men strolling together in the most leisurely manner in the world.

"Do you see now?" the Vicomte asked.

Cadoudal was gazing at them with fierce intentness.

"I see five men who take their time, *mordieu!* You say

they're agents watching us. Well, you've come in right under their noses and I've been here all night. What are they
waiting for, these agents of yours?"

"They're waiting for their friends," the Vicomte said,
and he pointed down the way he had come.

There, less than fifty yards away, another group of men
about a dozen strong came into sight, moving towards them
along the centre of the road; the rays of the sun slanting
down the rue Saint-Force shone full on them, so that they
seemed to be marching on a golden carpet laid across the
paving of the street. There was no mistaking their purpose,
the superior activity of these agents of Réal, and Georges
was the last person to persist in a delusion. He stepped back
from the window and, laying a hand on his friend's shoulder, said in a voice of resignation:

"You're right. We've been betrayed. Querelle, de Lozier,
and now a third."

Wounded though he was, the Vicomte was in the mood
to expect a more vigorous reaction. The whole process of
antlike industry that had been set in force by the capture of
Querelle would have seemed as irrelevant to him as the
sufferings of the victims who had brought them to this pass
or even their identity; he was not concerned with the betrayal but only with its results, and he was shocked to notice
in his friend a quality of lethargy so foreign to his own
nature that it filled him with bewilderment.

He shook himself angrily free from his leader's hand and
turned towards the door, hearing the voice ask behind him:

"Where are you going, Charles?"

"To save you," the Vicomte said, and so intent was his
face, so filled with an evident determination, that the words
were robbed of all bombast, and even of humour.

Cadoudal saw this. Glancing down into the road again

at the advancing cordons closing in on them from opposite sides, he asked kindly and without irony:

"How will you do it? They're ten to one. You were acute, Charles. Even romance is taking a practical turn outside."

"So you'll surrender?"

Cadoudal looked down at himself, at the great barrel of a chest, the vast arms and thighs and the hands with their powerful, square-cut fingers. He said without emotion, in the tone of a man who utters a self-evident truth:

"I shall never surrender."

"You'll fight them?"

"Yes."

"At odds of ten to one! And you'll pull the house down on them like Samson, I suppose?"

A smile crossed the face of Cadoudal. He found the fancy amusing.

"That had not occurred to me."

But the young man had not discovered such reserves of resignation in his soul. He burst out urgently:

"Well, I've a better way."

"Of fighting them?"

"Less heroic. Of escaping."

"And now you interest me."

"Yes, listen." And he began to draw his leader behind him down the stairs, explaining as he went: "You must use the secret way."

Georges was shaking his great head ponderously from side to side.

"Ah, my dear friend, I was afraid you'd think of that."

"Why afraid? The way exists."

"Yes, and where does it lead to? Ask yourself. Into the cellars of the house behind. Do you imagine they haven't covered the whole quarter, and won't search it if necessary till they dig us out? I prefer an attic; it gives one some advantage." At that moment they heard the sound of footsteps marching in unison in the street, and he added: "It's an advantage we shall need."

"I can give you another," the Vicomte said.

"Another advantage?"

"Yes, of privacy."

"What do you mean?"

"That they won't search your cellar. That you'll be alone when you step out into the street."

"How will you work this agreeable miracle, may I ask?"

"Listen to me," said the Vicomte, clutching at his friend's arm with a fierce, impatient grip as he heard a clash of muskets outside the door. "Go down the secret stair. Watch your opportunity. In about five minutes the way should be clear into the rue des Dames. It should be clear because I shall have led them off—yes, along the rooftops. They'll shoot; they'll follow. We know their discipline and intelligence after Biville. I shall be the fox and I shall draw them all."

Georges was looking speculatively at his friend.

"For how long? I see you're wounded."

"Yes."

"You'd have no chance."

"You're the one to have the chance, and you're wasting it. You've little time."

And as a commentary on his words there came a loud knocking at the door.

At that sound a change came over Cadoudal, who, in the shock of the discovery that he had been betrayed, had shown a supineness like that of Danton on the night of his arrest, a condition of mind highly uncharacteristic of these two resourceful men; the alert look returned to his eyes and he started rapidly down towards the room where he had slept, a dogged combativeness in every line of his body that moved with an extraordinary speed and lightness over the loose boarding of the stairs.

Like the good soldier he was, the Vicomte recognized the change, and rejoiced in it. He was responsive to leadership and to the personal magnetism of Georges, which acted on his associates with an effect that was almost physical. He made no further attempt to impose himself, but asked in the voice of a subordinate:

"Will you do it? Shall we try that way?"

Cadoudal had flung a cloak over his shoulders and was thrusting a pair of duelling pistols into his belt. He spoke over his shoulder in the most matter-of-fact of tones: "Naturally. It's the only chance." For once he had seen a possibility in the plan, it no more occurred to him to refuse the sacrifice than it had to the Vicomte to uphold it; they were servants of the King, and knew their respective worth to the service that had brought them both to France.

Another loud crash sounded from below and the cry of voices in the street. The two men looked at one another, and a smile passed between them—a legacy of those last minutes on Biville cliff when the storm of indiscipline had broken out among their enemies, in confused shouting, contradictory commands, a fusillade of shots from the sentry posts that had promised—and probably achieved—the most lethal and suicidal results. For such antagonists it was impossible not to feel contempt, increased by memory of the charade that had been played below their windows; even so, they would waste no time, for the door was not impregnable, and already the battering of muskets was sounding against its woodwork and against the shutters on either side.

The panel leading to the secret stair was at the head of the landing on the first floor, an ingenious arrangement similar to that devised by Spein, the carpenter in the rue Carême-Prenant. As Georges placed his hand against its hinge a portion of the woodwork swung wide to reveal an opening with rough steps leading down into its depths. For an instant the two men peered at it; then Cadoudal stepped forward and edged himself into the gap, hardly wider than those great shoulders in the heavy cloak. He did not say a word of gratitude for the Vicomte's selfless act; he did not wish him well, though he must have suspected that he was seeing him for the last time; but his left hand fell naturally on the shoulder of his friend, a companionable gesture full of rough sympathy and affection.

Next instant his body had slipped out of sight in the recesses of the stair, and the Vicomte was pressing the catch to release the panel, which slid smoothly into place. Even as he stood in momentary indecision like a man who by some action has closed a chapter of his life, a tremendous crash rang out from below him, and he heard the splintering sound of wood, and loud, triumphant voices through the broken door.

# Chapter Eighteen

THE VICOMTE TURNED AND RACED UP the stairs to the attic. As he lifted the skylight and climbed on to the roof, he heard the entry of his enemies into the hall below—a wild stampede of movement in which he could distinguish the clatter of heavy boots and muskets, the clash of sabres, mingling with the raised voices of the huntsmen encouraging each other —rather noisily—in a chase which, in view of Georges' reputation, might be expected to have its harsher side.

From his vantage-point he cast a quick glance around. Below him in the rue Langrais and in the parallel rue des Dames small groups of police could be seen, watchers at the bolt-holes along the route; it would be his object to attract their attention and draw them after him down the street, but for the moment he must take stock of his position, and study that quaint, tortuous skyline into which the turrets and gables and chimneystacks of the quarter obtruded like rows of soldiers on some lunatic parade.

He was high up in his eyrie. Around him on every side he could see the panorama of the city bathed in a misty golden light filtering through the smoke of a thousand fires: he could see close at hand the Cordeliers district and the

Panthéon and the Palace of Luxembourg; beyond them Notre-Dame and the delicate Gothic of the Sainte-Chapelle, the vast bulk of the Louvre, and the Tuileries gardens where the little Dauphin had once played; the hill of Montmartre to the north beyond the roofs and steeples; the grey twist of the river that seemed to draw towards itself all these elements, the mass of the town in all its formless detail, giving it the harmony of a work of nature.

The Vicomte saw in it a military problem, and one of a peculiarly complex kind. Once beyond the range of his enemies, his chances of escape in the maze of streets were excellent, but there remained the fact of his exposed position at the centre of a ring. The disadvantages of this situation were all too obvious: he could be caught at the vortex, a target for the whole circle of his pursuers; but his trained mind, appreciating this, knew also that if properly exploited there were advantages to compensate—the central position was perilous or helpful according to the use one made of it, and by descending suddenly from the spine on to one side or the other he could halve the number of his enemies.

But once down? Even half the patrol would be too much for him in the bare exposure of a street. It was at this moment that he caught sight of a garden whose lawns stretched back to the rue des Dames, which made a sharp turn to the south to skirt its wall. Suppose he could reach it in safety: he would be free for the moment from the attentions of the patrol in the rue Langrais, and might hope to outwit the parallel smaller group, which could possibly be lured from its strong position in the street into the mazes of a garden, where chance would favour the resourceful. A great deal depended on keeping clear of the party that had burst in at the door and which might be expected shortly to share his central position with him; he could hear the loud voices as they searched inside the house, rising in crescendo towards the skylight through which he had just climbed, the obvious avenue of escape in the light of simple minds.

The time had come. He could wait no longer, and as the determination came to him he stepped out from behind the gable into full view of the agents in the rue Langrais, a small, fast-moving target in the sunlight. A cry went up from the street; he saw the glint on the barrels of the muskets, and next instant the balls—excessively ill directed —were bursting against the stacks and parapets; it was balm to him to hear from the side of the rue des Dames a similar commotion on the part of marksmen who had no chance of seeing him but who discharged their pieces with enthusiasm—a *feu de joie* whistling harmlessly over his head.

After that first exposure of himself, a necessary part of his plan for saving Cadoudal, the Vicomte showed the greatest respect for his own safety; he adopted a half-crouching position as he ran, darting along in the shelter of the chimneystacks, so that he seldom presented to his pursuers more than an excuse for a random shot. They continued firing, all the same, at the best speed of their cumbersome weapons, using, in the words of Fouché when the affair came to his ears, "more powder than Bonaparte at the siege of Saint-Jean-d'Acre."

The Vicomte was less concerned with marksmanship than with the terrain: on the incompetent level of the one he could rely, but he had never imagined such tortuous variations as now confronted him in the others—a fantastic jumble of gables and drops and gradients that seemed more in keeping with the old ruffianly Paris of Villon. There was good cover, that much could be said for it at least, but it did not escape him as he ran on his elusive zigzag course

that both the patrols in the rue Langrais and rue des Dames
had ample time to anticipate his plan. He could console
himself with the success of it, for he could see that the
effect of his escapade had been to draw every available man
after him; perhaps they believed that there were two fugitives up there on the rooftops, and he did his best to
heighten the illusion, appearing with an astonishing
ubiquity now on one side, now on the other, and drawing
always the tribute of a cannonade.

Till now he had been free of the most pressing danger—
pursuit by the men who had forced their way into the
house—but he could not hope that this immunity would
last. He could see nothing beyond the maze of stacks that
lay between them, but through the rattle of musketry from
the street he heard the crash of the skylight as its frame
dropped back into place, the sound of the voices of the adventurous as they emerged into the strange rooftop world,
the clatter of their feet on the uneven surface of the tiles.

The garden lay close ahead, a labyrinth of shrubs and
evergreens and the bare skeletons of trees whose branches
began to be touched by that indefinable first stirring of the
spring. One could feel it in the air and in the sunlight pour-
ing down on the roofs with all the promise of flowers, the
willows along the Seine, the candles of the chestnut trees.
He had not seen spring in Paris for six years. How long ago
since he had walked in the fields beyond Saint-Germain and
seen in the distance the young ladies of Mme Campan's
select establishment, each one in her white dress a denial
of the Revolution and the Terror, of Robespierre and
Hébert, and the guillotining of the King!

As he sped along the sloping roofs, doubling from one
point of cover to another in the crouching run of a hunted
beast, this recollection flashed into his mind, the result

perhaps of some premonition of disaster, followed by the remembrance of events still further back—his youth in the warm highlands of the south, the round of the small noblesse that had seemed rooted for ever in an earlier, more patriarchal time. These memories of the secure, ordered days were the background for the reality of the present that now, on this sunlit morning, showed him the Medusa's head of his mortality.

The patrols were there below him. He could see their white faces upturned to his, the scurry of their movements, stilted and absurd as one looked down from this height; he could hear the voices of the men behind him as they stumbled clumsily along, the door of the trap into which he had ventured of his own free will. But not for an instant in the course of these melancholy thoughts did the Vicomte doubt the necessity for what he had done; not for an instant did he lose his hope or courage.

He could see the details of the sanctuary more plainly now: the paths that ran in ordered lines between the wilderness of lawns and shrubs, the wreckage of a formal garden that once, in the days of the old regime, must have been trim with conscious aspiration, a miniature of one of the great creations of Le Nôtre. One could see the evidence still, even in the time of its decay: in the neat geometrical arrangement of the paths, the pavilion with its classical colonnades, the fountains whose waters—alas!—were now covered in green scum, in the perspective of the central avenue, a pleasant conceit of a Grand Vista that ended in a suburban wall. But it was at the trees that the young man was looking, approving them even in their present bareness —one in particular, a huge sycamore whose branches reached out towards the rooftops, against which in summer the leaves would nuzzle in a delicate caress. Here was the ladder he was seeking, a way down into the garden that would make few demands on his agility.

The Vicomte was now approaching the edge of the roof where it sloped down under the topmost branches; he could see below him the great trunk of the tree, foreshortened so that it appeared massive and top-heavy; to his left the parapet sloped down, exposing him to the marksmen in the rue Langrais, then rose in a line of gabling till it towered high above him, cutting off all but the tallest branches of the sycamore from the sight of those below.

The way down was obvious enough. He could clamber along the inner surface of that protecting wall till he reached one of the jutting branches of the tree. Nothing could have been more agreeably and conveniently arranged. But once down, was there a way out again? His gaze passed rapidly round the garden, taking in the walls that rose with the uncompromising abruptness of a fortress, the two gates on either side of the central avenue, studded and barred with rusty iron, guardians that held this small plot of nature in captivity.

In action the Vicomte was a realist, and in that one glance he recognized the truth about the place that he had imagined as a refuge: he saw that once inside the garden he was doomed; the walls could not be climbed, the gates could easily be held, and, indeed, the patrols on either side were already moving into place to guard them. As the realization came to him he stood still, oblivious of the marksmen in the street: it was the most terrible moment of his life, the more terrible from the fact that he had advanced so gaily, so confident in his cleverness, with such hopes. A trap in front of him; the patrols on either side. He heard not more than two hundred yards behind him the sound of hurrying feet.

And suddenly the Vicomte knew what he would do—
knew it with a certainty that took account of all the risks,
the obstacles in his path, the tenuous nature of his chance,
and yet accepted them joyously as part of a supreme gamble
appealing to his energy, his boldness, his sense of irony.

His pursuers on the rooftops were not yet in sight: it was
on their slowness and their gullibility that everything depended. He ran suddenly towards the low edge of the parapet above the rue Langrais, exposing himself there till he
drew the cries of recognition to which he had become ac-
customed—those and a few random shots which he accepted as part of the price of the deception—then, satisfied
that they had placed him on that side, he moved out of
view behind the gable and dropping swiftly along the glacis
of the roof, reached the projecting ledge above which the
branches of the sycamore hung invitingly to hand, the first
rungs of the ladder that led downwards into space.

He was concerned with an illusion and spared no pains
with the execution, dragging at the tree with all his strength
till the movement was echoed in a rustling up above; cast-
ing down loose tiles; achieving a *tour de force* of stage
management that drew the reaction he most coveted—
voices from the rue Langrais that cried out insistently that
he had left the roofs; they had seen it, with their own eyes
they had seen him take to the branches like an ape. He had
given them credit for so much gullibility, if not for the vivid
detail in which it was expressed; he continued the illusion,
shaking the branches with diminishing force till he might
be judged to have reached the garden; then, turning rapidly,
climbed back in the shelter of the gable and crawled on
hands and knees past the low part of the parapet into the
safer ground beyond.

The noise of firing had ceased as his enemies closed in on

the garden for the kill; the only sounds now were the voices that still called their comforting misinformation from the street, and the footsteps of his pursuers on the roofs as they clambered painfully over the obstacles of pitch and gabling that he had taken in his stride. Here were the men with whom he had to deal, a mob no longer, but individuals—four, he reckoned from the sound of them, four men stumbling along just out of sight; their presence gave the colour of personal conflict to the work ahead.

He looked urgently around him. There was a good deal of cover on the roof, forming a screen that still shut off a view of his pursuers, though they were so near to him. How were they grouped? Were they moving together or strung out in line? Until he could be sure, the selection of a refuge would be a gamble, but one that he must take; and with beating heart he made the choice: a pyramid of stacks on the side of the rue Langrais, through which spirals of smoke—ironic flavour of domesticity!—curled gently into the still air.

Hardly had he taken up his position when he saw the first sign of the patrol—an officer of police climbing among the eaves with the earnest concentration of a man who walks a tightrope, followed an instant later by three others, to confirm his guess and warm his heart with this evidence of the herd instinct of his enemies. On they came in a compact group, moving along the central axis of the roof on a line that would take them wide of the cover where he lay; he could see every detail clearly: the heads that turned suspiciously as they searched, the glint of the sunlight on the barrels of the pistols they carried in their hands. They had reached the top of the steep edge of roofing that had so sorely tried them, and stood now on the level platform that extended to the verge of the glacis below the sycamore.

And suddenly the Vicomte felt his heart stand still, as at a gesture from the leader two of the men turned outwards, one moving towards the rue des Dames, the other towards the parapet that overlooked the rue Langrais.

He reached it. Not fifteen yards divided the man from de Bellac in the shelter of the stack.

The impulse to stir was almost irresistible, to move away, backwards towards the garden, inwards towards the rest of the patrol, to be free in some way, even by surrender or in the fierce action of attack, from the menace of this figure that he could no longer see but whose steps came to him with a dreadful clarity. Soon only the width of his cover would lie between them. He could imagine the hand reaching out, feeling with a slow inquisitiveness; the sudden touch; the startled, incredulous expression of the eyes.

More slowly the gendarme came on. What was guiding him? Chance? Or was it possible that they had caught a glimpse of him in silhouette against the long slanting rays that played upon the roof, striping it with bars of shadow, thin and elongated like so many projections of the figure of a man? It was possible. He had known from the beginning the dangers of his plan, the nature of the cover on which he must rely. But he could not tell; he could do no more than guess the intentions of his enemies from the sounds he heard: the noisy clatter on the centre of the roof, those nearer movements that paused now by the parapet and then started into life again, loud, abrupt, terrifyingly close at hand.

The Vicomte's fingers closed on the butt of his pistol. He no longer doubted that he had lost the game, but so far from knowing the resignation of the failed gambler he was borne up by a wave of energy that took no account of his wounds or desperate position—a flood of pure pugnacity that rejoiced in the call of action after the long flight that had been of so little profit to him, that had not saved him from the indignity of being baited at the last.

Well, it had ended; he would not be surprised; he would do some surprising of his own; and he was crouching down, poised to launch himself at his pursuer, when he heard a voice calling from the street:

"You there! What are you doing? They're in the garden. They went down the tree."

The footsteps came to a halt in indecision; there was a moment of silence and then the voice from the road again, confident, buoyed up by an enormous assurance, the superiority of the secondhand:

"They're down, I tell you. Down in the garden. Move yourself. Close in and spot for us."

From his cover the Vicomte could almost share in his enemy's dilemma—two sets of orders that were grossly contradictory. One solution would be to temporize, and a sudden scraping of feet announced the accuracy of this guess: the man had moved back from the parapet, insufficiently far, as it appeared, for the voice—an authoritative one by all accounts—continued with its exhortation:

"Move, I tell you. Get up to the garden side and give a line on them."

The order was imperative, and it was obeyed. De Bellac was suddenly aware of a body that moved past the corner of the stack. As he swung himself round, turning noiselessly on his toes, he caught a glimpse of his antagonist—a large, uncouth figure almost within touching distance. He had never realized, even in his worst imagining, the minute space that had divided them, so small a gulf that he could not credit that he had not betrayed himself.

But the fact was that the man was moving away towards his friends: there was a murmur of voices and then the tramp of feet as the patrol passed on towards the garden's edge in the shadow of the sycamore. In that moment the Vicomte saw the chance of escaping from the trap, but the effect of the knowledge was to make him doubly cautious as he crept out from his shelter and began to work his way towards the house from which he had emerged not ten minutes since in a cavalier spirit of defiance.

It was strangely peaceful after the storm of firing that had accompanied his progress: the sun shone benignly through the lifting haze, drawing a sparkle from the glass of the skylights and from the pools of rainwater that lay in hollows among the eaves. Close ahead of him lay the house, and for an instant as it came in sight he relived the moments that had passed there: Cadoudal rising like a wraith from sleep, the view from the window, the secret stairway, the wild beating at the door. Nothing could have seemed more ordinary than it now appeared—at one with its neighbours in unimpeachable respectability, a particle of the city that basked so comfortably in the rays of the sun.

In spite of this it was with extreme caution that he approached it, alert for any sign of his enemies. But when at last he reached the skylight and peered down, all that met his gaze was the bare floor of the attic littered with broken glass, and the chair that he—and others it seemed—had used to climb up to the roof, lying on its side where it had fallen under the thrust of the last man of the patrol.

He bent down, and slipping his hand past the broken panes, found the catch and lifted the sash towards him;

then swung himself through the opening and dropped softly to the floor. He stood listening, but there was no sound except that of distant voices calling to one another from the roof and garden and surrounding streets: the tide had flowed on past this silent place, to break—how impotently!—in that tangled wilderness beneath the trees.

Slowly, still moving with immense caution, he began to descend into the house, though it was not till he had reached the turn above the landing that he saw the flotsam that had been left behind—the agent of police below him on the stair.

# Chapter Nineteen

THE MAN WAS FACING AWAY FROM HIM towards the panel that concealed the hidden door. De Bellac, looking down, could see the stooping back, the head thrust forward, all the evidence of an intense curiosity—a fortunate curiosity, for it had masked the sound of his own approach. The enemy who might so easily have been waiting for him in the shadows was at his mercy, and as he appreciated this lucky chance he shifted the grip on his pistol to the barrel and crouched down.

At the last moment he was incautious, the result of the unbearable strain of knowing that there might be other agents in the house and that he must finish the matter with one blow; his feet grated on the stair, and as he sprang he realized with a terrible certainty that the man had heard him, that he was turning, that the stroke was wide.

The two bodies cannoned into one another and fell apart, de Bellac sprawling at full length and striking his head against the wall, fair game for an antagonist who recovered much the more quickly, who now flung himself upon him with a speed and fury worthy of Morillac, pinioning his arms and grasping at his throat. At this moment full of the bitterness of failure he had one small consolation in the knowledge that they were alone in the house, for the man did not cry out; he seemed to prefer more silent courses, for just as the Vicomte was acknowledging his good fortune he saw the glitter of a knife in the clenched right hand.

De Bellac felt the shift of weight as it was carried back, and with a supreme effort rolled over sideways so that the thrust, delivered with a lunging movement of the arm and body from the level of the waist, took him in the shoulder close to the spot where Morillac's sword had struck. It was a glancing blow, and at this moment in the struggle for his life he felt no pain, but only the stimulus of a burning anger. His right arm had been momentarily freed as his enemy leaned forward, off balance with the blow, and he struck out with it, a tremendous buffet that caught the man between the eyes, driving him back so that for the first time the Vicomte was free of the weight that had held him down.

But if he had freedom of movement, so had his antagonist. The second blow came; he parried it desperately with his cloak, which he held in his damaged left arm like a shield; the third slipped under it, a cleaving upward thrust, fortunately turned by the stiff material of his coat. The Vicomte seized his chance. Leaning forward, he pressed both knife and hand against his breast, then with a convulsive movement wrenched at his enemy, drawing him within reach of his right arm. With all the force he could summon he struck out, feeling with a fierce exhilaration the crunch of his knuckles against the yielding flesh, the weakening of the hand had held the knife.

The blade still lay close against him, doubled back so that its point pressed into the sinews of his wrist, held there by the pressure of his own left arm and body and an iron

strength of will. Suddenly he pounced with his right and
seized it, searing his own flesh in the movement that tore
it from the grasp of his enemy and flung it far from them
down the stairs. He was the master now. The man's left
arm was still imprisoned, and he drew it tighter with a
savage pressure that turned the victim on his side; then,
half rising, he struck out with his fist again and again, continuing till all resistance ended and he could feel a limp
body pressed against his own.

For an instant after he had realized this the Vicomte remained motionless, slumped against the enemy he had
beaten down, overcome by a sense of weakness that he
found unaccountable till, looking at his left shoulder, he
saw the spreading stains of blood. With his good hand he
ripped away the sleeve and did his best to stop the flow.
The blood was welling freely from the recent wound but
had congealed around the first, and once he had put the
improvised dressing on he felt a resurgence of energy, partly
the result of the discovery that they were clean, straightforward wounds, more formidable in appearance than in
reality.

He rose to his feet and looked around him, but no one
stirred; he stood listening, but there was no sound except
the distant voices. It seemed incredible to him that the
struggle could have taken place unheard near the centre of
so much violent action. Yet so it was. There was the house,
as silent as at that moment when he had entered at dawn;
there was his enemy at his feet struggling back to consciousness, and just beyond him the panel to the secret stair.

As he leaned forward and pressed the catch the door slid
open, and without a backward glance he stepped inside,
closing it behind him till the dim light from the house was
cut and he was standing in pitch darkness, reaching with

outstretched hands for the guide-rope that led steeply into the depths.

Step by step he began to feel his way down the stairs, whose woodwork creaked beneath his weight—little spurts of sound, matched once from far off down the corridor by a scurrying—of rats, most probably, in the hollow walls. There it was again, now sounding below him, now in the rafters above his head, evanescent as an echo of human footsteps moving in the void ahead. There could be someone there—Cadoudal, of course. It would not be pleasant to walk on and feel suddenly the touch of a body against his own, and as the uncomfortable nature of the thought imposed itself he called out softly, "Georges, Georges!" hearing the words reverberate in a whisper so secretive that it seemed to him that it reproached him for his folly.

No answer came, only the rustling and scurrying of the creatures of the night he had disturbed. His courage returned, and he moved on through the fetid air that hung like an emanation from the cold, damp walls, the breath of darkness and corruption. He was at the end of the staircase now. He stumbled as his foot, reaching out, found the level of the corridor that led, still at a slight downward angle, towards the entry to the rue des Dames, flagstoned with large uneven blocks, the original paving, on the foundations of which the more modern houses of the quarter had been built.

From now on the size of the tunnel altered perceptibly, dwindling to a narrow conduit between two floor levels, along which he was forced to crawl painfully on hands and knees. There was still not a vestige of light to guide him, even when he felt the face of the wall close in ahead and knew that somewhere above him, marked by an iron ring, was the trapdoor, a solid block of stone fitting into the patchwork paving of the cellar. He reached up for it, stirred by a wave of panic as his hand searched over the cold, damp surface of the roof, a void of darkness that mocked his knowledge and blind sense of touch; then suddenly his fingers brushed against it and he seized hold, lifting himself from the tunnel floor till his shoulders were set against the stone.

With all the force of his body he thrust upwards, pushing away the darkness as the door moved from its bed; a grey light slanted in, widening with each instant till he could look from the burrow through which he had come into the gloom of a cellar festooned with cobwebs that trailed their dingy draperies between the shelves and broken casks. It was a melancholy scene, this deserted wine store in a deserted house marked already by the sickness of decay—the rotting woodwork, the door aslant on its hinges, its panels seared and cracked—but de Bellac saw an ally in it and in the surrounding pall of silence; he raised himself like a sexton from a grave and threading his way between the bins, passed up the stairs into the flooding morning light that shone on the mouldering tapestries and carpets—and on a line of footsteps in the dust.

The Vicomte had expected them. He recognized the marks of Georges' passing with a conviction of mind that made small impression on his instincts, on those wayward fears that reacted with increasing stridency to each alarm. He had been too hardly tried. As he approached the door that led into the street, he was aware of a recurrence of weakness not all due to his exertions and loss of blood, a tension far greater than he had felt at the other events of the morning—the sight of Morillac, of the patrols, of the figure on the landing near the secret stair. Filled with morbid imagining, it was with reluctance that he set his hand to the latch, the trigger to effort from which his body shrank. It was peaceful in the house after the firing and the shouting in the streets. He was called on for no action there; he could stay quiet; after a while his enemies would go away or they would come and take him, and in either case he would be free from this torture by fear and hope that would have earned the respect of the Inquisitors. These were traitorous thoughts, foolish ones too, for only the final test awaited him, and as he saw their drift he responded with his usual directness, opening the door and stepping out into the sunlight of the street.

To the right the road was empty. To the left—but the Vicomte did not spare a second glance for the distant hurrying figures of the patrol. He heard a voice call out, the sound of a shot echoing in the cavernous street; next instant he had reached the junction with the rue des Fossayeurs and plunged into the maze beyond, a world of narrow alleyways with central troughs of gutters down which the turgid water flowed, tall mediæval houses, a square gay with the toadstool growths of booths and market-stalls.

He was safe here; there would be little chance of their finding him in this thronging hive. But the Vicomte could not so easily rid himself of the sense of danger, the result of experiences that had left their mark not only on his body but in his heart. He hurried on with anxious steps through this world of a bustling, cheerful vagabondage, a third force whose citizens cared nothing for Bonapartists or Bourbons, and would have judged the struggle that had just taken place between them with the disenchanted eye of veterans of the Bastille, of the September Massacres, of the Champ de Mars and the storming of the Tuileries. De Bellac, with his wounded arm and furtive manner, was no surprising sight to such men—or to such women, sisters of those Amazons of Les Halles who had made the liveliest audience around the guillotine—though they would have been intrigued if they had known his business: a royalist émigré, a member of the noblesse, passing through the quarter where Desmoulins had penned his scurrilous invective, where Danton had worked and dreamed, where the tocsin calling the people to the overthrow of tyranny had rung on that hot August night from the steeple of the Cordeliers.

Down the rue des Boucheries he went, into the rue du Colombier near the Jacobins, then, by a roundabout route, along the quai Malaquais, across the river into the place Louis Quinze and the rue Saint-Honoré—Robespierre had lived close by with the Duplays, in whose house he had written his last smug philippic—streets alive with memories of Revolutionary Paris that had devoured almost all but one, the most formidable of her children; until ahead of him was the Palais Royal and the lodging of Méhée de la Touche, where he could find security and sleep.

It was late when he awoke, to find the room falling rapidly in the shadows: beyond the windows the houses across the street could be seen lit by the soft radiance of the afterglow, a colouring so reminiscent of the morning that in that waking moment his mind harked back to it and he was on the road again, surrounded by the shadowy figures of his enemies.

But it was Diane who came. He did not start at the sound of her knocking at the door; he had never doubted that she would keep her promise, though not till they were alone together with the shutters closed and one guttering candle for light, did they realize, without embarrassment, what that promise was.

She looked around her at the narrow, ill-conditioned room, its furniture a few rough chairs, a table, and the bed where he had lain. It was how she had imagined it, it was how she wanted it, she told herself, recognizing the presence of deep-rooted instincts that would be satisfied in the place and the way.

But when his kisses deepened she shook her head and drew back from him: he believed it was part of the game of love until he saw her eyes fixed on his bloodstained shoulder, still bound with the rags of his torn cloak. He was wounded and she had forgotten; and almost as a penance she set herself to cut away the edges of the cloth, to bathe the torn flesh, aware all the time of the impatience of the man beside her, communicating itself so that in spite of her earnest care her fingers forgot their office and strayed along the firm line of the muscles of his arm.

She reproved him even as they kissed. He was distracting her. He must wait. There would be time. They had the whole night before them; she would have been surprised to know how urgently she herself was hurrying.

He sank back against the pillows, full of a flooding sense of well-being as the pain of his shoulder eased under the pressure of her hands. He would be patient, imagining the moment, now so close, when she would be lying in his arms to crown for ever the memories of this small, bare room, so far a cry from the salon of the cupids and the great four-poster with its silks and tapestries, its opulent, suggestive promise.

But when the last dressing was in place the Vicomte found that he did not suffer any sense of deprivation. The room was suddenly plunged in darkness. For an instant he could not see her, though he could hear the sound of movement, the soft rustle of a dress; then dimly in the last glow of dusk he caught sight of the white figure at the bedside and reached out for her, his fingers brushing against the powdery softness of her skin.

Slowly he drew her down. She was very small and pliant in his arms, the gentle agent of love on whom he lavished all his pride and strength, all the joy and tenderness and ecstasy that mingled in his body and his heart.

# Chapter Twenty

**B**EFORE DAWN THE VICOMTE WAS awake. He lay on his side watching the glow of the morning lighten beyond the shutters, to penetrate through the broken places in the slats in bands of dappled colour; one shaft shone directly on the bare column of her neck, and with the attention of a lover who for the first time sees his mistress sleeping in his arms he watched it, a ray that picked out the faint pulse that beat against the whiteness of her skin.

A wave of tenderness flooded over him at the sight of her figure touchingly revealed in the candour of sleep, the slight breasts, the firm moulding of her thighs; he did not move as she stirred against him, turning her face so that the sunlight caught for a moment against her lips, slightly parted as though in the memory of some agreeable experience that still lingered in her dreams. After the happenings of the night, it was strange to lie there and watch the passing of an emotion he could not share, and he felt an irrational jealousy and sense of grievance, dispelled when her hand touched against his own.

The morning was brightening around them. He wondered that she could still sleep with that light beating down on her, a sharp arrow of sunlight in whose gleam he could see the dancing particles of dust. It was certainly ironical that the supreme experience of his life should have happened in such a place, that they should lie together in the cold morning with only his cloak and a rough blanket for a covering. He saw that she had shaken herself clear of them in turning, and he reached over her to draw them into place, feeling as he did so her body against his hand, so relaxed and trusting, yet recalling such vivid memories that his grip tightened, bearing down on the roundness of her shoulder that showed startlingly white against the soiled texture of the cloak.

Suddenly he knew that she was awake. The dark eyes looked up at him, grave and watchful as though weighing the quality of what he did, without reproach, without encouragement. Where was the true woman? Here in this moment of waking, or in the passionate yielding of the night? He was filled with a sense of sadness at this proof of the fitful quality in love, but when he released her he felt her stir against him, the gentle pressure of her lips.

"Charles."

He did not move.

"Charles, what is it?"

He could not tell her; he could not express the effect of his fugitive life, his fears of the day that stretched out ahead of him, the need he felt for her kindness and the assurance of her body in his arms.

He said coldly:

"It's nothing. There's nothing wrong."

She lay close against him, fully awake, and of course she understood. She whispered:

"There is. I can see now. But I said you should be patient."

"Patience is a virtue for people who have time, Diane."

"And we have time."

"No, you're wrong." He was looking towards the street—already alive with the sound of voices and hurrying footsteps—seeing the long, dangerous road. He said sadly: "We may have very little. You know how I'm placed."

"I know how you've placed yourself. This foolishness of yours could be ended any day."

"How could it be ended?"

"By leaving France."

"Do you want that?" he said, looking at her with a significance that she certainly did not mistake.

Did she want it? She had not always done so, for there had been a time when his mission had seemed an agreeable adventure, gay, romantic, utterly impractical. It would have been a deprivation if he had left the country in those early days: she would have missed the excitement, the delicious reactions at the Tuileries, the sense of thwarted power. Even the torture and confession of Querelle had not convinced her that it was not all a game, for she knew the Vicomte's chivalry, she believed in the moderation of Bonaparte, and had looked for some ending that would satisfy honour and her own warm inclinations. But the pattern had altered. She could no longer recapture these feelings from the past, for there stood between them new memories, new sensations, the realism of the heart.

What should they do? They could stay together. It was what he seemed to want. It would be very pleasant, she thought, looking at him with calculation. He was an admirable lover, tender, passionate; she had not been deceived. They could share a few more nights—there in that house before it was its turn to be betrayed; indeed, there was much to be said for a fatalism that could be reinforced by so many sensual memories. All these thoughts were in her mind. But she answered simply:

"Yes, I want it. If you save yourself now, then one day we shall meet again."

"If I save myself," said the Vicomte slowly, as though testing the pretensions of the phrase. "If I desert my friends, you mean."

"Desert them! Why, they denounced you!"

It was clear that the one was astray in her logic, the other in his loyalties. Both were angry. It was their first disagreement. Neither saw the humour of the fact that they were divided by the fruit of the unselfish, reckless courage that had been his chief attraction in her eyes, and by the very success of the night they had spent together. Everything was changed for her now that she knew she loved him; all things were swallowed up in that; and the knowledge that he could keep an independent mind, could conceive of duties and ambitions apart from her, struck her with the force of a betrayal. It was unfair of him. It was perverse.

She was sitting bolt upright in bed so that the sun shone full on her, lighting below the skin a flush of olive and the delicate tracery of veins, but for the moment her lover was not responsive to these impressions of her beauty. He replied sharply:

"You judge everyone by Querelle."

"And by what happened yesterday. Querelle denounces de Lozier; de Lozier a third; and that third denounces you."

"Three men among so many. Three weak men caught by circumstances."

"Yes, and the circumstances will grow more catching, the men weaker, you can be sure." He nodded his head, not in agreement but in tribute to the quick, argumentative bias of her mind. Dimly she understood this, for she put out a hand to touch him and said with passionate earnestness: "They'll all betray you. You will see."

He looked at her sadly, touched in spite of himself by this evidence of suspicion and distrust, inbred by her experience of courts. She might be right. Even Cadoudal might betray him. But to admit the possibility was to rob himself of something, not just a hope, a wishful dream, but an ideal that had its uses, as worldly in a way as any that existed in her empiric scheme of things. Placed as he was, it was necessary that he should believe, for conspiracies were by their very nature acts of faith, and to approach them in a questioning spirit, obsessed with the weakness of men, was to destroy them at the root. He could not explain this; he could not find the words; he felt divided from her, unable to appeal to loyalties which he knew to be complementary, but which she would feel in her woman's heart to be conflicting.

So he kept an uneasy silence. His doubt and hesitation were very marked; she saw this, though she misread the cause, and hurried her arguments into the breach—arguments he could have made for her, for he knew them all, no one being better acquainted with the failure of the conspiracy, no one more familiar with the activity of the police and his own poor chances of survival. He listened to what she had to say. But when once more she pressed her plan on him, begging him to leave the country, he shook his head slowly, without emphasis, unwilling to let her see how little her pleading weighed with him. At this moment he did not understand himself. He loved her, he wanted to live for her, there was nothing suicidal or heroic in his thoughts, only the extreme stubbornness of a man who tries to be true to his own beliefs.

It can be imagined with what exasperation she watched so much truth, so much logic, so many unanswerable arguments, go to waste. She could have forgiven him if he had denied things, if he had protested his wisdom or his safety. But it was clear that in his heart he expected to be taken, with all the consequences that must flow; he had not defended the chances of the conspiracy, or its ideals, or even his own reasons for remaining—illogical, unreasonable silence that imposed itself on her in spite of all her eloquence, so that in despair she turned from him, crying out:

"You won't save yourself. You're stubborn. You won't do it. So I must."

He looked at her indulgently. He had much cause to be grateful to her. She had behaved well; she had made little fuss; she had not intruded their love for one another as an argument, as he had been afraid she would; and he could hardly object when she engaged in fancies born of her care for him. He reached out and touched her hand, saying in a tone of gentle irony:

"You're so kind today. And you have such unreasonable ambitions."

But she drew away, looking at him in no friendly spirit.

"It's certainly unreasonable to hope to remain with you or become your wife. But there's a chance, for all that. I shall beg for your life."

"Diane!"

"Yes, from the First Consul when he comes to visit my mistress in the rue Victoire."

He cried out:

"The rue Victoire! The First Consul! When?"

"In ten days."

"At what time?"

"The afternoon."

"And why's he coming?"

"Hortense has appealed to him. She wants support. Her husband has pressed for my dismissal."

She had answered mechanically, taken by surprise by the force of emotions which she did not understand. The fact was that in those few brief words he had seen the chance for his most cherished plan, the interview with Bonaparte that from the outset had filled his chivalrous, sanguine mind. It was opportunity of the kind of which he had dreamed since his first meeting with Artois; and as he recognized its significance and fitted it into the pattern of the conspiracy, he was seized with a burning desire to see Cadoudal, to share this knowledge that promised great results.

She watched him silently as these thoughts were reflected with almost laughable candour in his eyes, but when he rose from the bed she began to feel that the comedy had gone far enough and asked:

"Where are you going?"

He replied:

"To find Georges, of course."

"So you're set on being foolish?" She saw his evident determination, and there came the glimmering of a plan. "Where will you find him, do you suppose?"

In his excitement he had not stopped to think of that. From the moment he had emerged from the tunnel he had not thought of Cadoudal at all; it had been enough for him that his leader had escaped. As he looked up in perplexity, he saw that she was smiling.

"Where will you look, Charles? At Clichy? Or Montmartre? Or Chaillot? You could look all over Paris."

And so he could. But she would try to keep him there in that room in safety till her plan unfolded at the rue Victoire.

Suddenly the room seemed very still. She had made only the slightest movement of invitation, but he caught the warm inflexion of her voice.

"Or you could stay here until he sends for you. That would be sensible. You could stay here with me."

But towards evening the summons came.

As soon as she heard the footsteps, the rapping at the door, she knew her plan had failed. She had no hope of keeping him in safety once he knew where he could find his friend; she submitted with good grace, touched by his anxious tenderness, caresses so tentative, so delicate, so unlike the treatment he had shown her in the first confidence of love. The melancholy of parting held them both. There seemed so many things to say, inexpressible things that they could not share even with their bodies—the secret, hoarded treasures of the heart.

The knowledge of that failure accompanied him as he set out through the darkening streets. He had said he loved her—as they had clung together he had told her so again and again—but he had felt the meaning diminish as the reality increased. What was love? A division within a union. A simple thing. The consciousness of one's loneliness wrapped up in a glut of appetites that could be shared. Well, they had shared them. He had been fortunate in her. No man could have wished for a more desirable mistress, but at this moment it was her grief and gentleness that he remembered, the fear and pity for each other that had gripped their hearts.

These thoughts, interacting in a thousand combinations, all melancholy, all disturbing, persisted until he found himself approaching the place of rendezvous; then they began to merge in the other anxiety of his life. He knew that he was on the way to a decisive meeting. There could be no further delay in the affairs of the conspiracy; it must dissolve, or strike, or perish. But what a sad pass it had come to: a band of fugitives scattered around Paris in a score of lodgings, *maisons de confiance* no longer, from which they flitted with an unhappy fitfulness of which their leader's odyssey was the clearest illustration—from the inn of the Cloche d'Or in the rue du Bac to the house of Mme St. Legier at Chaillot; from Chaillot to Spein the carpenter in the rue Carême-Prenant; to the rue du Puits de l'Hermite near the Jardin des Plantes; back to Chaillot; back to the rue du Puits; to the rue Langrais; and so to a room above a fruiterer's shop in the rue de la Montagne Sainte-Geneviève in the shadow of the Panthéon.

Was there something symbolical in this last refuge? A man like Georges would have seen a pleasant irony in the thought that one day a grateful France, restored to her true allegiance, might find a resting-place inside those mausoleum walls for him, successor of the other martyrs who had been carried there with grand Revolutionary pomp—Mirabeau, the man of '89, Marat, the Friend of the People, the idol of the sansculottism of '93; he might even have spared a smile for the turn of fortune's wheel that had seen those hallowed bodies bundled out again.

Such were the ways of revolutions. But they were concerned now with something as ruthless and sinister and vastly more efficient—the machinery of the dictator who ruled in France. The shadowy figures in the gloom of the evening might be his servants: the soldiers of his armies, the agents of the police forces that had grown like so many mushrooms out of the spawn of the unsettled years— the general police, the *gendarmerie élite*, the police of Savary, of Berthier, of Duroc, the army of the plain-clothes spies.

It was with hesitant, uneasy steps that the Vicomte approached his rendezvous. It was growing dark; houses and streets began to lose their outlines; a faint trace of river mist through which the pinpoints of lanterns glowed suggested half-forgotten memories—the sullen Thames rolling between her wharves, fog lapping the grey London stone, the meeting with Artois that stood at the beginning of his adventure. What high hopes he had had then, and how sadly they had been dashed by the reality! He would continue to serve with the same loyalty, but in the light of failure he could recognize royalism for what it was in France—a belief that had become a cause that had dwindled to a sentiment.

He was close enough now to see the details of the refuge that his friend had chosen; they were sufficiently dispiriting —a grey, shuttered house from which the paint was peeling, a ground-floor booth in whose dim lamplit interior piles of boxes could be seen, mostly empty, showing here and there the gleam of orange, lemon, red, and the deep purple flush of muscatel. From his position in the shadows the Vicomte watched. There were no loiterers in the street, only the good housewives with their baskets, engaged on a round that could not greatly have encouraged the tradesmen of the quarter. They made few purchases, none of fruit, though the fruiterer himself could be seen at his post behind the counter, alert for custom like the good bourgeois that he was. He seemed to be keeping a keen lookout, for as the Vicomte stepped from his point of vantage and began to cross towards the shop he saw the man's figure slip into the shadows beyond the counter near the rear communicating door, to emerge on the threshold, full of a most volatile obsequiousness.

He wished the citizen good evening—this with a pleasant bow. And what did the citizen require? The citizen would appreciate the season. Choice was restricted, stocks were low. Grapes, perhaps? Or oranges? There had been a consignment from the south. Let the citizen say what he desired! It was remarkable what Revolutionary manners this little royalist had.

De Bellac, patient under this byplay, began to smile, but as the man turned towards the lamplight it could be seen that under the ingratiating manner he was desperately afraid. Of course! The vigil in the shadows had been seen and misinterpreted, and filled with compassion, the Vicomte reached out and pressed a square of paper into the fat, trembling hand, the note of assignation that Cadoudal had sent.

For a moment the man did not seem to appreciate his good fortune: he looked from the customer to the note and back again, as though expecting the most unpleasant metamorphoses in them both; then suddenly reaching out, he clasped the Vicomte and drew him deeper into the shop, whispering in a low and rapid tone:

"Monsieur is a friend?"

"Of course."

"Yes, yes, this paper says so. I see that. You will forgive me. One can't be sure. There was a man this morning watching—yes, monsieur, across the street exactly in the place where you were standing. It was not agreeable to think that he had come again." And he raised his moon face to the Vicomte's, showing his fear in the dilated pupils, the anxious, doe-like eyes—a most unlikely, a most unwilling hero.

De Bellac could have embraced him. But time was pressing; the words that had been used had not encouraged his patience or peace of mind; he felt all around him the web of his enemies closing tighter with every hour; and laying his hand gently on the man's shoulder, he turned away towards the door that led to the private apartments of the house.

The patter of footsteps followed him, the murmur of a voice, more assured now and with the traces of a natural officiousness:

"Monsieur will permit me and I will lead. This way. Monsieur will follow, please." And as he issued these directives the good fruiterer bustled to the private door and opened it, removing his compromising guest, not out of the house—for that happy moment would have to be deferred —but at least out of the holy-of-holies of the shop.

Once accomplished, this seemed a great relief to him and he chattered freely in the darkness of the stair. "Twenty steps, monsieur, twenty exactly, it's as well to count them. The spiral is to the right. And here's the room now just ahead. If monsieur will wait until I knock." There followed three raps on the door, a gruff reply, and then the fruiterer's voice, round with the credit of good news: "Monsieur, I bring a friend."

The door swung open, and over the shoulder of their host the Vicomte saw the figure of Cadoudal in the flickering candlelight, a huge shadowy bulk dwarfing the chairs and table and rickety trestle bed—the new Gulliver in a gimcrack Lilliput. And suddenly at that sight he felt profoundly moved. He could not have said why, but it seemed to him for the first time that there was something to pity in that giant strength, something lonely and defeated, a defencelessness that touched the heart. As the two men embraced the Vicomte's grip momentarily tightened on his friend's arm, the response to his presentiment; he quickly drew back, ashamed of his emotion, rebuked by the solid strength of Georges' body, hard as iron beneath his hand. But it was with a heartiness that rang noticeably false that he cried out: "It's good to tell that you escaped them! You're real enough. There's nothing of the phantom about you." And then, as the footsteps of the guide echoed on the stairs, the politic smiles faded, and they looked at one another, seeing in each other's eyes the awareness of the miracle of their safety, the knowledge of their isolation, and the dangers that closed in on every side.

"And now?" the Vicomte said.

Cadoudal had kept a hold of his friend, a bearlike hug around the neck. He shifted it slightly as he replied:

"And now action, naturally. We can't wait any longer. Artois will never come now; Moreau's failed us; we've only ourselves."

"How many of us?"

"Twenty. Nineteen—I was forgetting the one who betrayed us. The poor wretch was taken before dawn yesterday. Nineteen only, and no hope of Moreau or Macdonald or any of the men we counted on. There's no hiding the fact that things have gone from bad to worse."

"Except in one particular."

"Why, what do you mean?"

"That ten days from now Bonaparte will be with his stepdaughter in the rue Victoire."

An expression of intense excitement showed in Georges' eyes; he seemed about to express himself in a flood of words; suddenly he checked himself, all enthusiasm left him, and when he spoke his voice was as enigmatic as his face.

"With his stepdaughter! In the house where you have the entrée?"

"Yes."

"And what exactly are you proposing, Charles?"

The young man needed little prompting, but launched out into the plan that had engaged his mind from the beginning; it was indeed a reflection of his character—bold, direct, honourable, and intensely trusting. Why, he reasoned, should they not go to Bonaparte as the King and Artois had once envisaged, choosing the house where he would be *en famille,* his unofficial self, and accessible through the medium of Hortense? They would use the letters that Artois had given them, letters that would act as passports and give them the status of ambassadors of the King.

"Ambassadors without immunity," was the objection of Cadoudal, who asked why in such case the First Consul should not arrest them. But the Vicomte, in the full flood of eloquence, was ready with his answer—it was no illogical one, for had not Cadoudal gone once before to Bonaparte after the campaign in Morbihan? What immunity had he had then? What guarantee? Yet the First Consul had acted like a man of honour. The implication was clear: he *was* a man of honour, and would act honourably again; in any case, he must know the advantages of coming to terms with monarchy, a movement that could call on the allegiance of such devoted men.

It was when he came to the alternatives that the Vicomte found himself on the firmest ground. For essentially there were none. All the great men for whom they had come to Paris had proved too cowardly to rise. There was too little money left to finance rebellion, even if it could be raised.

What remained? Only the plan he was advancing. It might fail—of course it might fail—but it pointed to some chance. "At least," he concluded, "it has the advantage of boldness and simplicity."

A man of unbiased judgment—Joseph Fouché, say—would have seen a delightful aptness in this choice of words, though he might have thought "simplicity" an understatement. But Cadoudal did not seem to be capable of so much perception: he was nearer to the fray, he had the benefit—or burden—of his friend's eloquence and force, and there could be no doubt that he was listening.

He said slowly:

"So that's the plan?"

The young man waited, encouraged by the note that had crept into his leader's voice. He had expected to be overruled, almost contemptuously; such had been the fate of all his earlier suggestions. But this time it was different: Cadoudal had begun to nod his head, a movement to match the words that now came ponderously:

"Yes, Charles; yes, I see. At least it's a course of action, something definite, a plan, and as such has merits. I should be seeing Bonaparte again." And at this thought he gave a sudden laugh, so vibrant, so out of character, that he himself felt called on to explain it: "Just something that came back to me—just a memory of something I once said—a thought that once occurred to me."

"A pleasant thought?"

"A very pleasant one. Charles, there is really merit in your plan; there are distinct possibilities that I can see."

The Vicomte almost blushed. He would have said no more for it himself.

"Distinct possibilities," Cadoudal was continuing. "And one objection—my admittance to the house."

The young man said eagerly:

"I can arrange it."

"Then do so secretly. There's this misfortune about me, that in the eyes of the good Hortense I might appear an ogre." And as Georges leaned forward with his great arms extended in front of him, his dancing shadow monstrous on the wall beyond, it did occur to the Vicomte that he looked like one.

# Chapter Twenty-one

THE SUBSTANCE OF THIS NEWS, AFTER making the rounds of the conspirators, was passed on to Fouché some days later by Méhée de la Touche; it created so excellent an effect that the Senator, one of the least demonstrative of men, broke one of his own rules in congratulating his agent: "You have done well"—how well was to be seen in the reward, handed over on the spot with that lack of delicacy that showed that the donor knew the difference between a purchase and a gift. The lesson was not wasted and certainly not resented, for the recipient was the last person in the world to be offended by a bag of gold.

It was pleasant to see such harmony between master and servant, two men who agreed over the soundness of the information and the reward—no lies in the one, no paper money in the other. Both were justified in a faith that would have seemed more like gullibility to their enemies, who could hardly have been blamed for failing to see in this agreement between rogues the elements of a deep and true affection. Of course they did not recognize this, either, and would have been horrified if they had, feeling with justice a reflection on their own abilities: they were spared the knowledge of emotions that they would certainly have classed as weaknesses and were only aware of others far more practical—Fouché was thinking of the price he had had to pay, Méhée of the lamentable fact that there would be no more payments.

For the case was ending: with Cadoudal in the rue Victoire and Bellac in the salon of Hortense, there was every sign of that. Their relationship might be continued, with the Senator back at his Ministry and Méhée diligent as a paid informer; but there could be no doubt in the latter's mind that his salary would fail by the standards of the princely present, for he could hardly hope to find another group of royalists of such eminence to betray.

"It should be all over soon," he said, and the sadness in his voice was marked.

His master naturally did not share this mood of nostalgia, but replied with relish:

"Yes, it should be over. They are moving very nicely to their places. It only remains now to see that Réal gets there too."

"How will you do it, Excellency?"

"By telling him, of course. We must be sure that the arrests—particularly of de Bellac—occur at the proper time and place to provide the maximum embarrassments to Bonaparte. I won't disguise from you that it's my intention to return to the Ministry—or even higher—on the indiscretions of this fortunate young man."

They looked at one another and smiled, expert stage managers who by their virtuosity would surprise not only the audience but the players too.

"Let us hope," said de la Touche, "that he does his part."

"You may be sure he will, provided your cousin Florian's still there and hasn't by some fatality been dismissed. He'll be indulging his good fortune. He'll be in the house near the one woman or the other, and it can be made to look compromising either way. That's the best of the Vicomte: one can rely on him; he's a truly remarkable young man."

"Most remarkable, Excellency."

But the Senator had spoken in no perfunctory way. He was intrigued by de Bellac, admiring an activity that needed little direction and—best of all—no payment. So nearly did his feelings verge on the paternal that he could shake his head over the obverse of all these sterling qualities.

"But too impulsive, Méhée, far too impulsive. It was agreeably impertinent to choose a mistress in the household of the First Consul's brother; it was enterprising, to say the least, to climb through her window to enjoy her; but the spy Morillac was another matter—it was foolish to fight him, and quite criminally negligent to leave the job half done."

"So the man's recovering?" asked Méhée, in tones that proved him to be rather lacking in professional spirit and sympathy.

"Being the devil's brother, naturally. The thrust missed his lungs and everything vital. His illness was more the result of shock than anything. In a few days he'll be about again, almost as good as new and a great deal more revengeful; furthermore, he's to be transferred into the First Consul's service—presumably to relieve Hortense—where he'll be ideally placed to do most harm. Yes, believe me, Méhée," said the Senator with a gentle smile, "in arresting this young Vicomte we are doing him a favour; we're preserving him from Morillac and from a denouement that might have been uncivilized."

On that note they parted, Méhée returning to Cadoudal, Fouché taking his coach towards Saint-Cloud.

It was late when he reached the palace, but lights still shone from many windows, for there had been a reception there that night—a small reception for the "Savants," in whose company Bonaparte delighted. It was with these men, many of them companions of his Egyptian expedition, that the First Consul felt most at home. It had always been the same. On the decks of *L'Orient,* by campfires and in palaces, on the darkened frigate bringing him back to Fréjus through the screen of English cruisers, he had found in science and philosophy the antidote to every care and even to his own ambition. The existence of God, Truth, Justice, the structure of the universe, these were the preoccupations of the victor of Lodi and Marengo, a man of action who never showed his genius more truly than in his deference in the realms of thought.

He did not only seek enlightenment, but entertainment too. There was the East to speak of, the magic land to which his thoughts were always turning, and which he loved with a passion that was a strange mixture of the romantic and the practical. Everything about the East intrigued him: Islam and the Sultanate, the Pyramids, the Mameluke cavalry, the Rosetta Stone, the march of Alexander, the ruins of past grandeur that lay out in the desert half buried in the dust of centuries; he carried this preference down to the smallest details, in his love of dates and pilau, in his fondness for the little gazelles that roamed in his park at Malmaison, which he would feed—rather ingenuously—with snuff. These were the innocent diversions, the relaxations of an Olympian mind, but when Senator Fouché was at last admitted through the picket line of Duroc's sentries to the inner sanctum, he found they had been put aside with the departure of the guests from the salon; the man of destiny had returned.

Bonaparte was not at his desk, but was sitting on a settee protected by a screen from the heat of a banked-up fire. On a table beside him lay piles of state papers, neatly arranged by Ménéval, and already in the process of being disarranged, for the First Consul was not by nature a tidy man. He wore his favourite uniform, its waistcoat comfortably unbuttoned, nankeen breeches and buckled shoes; in the candlelight the skin of the face and hands glowed with an olive tint, an Italian colouring that the milder air of France would tone down till in the end men would speak admiringly of its whiteness. Fouché, a keen observer, could see already a slight fullness of the jaw, the sensuous curve of the lips, the gradually increasing corpulence, which he contrasted with the figure of the young soldier of Toulon, thin as a scarecrow on short commons and the itch of unrealized ambitions.

What an impression that figure had made on Paris in those early days! The Senator, remembering, could smile at judgments that had long since been falsified—at the sneers of the salons that had found a butt; at the gullibility of Barras, who thought he had found a tool and cuckold; at the frivolity of Josephine Beauharnais, who had made what she had believed to be a marriage of convenience. There in front of him, with the piercing blue-grey eyes and head that seemed already modelled for a crown, was the answer to these credulities. It was astonishing to think that anyone could ever have misjudged him; yet it was so, and even Fouché, whose political instinct was thought infallible, had at one time opposed and overlooked him, and, what was more, was doing it again when all the original powers had suffered a reversal of their roles—the members of the salons becoming courtiers; Barras, rather against his will, a country gentleman; Josephine, a wife who waited with increasing longing and anxiety for the sound of her husband's footsteps on the stair.

It was dangerous work. The Consulate had made its bow without bloodshed and had continued mildly, but dictatorships sooner or later demand the blood of victims; they cannot be expected to subsist for ever on the discomforts of a few deputies hustled into oblivion at the bayonet-point. Fouché knew this; he distrusted regimes that began on too high a note of comedy, sensing already that change of mood that was to lead to the bloodstained epilogue with d'Enghien in the Vincennes moat. This knowledge did not affect him personally, it did not in any way impair the confidence with which he faced his all-powerful adversary, though he disguised this for appearances' sake with just sufficient of the humility that Bonaparte was beginning to demand. No courtier could have been more accommodating, but even so it was some time before the Consul deigned to notice him, and the first words were not encouraging:

"Ah, you're here! More police process, I suppose."

Fouché bowed, but did not salute this sarcasm with a smile.

"Yes, General."

"It seems to be your one concern. Isn't there employment for a Senator in France?"

The First Consul knew very well that there was not, for he was busily engaged in whittling away all free legislative powers. His aim was the kind of Senate of the Claudian emperors—a highly decorative club about as useful to the body politic as a strut of peacocks. Fouché in his gorgeous uniform represented one stage in his plan of government: if only he would stay like that he would heap gold and worthless titles on the man till he was buried under the weight of them.

But it was not to be so easy. The Senator replied with the utmost sententiousness:

"Your safety, General, is the concern of every man in France."

"Yes, yes, my safety. I keep my police for that."

"Evidently. And we know how well they are informed."

"More criticisms," said the First Consul, taking from his pocket a small oval snuffbox of tortoise-shell. "Always criticisms. Nothing will satisfy you but a return to office."

"It would be one way of getting rid of me."

"But I don't want to get rid of you, you see. I need your services and advice in more important matters, and it's no fault of mine that you persist in bothering yourself—and me—with detail. I have one consolation: these intrusions of yours may be distracting, but they're diverting too."

The Senator bore this sarcasm with the same composure with which he accepted insults, though he found it harder. He was not insensitive, but only appeared to be so; and this delicate reminder that his master found him laughable would have hurt abominably but for the prospect that he would shortly be doing some laughing in his turn. He replied coldly:

"Detail, if I remember, was one of your maxims for good government, and I'm not ashamed of being your pupil. In my days in office we paid attention to it, and the result was a state of security I don't see today."

It was true, and the First Consul knew it. In his irritation at this reminder of the value of a discarded servant, he burst out with the unfair comparison:

"Security! In your time St. Régent went within an ace of killing me."

"But that was different. France was full of such men when the Consulate began. I cleared them out for you.

Now they're returning. There are twenty St. Régents in Paris, and your police can't tell you the address of one of them."

"Can you?"

Fouché said in his gentlest voice:

"I can."

"What! You know the addresses! You've come to tell me that you've arrested them?"

The Senator did not speak, but with a gesture of the hand, slight but of the utmost eloquence, conveyed the sense of his own helpless state—a watchdog muzzled by the ill-advised order of his master.

"Well, then," said Bonaparte, closing the lid of the snuff-box with a convulsive movement, "you've passed this information on, no doubt?"

"To the police, General! Without telling you! I am not so lost to my responsibilities."

"Your responsibilities! Let me tell you that you've taken responsibility on your shoulders—the responsibility for high treason."

"High treason, General?"

"Yes, in the suppressing of evidence vital to the State."

The peculiar logic of this charge appealed greatly to the Senator; it reminded him of his own days at the Police.

"And the proof of it," he murmured, "is in the fact that I've come here to divulge it."

"What's that?"

"I was reminding you of the reasons for my visit."

"Reasons for your visit!" cried the First Consul, working himself up into one of his rages that were never quite divorced from policy. "I know the reason for your visit. You came to bargain with me."

Fouché's face did not change in expression, but in its

natural state it was perfectly suited to give the lie to this—
a long, bony face, ascetic as a priest's, entirely free from
traces of the commercial spirit.

"Now I fail entirely to understand you, General."

"To bargain with me," repeated Bonaparte, who knew
the trade the Senator had engaged in all his adult life.
"You've found out something through some channel of information illegal in itself, and now you've come to offer it
to me."

"As was my duty."

"In exchange for your Ministry, no doubt?"

"You believe that of me, General!" said the Senator in
tones that seemed to struggle against so unnatural a
thought.

"I know it of you."

"Then permit me to say that you deceive yourself. I have
the information, it's true. My source is not illegal, it's
merely alert and accurate. As to the Ministry, it's also true
that I should like to be restored. My aim is to serve you. I
know—may I say it?—my own abilities and the office where
they would be best employed."

"Yes, yes," cried the First Consul, who rather preferred
the unregenerate Fouché to this catalogue of the virtues.
"You are nominating yourself again."

"But to bargain the one for the other! No." The almost
too pressing eloquence faded from his voice and he added
coldly: "You must imagine I'm a simpleton."

This was the last description that the First Consul would
have applied, and he was so surprised by it that for the
moment he could not speak.

"Yes, General, a simpleton. What is a bargain? It's an
agreement between equals; it's something enforceable in
law. Consider this case now. Where is the equality between

us? Where should I look for the enforceability? Either you will give me back my portfolio or you will not. Yours is the absolute power. I cannot bargain: I will not plead."

And with these words the Senator looked straight into the First Consul's face, adding the force of his enigmatic personality to this plea that was not a plea, to this confession of weakness that was not weakness, to this appeal to power which, under the impact of so much artistry, doubted whether it was powerful.

Bonaparte took a deep breath.

"So you come to volunteer this information, that's what you're telling me?" he said.

"Certainly, General."

"And you want nothing from me?"

"Three small things only—three things in one: your indulgence; no questions for the moment; Réal, not under my orders, but under my guidance for a day."

# Chapter Twenty-two

EARLY ON THE AFTERNOON OF THE FIRST
Consul's visit Hortense sat in front of her mirror in
her dressing-room, engaged in a ritual that she had
inherited from Josephine. Her dress was of white,
cut very low to display her magnificent shoulders and neck
adorned with a double string of pearls; she wore no other
ornament; there was about her an air of elegant simplicity
that can only be achieved by the best taste and the most
expensive dressmaking; and as she tilted her head, moving
herself to and fro in front of the mirror, she nodded in a
pleased way at her reflection, measuring her beauty and
ability to please.

The effect was charming, the complacency forgivable,
though it would have been censured by her mother, who
served more exacting gods and in matters of the wardrobe
was now so much the *dévote* that she no longer dressed to
impress others—or even to annoy them. That clothes were
ends, not means, was a lesson that Josephine had done her
utmost to impart—unsuccessfully, for here was her daughter satisfied with a mere effect; she would have thought it
as incongruous as a saint being satisfied with his own
sanctity.

In half an hour Bonaparte would come to her from Saint-Cloud; he would be sure to be punctual, for that was his religion, as Hortense knew. The care with which she now prepared for him, the look of anticipation in her beautiful, expressive eyes, would have been grist to the mill of her accusers: they would have been sure to find the evidence of an incestuous attachment in this love for her stepfather, the one man in her life who had been kind to her, who had given the most recent proof in the way he had taken the convalescent Morillac from her husband's household into his own.

It was certainly true that she had dressed for him. As she studied herself in the mirror she found a smile—a very gentle and indulgent one—for his preferences, always conservative to a fault. He was a creature of habit, who liked familiar faces, familiar things, a round of repetitions in all the minor details of his life—the same uniforms to wear, the same barbers and generals, valets and ministers and aides-de-camp, the same style of hairdressing for his womenfolk, and the classical white dresses that gave his court the agreeable flavour of a scene in Arcady.

His preferences were met in the face and figure in the mirror; she had added on her own initiative the rope of pearls, a great extravagance which he would forgive her, though the pearls of Josephine were quite another matter—they were seldom paid for, and were apt to precipitate domestic scenes. A white dress, ringleted hair in imitation of her mother's style—all would be as he would like it. She would give pleasure. That was what made this toilet of hers a labour of love, because after a gap of many weeks she could count once more on admiration and friendly words. It had to be confessed that the First Consul's pleasantries were not always pleasant or even in good taste, for he was afraid of women and society and knew his own deficiencies in grace and refinement, for which he had never found the time. She understood him well and made allowances for these things, seeing behind his gaucherie and boorish ways the small boy born to hardship, the young man of the disastrous Corsican adventure, the officer of the Revolution, always lonely and misunderstood.

She was young and only knew of these events from hearsay, yet she felt sure that she understood him as no one else had done. No one else had ever loved him as he wanted to be loved, with an unselfish love. His servants feared him; his family had no feelings beyond ambition; as to his wife, Hortense could see her with a daughter's affectionate but clear eyes, without illusion, and knew that she was light and fickle and had been unchaste. That was one of the many things she had not understood in Josephine. It was inconceivable to her that any woman married to such a man could first have betrayed him, and then have sent her children to kneel before the returning conqueror of Italy to beg back the shreds of chastity, badly tattered in the bed of Captain Charles. That was how her mother had behaved, and now was the time of retribution, for already there were rumours of mistresses; already—and far more terrible— there were rumours of divorce.

But it was only for an instant that these thoughts intruded. Half an hour. Less now. She had not seen him for six weeks. Once it had been different. Before her marriage she had been in his household, part of the round of receptions at the Tuileries, balls at Saint-Cloud, the family group at La Malmaison, with its beautiful park and the little theatre where she had played—how seriously!—under the direction of Talma who had taught her to declaim. Those had been happy days. She could see her stepfather still:

among the audience applauding her small triumphs; sitting at the chess table in the candlelight, playing—very badly, with a precipitancy which he fortunately never showed on any battlefield.

In those days people had found her gay. She had certainly had no anxieties as she had stood on the threshold of the new century that stretched out before her, glittering with the promise of fresh ideals and fresh fulfilments. No one in France had seemed better placed, a young woman with the world at her feet who could look forward to years of pleasure, political influence, devotion, love.

Yet every one of these hopes had been disappointed. She had loved de Bellac, but he had remained in exile—that had been the end of her childhood dream. In maturity she had found Duroc and had believed herself beloved—Duroc who never cared for anyone in the whole course of his passionless, dedicated life, who had rejected her with a callousness that would always rankle in her heart.

So they had made a marriage of convenience for her in exchange. The match had suited her mother, who had thought to detach one brother from the hostile junta of the Bonapartes. It had suited her stepfather's ambition, for the Beauharnais were of noble blood. These had seemed unanswerable reasons for a union that only the principals detested, and for which they were now paying with the ruin of their lives.

As she looked into the mirror she could see in her mind's eye her partner to this contract, the sullen reproachful answer to her dreams. She had never wanted him, she had wept bitterly when they had told her what she must do, for she had always feared him and his air of virtue that hid such a cruel and calculating heart. Never from the outset had she had cause to doubt the aversion that he felt for her. She wondered about it sometimes, for she did not appear to herself as ill favoured as he seemed to find her, but the evidence was with her constantly in the look in his eyes, in the tone of his voice when he addressed her, filled with contempt and bitterness. She was so used to such treatment that the injustice no longer hurt her. In the early days of their marriage she had done her best to please him and even to pretend to an affection she had not felt, moved by pity for a man who was, like herself, a sacrifice on the altar of family ambition. She had dressed for him then—she who had been one of the leaders of fashion—risking her stepfather's anger in a display of semi-nudity that had verged on the heroic.

But it had all been in vain; he had never felt a kindly thought for her, and now she herself had ceased to care, so that it was only on rare occasions that people saw in her the ravishing young woman who had ruled at Malmaison, whom so many had desired. She was not strong, she was not a very enduring spirit, and already she was bowing under her misfortunes, the traces of which could be seen in the network of lines around the eyes, in the complexion, once so brilliant, now dull with an unhealthy tinge, in the droop of the lips, full and sensual still, so that they could stand as proofs of all that she had wanted and all that she had been deprived of in her life.

There was so little left—a visit such as this, when for a brief while she could forget her wasted life. She would pay for it soon in the reproaches of her husband, delivered with an artistry which he could conjure up for her alone. She knew he hated her: not her fading but the beauty that survived, a quality that had pleased and might still be pleasing other men. She must endure this jealousy, which was inexpressibly painful because it was not the result of any care for her; she must endure his contempt and loathing and those moments—perhaps the fruit of carnality, perhaps of more subtle and depraved emotions—when he exercised his husband's rights. All this she would suffer uncomplainingly as the price of one brief visit.

Soon her stepfather would be there, and she would be happy. The time would be short; there was not much that they could do or say. But no fears of Louis' hatred would spoil for her the joys of this reunion, the strange sympathy that existed between the man of genius and a woman, not particularly beautiful or clever or courageous, united to him by what bonds of love or kinship? Her husband would tell her soon enough, the usual accusations that never failed to cut her to the heart—perhaps because of the slight—the very slight—element of truth in them. Napoleon would be coming soon. That was all that mattered. And with a last look into the mirror that gave back its usual enigmatic answer, she turned towards the window, seeing the glow of the torches and braziers that her servants were lighting in the dusk.

# Chapter Twenty-three

D IANE."
"Yes."
"Nearly time now."
She said drowsily:
"Yes, he'll be punctual. It's nearly time."

He was standing at her window watching the sunset over the roofs in the rue Victoire—a field of gold crossed with long parallel bars of cloud, one behind another like the raised backdrops of a stage. A blaze of light shone down, an extravaganza of lighting too brilliant for the mundane things beneath—the streets, the bare trees, the houses in their sober lines that appeared to blush resentfully at this invasion of their privacy.

He said half to himself: "Even nature seems to wait for him and set the scene." And as she was puzzled and asked him to explain; he did so. "Why, it's the light, Diane—a special light."

As soon as she had joined him at the window she saw what he had meant: the curious shades of everything around them—houses, grass, and trees—as though each colour had purged or added something to itself, red showing a gleaming orange-red, green the most brilliant emerald, shades that lingered expectantly and shone with a suffused glow even when the sky darkened above them, the bands of black and gold becoming tinged with rose and merging at last into a violet flush extending high above the horizon to the west.

With the coming of darkness the wind fell and noises from the houses and streets around them became magnified in the heavy air—voices, footsteps, the distant howling of a dog, a sound so desolate that instinctively they moved closer together, as though there had been some message for them in that cry of brute hunger and despair and loneliness.

"He feels it too," she said.

"Yes, poor beast. The world's out of joint for him and he tells it so."

"I could act like that."

He pressed her hand.

"I could, Charles. It's out of joint for us. I could wail my own sorrows to the moon."

The Vicomte believed he knew the cure and kissed her. But she drew away.

"You don't understand," she said.

"What don't I understand?"

"Oh, I don't know. So many things I can't explain. My feelings for you, for one."

"Your feelings! They're so unfathomable!"

"You think you understand them," she said, catching the tone in his voice, that triumph that she knew to be inseparable from the male view of an affair. "You think I love you." His brow clouded and she added hastily: "Well, I do."

"I knew it."

"You knew it! With what, Charles? What perceptions

men have—perceptions of the body! You knew it because I kissed you, because I've been compliant."

"Is that the best word you can find?"

She said significantly, calling up memories of the night: "I leave those words to you."

It was not to be expected that he would miss her meaning. But she stayed for only a moment in his arms.

"That's how you judge my love, you see. That's the man's view of love."

"And the woman's?"

She did not reply for a while, for she was listening to that distant wailing that rose and fell eerily on the still night air. At last she said:

"Well, love's not an interlude for us. Love's a serious thing, a sad thing, the matter of a lifetime."

"Don't you think it is for me?"

She looked at him and shook her head.

"No; you don't really know its meaning. You think you do. You tell yourself you love me. You even think you've proved it."

The Vicomte had certainly believed as much, and could not see how in the light of all that had passed between them either of them could doubt it for a moment. Before he could protest, he heard her voice go on:

"But you haven't proved it. What you've proved is something else—that we suit one another, that we agree. That's all very well and most satisfactory in its way, but if you really loved me you'd act differently."

"How differently?"

"Well, you wouldn't use love as a kind of entr'acte, Charles, something to fill in the time between one folly and another."

He cried out, shocked to the bottom of his soul:

"How can you say that?"

"How can you do it? You know that it's the truth. Cadoudal, Bonaparte, they're the important ones to you."

Charles recognized the ghost of an old argument. It was wonderful with what persistence she returned to it, though he had believed with touching faith that his kisses had exorcized it in an afternoon. He said impatiently:

"You're wandering. What have they to do with love?"

At that she shrugged her shoulders and turned away from him.

"There, you see! You'd do better not to use words you'll never understand; you'd do better to treat me the way you've treated others. We'll forget more easily."

"Diane!"

But she would not be comforted. The lamps were being lit at the main entrance to the house. In their gleam, in the long flickering shadows, in the urgency of the attendants hurrying to and fro, she recognized the approaching end of this romance that had started in so light a spirit and now engaged the profoundest feelings of her heart. It was unendurable that it should end so soon. They had known one another such a short time, they had been so happy, they were young and could have had great hopes of the world. Yet they had both willed this ending in a way—he in response to an absurd, quixotic loyalty to his friends; she in loyalty—still more ridiculous—to him. That was the most monstrous thought of all—that she was helping to arrange a meeting that must prove fatal to them both—and at this realization she cried out:

"I should never have indulged you. I should never have allowed you in this house."

He tried to reason with her, but her voice ran on, a sharp little voice, anguished and despairing:

"I shouldn't have allowed it. I was a fool. I've given way to you. And you don't know Bonaparte. You don't know what you're doing."

He said coldly:

"I know very well."

"But you don't. I've tried to tell you, but you won't listen. You think he's like yourself—a man of honour. You're wrong. He has no sense of honour—only of self-interest."

"That's what I shall appeal to. Yes, listen. It's in his interest to hear the proposals of the King."

She had believed for a moment that he had some fresh solution, some new hope—for love of its very nature expects the marvellous—but at these words she saw that he had no more to offer than an old illusion, and burst out with bitter disappointment:

"Interest! In the King! Bonaparte has no interest in him; he has nothing to hope from him. He might interest himself enough to guillotine him if he came to France—or to shoot him, perhaps, as a concession to the faubourg Saint-Germain."

He greeted this with an uneasy laugh, but she ignored him and hurried on:

"It all comes of this passion for seeing a Monck in him, a king-maker, while all the time he has the instincts of a Robespierre. I've told you. You will see. Such false estimates are laughable. But he won't laugh. Politics is a serious business with him—even your sort of politics."

"I must point out that you don't know my business."

She cried contemptuously:

"One doesn't need to. There's nothing the King could offer him that would add up to an inducement. Bonaparte has everything—the army, the administration, the finances —and the King has you."

The Vicomte drew himself up. He would not have let these words pass, even from her, but as he was about to reproach her he caught sight of her face, not mocking, as he might have imagined from her words, but full of passionate earnestness. He said gently:

"You were wrong to allow the King so little."

She was alarmed by this reaction, knowing that she had hurt him, that she had gone too far.

"Charles, I didn't mean it."

He continued in the same level voice, just as though she had never spoken:

"And you were wrong to allow me so little sense. Of course I know the danger. But I know the necessity as well."

He stopped, and in the silence that followed both caught distinctly the sound for which they had been waiting—the distant drumming of horses' hooves.

Next instant she had thrown herself into his arms, no longer pleading or reproaching, but concerned only with his presence and the passion that she felt for him.

She had little time. In those moments while they clung together she remembered all that she had experienced since the day she had first seen him, all that she had wanted to do and say. But love, which she had believed she understood, now had its revenge: she found that she could no longer express in words or with her body an emotion that had once seemed simple and which she now saw to be of a profound complexity. She loved him, she had never been more sure of it. But how was she to tell him? How was she to express in the few moments left to her all the thronging feelings of her heart, so much truer than words, so much more tender than her most tender kisses? She had always foreseen that she might lose him. She had been courageous about that—absurdly so, she thought now, seeing that she had always doubted the reality of this danger and that her courage had been a fraud. Now the event was upon her— she could hear the pounding of hooves, the rattle of carriage wheels, the jingle of harness and equipment—and she knew that she was not brave at all. She was afraid for him and for herself—most terribly afraid.

To lose him. Never to see him again. She had not even the comfort of ignorance, for she knew the real character of Bonaparte, the instinct of the Corsican that treated all opposition in terms of the vendetta. She knew that her lover would be lost the moment that he entered the First Consul's room, but she could no longer plead with him; the thought of the few brief moments left to them prevented her, so that she remained silent in his arms, responsive to his kisses, but hearing beyond the whisper of his voice the clatter of movement swelling out of the darkness of the night.

Soon the leading horsemen of the escort could be seen, shadowy figures in the gloom, the light from the torches and braziers reaching out to them and striking here and there a gleam from a sword or a cuirass; as they advanced the pattern of the uniforms appeared, opening into view like the petals of a flower. On they came till the light, shining fully on them, revealed the dazzling movement of the parade—a screen of horsemen wheeling under the windows of the house, the tossing plumes, the gleaming saddlery, the arched necks of the horses dark with sweat, and at the centre the grey caterpillar of a coach.

A door was opening.

There stepped from it an aide-de-camp of resplendent

brilliance, then a small figure in a plain surtout and three-cornered beaver hat adorned with a tricolour cockade.

The escort was fanning outwards, its outriders already moving towards their posts behind the house, when the Vicomte's quick ear caught the faintest of sounds from the far end of the apartment, where a barred door at the bottom of a flight of steps gave access to the garden. He had been expecting it, and turned immediately from the window.

But Diane had heard it too.

"What was that?"

The sound was repeated, a soft and furtive tapping at the door. He had not replied, but she saw that he had moved away from her in the direction from which the noise had come. She said in a louder voice: "Charles, what is it?" And at that moment, as she noticed for the first time the curiously withdrawn and secret expression on his face, old suspicions were reborn, old memories returned: the face of Morillac in the lamplight, the cruel and solemn words—"He has come to assassinate the Chief of State."

"What is it?" she said. "Why do you look like that? Who's there?"

She did not catch his murmured answer: she knew with absolute certainty that it amounted to a lie.

"You know who it is?" She had followed him down the room, a small accusing figure, astonishingly changed from the woman who a brief instant before had been lying in his arms. "You do know. Tell me. What game is it you're playing?"

Her voice had risen dangerously, and suddenly he turned and faced her, saying with a most unhappy attempt at authority:

"Diane, you must be quiet."

She looked at him, seeing the extreme pallor, the nervousness of his movements, hearing the voice of Morillac, "That's what he's come for, of course," and then the question in all its knowing, sly simplicity, "Do you imagine his only aim's to sleep with you?"

A flush mounted in her cheeks and she moved towards him.

"No, I won't be quiet. I want to know."

The Vicomte paused. In the silence that had fallen on the room they could hear the movement of sentries round the wings of the house, and the tapping sound again, filled, as it seemed to them, with a note of desperate urgency.

And suddenly he came to a decision.

"It's Cadoudal," he said.

"Cadoudal!"

"Yes." He began to speak quickly, persuasively, in deadly earnest. "Yes, he's to come with me. We'll go together, ambassadors, as I told you. It's our only hope. We'll go together, just Cadoudal and I."

She stood close beside him, the prey of emotions so conflicting that for the moment she could not speak. He had deceived her grossly, unforgivably. But an assassin! All her instincts revolted against the thought. He could not be. He had deceived her, yes, but first he himself had been deceived. And then she knew with certainty two things: that she loved him still, and that she was consumed with a furious, burning anger against him for all that he had made her suffer, for his gullibility and monstrous weakness.

"Just you and Cadoudal!" She saw his face still full of a bland assurance. "Ambassadors, I think you said!" A hot wave of feeling overcame her and she rounded on him with clenched fists and blazing eyes. "Assassins, you fool; that's what they are. Can't you see it? Can't you see they've used you? A man of honour!" All her hatred of the deception burst out, though it was directed most unjustly against him who was the victim, and she cried: "Artois used you. They planned this. It was planned from the beginning."

The Vicomte had gone deathly pale. He did not deny her words, but backed towards the door on which the tattoo still beat insistently. She followed him, her eyes fixed on his, wide like a sleepwalker's, in the throes of a passion she was barely able to control. "Just you and Cadoudal! Before you dishonour yourself and ruin France, perhaps you'll take a look and see."

It was late for such precautions. Her words had had their effect on him, correcting that trust and generosity that were the mainsprings of his being, but in spite of them it was with confidence that he unlatched the door, sustained by many memories—the cliff of Biville, dawn in the rue Langrais, the parting by the secret stair. He was prepared to stake his life on Cadoudal, and on a comradeship that had survived so many dangers, so great a disillusion.

But when the door swung open the light from within the room shone on Georges and on the group of men gathered round him in the shadows—and on the glint of steel. In that instant many things happened. He heard Diane cry out, saw the flash of sword-blades as he moved to slam the door against the friends who had betrayed him, and turning back into the room with a warning on his lips, stepped almost into the arms of Councillor Réal.

# Chapter Twenty-four

THE FIRST CONSUL RETURNED IMMEDIately to Saint-Cloud, where he shut himself up in his study and called for a report. He had had ample time to appreciate the ineptness of his servants before Méneval came to tell him that Fouché had arrived—Fouché who had been the instigator of the whole enterprise, and, on the face of it, the most inept bungler of the lot.

A lesser man would have refused to see him. But Bonaparte had scented danger. He saw that the cap would not fit, that there was no similarity between this figure and the Fouché that he knew; and where many would have seen only incompetence, he was sufficiently psychic to catch already the horrid glimpse of an intrigue. What was its shape? That was the problem. One thing was certain: it was no good guessing at the repertoire of so supreme an artist. He knew that he would do best to wait and see, and accordingly kept silence, though not without effort, for there were many things that he wished to say to this blundering servant, the creator of the late debacle, to say nothing of that other Fouché that existed in the selfsame body, the scheming, diabolical familiar.

The Senator, for his part, was in the best of humours. He had waited a long time for this moment, the mere thought of which had been sufficient to warm him in the chill of the outer darkness into which he had been cast: his heart was aglow with that most delicious sun of preferment that was rising on him, and he had to struggle with almost the same intensity as Bonaparte to prevent his feelings from showing in his face. What made it all more difficult was that the most delightful form of greeting was trembling on his lips—congratulations to the First Consul on his escape from death. He struggled against this formula, which might confidently be expected to send the man into a decline, then substituted another and rather better one: "May I congratulate you, Citizen First Consul, on the brilliant outcome of the day"—all of which had an excellent effect, for the victim could keep quiet no longer but exploded: "And I congratulate you too."

The Senator looked deserving.

"Yes," the First Consul continued, "you deserve all praise for the arrangements made in rue Victoire."

"For your protection and convenience, General."

"Police officers inside the house, a garrison of police officers, and all unknown to me."

"It was known only to some of the servants, General— even the lady of the house was ignorant. It was done that way to spare you."

"And to spare the conspirators, as things turned out. One man was taken."

The Senator replied that he rejoiced to say so.

"A young ruffian called de Bellac," the First Consul said. "Cadoudal escapes me, and I'm presented with a pawn."

No one would have looked more pained than the Senator at this description. It was all very well for Bonaparte to speak in such a way: he had not nursed the man with anxious care through intrigues and sword-fights and love affairs or hung a whole chain of hope and policy around his neck. He said reproachfully:

"A pawn, General! I wouldn't have used that word."

"You wouldn't? Why?"

"Because of all the conspirators the young man was nearest to your person, therefore the most dangerous, therefore the most important of the lot. I would draw to your attention, General, the fact that he was taken actually *inside* the house."

An ear less keen than the First Consul's would have detected the suggestiveness that had crept into the ex-Oratorian's voice.

"Inside your stepdaughter's house," it said. "Inside your stepdaughter's apartments. Near her bedroom—such was the young man's insensibility, I regret to say."

The First Consul had half risen from his chair. He said in an ominous voice:

"Is that an allegation?"

"An allegation, General! Against whom?"

"You may well ask that. Was it not in the apartment of the maid-of-honour that the man was found?"

The Senator almost eagerly concurred.

"Indeed, yes. Diane de Florian, the man's mistress. It was certainly in her room."

"I'm glad that you admit it."

"But naturally. It was the truth. There is always the fear, however, in such cases of what the ill-intentioned everywhere might think."

The First Consul did not reply, leaving it to the Senator to say what the ill-intentioned everywhere were thinking—a task for which it had to be admitted he was ideally suited.

"Well, for instance, they might imagine this Diane to be no better than a go-between," he said.

Bonaparte repeated the words, "A go-between," as if he had not understood their meaning, though it was in fact their daring that had astounded him, for since Brumaire he had been treated with such deference that he had almost lost the art of assimilating insults: so greatly was power corrupting him. While he was still floundering, he was astonished to hear his subordinate become even more explicit.

"To be plain with you"—as if the man had not been sufficiently plain already!—"there would be danger that some might attribute the young man's presence not to the frailty of the maid but of the mistress."

"My stepdaughter!" said the First Consul in a strangled voice.

"General, yes. It is inconceivable to me that such things could even be imagined. They are grossly out of character. Everyone knows that Mme Hortense is a model of wifely and—may I add?—filial devotion; everyone knows that she mirrors you in word and deed. In the circumstances, and taking into account her most intimate connection with you, such accusations smack almost of lese-majesty—to borrow a word from the vocabulary of your distinguished predecessors."

The First Consul's reactions to this summary of all that the Court had been whispering, served up to his face and garnished with the choicest sauce of words, were of remarkable intensity. He was furiously angry—more angry than he had been since the Five Hundred had insulted him in the Chamber—but whereas he would act the tyrant over trifles, with livid cheeks and flashing eyes, real anger, a more exacting prompter, only made him tremble and drained every spot of colour from his face. At such moments he was really quite a primitive person who would have terrified most men, but not the Senator, who knew the strength of his position, who respected the First Consul but regarded the Corsican *bandito*, now appearing like a changeling, as a very much less formidable enemy. It was clear that the very force of the insults made for his protection, implying as it did a position of great power. No one had a better knowledge of safety margins, and where most politicians would have hurried from the room, and probably from Paris, he turned with relish to the treatment as before.

"You surely don't imagine that I share these misguided thoughts?" he said.

The First Consul knew that the man had not so much shared them as actually inspired them, but for the moment he was beyond rational speech.

"You should not imagine it. That Mme Hortense, placed as she is, should feel an attachment for an obscure young man strikes me as ridiculous; that she should knowingly have taken part in a plot against your life, incredible and utterly obscene. Unfortunately there is public opinion to be thought of."

He paused as though to see whether the First Consul was yet fit to take an intelligent part in this entrancing game, then, as he saw that he was not, went on:

"Public opinion is invariably immature; it has a passion for celebrities; it is also inclined to be lubricious. Apply these precepts to the present case and what does one discover? That the public—if it gets to know, of course—will believe that the young man was in the ladies' quarters of the house for something rather warmer than political discussion. Yes, indeed! It expects a certain liveliness from young men and young women, a disposition to be sportive, and it will be cheated if it doesn't feel that these persons ended up in bed. Of course we know Florian's place in this. But maids-of-honour have little general interest. It is great personages that men in the street admire and talk about, and whom they passionately desire to see in compromising situations. To sum the matter up: we know that Mme Hortense is innocent, but France will believe that she is guilty. France will positively insist on it, in fact."

"You will insist on it, you mean."

The Senator shook his head, not so much in denial as in sympathy for an antagonist who still laboured below his best.

"You're joking, General, I can see. My feelings in this matter are purely of disbelief. I don't believe in Mme Hortense's guilt, even though I know—and this is a matter where a disclosure to the public might be fatal to the regime—even though I know, as I was saying, that your stepdaughter and de Bellac were childhood friends, that they had a partiality for one another—quite innocent, of course —and that it was through the good offices of Mme Hortense and of your wife that this royalist, this traitor to the Revolution, was able to escape the guillotine. I don't believe, in spite of all these things." He raised a shoulder, the first gesture he had made since entering the room, and asked with a melancholy forecast of the answer: "But won't the public?"

Of course the First Consul, with his acute perceptions, knew all too well what the public would believe: it would believe the worst with enthusiasm, nicely divided between censure and ridicule. Republican institutions could survive such blows—for had not the Revolution survived even the Festival of the Supreme Being and the Cult of Reason? But that was small consolation to a man who already aspired to be an emperor and could see as clearly as the Senator that royalty was an intensely personal, intensely vulnerable, state. *"Che coglione!*—What a pity!" he had exclaimed as the last sad parade of royalty had passed to prison through the Tuileries gates. Personal faults had brought them there —the Queen's levity and treason, the fatal moderation of the King. These had counted for more than centuries of oppression, so that it had been at the "Austrian Woman," at "Little Capet," at "Fat Louis," that the brutal, jeering crowds had flung their hatred.

Now his own dynasty was threatened before it had properly begun, threatened in the person of the one who was closest to his heart. He could hear already the shocked disapproval of the moralists, the laughter of the scandal-loving who would see in his own position a kind of cuckoldom— that hurt; it hurt more than all the monstrous whisperings of incest; it was almost as unbearable as the voice of his tormentor running on: "But won't the public? We know its weakness, its fervour to believe." He could stand its silky tones no longer and burst out, less as an argument than as a means to stop the flow: "There's nothing to believe in beyond a boy-and-girl attachment."

But Fouché slowly shook his head, as though marvelling that his master should be so blind to men's depravity.

"If they heard of it, they'd think the worst of it," he said. "Suppose they heard of this new meeting? They'd *know* the worst of that, and who can tell what they'd say or do?" A smile, the gentlest of smiles, crossed his face, for his hold on his sardonic humour had slipped at last, and he added in the most reasonable manner in the world:

"So to protect the regime—and public morality, of course —I suggest my reappointment to the Ministry of Police."

## Chapter Twenty-five

THE MINISTRY OF POLICE! NEVER IN HIS life had Bonaparte been so outfaced. Once before he had accused the Senator of levying blackmail, but the thing was still outrageously surprising when it came; and for long after the man had left the room he sat tortured by his impotence in face of that urbane manner that had concealed, he knew, the liveliest triumph in his discomfiture, and by the knowledge of the remorseless truths that had been uttered. Worst of all was the realization that he could not safely kill a man who had so many loyal—and potentially talkative—familiars; for rumour was Cerberus-headed, and Fouché was master of the beast. It was a terrible frustration, and he trembled with the force of it, so that in spite of his shrinking from personal violence —natural in so small a man—he had a fierce longing to hurl himself after that wraithlike figure and tear it to pieces with his hands.

But this impulse, like the arguments and expedients that now ran in his mind, was as late as it was ineffective, for with his immaculate sense of timing the Senator had taken himself away before the guttersnipe in Bonaparte could even think of insults or actions to destroy the unruffled dig-

nity of his retreat; it was really remarkable how the air of
the grand seigneur—the one attribute that could daunt his
master—had found its way into this parvenu regicide.

The honours of war had gone with him—or at least as
many of them as the Senator had thought it prudent to
take away: not the portfolio or even the promise of the
portfolio—for there were limits to the amount of yielding
to be expected of a dictator in an afternoon—but enough
to satisfy a man who always preferred the reality to the appearance and liked to proceed by a strategy of limited ob-
jectives.

It was at such times that Secretary Méneval paid for his
position. He had to answer for many defaults and many
people: for the stupidity of Réal, now engaged on his in-
vestigations—probably wisely—at a distance from Saint-
Cloud; for the frailty of Diane; the good nature of Hortense; and all the subtleties of Fouché's mind, for which the
devil himself might not have liked to feel responsible.
Trained to subordination, the young man did his best, but
no amount of his helpful masochism could cure his master
of that bitterest of maladies, defeat: nothing could cure him
but the most unlikely of phenomena—a repentant Fouché
on his knees.

That he should have been tricked and browbeaten in
such a way! The First Consul returned to the theme again
and again, pacing the office with abrupt steps, backwards
and forwards, hands clasped behind his coattails and head
bowed on to his breast. The means used roused his special
fury: an attack through the family and particularly through
the women of the family. All his Corsican instincts were
aroused by the mean advantage that the Senator had taken
in using members of this sex, politically beyond the pale,
for the purpose of an intrigue—he could hardly have been

more surprised if they had suborned his horse to throw him
at a review.

The damage was done now. He had been compromised.
If Fouché spoke—and there could be no doubt of the size
of the audience he could command—then the people he
was dragging slowly back to public order and respectability
would think Hortense an Antoinette or a Messalina or a
mixture of them both—they would think him another
Claudius or Louis Seize, and that was worse.

And suddenly the First Consul was seized with the urge
for talking the matter over point by point in all its humiliating detail: not with Méneval, from whom he must keep
so many secrets, not with Talleyrand, who would be sure
to worm them out of him, nor with his wife, who had secrets of her own; but with someone he could rely on and
at the same time reproach. There was only one candidate—
Hortense.

What harm she had done him in her innocence and
blind trustfulness! He reflected on it as his coach lurched
down the roads on the way to Paris, flanked by the glittering cordon of the Guard. But gradually a questioning spirit
crept into his thoughts. Innocence? Ah yes. But was it perhaps too absolute a word? What had she told him in those
hurried moments after the arrest? That the young man
was the lover of her maid-of-honour, that he had come
that afternoon in the hope of interview. A likely tale, with
Cadoudal and his assassins at the door! Why, if any other
woman had told him that, he would have known her for a
liar or a fool! What were the facts? That to Hortense's
knowledge an old admirer and proscribed royalist had been
admitted to the house.

He sat up abruptly in the coach, so white of face that if
Fouché could have seen him he would have been charmed

to find that he had sown so very much better than he knew.

Why, if any other woman had told him that, he would have thought her either a harlot or an accomplice! He would have had no choice in face of the compromising situation, the convenient female "go-between" (the Senator's barbed word), the conspirators waiting in the darkness: it all added up to a picture more sinister than any he had imagined since those agonizing hours when he had first suspected the infidelity of Josephine.

Hortense a light woman, a traitor to him! He suffered these imaginings, perhaps as a punishment on himself for his failure to discipline his family; it was certain that even in his worst moments he never quite believed in them, for he loved his stepdaughter and the memory of her candid, trustful nature was there to guide him.

But what his heart knew and what his intellect suspected were two different matters; and Fouché's accusations, even when robbed of their worst meaning, still pointed to a most appalling indiscretion. Hortense had acted with a reckless disregard of her position, and as he thought of it his anger, reinforced by the doubts that he had half managed to shuffle off, boiled up against her, only restrained within bounds because his companion was Duroc, a man indifferent to passion.

It was in no pleasant spirit that he entered the salon of reception to find his hostess, no longer dressed to please, a rather bedraggled figure with red-rimmed, anxious eyes. It was an additional irritation, for he detested tears—except sometimes those that he himself had caused—and loathed slovenliness in women, as inexcusable in these pretty creatures as cowardice in a guardsman.

This, he thought, was the person who had compromised him and exposed him to defeat, a weak woman who allowed herself to be surprised, even in the afternoon, so that she looked as though she had just risen out of bed. In that light and costume, indifferently rouged, she seemed already old —dark lines under the eyes, a greyish pallor, irregular and faintly discoloured teeth. Women should not look like that. Even disorder should have its charms—he had noticed it often in his wife, who knew to a hair's breadth just how much of the slattern a masterful man desired. It did not matter what the relationship was—mistress, wife, sister, daughter, friend—they should not look like that. It was a betrayal of their sex, or worse, even a denial of it and the uses for which they had been brought into the world.

As these irritations mounted up, aided by contrasting memories of how she had greeted him the day before, he began without introduction to reproach her, his voice rising querulously, the Italian accent creeping back as he expressed emotions that had their origin in the customs of the island of his birth:

"It's a fine thing you've done—entertaining admirers in your house, traitors who might have killed me! You owe a duty to your husband. You owe me a duty. A fine way you've shown it! A woman can only lose her reputation once." He repeated the words, stung by memories of that patriarchal society in which an erring woman was apt to lose not so much her reputation as her life. "You've been too well treated. I took Morillac into my service to please you: I should have left him to watch over you. You think you're emancipated—all you devils of women think that today. There's no modesty among you. Modern manners have corrupted the whole sex. I find it everywhere: among the people, at Court, among my own sisters—and now you!"

She remained silent under this abuse, too frightened to

dare to ask him why he had kept silence on the afternoon
of the event and now returned to heap reproaches on her.
It was as well she did so, for the shadow of Fouché, which
would certainly have been materialized by this reminder,
was no suitable companion.

"You think everything becomes you. We can bring our
lovers into our houses now." She stirred protestingly and
he, anxious not to spoil his case, amended: "Old admirers,
if you like, even when they're traitors to the country, royalist scum sent here to kill me. *Sacré bleu!* Was there ever so
much disloyalty in a family! That rascal Egalité served the
King no worse."

At that she began to weep. It did move him a little, but
he was too well embarked on his tirade, word firing word,
balm to his heart after all that he had suffered at Fouché's
hands.

"Ah, you may well do that. Does it occur to you that
you've made a simpleton of yourself, if nothing worse? Can
you perhaps conceive that you've made a laughingstock
of me?"

He watched the tears coursing down her cheeks, the
puckered face, and moved almost to fury by the pity for
her stirring in his heart, cried out:

"That's how you've repaid me! I brought you up. I took
your family off the streets—pensioners of Barras. I gave
you everything: money, protection, position in the world"
—he had nearly added, "and a husband," but had the delicacy to suppress that particular advantage. "I did all those
things for you, I never asked for a return. It was enough
that you should think of yourself as my daughter and act
as one. It was inconceivable to me that you'd entertain my
enemies behind my back."

She had sunk down on a divan, her face, blotched with

runnels of tears, raised piteously to his. He was reminded of another scene: this girl and her brother, two children on their knees before him, the ambassadors of Josephine staring up at him with wide, imploring eyes. He had been touched then. He had received back his faithless wife because of them: those children had always had his love, and no hard words had ever passed between them. He looked down almost with an air of puzzlement into those same eyes, as beautiful and candid as on that day—how many years ago?—hearing his voice, harsh with anger, demanding: "What sort of enemies! A pack of murderers and assassins!" —and her denial, so soft and blurred with weeping that he could hardly catch the words: "I didn't entertain them. I didn't even know that they were there."

So she was answering, defending herself. Well, he would give her the chance for one more contradiction.

"And Bellac? Are you going to plead the same ignorance of him?"

As soon as he had spoken, he found himself wishing with all his heart that she could deny him too. He wanted to believe in her; the need for it came over him like a wave, wiping out all other feelings, even his instinct for the truth. His daughter—the grave little girl in the long white dress.

But of course he knew what the answer to his taunt would be. She had drawn herself up, and he could catch the note of resolution in her voice.

"He was my friend. I told you I knew that he was in the house."

The First Consul sighed, for a mood of profound sadness was stealing over him—he could not have told the cause.

"Your friend! A royalist! Were you in love with him?" He looked at her, seeing the denial in her face but unconvinced by it, for he had learnt in a hard school—too hard a school—that there was no truth in women. He added: "You were once. You loved him. What happened to this fine romance?"

When she began to cry again he watched her, quite unable to understand the conflicting feelings that raged within him. She was his daughter, he had always thought of her as such, always loved her with a tender and pure affection —the dream figure, child of his body that had been denied him—and as such he loved her still. Why, then, should the thought of this young man affect him with a bitterness that cut him to the heart? An old attachment. They had been children at the time. And if there had been a revival of it —sighs and kisses, a warmer consummation—what should that mean to him? It was a matter for her husband, whose jealousy would be more than sufficient for the whole family. Why, then, did it affect him so directly, as though there were some substance in those whispers that he told himself were lies?

This man, this woman, they were young and foolish, they were of an age.

He said in a harsher voice:

"What happened to it? Wasn't he constant? Was it, after all, your maid he came to see?"

And then he caught sight of her face, so anguished that in spite of his distrust for her sex he knew the truth. She wasn't acting; she was innocent, or at least her body was; she had cared all the time, but something had held her back —perhaps the thought of her fading beauty, a defeatism that shrank from the warmth and loving of the world.

He said slowly, seeking for a reason, and aware all the time of the strange fact that this knowledge had the power to hurt him:

"But you saw him? You had him in your house?"

"Yes."

"And you protected him. You said he was your friend."

Suddenly she burst out, as though defending everything in a breath—her disloyalty, her love, even her abnegation, the one indefensible action of her life:

"Yes, he was my friend; always gentle and kind to me. He was in danger. Do you imagine I could forget so soon?"

He looked at her, surprised that she should not have seen the irony behind her words. Women! What could one make of their unreasonable loyalties? Sometimes it seemed to him that they reacted only to the stimulus of pain.

"No," he said, not altogether unkindly, perhaps to point the moral to himself, "no, it's clear you'd not forgotten."

"Nor had he. That was why he came to me. He just wasn't a child any longer, that was all."

The First Consul gave an unpleasant laugh. Words again! The words she used!

"A child! I should imagine not. He'd matured since then. He'd promoted himself to an assassin."

He was astonished to see the transformation worked by that abuse. She jumped to her feet, her eyes shining. He could not know the relief that came in answering this false and monstrous charge, so much easier a defence than the one she had undertaken against the accusations of her heart.

"He was not! He was too honourable. Do you think I didn't know him? He came here from the first as an ambassador of the King."

"From the first," Bonaparte said slowly. Then, as an idea struck him: "How many meetings did you have?"

"What does it matter? Three—four. I can't remember."

He shook his head. It was incredible that she should give such answers. Was it possible that she was ignorant of her position—a regular part of a conspiracy?

"Four meetings! Well, you astonish me. Four meetings in your husband's house and under the nose of Morillac!"

"No. Elsewhere."

Immediately he became watchful as he sensed an extension of the plot.

"Tell me," he said. "Where? I'm curious. Be detailed. You can be sure that I shall find out everything."

She looked into his hard, compelling eyes, feeling her determination ebb away.

"In a house near the Palais Royal," she said at last.

"Whose house?"

"Of a M. Méhée de la Touche."

And suddenly, miraculously, he was smiling.

"In Méhée's house! Ah, that's another conspiracy you've become involved in—a conspiracy of another colour, as a friend of mine will find."

# Chapter Twenty-six

THE VICOMTE HAD OFFERED NO RESIST-
ance. His docility had pleased the police agents,
who could pride themselves on their cunning and
the complete nature of the surprise; they were not
to know how greatly he had been affected by the trick that
Cadoudal had played on him, that he had lost the will to
save himself.

He sat, hands tightly bound, between his guards as the
heavy berlin jolted on its way towards the prison they had
chosen for him, an object of wonder to simple men so
nourished on tales of his exploits at Biville and in the rue
Langrais—already grown to the size of legends—that they
half expected him to vanish like a phantom through the
windows of the coach.

But he made no movement; he sat grim and silent, listening to the sounds around him, which seemed to match his
mood—the creaking of springs and axles, the menacing
clatter of the escort's hooves, almost drowned before they
had gone far by the storm that broke over the town, the
drumming of raindrops on the roof like the sound of a
distant cannonade. There was little he could see: the dark
runnels on the windowpanes, a view of a horse's steaming

flanks or a sodden uniform caught in a gleam of passing light, the grey faces of the policemen at his side turned towards him with the stolid look of cattle gazing at a stranger in their field. There was little to distract him from the morbid pattern of his thoughts.

Well, he had been taken. But he would have this to say of his enemies: they had served him no more treacherously than the men he had believed his friends. Through all the weeks of danger since he had boarded the *Vincejo* he had been sustained by his loyalty to his comrades, to Artois and the King. Yet they had never wanted him, only his services. From the beginning he had been the dupe of those who had used him to bring them close to Bonaparte. The knowledge was very bitter after the remembrance of all that he and Cadoudal had done. He had never thought to take credit for these actions until the moment when he saw them in perspective against the opinion they had held of him, but now they were tinged with bitterness so acute that he could find it in his heart to wish that he had been killed on Biville cliff.

The coach rolled onwards through the darkness, more slowly as the horses began to struggle and slither in the mud. Poor beasts, how miserably they were being mishandled! He remembered his own ride to Paris, the quiet farmhouses tucked away in the golden autumn countryside, the exhilarating gallops in the moonlight across the stubble of the plain. He had had faith then, he had believed passionately in a course which he now saw no one but himself had ever held. He remembered how the first sight of the city had affected him, the challenge of that skyline under the morning sun, and how in the absurd gaiety of homecoming it had seemed a small thing that they were doing in setting themselves to overthrow the master of her choice.

And then that other ride northwards to the coast—his horse's breath in the frosty air, the iron-hard ground beneath them, the ominous silence that had heralded the snow. That had been the start of his friendship with Cadoudal, a comradeship so strong that he had not hesitated to risk his life for him in the rue Langrais. But all that time Georges had despised and distrusted him for a moderate, had used him as a decoy, and had finally left him to his fate. They had thought him unimportant, worthless, a fault that could not be laid to Councillor Réal's door: indeed, in some strange way it was a solace to him to see the faces of the gendarmes turned to him, full of a dull, portentous care.

The cavalcade was slowing now. His keen ear could catch the sharper ring of the horses' hooves. They were close to some building from whose walls the sound rebounded; and leaning sideways—a movement reflected next instant in a sudden stir of uneasiness inside the coach—he glimpsed through the window a massive barbican and gateway silhouetted against a light beyond.

They were entering the bailey of a castle. The choice of such a prison was a compliment in itself, he thought, as he was thrust from the berlin and could look up at the formidable line of battlements that rose against the sky. They did him too great honour, though not, as it appeared, in the civilities of arrival—the bayonets held uncompromisingly against his back, the rough hands that dragged him through a doorway towards a table at which a man sat writing by the light of a shaded lamp.

He recognized the technique made familiar through a thousand anguished stories of the Terror—the manners of Revolutionary officialdom. That every judge should look like a jailer and every jailer an executioner was a piquant refinement that even the Consulate had not thought fit to change, and the Vicomte could not for the life of him have told which of these functionaries now faced him in the figure sitting at the table; he only knew that the tactics of reception had been perfectly understood by a man who had provided the setting of shadows, the silence broken only by the rustle of a pen.

Curiosity—that was the most effective weapon of them all. The young man was not impatient, he was not easily impressed, but as the minutes passed he felt the stirring of a mad desire to see over the writer's shoulder and to know what was being written—the details of his death or only the receipt for his body, as formal and businesslike as for a load of merchandise.

There was nothing to be told from the writer's face, nor were the manners of the warders more revealing as, at a signal from their master, they closed in on every side. Manacled between two agents of police, the Vicomte was half dragged, half carried from the *corps de garde* into the long stone corridors of the fortress, along whose walls the shadows of their passing were flung like those of lovers in some grotesque, debauched embrace. He cried out, not in fear but in shame at the indignity—a forlorn sound echoing and re-echoing through the vaulted tunnel that led downwards into the bowels of the castle, succeeded by a softer noise almost lost in the clatter of marching feet, the blow in the face that rebuked this breach of the proprieties.

The Vicomte had not expected it. With the rather naïve optimism of a soldier, he had believed he would be treated with some respect for form even in the torture chamber; he made few allowances for the fact that his warders thought of him as an assassin, and less for the influence of this dark and secret place so distant from the light and reason of the world.

But there was no mistaking the fierce grip of the hands now laid on his body. He did not cry out again. He knew that if he did so he would receive the treatment he had once seen meted out to a poor servant of his family in Auvergne—a thrashing so severe and so monstrously humiliating that he carried the memory of it still. They would be glad to do it: he could sense it in every movement of these warders who had behaved in the coach with such correctness. He felt he could not have borne it. Pride made a coward—or a wise man—of him, so that he offered no resistance as they dragged him along the corridors and down the tortuous spirals of the stairs; he said no words as they reached the cell and flung him down with a last, almost regretful violence on to the rough stone floor. There he lay, listening to the grinding of metal as the bolts were driven home and to the footsteps of the guard, a dull and hollow echo fading into the distance like the sound of mourners retreating from a tomb; then rose and looked around him, half expecting to see some trace of the glow of a lantern, some fugitive chink of light.

But he was surrounded by a pall of darkness so impenetrable that he had not the least idea of the shape or size of the prison that enclosed him. He began to walk with hands outstretched till he felt the solid stone ahead, then carefully followed the circuit of the walls, aware all the time of the uncomfortable feeling that there might be some well or trapdoor gaping at his feet. The cell was a rectangle, he discovered, seven paces by ten, faced with massive blocks of masonry. There was an air-vent somewhere—it was the sole concession that the builders of this oubliette had made—a small one, as could be deduced from the foulness of the air, but he was persistent and traced its course at last—a shaft high in the wall opposite the door.

When he had carried out this investigation and made above a dozen crossings of the dungeon, the Vicomte found that for the time being he had exhausted his curiosity about the place: it was empty; there was not so much as a stone bench for him to lie on. He sat down in the angle of the wall beneath the shaft, where the air was purest, and in the most philosophical manner in the world prepared for sleep, unmoved by his prospects or by the chill dampness rising from the floor. All traces of the morbid feelings he had experienced in the coach had left him as a result of the ill-treatment he had received. Indeed, he felt almost grateful to the guards for giving him the purgative of a new and overriding indignation, a warm and comfortable feeling that was proof—but only for a little while—against the cold that came seeping through his clothes.

When he awoke he had lost all sense of time. Morning might have broken in the world beyond, but no glimmer of light showed in that black pall that seemed to be pressing down on him from the low roof of his prison.

He began to exercise himself, stepping briskly between the walls, recognizing each in relation to the door and the air-vent by rough irregularities of stone that grew to familiarity under the searching touch of his hands. It was surprising how rich in detail the pattern was—one wall was faced with smaller blocks than the others, it had the sharpest angularities; the surface beneath the vent was the smoothest of the four; there were two iron rings set in it at a distance of a yard apart; most exciting of all, a series of shallow grooves cut in the angle where they would be hidden by the opening of the door revealed themselves as letters—L. C. LEON DE C.—and one unfinished, as though discovery, or perhaps the release of death, had cut the writer short.

Who had he been? The Vicomte became greatly exercised by the problem: the presence of this unfortunate still seemed to linger, a sad but companionable shade. He wondered if this was the man who had been chained to the staples in the wall, the marks of whose feet and manacled hands could be traced in shallow indentations in the stone, and whether that had been his punishment for an offence of too great individuality, the urge to leave some trace behind in letters carved with such painstaking, loving care. How deep, he thought, was the urge to immortality! It was strange, too, that this pathetic gesture should have had a use, that it should reach out across the years to another man confined in that same darkness and have the power to comfort him.

And then there were other points about the cell. He found that the floor sloped quite sharply towards the door; water collected there, the moisture flowing in a shallow but definite channel diagonally across the room. The dryest place was the one that he had instinctively chosen, and returning to it with a surprising sense of property, he lay down at full length, easing his body in a depression in the stone, and let his mind wander over the events of crowded days.

He began to realize how desperately tired he was. His sleep had not refreshed him, his body was bruised and aching, his emotions exhausted by the extremes of fear and happiness that he had experienced from the moment—it seemed a century before—when he had climbed to the bedroom of his mistress. Into his tired mind the oddest thoughts came, shadowy, inconsequential, without any relation that he could see to Georges, or Diane, or the other preoccupations of his conscious mind, shading down imperceptibly into a dream—of the sword of Morillac, glittering silver, the letters on the wall, monstrously elongated till they seemed to fill the narrow cell, letters of fire, bright before his eyes.

He awoke. A light *was* shining, a soft glow that lit the walls of the oubliette, a picture so astonishingly unlike the one that he had created with hands and imagination that he hardly recognized the source of it—a lantern that a man was holding high above his head.

He lay still, uncertain whether he was not faced with an image of a dream—the tall figure muffled in a dark redingote, the sallow face on which the lamplight was shining, lighting it against the background of shadows with an effect that was indescribably macabre.

It moved, and as it did so the Vicomte sprang to his feet. He no longer thought he saw a ghost; he believed that he saw his executioner, the man who had been writing at the table in the *corps de garde*.

"Citizen Bellac."

"Charles Louis d'Esperé, Vicomte de Bellac," the young man said.

There was no sign of a response, even of irritation, on the Commandant's impassive face. Such fictions no longer had more than an amusement value in a society that instinctively felt it was preparing some resounding titles of its own.

"Citizen, it is my duty to read you a copy of a government decree minuted for delivery at the castle of Vincennes."

"So that's where I am!" the Vicomte said, seized with a reckless humour at the formality after all the secrecy that had gone before.

As a mood it was contagious.

"Yes, at Vincennes—to be specific, in one of the cells used for the incarceration of detainees by *lettres de cachet* under the late tyrannical regime. The Commission." And handing the lantern to a subordinate who had appeared at his elbow, the Commandant drew from his pocket a document plentifully embossed with seals, which he unrolled and began to read in a mechanical, high-pitched voice.

"*XII year of the Republic One and Indivisible.*

*IV, Ventose.*

"*The Government of the Republic decrees as follows:*

"(1) *The Citizen Charles Bellac, formerly so-called Vicomte de Bellac, accused of having borne arms against the Republic; of having been, and still being, in the pay of England; of having participated with others in the plots devised by England against the internal and external safety of the Republic; of having attempted in his own person the assassination of the First Consul for Life; shall be delivered up to a military commission composed of seven members named by the General, Governor of Paris, to be assembled at the castle of Vincennes.*

"(2) *The Grand Judge, the Minister of War, and the General, Governor of Paris are jointly charged with the execution of this decree.*"

The Commandant drew himself up, and with the intonation of a priest calling on the god behind the curtain, added:

"*Signed, Bonaparte,*"

and almost as an afterthought:

"*Hugues Maret.*"

The Vicomte was breathing heavily.

"In the pay of England! The safety of the Indivisible Republic! Signed by the man who will shortly murder it." His voice rose with an almost painful clamour in the narrow cell. "Do you think I'll listen to this hypocrisy—to these lies."

"It will be the least of your troubles," said the Commandant.

"To call me an assassin!" He was about to go on, to justify himself, when he caught sight of the man's face set in an expression so uninterested and withdrawn that he realized the uselessness of it and threw himself back against the wall.

"Well, now you've read it, your Commission; you've completed your formalities, for what they are. Leave me in peace."

"Formalities!" said the Commandant, who was not without a certain waspish humour. "The reading of the Commission was not ordained by law. You have received special and preferential treatment."

"Yes"—and the Vicomte was looking slowly round the cell. It was smaller than he had thought, and the flagstones glistened with dampness even in the corner where he had lain.

His jailer caught the glance.

"Have you complaints? It's part of my duty to attend to them."

"Why, what complaints should I have? Things are excellently ordered. Everything's provided here except a spade to bury me."

"You should be patient, citizen. In the meantime, I ask you formally whether you wish to register requests?"

"And what happens when I do?"

"They're registered, that's all. No harm is done. There are practically no limits to the things you may ask for. We live in enlightened times. You should reflect that your predecessor, whose workmanship you may have discovered by the door, probably never saw his jailer or heard his voice until he died."

The Vicomte turned his face to the wall.

"Is there nothing that you require?"

There was no reply.

"One must admit you're not exacting. You don't ask for a light or writing materials for the preparation of your defence—which certainly shows your realism. You don't even ask for food. Duval!" A second warder stepped into the cell. "The food, Duval."

The Vicomte watched the man move towards him carrying a bowl of soup and a slice of coarse black bread, and heard the mocking voice from the doorway of the cell: "You don't mind if we leave you? You'll have a good appetite, I'll warrant, even in the dark."

But not till the footsteps of his jailers had faded into the distance did he dare to unclasp his fingers from the object that Duval had pressed between them. He had no glimmer of light to guide him. It was some moments before he recognized with wildly beating heart the heavily embossed signet ring that he had seen a thousand times on the hand of Cadoudal.

# Chapter Twenty-seven

MÉHÉE DE LA TOUCHE HAD BEEN SO long inviolate and had felt himself under such secure protection that it was the greatest shock to him when he awoke to find a group of armed men in his house—soldiers, which made the entry and his own arrest irregular, as he pointed out—perhaps with too touching a faith in legalism—to Duroc. He continued to protest this irregularity and his own spotless character throughout the drive to Saint-Cloud—he couldn't think what they wanted with him. Indeed, so great was his sense of outrage that when to his horror he was sent into the presence of Bonaparte and Talleyrand he could still repeat them—in a suitably amended form.

"Armed men, Excellencies! Guardsmen who treated me as though I were a criminal."

"Or even a conspirator," the First Consul said. "Talleyrand, it's clear that Duroc exceeded his instructions. Devil take it, doesn't the man know that if Citizen de la Touche had been a suspect I would have sent those incorruptible agents of police!"

Méhée began to detect the presence of some very undesirable humours and emotions, for when Bonaparte began to talk—and look—like Joseph Fouché, it was time for men to beware.

"Yes," the First Consul continued, now addressing him directly, "you must forgive Duroc, a keen officer who most certainly misunderstood me. As it happens, I did no more than express a wish to see you and thank you again for the valuable information that you gave me once."

"About Querelle, Excellency?"

"Yes, about Querelle. That information led to great results—to a fiasco at Biville, to another incident in the rue Langrais of which I can hardly trust myself to speak, and the culminating triumph in the rue Victoire." He held up his hand as he saw that Méhée was about to defend himself. "Don't misunderstand me. The information was good—the *only* good information I received." He added in a softer voice: "Though I've often wondered why it wasn't better."

De la Touche excused himself with eloquence. He was one man with one man's body and brain and only on the fringe of the conspiracy. He had told everything he knew. He had done his best to penetrate the designs and get to know the leaders, but in spite of all his efforts he had failed. "The fact is," he concluded with an air of pained surprise, "I don't somehow think they trusted me."

"Not even de Bellac?"

Méhée inclined his head to one side: such questions always found him hard of hearing.

"De Bellac," the First Consul repeated. "You must have heard of him. The young man who performed such prodigies at Biville. You should know him. You lent him your house."

For one shattered instant it seemed as though Méhée had been so unmanned that he would fall back on a denial. At the last moment he avoided a crudity that would have been unworthy of him and managed a smile of acquiescence.

"So you admit it? This traitor had access to your house?"

"Yes, Excellency."

"But it seems to me," the First Consul said, "that you neglected to make one of your indispensable reports of that."

De la Touche was beginning to recover his composure. He was all things to all men, and, since Bonaparte required it, was now ready with a falsehood which, like all the best lies, was wrapped up inside a truth.

"It seemed unnecessary to me. The personage that the young man met there had the honour to be your Excellency's stepdaughter. I have no doubt that this meeting was part of your Excellency's plans. Since Mme Hortense was your agent, it would have seemed not only unnecessary but interfering in me to report."

The First Consul exchanged a glance with Talleyrand. It was clear that both were of the opinion that such a man was a loss to the Diplomacy, for here at one and the same time was an ingenious excuse, and the same suggestion—though more decorously phrased—that Fouché had made against the reputation of Hortense. What was a threat from the Senator, however, was no more than a divertissement in his servant. The First Consul turned to Talleyrand and asked for his professional opinion.

"Just specious enough to sound like truth," the Foreign Minister said.

"Excellencies, it *is* the truth. These meetings took place. Should I doubt the loyalty or competence of a member of the First Consul's family!" He looked from one to the other of his accusers, and at the expression on their faces he cried out: "If I was deceived, it was no fault of mine. Was I to blame if I found myself in an intrigue!"

Fouché, who alone knew the extent of the warren that his subordinate had been digging, would have seen the humour and the pathos of that lament.

Bonaparte only made a text of it.

"Whose intrigue? My stepdaughter's?"

"It was just a contingency that I mentioned, General."

"Yes, but the intrigue, though nothing to do with my stepdaughter, was unfortunately a fact. Talleyrand, you had some observations on that point, I think. With whom did you believe that Citizen de la Touche was working?"

"With Fouché," said the Foreign Minister, achieving over the name rather the same tone of ineffable distaste that the Senator reserved for his.

The effect on de la Touche was electric. He gazed at his accusers with an expression that was probably the greatest of all testimonies to his talents. He was desperately afraid, yet somehow contrived to look as though his terror were inspired, not by guilt, but by the discovery of the depths of the pit into which he, the innocent, had had the calamity to fall.

"Senator Fouché! Fouché and myself!"

"You deny it?"

Méhée did deny it: he did so with a vehemence that was not afraid of being too eloquent. Fouché the arch-plotter! The disgraced Minister! That his name should ever be associated with so great and so damnable a man!

"One thing's certain," said Bonaparte, as this virtuosity came to an end, "and that's that our friend himself wouldn't thank you for what you've said."

He added in a thoughtful aside:

"Or what you'll *say*."

"Excellency, what more can I say? Except that I execrate the man."

"'That was not quite what I was meaning," the First Consul replied. "Something more in the form of an indictment was in my mind—a statement connecting him with yourself, with de Bellac, with Cadoudal."

For once in his life Méhée found himself unequal to a situation. To bear witness against Fouché was an act that he had never considered in his wildest nightmares; it conflicted with his interest, his prudence, and strange to say, his loyalty.

While he was still stunned by this blow that had fallen so suddenly upon him, he heard his tormentor's voice:

"You look astonished, citizen. And yet, what is so surprising? You're an old confidant of Fouché's, we know that. You were a member of this émigré conspiracy, we know that. And when we find that the Senator, though out of office, knows more about this matter than the whole of my police, is it so strange that we should put two and two together and assume that you're a confidant of Fouché's still?"

"But I'm no conspirator," cried Méhée, who retained the rather naïve belief that arguments could save him. "Those that I knew of I denounced."

"To Fouché, you scoundrel."

"No, Excellency. Believe me, no, no, not a word."

Bonaparte rose from his chair. His bantering manner had deserted him, and his eyes shone, as they did when he was roused, with the cold glint of steel.

"Guileless, the pair of you! Unthinkable! Furthermore, in any case it's not my intention that the unthinkable should be thought."

"What can I do to prove my innocence?" the agent cried.

"It would be more realistic to consider," came the voice of Talleyrand, "what you can do to prove *his* guilt."

"You had better tell him, Citizen Minister," said Bona-parte, watching with ferocious satisfaction the beginnings of the collapse.

The Foreign Minister was drawing a document from his pocket, handling it with all the care he might have shown a treaty—as in a sense it was.

"I have here your confession," he began.

"My confession! Excellency, this is a game."

It could be seen from Talleyrand's face that he was of the opinion that a man who could think that could think anything.

"In seven articles, to be exact. You admit to associating (*inter alia*) with Artois, Moreau, and Cadoudal; to arriving in Paris along the royalist secret route; to being privy to the illegal acts of resistance at Biville; to failing to acquaint lawful authority with the presence of proscribed persons; to harbouring a proscribed person in your house; to being associated with Fouché in the ordering of the above and other acts; and, in particular, in a joint design with the said Senator Fouché and the said Cadoudal to assassinate the First Consul in the house of Mme Louis Bonaparte."

Méhée's eyes had widened throughout this recital, but it was not till the last charge of all that he appreciated the quality of his danger. He stared at the two men, his mouth agape, temporarily bereft of words.

"That is the substance of the confession. Only the formality of your signature remains."

Méhée shrank back from them towards the wall.

"Why, you're refusing!" There was a note of genuine distress in the Foreign Minister's voice. "Don't you admit the charges?"

So monstrous a question had the effect of loosening the

victim's tongue. The words spilled out in a torrent of reproach and anguish.

"Admit them! That I was privy to Biville, when it was I who put you on the scent! That I didn't denounce conspirators, when you've the example of Querelle! And then to accuse me of an abominable crime!"

Bonaparte had listened to this tirade, his head on one side like a bird's.

"Oh, we shall do more than accuse you, never fear."

"But why, Excellency? Why repay me in this way?" And as the thought occurred to him what that repayment all too probably would be, the victim clasped his hands together in a gesture not without a certain poignancy.

"Why, indeed!" the First Consul said. "You should ask yourself that question."

"You have decided to destroy me."

"To destroy *you*, citizen!" It required the voice of Talleyrand to point the insignificance of the victim and to convey the delicate intimation of a deal.

Méhée, who remained even in his terror a very sensitive detector of such nuances, understood him perfectly. Only an act of betrayal was demanded; the thing was common form to him. One small action—a signature, an accusation—it was easily made. On the one side was death and torture; on the other, life and the possibility of a reward: it was remarkable in the light of that that he should have hesitated, even for an instant.

But he did.

It was partly out of fear—fear of Fouché, a simple and direct emotion. But what had held him on the verge of an heroic action—held him there so firmly that he was in imminent danger of disgracing his good sense and falling into it—was quite another feeling, one that he would have been distressed to recognize in himself—an affection for his old friend and master that was lodged like a changeling in his corrupt and twisted heart.

Even the Senator might have been surprised at the downcast eyes, the faltering voice in which the betrayal was finally effected by the man who had made an art and speciality of the job. But as a realist and the one most intimately concerned, he might have preferred less sensibility and more fortitude.

# Chapter Twenty-eight

FOR LONG AFTER THE STEPS OF THE WARD-ers had faded down the corridors the Vicomte re-mained in the centre of the cell, turning the ring caressingly in his hands. Few things in his life had had so profound an effect on him as that one action of Duval's, for even his courage had not quite been proof against the darkness and the insidious memories of be-trayal, and then suddenly there was this link with the world outside his prison, the awareness of comradeship, the knowledge that he would not be left to die forgotten and alone.

Hope revived, and with it the urge to action. In a sense these were unsuitable emotions for the place in which he found himself, for the vigour of his mind passed to his body and he began to move about—ten paces, and then ten, the steps of a caged animal, wheeling by instinct short of con-tact with walls that would have set an unbearable limit to his thoughts.

The ring was a pledge that his friends had not abandoned him but would attempt a rescue. Nor, in this state of mind, was the Vicomte unduly doubtful of the issue, for hope is no logician: he had the signet, Duval, the implied promise

of his leader, and found in them, and in his memories of
Biville and the rue Langrais, reassurances to warm the heart.

Ten paces by ten. But he was already out beyond in the
green countryside of the spring. It was strange how vivid
his imagination could become in this dark cell so far from
the wind and the light of the world, but he seemed no
longer to breathe its air or feel the runnels of the water
along the floor; the physical features of his prison had
ceased to matter to him, so that he would have thought it
remarkable that a few hours before he had traced with such
care that message cut in the stone behind the door.

Backwards and forwards, backwards and forwards, the
noise of his steps setting up a continuous vibration into
which other sounds far away beyond the maze of corridors
would fit at times in a mournful harmony—the clash of a
door, the jingle of keys, the hollow tread of feet. Each time
he would stop in his tracks to listen, hearing the murmurous echo of his own steps reverberate between the walls,
dying as though in discouragement as those distant sounds
faded in turn into the oppressive silence of the fortress.
How still it was at such moments! A great weight of silence
descended on the mind, obliterating all the pictures he had
created, so that to revive them he would begin to walk
again, moving on his way like a man who hastens to his
mistress. Then he could weave the fancies of the imagination—Diane, life, liberty, spinning in a thousand patterns
on the loom, and always behind them the figure of Duval,
a reality merging, as the long hours went by, into that
shadowy world that surrounds our dreams.

Worn out with his exertions, he had taken up his old
place against the wall when he heard the noise of footsteps
coming to the cell. They were unmistakable—thunderously
loud under the stone vaulting of the corridor, utterly unlike

those other sounds, as remote as the world from the grave, that had tantalized him in the night. He was on his feet as the door swung open to reveal Duval, a small man, he noted, seeing him consciously for the first time and with an interest so acute that even the poor lamplight could not prevent the impress of every detail of face and figure on his mind—a small man with a curved nose and dark and shifty eyes.

The impulse of the Vicomte was to seize his hand, to draw this scarecrow figure to his heart. It was not without effort that he restrained himself, warned by his own instinct and by the appeal in the jailer's eyes that seemed to indicate that there was another person in the corridor beyond. Silently the wooden platter of food was handed him. Receiving it, the Vicomte felt the moist hand of Duval against his own, and looking down, saw reassurance, understanding comradeship, attempted rather than offered in that irresolute and apprehensive face.

It prepared him in part for the ordeal that followed within the hour: the visit of the Captain-Reporter of the court-martial that had been convened; the searching questions, the answers written down with a schoolboy's concentration, the pressure to sign his name and incriminate himself.

When these men had gone, the prisoner began to pace the cell, holding the ring clasped between his fingers as though its presence could make up for the other thoughts that came thronging to his mind. The proceedings against him had begun. There had been no second message from Cadoudal. It was all too easy for sombre thoughts to take the place of rosy images; for him to recall the betrayal in the rue Victoire, and to imagine a halfheartedness in friends who had chosen this poor Duval as the link between them.

And yet there was a link. His mind, repelling for a while the fears dictated by the solitude and darkness, recognized it for the marvel that it was, even in the form of the jailer with his timid, untrustworthy eyes. The man could do no worse than those others who had been his honoured colleagues—Querelle whining in his prison, Bouvet de Lozier, cut down from the rope by which he had tried to hang himself, blurting out a whole miserable catalogue of betrayals. What weaklings the monarchy had enlisted! There were no men now to dedicate themselves to good causes as Ravaillac and Felton and Balthasar Gérard in other times had done to evil ones—Gérard, assassin of the Prince of Orange, who had remained constant under the most inhuman torture till that moment when they had torn his heart from the living body and flung it in his face. When the time came, would even Cadoudal, he wondered, rise above the pitiful level of his friends? Would he himself?

As the thought occurred to him, the Vicomte stopped and leaned against the wall. From the moment of his arrest he had regarded his own trial and execution as the certain end, but he had never considered himself in the role of a Querelle, being perhaps too reliant on his own position as an officer and the ability of his enemies to recognize it. That they might fail to do so was an unwelcome thought, one that invested every movement in the corridors with an added significance, conjuring out of the darkness behind the Captain-Reporter and his writings, the menacing figure of Réal.

He had little to betray. That was the best answer to these fears, the result of a weakness that he only began to recognize in his mind and body, worn out by his exertions and the melancholy of failed hopes. At the worst, he could do no more for his enemies than give them addresses from which the birds would certainly have flown, so that his victims would be little men like the fruiterer in the rue de la Montagne Sainte-Geneviève, comfortable men of placid lives and small ambitions. It did not make the thought of betraying them less odious to remember that such bourgeois supporters—no enthusiasts for royalty—must certainly have been bought. Duval, too, had been bought, of course—at no high price, from the look of him—and yet in some strange way the Vicomte felt comforted by the mere idea of the relationship, for he had seen enough of ideals to be glad to rub shoulders with the mercenary for a change.

Many hours passed before he again had the opportunity, before he heard the ringing footsteps in the corridor. So intense was the echo that it was impossible to be certain whether more than one person was approaching, though he believed that he detected two—two sets of steps that gave the odd impression that one was trying to walk apart and one in unison. Duval came into the cell alone; again he did not speak; but this time, though no sound of further movement reached them, the Vicomte became certain that another person was in the corridor, even before he caught the glint of the lamplight on the barrel of a musket levelled at him from the shadows beyond the door.

It explained much: his friend's silence and anguished expression, also his status, which had puzzled him from the beginning. Duval was no jailer but a servant, and not a very trusted servant, judging from the secretive performance of the guard. What was authority expecting him to do? Attempt to corrupt Duval? Authority would certainly not expect him to continue to keep silence; it would seem suspicious, or at the least be inartistic; and the Vicomte, appreciating this, spoke out.

"Well, monsieur, what are they planning for me? When's this precious court of yours convened?"

From the expression in Duval's face it was clear that he was not thinking in the same terms of play-acting as the prisoner; words of any sort seemed compromising to him, with that lurking figure at the door. He rolled his eyes in so alarmed a way that the Vicomte, though touched by this evidence of care for himself—and a measure of self-care too—could hardly keep from smiling.

"Well, why don't you answer? Are you dumb?"

Over the shoulder of his friend he could see a movement in the corridor—the guard was showing signs of interest.

"You must be dumb."

Duval had handed him the food and was backing hastily away.

"Dumb, you wretch! Are you deaf too? Why don't they send me someone who can speak?"

Duval's face retreating to the door was more eloquent than any words: it conveyed so strong a sense of bewilderment that the Vicomte, who had been pleased at his own ingenuity in deceiving the guard with this proof of his friend's innocence, began to wonder whether he had overdone things and frightened Duval into a state of uselessness. What had seemed to him a logical and indeed necessary ruse had clearly impressed his benefactor in quite another way, so that the last view the Vicomte had of his eyes, as the cell door closed upon them, showed them to be round with a kind of wonder that was making few allowances for his charge's sanity.

Under other circumstances he might have been amused by so quaint a misunderstanding, but his present position did not encourage refinements in the way of humour; he waited with a gnawing anxiety through the long hours, reproaching himself for a miscalculation that might have the worst results. In this mood he did not fail to recognize in himself proofs of a deterioration in judgment and resolution that began to frighten him, for he had believed in his own constancy and was distressed by the alternation of hope and despair that seemed to be playing leapfrog in his thoughts.

His predecessor in this place, who had lived through the cycle that had enlarged itself in the pattern of a lifetime, could have explained the matter and given the credit to the cold and the darkness and the narrow boundaries of the cell —surroundings that roused the mind to fancies soon to be exposed for the pitiful stuff they were. The Vicomte, young and active, with memory not distant but at his elbow, reminding him of the sunlight that he knew existed as a fact and not as a matter of faith, was more easily a victim.

Starting as a weapon of his jailers, a means of reducing him, the darkness began to emerge as an enemy in its own right, hostile and malignant. It was so absolute; it seemed to fill the world. He had not appreciated before the blessed quality of sight, or of how much its possession or its frustration could mean to him. The walls of the cell were there and the floor and the air-shaft above, but he must visualize them with other senses. This came to him with the force of an almost unbearable deprivation. His eyes were open, straining into the darkness, but he could not see. He pressed his hands to them, feeling the lids, the delicate antennæ of lashes, the wall of the eyes themselves.

It was not so much that he feared that he was blind. There came a moment when he would almost have been relieved by such knowledge, bringing to him in its train a kind of kinship with the darkness which he could have accepted and against which he would not have struggled, feeling its waves lapping close around him. It was no use reproaching himself for a weakness that his intellect despised. These moments might be brief, but while they lasted they had a quality of eternity; and it was pointless to reflect that next day he might be dead, or that if he were allowed to live he would make a conquest of his enemy such as his predecessor in the cell had made.

But it was not a conquest, the Vicomte thought, seeing those letters on the wall as they had shown in the light of Duval's lantern—futile scratchings at the stone that only his blind captive's touch had made to seem regular or significant. The prisoner himself had never seen them; he had not recognized the evidence of his surrender—actions that had made him at one with his prison and had proved the truth of his captivity. It would have been better, thought the Vicomte, if he had left the cell as he had found it, without admitting the triumph of inanimate things over the spirit of a man and without leaving his signature to prove it.

Nothing else of his survived.

The Vicomte had never actively disbelieved in the occult. It had seemed reasonable to suppose that places intimately connected with the joys or sufferings of a man might carry the echo of them long after he was dead—a feeling, if not a manifestation that could be seen. So might the memory of the Dauphin, Louis-Charles, haunt that bare room in the Temple where he had died, and that of his mother, Antoinette, the pavilion of the Petit Trianon.

The cell he now occupied was such a place. Yet even that aura of the man's presence that he had believed he had sensed beside him had now faded from his mind. It had never existed, he supposed, except as an emotion arising in himself, the response to a sentiment or a wish. He could not even re-create that now. Was it true, then, that the place *was* empty, that man left nothing behind him in his journey through the world except the works of his hand that must decay? Or was it a matter of the presence or absence of sympathy in the observer, so that, in the act of seeing what the dead man had been, he had forfeited the knowledge of what he had become? He remembered the strange sense of well-being and peace that had pervaded him on first discovering the cell, and remembering, could not place such felicities for certain in his own bewildered heart.

More patiently, as these thoughts took root in him, he set himself to recapture an atmosphere—or was it just a mood? He sat down in his corner against the wall and closed his eyes, as though moving through this gesture into a comfortable private darkness of his own. He began to see his own past and even his future in a less tragic light. He had had great good fortune—a life of gaiety and adventure that had been summed up in one supreme experience. He must not regret that or allow his dreams to poison a past reality. And death had at least the advantage in his case of seeming singularly uncomplicated, demanding no decisions and making no claim beyond submission.

There remained the possibility of rescue, at which his heart began to beat so fast that he was forced in self-defence to try to edge the thought aside. He must look on rescue in the same light as other things—as a fact outside his power. But the thought was not to be disciplined so readily; it continued to peep out under the cover of more controllable emotions, overturning his acceptance of fate with other visions full of passionate tenderness. The truth was that he was too young to find a place for love in a philosophy; he could not be resigned while he could still feel the worn gold circle of the ring against his hand.

# Chapter Twenty-nine

ARMED WITH MÉHÉE'S CONFESSION, BOnaparte sent, through Méneval, requesting the pleasure of Fouché's presence at Saint-Cloud. For the first time for months he was able to contemplate a meeting with this man without those feelings of self-doubt that affected him like a disease: he promised himself a pleasant afternoon, all the sweeter for the humiliations that had gone before.

Talleyrand, who in one sense had been the architect of this recovery, had hoped to be present at the meeting: he had urged the production of Méhée and a confrontation of the two men that could not fail to be diverting. In this he was rebuffed. He was not perhaps to be blamed for failing to detect one reason for this refusal—a distrust on his master's part, an unwillingness to let one Achitophel triumph too patently over the other—but such was his subtlety of mind that he discerned the second—a peculiarly Corsican feeling for the private nature of the vendetta.

Talleyrand knew that Bonaparte was in some ways an elemental man. He looked with confidence for the results —a trial unencumbered with too much justice (though it would be full of legalism of his own manufacture), followed by a killing or a deportation, and though not admitted to the office, he contrived to see his enemy arrive, bowing to him in the anteroom in a way that hinted at these prospects and his own pursuit of a private vendetta of his own.

The Senator, for his part, thought nothing of it, for his relations with the Minister were always marked by that vibrant quality that precedes the beginning of a cat-fight; he inclined his head in return, swept Méneval with an expression of distaste, and strode into his master's room with the look of a purchaser who has called to collect a bargain. He *was* a little shocked by the sight of his man at the writing-table, for there was a repose about him, a roundness, a good humour, that the First Consul notoriously only showed in the camp. It was to be a battle—and Fouché braced himself, reviewing his weapons, which were in excellent order. *"Que messieurs les Anglais tirent les premiers!"* He would wait on the defensive and allow this already defeated enemy the privilege of first shot.

It came—a sarcasm, of course. He had expected it.

"You'll observe that this time, Senator, it is I who have solicited a meeting."

"I do observe it, General."

"And has it occurred to you to wonder why?"

It had occurred to the Senator. At the last meeting he had made a request—it was now to be granted him. This being so, he was prepared to allow a certain saving of face on the First Consul's part, for such a man could not be asked to surrender without a struggle or the appearance of a struggle. Provided he got his Ministry, he, Fouché, was for the time being prepared to make it look like a gift, or a purchase, or a concession, or anything that might appeal to the General's somewhat Oriental mind. At their last meeting in the moment of achievement he might have shown a certain vulgar triumph, but essentially he was a reasonable man and could win a game with the utmost magnanimity.

"It is because you have some commands for me, of course," he said.

"But if I remember, Senator, at our last meeting it was you who had commands for me."

"For you, General!"

"Commands for your reinstatement at the Police."

Fouché began to look embarrassed. All things considered, it was probably in his long-term interest that the surrender should be painless to the Consul, yet here was the man probing in the most morbid fashion round the wound. That was not the way to do things, and knowing this, he could not help but feel aggrieved, like an actor whose colleague is blundering with his lines.

"They were suggestions, and naturally no more than that," he said.

"Suggestions, were they! They were strongly phrased."

"It was the arguments that were strong, General. That is what you will have remembered."

"But, as it happens, I do not. I have the clearest recollections of other things. Of your treasonable words, for one. And of your treasonable acts."

The Senator shook his head, regretting that he must build his whole case again. It all came of his own dilatory nature, he thought reprovingly to himself. He should have insisted on the Ministry from the start. But though pained by this new Bonaparte, he was not afraid of him. He would just have to return to his muttons and make a better job of it.

"You will recall, General," he said, "that I was *reporting* treasonable acts. The acts of the man Bellac. Who was discovered, you'll remember, in circumstances that might be said in some way to compromise Your Excellency."

The phrasing was as suggestive as ever, the evidence on which it was based remained as solid. What was it, then, that made Fouché, even as he spoke, feel a sudden sense of inadequacy, as though Hortense and de Bellac and the whole plot on which he had buoyed up his hopes had slipped into the sea?

The counterattack was immediate and in his own best manner. The First Consul leaned over towards him and said in a surprisingly gentle voice:

"Ah, those circumstances! You will find, my friend, that it is *you* whom they have compromised."

The Senator could see the absurdity of this—but only with his intellect. A sudden fear was clutching at his heart.

"Say defiled, General. Pitch defiles."

"So does ambition, even a small ambition—like seeking to return to office. You have sought this. You will agree?"

Fouché, who had believed he had not so much sought as actually attained, lowered his head. He was thinking rapidly. But the conversation was no longer under his control —a mortification in itself.

"So you do agree? You have wanted office. You have intrigued for it. That's only natural, your name being Fouché. But in the process you have had the misfortune to conspire."

That word brought the victim's head up with a jerk.

"Conspiracy is a serious word," he said reproachfully.

"It's a much more serious action. I confess that from the outset I was puzzled by the superiority of your information over mine. You knew far more about this conspiracy of Cadoudal. The reason is now apparent—you were part of it."

It was a deadly thrust, but Fouché displayed none of the weakness of indignation that de la Touche had shown when he had discovered that his name had somehow got itself linked up with the devil. Perhaps the knowledge of his innocence helped to give the right tone of gravity to his voice as he replied:

"You've been told a lie."

"So you deny this? My information is still inadequate, I suppose!"

"I would be very glad to hear who my accuser is," Fouché said in unctuous tones.

"I very much fear that you won't be glad at all. Shall I tell you? Can you guess?"

It *was* a puzzle to the Senator. He inclined to the belief that the accusation had been planted on de Bellac, the most recent captive, perhaps as the price of life. It did seem ironical that it should have been his own information to Réal that had led to the arrest and the attempted blackmail now in progress. He was not too greatly frightened by the development which he believed he could control, though he did shake his head over the weakness of the young Vicomte who had become in recent months almost his favourite dupe. One thing was certain: he was not so far reduced as to blunder into the trap of the First Consul's question and accuse himself.

So he shook his head and wondered with Bonaparte about the identity of his calumniator.

"Then I'll tell you. Or, better still, you can see for yourself." And taking Méhée's confession from the table, the First Consul handed it to his victim with the care one bestows on a very interesting and precious work of art.

The Senator received it; he glanced at the signature; he read the seven heads of the indictment that Talleyrand had so thoughtfully provided. Instinctively he had braced himself, but as he returned to the signature, just for an instant his guard was down and there shone in his face neither terror nor bitterness, as the First Consul, avidly watching, had expected, but a look of almost wistful sadness.

That signature tucked away in the corner of the paper as though turning its back on the betrayal—how typical of Méhée! By itself it disproved a forgery. The letters jostling against each other, trying to lose the wood in the trees— that was Méhée. One had the feeling that he was even denying the fact of the betrayal: the words were not his own, the accusations were false, the signature no more governed them than a man governs his soul and body at the moment of his death. Yes, that was Méhée; and in a flash of understanding the Senator was seeing all the other betrayals that were not betrayals, the faces of Le Bourgeois, Querelle, and de Bellac, and behind them the agent disclaiming each of them. He was a man; he had a sense of the tragic and of the comic like other men; and in face of these visions there was no reason for wonder at that fleeting look of melancholy that had disturbed the First Consul with the shock of the incongruous.

"He has signed that," he said.

"Evidently," the First Consul replied, though the words had not been spoken for his benefit but rather as a kind of epitaph. "You ought not to be surprised: such denouncements were the man's speciality, after all.

"But you *are* surprised," he added, with a shrewd glance at his enemy, for he was discovering beneath the outward shell all manner of emotions that he could hardly have suspected. The Senator had a heart, he had loyalties, sensibility. These were strange and not altogether agreeable discoveries; there was something almost monstrous about their presence in this frame. "You believed in him!" he exclaimed, turning to sarcasm in relief. "In Méhée! Yet it was he who betrayed Querelle to me. He was mine from the beginning."

That was what the First Consul apparently believed. Fouché knew better. But no sooner had this small consolatory thought occurred to him than he remembered that he personally had believed this same thing of de la Touche. He had thought the man was his. He would never have spoken of it and had disguised his own feelings even from himself, but the fact remained that he had trusted Méhée, endowing him with loyalty and courage, qualities of sentiment that had crept in the clothes of cynicism into his harsh and factual mind. The more he had known of the man's duplicity, the more he had relied on him. What a paradox! Honour among thieves! Was there ever, wondered the Senator, a more ridiculously optimistic, ridiculously moral, precept?

Bonaparte was saying:

"You will appreciate what this means?"

He appreciated right enough. His sentimentality had destroyed him. He had lost the game. Lesser men might have bluffed and argued, they might have denied everything—as if denials mattered!—or might even have threatened exposures at the trial—as if there would be anyone at the trial to hear them! But the Senator knew when he was beaten; he knew also that defeat, if properly handled, had bargaining counters of its own.

So he bowed his head, not with too great humility which would have an irritant effect, but with all the dignity of a surrender.

"So you do appreciate where your double-dealing's led you?" came the voice of Bonaparte.

The head sank lower on to the breast.

"You see the foolishness of crossing me?"

And as he said that and saw the result of this folly and the extent of his own success, the First Consul rose from his chair, feeling within himself that thrill of triumph which was the due of the victor in the field. His tendency was always to see events in terms of war, and there before him might have been the emissaries of Melas, of the Archduke, the plenipotentiaries of Campo Formio. It gave him a warm feeling of pleasure that extended its aura around him to include even the figure of his enemy.

He had been afraid of this man. He was no longer afraid —or so the impulse of the moment told him. Those eyes no longer looked into his with the challenge of equality. They were not equal. His was the power. He could order this man to exile or death. The man deserved it. There would be disadvantages, of course: the voice of scandal, the appearance of tyranny, the waste of talent. He could do it. Some things were hardly wise, but he could do anything he wanted with the man.

And suddenly the urge to do something, to show this power that he boasted to himself, swept over the First Consul like a flood. He drew himself up, seeing below him the draped eagles, the muffled drums, the sword of the defeated.

"You're beaten," he said. "You know it. I should have you shot. Instead, I shall restore you to your Ministry." He laughed—not a very confident sound, for somehow at the last he had to call up his cynicism to still the warnings of his heart—and he added: "So that you can watch Talleyrand and catch Cadoudal for me."

# Chapter Thirty

ALL THE HOPES OF THE VICOMTE IN HIS cell were founded on Cadoudal—as it happened, more justly than he knew. For from the moment of the discovery of the presence of police agents in the ruc Victoire the members of the conspiracy, apart from Georges and his two most intimate familiars, thought only in terms of their own safety: it did not occur to them to waste their sympathy on a fallen colleague whom they half suspected of betraying them.

For a time Cadoudal had shared this belief, and it was only gradually after his return to his lodging in the ruc de la Montagne Sainte-Geneviève that he began to piece together the events of the afternoon—the reported arrest of de Bellac, the ease of their own escape—and to deduce from them that the young man alone had been expected by Réal, and so far from selling anyone, had himself been sold.

From that moment onwards he determined to save him— an obsession nursed by a bad conscience and the opposition of his friends. There was one initial problem: the place of imprisonment. He discovered it at last—through Méhée de la Touche, performing (on the instructions of Joseph Fouché) what was to prove his last office for the conspiracy on the very eve of his arrest—and straightway sent his two most trusted supporters to Vincennes with the signet ring and a large sum in gold.

On the day after their departure, the gates of Paris were closed. The fruiterer, returning from a business visit to a warehouse in the city, came round-eyed with news of police patrols in the streets, armed sentries at strategic points, detachments of cavalry in the outer boulevards. The wildest rumours were current: that a royalist rising was imminent; that the faubourg Saint-Germain was arming; that Fouché was implicated and was under detention at Saint-Cloud.

Furthermore, there were the posters. Here Cadoudal could not help but notice that his host's face, that had been so alert with momentous tidings, had clouded over and had become full of embarrassment. There were posters in the streets. They were displayed everywhere: on hoardings, trees, the walls of houses—descriptive posters. In a sense they were threatening posters too.

And suddenly the man's meaning was clear to him.

"You're asking me to go."

The fruiterer's figure seemed to swell with the force of his decision. He was about to express himself—to explain with a thousand flourishes that this honoured guest must not think of leaving, though it was highly imperative that he should. It was the speech that was required by the occasion and which he had been rehearsing for some days. But even as he was opening his mouth he caught sight of Cadoudal's eyes fixed on his, and all this roundabout rhetoric was stillborn.

"That is what I am asking monsieur to do," he said.

Only after he had spoken did he realize the full sense of it, and he took a step backwards, appalled by his own boldness. Before he could cover up this enormity with words

that he now knew he should have used, he heard the voice
of Cadoudal asking with surprising mildness:

"Then where am I to go?"

At once he took heart. Nowhere in Paris, he explained,
almost breathless in the intensity of his relief. Paris was
too dangerous. But it was possible to leave the city, even
with conditions as they were. His friends at the warehouse
were royalist, or could be converted into royalists—monsieur would understand the way. The firm's wagons left the
city, trading to the Limousin and the valley of the Rhone.
Naturally there was danger in such an attempt, but it was
the lesser evil. His eyes were widening again. His friend had
not seen the streets filled with soldiers and police. They
would be searching the houses soon—and if it had not been
so tragic, his audience might have spared a smile for the
discomfiture which showed itself in advance on the fruiterer's face as he imagined the discovery of this compromising
cuckoo in his nest.

The friends of Cadoudal, whose judgment had not been
warped by the call of honour or by the knowledge that
Paris was plastered with descriptions of themselves, would
have seen the absurdity of this plan. But it happened that
it suited the mood of recklessness that had descended on
their leader, the deeper springs of his own nature that he
had suppressed in the interests of the conspiracy and which
now reasserted themselves in defeat.

The truth was that he had never been the man for a mission that depended on diplomacy. To win over Moreau, to
buy Macdonald, to control the myriad strings of a rebellion,
had been tasks quite foreign to him, and when at the end he
had turned to the actions that his instinct had favoured
from the beginning, it had only been to find that they had
come too late. His was an ardent spirit that throve on the

attack; it had been worn down by the hole-and-corner poli-
cies that he had been obliged to follow and by the strain of
his life in Paris, constantly frustrated by the fears and eva-
sions of weaker men. As a result, discretion and even confidence were deserting him, making him reckless where he
had been bold, and convincing him that he should no
longer skulk in cellars and attics for anyone. He would leave
Paris in any way he could, he would try to save the Vicomte,
and then he would retire on his old base in Morbihan in
the hopes of raising the standard of the King.

In the circumstances that ruled in Paris this was not a
policy, it was an abdication, and in proof of it he was soon
to find that he had ceased to be the leader. Only one man
besides the fruiterer—no lukewarm party in an enterprise
that would remove an embarrassment from his house—
could be found to help with the shaping of the plans—with
arrangements at the warehouse and with the ordering of
the cabriolet that was to meet Georges near the Panthéon
and take him across the city to his reluctant hosts.

But it was done at last, and on the following afternoon
the royalist leader, dressed in a heavy travelling cloak against
the blustery March day, descended the private stair to the
shop. Until this moment the fruiterer had hardly dared to
hope that he would rid himself of his incubus, but at the
sight of the giant's retreating back he was suddenly seized
with emotion, partly due to his warm heart, partly a tribute
that he felt he owed to the drama of his position.

"Monsieur is not angry with me?" he cried, running to
him and seizing him by the arm in full view of the street—
a kind of propitiation for his cowardice.

"No, my friend."

"Monsieur knows that it's not for myself that I'm acting,
but for him. Monsieur will appreciate my reasons."

"I do appreciate them. You're afraid."

Honesty welled up at these words, an obstinate honesty that elbowed all the glib denials out of the way.

"It's true. I am. You won't understand that."

But Georges was shaking his great head from side to side. "Why not? Everyone around me is afraid, except that poor Vicomte who has too little imagination, or too much. Fear has ruined us and made us what we are." He was looking through the doorway of the shop, seeing the windows across the street shuttered and barred as though for a siege, and he added slowly: "I too am afraid. I can tell you that I'm not finding this an agreeable experience."

"It's not agreeable for me, monsieur."

"Because you fear that you're being compromised?"

Emotionalism was returning at the gallop.

"No, monsieur—dishonoured. I've abandoned you. I've driven you out. I've betrayed my trust."

"You're certainly betraying your good sense," said Cadoudal, drawing his cloak around him and moving towards the door. Only half his mind was with his host in this quaint verbal flagellation, though it could divert him from the sombre thoughts of the ordeal that lay so close ahead. He added: "It's quite unnecessary to reproach yourself."

But the fruiterer would not be cheated in this way of punishment. He felt with all his heart that he deserved it, and was delighted to discover how agreeable the penance was.

"But it *is* necessary," he insisted. "If anything were to happen to you, how could I forgive myself?"

"Merely by forgetting, my good sir."

The man drew himself up. He could see that he was being mocked—not quite so satisfactory a form of masochism.

"Ah, you're laughing at me. You think my interest in

you has been a sham. You're wrong. You should believe that. I have cared for you and His Majesty."

"I know. And for my part I shall remember."

"But *what* will you remember?" cried the fruiterer pitifully, for he had had a return of that vision that never seemed remote from him—the Bourbons at the Tuileries and Cadoudal as Minister of Police.

"What, that you were good to me." A smile had appeared, a trifle incongruously, below those massive brows. "And that you ended by detaining me."

"I mustn't do that," the fruiterer said. "I mustn't detain you." But the impulse to rid himself of his visitor had gone in the moment of his victory; instead, he felt an urge to reverse the whole process, to keep his man there—at least until such time as he had talked himself back on to good terms with his conscience. He asked fussily: "You know what to do? You know all the arrangements that I have made?"—for this at least must count to him for virtue, since he had risked his life—and, what was quite as precious, his trade—in a disinterested passion to save his leader.

Cadoudal replied that he knew them well.

But his host was ready with instructions, just as though he had not spoken.

"Go to the corner of the place and rue de Fourcy. A cabriolet is waiting, cabriolet number 51. Direct the driver to the Luxembourg. He will take you to the warehouse in the avenue Laon. Ask there for Citizen Ducaze, saying you have a consignment for Limoges. There!" said the fruiterer, who may have felt that with these last picturesque details his conscience was appeased at last—"there! that's all that I can do for you."

"Thank you, my friend."

The man raised his round white face to Cadoudal's.

"You shouldn't thank me." And moved by an emotion that had no motive nor profit and which he was never able to explain, he turned and walked rapidly away into the recesses of the shop.

Georges was left by the door.

He knew the street from long acquaintance; he knew how tranquil and remote it was. Nevertheless, some superstition was assuring him that the first step was the important one, and he looked up and down its length with exaggerated care before venturing into the open. As soon as the decision was made, these fears deserted him and he began to walk briskly along, head up as though contemptuous of disguise, carrying his arms thrust out in that fashionably aggressive style that he had picked up during his stay in England, only slightly inconvenienced by the bulk of the pistols strapped beneath his cloak. His friend the fruiterer, he decided, had exaggerated, no doubt in his own interest, for the city appeared much as usual to him. It was true that many of the houses and shops were closed, but the tension in the air would only have been apparent to sensitive observers, and Georges was not the man to be impressed by anything but the physical presence of his enemies. Between the rue de la Montagne Sainte-Geneviève and the place Fourcy he did not see one soldier or agent of police, not even one of the famous posters that had been among the causes—and not the least—of his present odyssey.

With every moment his confidence was increasing. For seven months he had been moving through this city with impunity, passing under the scrutiny of gendarmes and their "noses" with an ease that owed much to his un-self-conscious attitude to life, to that small capacity for surprise that had accepted his presence in Paris as natural and not as a phenomenon only half believed in. So much self-knowledge was beyond him, but now that he was in reflective mood he did recognize the force of this immunity, which he put down to his good luck. Was it so unreasonable to expect a small extension—a walk, a ride through Paris, and those other moves that would carry him beyond the walls?

The first part was certainly ending as he would wish. There was the cabriolet drawn up in the angle of the square, exactly in the spot that the fruiterer had described; it gave him a pleasant feeling to see it standing there, part of the limbo of the city that had been drawn to him to shape his dream.

He had a lucky star, he assured himself as he sat back among the cushions, seeing the dangerous surroundings through which he had walked dissolve into a jumble of streets and roofs that danced before him with the motion of the carriage as it rolled and rattled its way out of the square. The rhythmic clip-clop of hooves, the comforting musty smell of leather, brought memories thronging to his mind. In just such a way he had entered Paris with Pichegru in the early days of the conspiracy, the safe days before the era of betrayals. And yet what precautions they had taken! He could smile still at the picture of his old companion, the conqueror of Holland, muffled like a strolling player in a grotesque green travelling cloak—Pichegru, taken these three weeks now, sold by a friend he had trusted for a hundred thousand francs. It was a large sum, and he had no doubt that they had offered more for him. But so far he had been fortunate with his betrayers, for like Bonaparte he had a lucky star.

The cabriolet seemed to be making a good pace, threading its way through the heavy traffic that was returning to the streets. Even in his time the pattern of it had changed, so that one saw rarely nowadays the coaches of the rich, of those ladies of fashion, with their monstrous headdresses, descending like a plague on the theatres, waking the bourgeois from uxorious beds with the arrogant clatter of their carriage wheels. Where were they now? Dead in nameless graves, their coaches burnt and looted, their horses long since slaughtered at the knackers' yards.

It was for that society that he had come to Paris and risked his life. There was no denying it, for he knew that time had only whetted the appetites of the exiles for a return to those privileged and spacious days. Artois would resurrect the whole crazy pyramid of caste. That was what he was fighting for. He would continue to fight, for he was a loyalist and it was his faith; but he knew that if those days should ever return, he, who had done more than any other man to make them possible, would find himself again, as he was now, an outcast. It would be a quaint ending to his efforts, he thought, with a smile for loyalties that he never attempted to explain. His support for the monarchy had always been different in kind from that of the nobles around Artois and the King, springing as it did from the conservatism of the peasant and not from any freemasonry of blood. He disliked the nobles; in other circumstances he would have burnt their castles with enthusiasm; and was it not another irony that it was on account of one of them that he was engaged on the most dangerous action of his life?

To spirit a prisoner out of the dungeons of Vincennes! His associates in Paris had declared the thing to be impossible, and even the success of his two loyal followers in corrupting a member of the guard had made no impression on a scepticism that was only too well founded on past misfortunes. In his secret heart Georges may have agreed with them, but his feelings for the Vicomte did not admit of too much reasoning. He would save him because he was his friend, because this was the one man whose spirit matched his own. Politicians like Lajolais; weaklings like Querelle; La Rivière and the brothers de Polignac, more royalist than an emperor, never mind a king, were not the men for him. Was it any wonder that such an ill-assorted company should have fallen into the habit of betrayal? But he knew that the Vicomte would not fail him; nor would he fail. He owed a return for the trickery he had practised in the rue Victoire; and he would succeed, he told himself, spreading his arms wide in an instinctive gesture of a gasconade, even if he had to tear the fortress guards to pieces with his hands.

The cabriolet was moving still more rapidly through the streets, its speed reflected in the dark, boxlike interior where the passenger was jolted violently from side to side. The sense of urgency suited his mood. He must hurry. He had little time, for already word had come from his agents in Vincennes that the court-martial would be convened within three days. There could be no doubt of its verdict or of the events that would follow; for there was not much to be hoped for from such a resolute young man, and in default of hope, authority would put him up against a wall without delay. Georges was not of a squeamish nature; he had shed few tears for Querelle or de Lozier; but the thought of this one death appalled him, perhaps because it was in his power—or at least his imagination—to prevent it.

He must hurry. He must be clear of the city before dark. The rattle of the wheels on the roadway kept pace with the flight of his thoughts, a wave of sound and imagination that merged in one all-embracing rhythm. They were moving fast; it would not be long before they reached the warehouse; already he had passed the rue d'Enfer by the Luxembourg, and he could recognize the houses of the rue des

Fossés-Monsieur-le-Prince etched against a sky of purest blue.

How beautiful the city was on this spring day! And how ill paved! he thought, as a sudden violent jerk shook the cabriolet, pitching him forward against the wall. They were slowing down. In the act of recovering himself he heard the scrabbling of hooves on the roadway, the confused sound of voices near at hand. An accident? They must have struck someone or some obstacle. But his instinct knew already what he would find when he had heaved himself up and flung open the carriage door—two men who struggled with the horse's head, swept along by its momentum so that they trailed from the harness like broken marionettes. The head and body of one was turned towards the carriage, and seeing this, Georges drew a pistol from under his cloak and levelled it, steadying the aim with his other arm. He fired. The sound of the shot volleyed between the houses, and the unfortunate man who had received the ball, throwing up his arms, was swept from his hold as the horse reared and plunged, striking its hooves down on the causeway, which was already dyed in blood.

Georges uttered a cry of triumph. He was filled with a terrible elation as the horse, under the lashes of the driver's whip, once more swung the carriage forward in jerky, shuddering movements, straining in the traces and flinging up its head. He leaned from the door of the cabriolet, and as the body of his remaining assailant came into view he levelled his second pistol and fired at him, wounding him with a lucky shot that brought a new surge of hope into his heart: it was not only his own life that was at stake, but far more—the life of the Vicomte, the safety of his colleagues, the rights of Artois and the King.

He was leaning far out now, well beyond the projecting

edge of the coachwork, from where he could see the driver still furiously at work and the poor beast in the traces struggling forward, its hooves slithering madly on the rough pavement of the street; but his wounded enemy had passed from his sight—the man, still clinging to the bridle, had swung himself close against the horse's flank so that he was covered by its body. Imperceptibly at first, but with increasing power as the momentum slowed under the urgent pressure of those hands, the carriage was being drawn diagonally across the street.

Against the background of men and women gathering around them, white faces with horror-struck and staring eyes, Georges recognized this movement and, in the same instant, his last chance of escape. He could not kill his man nor free the horse, but there was just the hope that he might be able to lose himself among the crowd. It was his chance and he would take it, and on the spur of this decision he leaped from the cabriolet, thrusting the pistols beneath his cloak. It was only then that he recognized the police agents among the people surrounding him, levelling their weapons at his breast: it was only when he caught sight—well in the background—of a face he knew, of Méhée de la Touche, that he realized how he had been the sport of his betrayers.

# Chapter Thirty-one

THE VICOMTE LIFTED HIS HEAD AS HE heard from far off the sound of feet moving in the corridor. He had learnt to count his days by measuring the intervals between the visits of Duval, and this noise of movement in the fortress, which he recognized at once as connected with himself, struck him with that irritant effect that can be caused to very sensitive men by a clock that keeps bad time. Not only was the event out of sequence, but its volume was out of proportion too. He resented this, and did his best to recognize the steps of Duval and his shadow, which now had the comfort of familiarity, but the pattern of movement would not fit; other sounds kept adding themselves one by one, individually at first, then swallowed in one thunderous murmur like that heard in a cave awash in the rising tide.

A wild hope rose in his heart, less a rational thing than a revolt against his instinctive knowledge of what these footsteps meant. But the vision of Duval and Cadoudal had faded long before the light from the lanterns shone into the cell; he sensed the armed escort of police and the fortress Commandant before he saw them framed in the doorway gazing in at him; he knew why they had come, and with that knowledge the last shred of surprise and fear was gone.

"Citizen Bellac."

He did not reply. Once he had challenged that address; he was astonished now to discover how meaningless such details were.

"Citizen Bellac, it is my duty to inform you that the court convened by government decree is now in session. I have been sent to fetch you before that court." The Commandant paused, just as though he himself had a judicial function and were waiting for some answer from the prisoner. As none came, he continued in a sharper voice: "You must come with me."

The Vicomte, who had been standing against the wall below the air-shaft, moved towards the Commandant, preparing to place himself between the guards. He had known without any conscious desire to irritate that this would displease his enemy, and he showed not the least resentment at the roughness with which he was seized and hustled out of the cell. Such treatment did not surprise him, for one lesson he had learnt on his family estates when very young was that a man's defencelessness is in itself a provocation. Armed with this experience, he could understand the feelings of the guards and even of their commander, all affected by a kind of inverted pity and by that suspicion that jailers have that their victims have found a secret weapon. It was true in a way—he had—but the fact was unimportant to him, for all his interest was concentrated on the journey they were making from the bowels of the fortress, rising towards the air whose breath he felt already on his face— he knew with an absurd conviction that it was the air of day, that the sun was shining, that the wind was rustling in the trees.

What a labyrinth of a place it was! He wondered with an

idle fancy what plans Georges and those others who had failed him had made to reach him across the gulf of corridors, for now that he was beyond the cell he could appreciate the vanity of the dreams that had seemed so reasonable—most clearly, by some irony of understanding, when he first caught a glimpse of daylight, a shaft stretching down from the vaulting high above with the air of being itself a prisoner. At once the castle rose into perspective as a place too strong for his friends' resources. They could never have reached him—a comforting thought in a way, for it gave him the assurance of the inevitable and he was distracted no more by regrets or hopes.

They were nearing the end of the corridor; he could see the shape of the vaulting enclosing within itself a greyness that gradually sharpened and invaded the tunnel's mouth. As they emerged, the Vicomte, glancing round at the escort, was struck by a sensation of release, for in the hall they had entered, with its steep-pitched roof, he seemed to be freed from the overwhelming physical presence of his enemies, and the lanterns that had glowed so fiercely, brilliant against the lowering walls, were thrust back into a kind of impotence. In one flash the mediævalism that still lurks underground was banished, swept away by the wind of the new age, and he saw around him not Inquisitors, but the prosaic, faintly absurd servants of the Consulate.

They for their part were quite unaware of any change in themselves, which made it all the more agreeable for him, but continued to hustle him forward from room to room with a watchfulness that had increased now that they were moving in the light of day. By the time they had brought him to the door of the hall where the court-martial had assembled, they had done him the service of putting him in the best of humours, so that when the call came and he was marched inside, he saw his judges only as the cast of a burlesque.

Seven men were there, seven men in uniform facing him across a table, an eighth by himself, a little way apart. All were watching him with that gravity that is so much part of the stock-in-trade of justice that it even affects its hangers-on, and he returned the compliment, looking at them steadily in turn, from the Captain-Reporter he had encountered in the cell, to the nervous junior officers in the wings, to the youthful colonel on the President's right—obviously the dominating figure with his ascetic face and cold blue eyes—to the President himself, one of those benevolent, paternal men who so often find themselves in the front seats at an injustice.

With rather muddled formality the trial began, the prisoner being relieved of his escort and his manacles, and placed in a low chair where he could be dominated by even the most junior of his judges. The Captain-Reporter rose, and having established the identity of the prisoner, began to read the charges that had already been published in the government decree, with the air of a man who by the rules must prove a theorem that is too self-evident for words. The prisoner, it appeared, disputed one charge at least—the most serious one, it had to be noted—furthermore he denied the competence of the court to try him; and from the Captain-Reporter's expression it could be seen that this was not the least heinous of the Vicomte's crimes.

"Is that true?" asked the President. "He denies the competence of the court?"

The prisoner himself replied:

"I deny its legality, even."

"But that means the same. You're saying we can't try you."

At this manifest fallacy there was some shaking of heads among the officers, and one of them, a jovial-looking man with moustaches that still carried the cachet of the sergeants' mess, put the thing in words:

"That's nonsense, for we're trying him."

"The prisoner will see the force of that," said Colonel Mordan, at the President's right, who was of that ruthless, busy nature that dislikes delay even in matters as agreeable as trials and executions. "The case should now proceed."

And before the President could so much as save his dignity by calling on the Captain-Reporter to begin, that dignitary had done so, speaking towards Mordan, with just a glance now and then towards the figurehead to see that the man was still in hand.

"Members of the court, you have heard the charges and the plea of the accused. It remains for me to make my report of the interrogation carried out by myself and witnesses in the prisoner's cell.

"The following took place:

"Asked his name and age, the prisoner replied: 'Charles Louis d'Esperé, Vicomte de Bellac, aged twenty-three.'

"Asked his employment, replied: 'A soldier of the King.'

"Asked whether or not he had landed from an English ship on Biville beach, replied he had.

"Asked whether he had associated in England with Charles Capet, self-styled Count of Artois, replied he had.

"Asked whether he had associated in Paris and elsewhere with the proscribed emigrant traitor Cadoudal, replied he had.

"Asked whether he had resisted the police in the execution of their duty on Biville cliff and in the rue Langrais, replied he had.

"Asked whether he had formed with other proscribed

persons, including the said Cadoudal, the plan of assassinating the First Consul, replied that he had not done so, that he was no assassin in fact or in intention.

"Asked whether he had broken by force and with arms in hand into the house of Mme Louis Bonaparte at a time when the First Consul was in that house, the accused did not reply."

"But he was found there," said the President in wondering tones. He turned towards the prisoner. "You were found in that house?"

"Yes, General."

"You admit that?"

"I do admit it."

"Do you not admit the forced entry into that house?"

The Captain-Recorder looked from one to the other, reliving the sense of mystery he had felt when he had seen the Vicomte in the cell. Alone of those in court he knew the truth of the circumstances in which the prisoner had been captured, but this knowledge was not helping him to understand the Vicomte's present actions. The man had *not* broken in. He had been admitted by a woman for services rendered or to be rendered in her bed, or in Mme Louis' bed—it made no odds. Here was the deadly charge of attempted assassination and here was the answer to it, the kind of sentimental answer that might sweep the President away, for Murat had blundered badly in putting such a dotard on a court. Yet the young man was dumb. One could only suppose—for the Captain-Recorder's was a "supposing" mind, one of those that always ferret out an interest—one could only suppose that the accused had been promised his life by Bonaparte in return for being discreet. That the Vicomte was obeying an honourable impulse would have struck him as in the last degree fanciful. It must be some deal with Bonaparte. He became quite certain of this when he heard the prisoner's voice admitting what he had only ignored before:

"It's true, General. I may as well tell you now in open court. I made a forced entry to the house."

"You agree to that now?" said the President, delighted to discover that his intervention had actually been of use. "That completes the admissions, does it not?"

"Except in respect of the attempted assassination charge," the Captain-Reporter reminded him.

"Ah yes, the attempted assassination charge. There was a denial there."

"Perhaps the accused would like to amend that also?" came the voice of Colonel Mordan. "It would regularize matters, and shorten them too."

A cheerfully brutal laugh from the moustachioed Major greeted this sally. Mordan quelled it with a glance, for he had much of that quality that had made Fouquier-Tinville such an ornament of the Terror—he understood the relationship of time to justice, and knew that the one wasted with the other.

"Do you wish to amend your answer?" asked the President.

The Vicomte rose from his chair.

"Never. How can you think such a thing of me? I am a soldier and a man like yourselves."

The members of the court were variously affected by this declaration that fell with the uncomfortable ring of truth. The President nodded. He saw that the young man was indeed a soldier and a man of honour. He would have liked to have clapped him on the back and drunk a glass of wine with him, but since he had been put up there to convict the man, it was at least a comfort to know that he was of the right material and would die decently. One could not expect the more junior officers to be so convinced of the solace of a soldier's death; as for the Captain-General and Mordan, they plainly doubted their affinity with a prisoner who had got himself at the wrong end of a firing squad.

"He appears to be repeating his denial," the Colonel said.

"I deny it utterly."

"This is the position, then," continued Mordan. "The prisoner admits to taking his orders from Artois, admits to association with Cadoudal, a notorious assassin and brigand, admits to entering by force a house where he knew the First Consul to be, admits having arms in his hands, and then asks us to believe his sentiments were as our sentiments. Does he take us for assassins?" The members of the court, except the President, echoed the question—five pairs of eyes turned on the prisoner, bright with offended rectitude. "Let me ask this: If he did not break into the house to kill the First Consul, what brought him there at all?"

His colleagues, remembering the light reputation of Hortense, held their breath and waited, expecting some claim to fornication at the least. From every point of view it seemed the only possible defence, and beneath the fear they all felt at having stirred up a hornet's nest was a pleasantly salacious welcome for the details that might emerge.

But the Vicomte did not hesitate.

"I broke in to see Bonaparte, not to kill him."

"Ah, to see him!" said Mordan, and his sigh of relief was barely audible. "And you must see him, of course, with a sword in your hand and a pistol in your belt?"

"I have the right to carry arms."

"A right, had you? May I suggest that you had not even the right to be in France? That's by the way. You were armed as I have described. To see him?"

"Yes."

"And Cadoudal and the other bandits waiting outside the door, were they there to see him too? Never were so many rascals gathered together since the robbery of the Lyons mail."

"Is that a question?"

"Answer," the President commanded.

"Very well, I didn't know those men were there."

"But they were your friends?" suggested Mordan.

"Yes."

"You'd lived with them for months?"

"Yes."

"And now you tell us that they came there, to that same house at the same time, unknown to you?"

"I'm telling you that."

"Why had they come?"

The Vicomte did not reply.

"They were armed, I take it?"

"Yes."

"Swords and pistols?"

"I suppose so."

"And they had brought this arsenal, of course, for a private talk with Bonaparte?"

"I tell you. I don't know," the prisoner cried.

"But you knew they were there?"

"I heard them."

"And is it true to say that at the moment you were arrested you were in the act of opening the door and admitting these brigands to the house?"

The Vicomte's face was flushed.

"No, no, I was in the act of closing it."

"Of closing it!" cried Mordan, and he looked round at his colleagues with so quizzical an expression that the

Major had to pay him the tribute of a great guffaw of laughter that rolled up to the rafters.

"Come, you are not telling us that, surely?" said the President, saddened by his subordinate's triumph and by the answers of the accused. "You admit the door was open. You admit your friends were there. And then you tell us that you shut them out!" There was no answer, and he continued in a gentle, chiding voice: "You would do better to tell the truth."

The Vicomte hesitated and looked around him. He would have liked to tell the whole story, if he could have done so without fear of consequences to third parties—the agreement with Cadoudal, the shock of the betrayal, the honourable impulse that had moved him to slam the door. One glance at the face of Mordan was sufficient to remind him that so much candour was unwise, and he began to speak, in rather halting tones, as though he suspected that truth is one of the few things that will not admit of compromise.

"There's something I should tell you."

"Yes?" the General said.

"I said in answer to that gentleman"—with a curt nod towards Mordan—"that I didn't know those men were there. That was true. I was not expecting them. I was expecting one man—Cadoudal."

There was a stir of interest in the court, and the Vicomte added:

"We'd agreed to go together to Bonaparte, the two of us as ambassadors of the King."

"Ambassadors!" cried Mordan, so delighted with the word and the picture it conjured up that he forgot his sense of urgency. "Here we have a new kind of protocol. Ah, my friend, you should have added Dubosq to your embassy to perfect it!"

At this reference to the notorious criminal and king of the Parisian underworld, even the President smiled. "Perhaps he was outside among the army of embassy retainers," was the Major's contribution, which not only provided its maker with his loudest laugh yet but also gave Mordan another text:

"Yes, what about these supporters in the street? Will the accused explain them?"

"Certainly. They were not part of the agreement. I think Georges must have brought them to guard against surprise."

"And not as assistant murderers, of course!"

The Vicomte said with an indignation that sounded false even in his own ears:

"They are no more assassins than I am."

"We must be grateful," came the voice of Mordan, "that we have a standard by which to judge them now. What is the prisoner doing? Accusing his friends? Or convicting himself?"

"I am trying to tell the truth."

"Then tell us," said the Colonel with a sudden pounce, "why you shut the door."

The Vicomte knew that he was trapped. He threw up his head.

"Because I was afraid of their impulses. They hadn't *come* to kill him. But I was afraid they might."

"Can you explain that sophistry?" the Colonel asked.

"Is it sophistry to try to distinguish between actions and intentions?"

"In your case, and from the legal point of view, it is simplicity."

"And do you imagine," the prisoner cried, "that I'm foolish enough to think that anything I say will weigh with you?"

This outburst, however natural, had an unfortunate effect. It takes injustice of a cruder kind to accept its own true nature, and this court-martial, born of an order of the Military Governor of Paris out of a Consular decree, was very conscious of its legitimacy. To assume that such a court was biased was a rebuff to the President and an opportunity to Mordan.

"General President, that is an insult to this tribunal."

"It is," the President said, and he gazed at the prisoner as though on some insubordinate ensign at Jemappes or on the ridge of Valmy.

At that rebuke, the Vicomte was instantly contrite.

"I'm sorry. Believe me, General, I have never questioned your fairness to me."

"Is the prisoner distinguishing," demanded Mordan, "between the President and the court?"

"I am making no distinctions. Distinctions sometimes make themselves."

A flush had mounted in the Colonel's thin, fanatical face.

"That's another impropriety. The President is as much aware as I am that the court as a whole is trying this accused. He has insulted the court. Let him make his apology to it."

"I have said all that I'm going to say," the prisoner declared.

"You have said too much," the President reproved him, driven by a sense of corporate loyalty in the opposite direction from his heart. "Captain Ricard."

The Captain-Reporter, glaring his solidarity at the prisoner, rose to his feet.

"Captain Ricard, have you further matter for report?"

"No, General President."

"Then let the witnesses be called."

"One moment," interrupted Mordan. "Do the witnesses include associates of the accused with personal knowledge of his motive?" The Captain-Reporter shook his head. "Then it's unnecessary to call them. The prisoner has admitted out of his own mouth every detail of the charges, with one exception. We have heard his version of events in the rue Victoire." A wintry expression passed over the speaker's face and he commented: "We shall know what to think of that. I ask the President if there is anything that need be added to what the accused has said, and whether time must be wasted in proving what the man himself does not deny?"

"It's true that the accused has made admissions," said the President unhappily. He was looking at the young man rather as though he expected him to round off the good work by admitting the justice and good sense of Mordan's last remarks, and seemed so uncomfortable with this legal problem that had sprung out at him from ambush that the Vicomte was tempted to oblige. "They were very full admissions," the good man went on—"comprehensive, I might say. I ask myself," he added with an expression that in fact asked everybody, "whether I am entitled to accept them in the form of proofs."

"What better proofs?" the Captain-Reporter said.

The President seized on this gratefully. "I have considered the matter, and I find there is no need for further witnesses," he announced at last, discovering a rich vein of decision in himself. "Except for the accused's own witnesses, of course." He turned to the Vicomte. "Have you witnesses?"

"None, General."

"Have you no one to speak for you?"

"No one."

"Then will you not speak for yourself?"

The prisoner shrugged his shoulders.

"What is there to say?"

"You might express remorse and detestation of your crimes," the Colonel said.

"I feel no remorse. I have committed no crimes." He looked up at the scandalized faces of his judges. "I am no more than a soldier who failed. If you had been royalist and not Bonapartist, you would have acted as I acted. I failed. I accept the necessity for this court and my own death. I ask you to believe one thing." Here the Vicomte, whose glance had ranged along the court, turned to the President and spoke directly to him. "I never intended to kill Bonaparte. That is the truth."

I believe you, was the message of the President's eyes, for all his chivalrous nature was called out by this appeal to the decencies by which he ruled his life. Soldiers fought hard but honourably. No soldier would do a defenceless man to death—and it was with the most painful sensation that he remembered that this was precisely what he was about to do himself.

He asked abruptly:

"Have you anything more to say?"

How much the young man could have replied! He knew the farcical nature of the trial; he suspected the faults of procedure and, beyond them, the deficiencies in charges that could not in strict point of law be brought at all. But he had known from the beginning that such protests would be useless; he had made the only plea that counted in his heart.

So he shook his head.

"Have you nothing more to say?" asked the President again.

"Nothing."

"Then you will leave the room. Captain Ricard, inform the escort."

The prisoner, manacled once more, was led away. He was not taken to his cell, but merely down a short corridor to the *corps de garde*, eloquent proof in itself of his warders' opinion of the time that would be spent in reaching a satisfactory result.

Nor were they mistaken. Ten minutes had not passed before the Vicomte was once more in the presence of his judges, who rose to greet him, not so much in deference to death as in obedience to some quaint formality of the President's devising.

"Charles Bellac."

He bowed, the odd thought occurring to him that this might be the last time that he would hear his name.

"Charles Bellac, you have heard the charges of which you stand accused?"

"Yes."

"The court finds you Guilty of each and every one of them. The sentence of the court is that you be taken from here and shot within the period of a day."

## Chapter Thirty-two

THAT SAME EVENING THERE WAS TO BE a reception and ball at the Tuileries, and soon after darkness had fallen Hortense began one of the few rituals that kept their power to please her. As she took from the jewel-case the rope of pearls that Bonaparte had given her and held it against her throat, she was aware that her maid-of-honour had entered and was standing in the room behind her.

For a while she studied her covertly in the mirror, wondering that anguish of mind should be reflected so imperfectly in the body's actions. Nothing apparently had altered in the face or figure of this beautiful young woman, and yet she knew that everything was changed. It was touching to see the effort that had been made to show the world a mask of courage that the world, for its part, would be sure to label callousness.

"Diane," she said.

The maid-of-honour came forward till she was standing behind her mistress' chair.

"Diane, there's something I want to ask you." She was turning the pearls in her hand so that the light caught their sheeny surface and the gleam of the diamond clasp. "Are you blaming me?"

"Blaming you? For what?"

"For failing you. You've always seen how I was placed. But even you didn't understand that I'd count for nothing, that I'd be told nothing, not even the place of his imprisonment. Does it help you to be angry?"

The maid-of-honour, looking down into the glass that reflected her mistress' neck and shoulders and the brilliant silver of her gown, replied that she was not angry. She thought she must have no feelings. She was not even angry with herself.

"No feelings!" exclaimed her mistress. "That's your illusion, your deception. But is it a helpful one, Diane?"

"Why not? I love him. I can't bear to think where he may be." She added, wondering even as she spoke at her unkindness: "It's different for you."

Immediately Hortense became excited. Her mouth began to tremble and she cried out:

"Why different? Haven't I feelings? Wasn't he my friend? It's wrong to think that I don't care about his death."

"His death!"

Hortense at once realized her error and began to soothe and minimize. But in the highly charged atmosphere surrounding them Diane had seen that her mistress had some knowledge that she had not shared, and she immediately pursued her. "Why did you say that? Why? What do you mean? You know something. You *do* know something!" And she laid her hand on her friend's shoulder, gripping her so roughly that when she released her hold the pressure marks of her fingers showed as smudges on the powdered skin.

Hortense said slowly:

"He's alive."

"Alive! You knew that for certain and you kept it from me! Where is he?"

"In Vincennes."

"And you never told me! Why?"

"Diane, be reasonable. I only learnt of it this afternoon."

"But you've known all this time that we've been talking and you never spoke. Perhaps you never would have spoken. Only it slipped out."

"Yes."

"And now which of us is practising your 'deception'?" The anger faded from her voice as a sudden cold feeling touched her heart. "Or am I wronging you? Have you been trying in your own way to break bad news?"

Hortense looked up at her friend, who was watching her bright-eyed, as though imagining that her mistress knew the answers to these questions. But she did not know them. She was following an instinct that had led her to a decision by paths more deliberate than she could ever have supposed, and in a voice which she struggled to keep calm she disclosed that the Vicomte had been tried, condemned, that he was to die in the morning.

It had been said. She tried to look away, but found in spite of herself that she was drawn back to the mirror and to the white face of Diane reflected there with a dreadful stillness. There was no sound in the room except the rustle of the pearls, which Hortense had clasped together and covered with her hand. There! she thought, I've told her— and suddenly some inner voice that she could neither control nor understand was whispering: "Why doesn't she cry out? Why doesn't she weep? Tears are comforters," though she knew that it was not only for this that she expected them but as decencies that were due. At this moment she was moved by genuine emotion both for the Vicomte and for the friend she loved, but it was as a ritualist that she judged. The girl had not moved, the eyes were reflected in the glass, bright and expressionless as a bird's. She longed to call out to her some message of hope, some conventional untruth that she supposed might be of comfort, but she was repelled by this detachment. She thought to herself, I care more, this thing means more to me, and then, as she returned to that white face of the sleepwalker awakening to a reality more terrible than the dream, she was suddenly given back her understanding.

"Condemned!"

Hortense caught the inflection in the voice, and filled with compassion, opened her arms wide to receive her friend. She expected tears, reproaches, the abandon of despair. But it was her fate that day to lag behind emotions. Before she could touch Diane or express the love and tenderness rising in her heart, she saw that the girl had changed —inexplicably—to one who lived for sentiment and could not see how grief had been only a moment in the act of awakening, before the will to save and live could shape it to a plan. She drew back, shocked by the vigorous words she heard—"Then you must appeal to Bonaparte." At other times she might have smiled at that suggestion and its tone; now she felt its unsuitability, the reflection on herself, and replied in a reproachful voice: "So simple! How little you know of him! And you imagine I haven't tried. How little you know of me!"

With another quick change of mood, Diane had dropped on her knees beside her mistress.

"You did that!"

"Naturally. At the Tuileries this afternoon."

"I should have known it. And he listened?"

"No, Diane."

The girl moved nearer, a frown on her face, as though she had not fully understood.

"But it's so little to ask. You've done so much for him and asked so little. How could he have refused?"

"My dear, how can I answer?"

"But he *did* refuse?"

"I've told you."

"Yes, but why? What can you have said to him?" Hortense drew herself up with a gesture of pathetic dignity. "Or what can you have failed to say?"

"Diane!"

"Well, you did fail. You've told me. So I was right. You must go to Bonaparte again."

Hortense had risen from her chair. Her training made it hard for her to forget, even at this moment, the claims of etiquette and this gross breach of them. "When you talk like that," she said, "what makes you imagine I shall listen?"

"Because there's a life at stake." The maid-of-honour paused and added in a softer voice: "And because you love him."

In the silence that had fallen the two women looked at one another, seeing between them the ghost they had both hoped to exorcize.

"You think I love Charles?" the mistress said at last.

"You've always loved him."

She gave a sigh that was barely audible even in that silent room. "How long have you known that?"

"From the beginning. From the time of your first denial."

"And you will believe it," Hortense said, "until my last." She reached out and took her friend's hands in hers. "Per-

haps you're right, Diane. We're companions in misfortune.
So I will go to Bonaparte again."

But that evening in the Tuileries she was to find that the
First Consul was not easily approached; he was already
swaddled like royalty in a protective blanket of guards and
servants—Constant at his bedside, Rustam, the Arab servant, at the door, Duroc in the antechamber, and the polite
M. de Rémusat in the drawing-room beyond. She saw that
each day by a piece of lace here, a new embroidery there, a
new dress sword, a cambric handkerchief or a buckled shoe,
the Court crept nearer to the tabernacle that the Revolution had overthrown; with every day the attendants looked
more like royal chamberlains, the generals ducal marshals,
her relatives Royal Highnesses, and knowing this, she found
it hard to blame her stepfather for feeling the Emperor
stirring in his heart. Destiny called to him that evening
from every member of the Consular procession forming up
in rigid order of blood and pride; it called to him from the
ranks that lined the walls of the great salon beyond the
double doors, the murmur of whose voices rose about them
as sibilant and restless as the sea.

As the First Consul took his place and the doors were
opened her gaze swept down the lines of the courtiers—
judges, savants, churchmen, financiers, soldiers, diplomats
—a sheen of faces that swayed towards her like a cornfield
before the wind. A morbid instinct was at work in her as
they advanced under the brilliant light of the chandeliers
down the lane of lowered heads. She looked around, seeing
here and there among the servants of his greatness the men
she distrusted: the Gascon Bernadotte, Augereau, the
young Marmont, Murat, Governor of Paris, the agents of
his fall; right in front limped the Foreign Minister, each
step a kind of herald of betrayal; her mother was in the

rank ahead; Louis Bonaparte, recalled from Compiègne for the occasion, was by her side; she could glimpse Morillac in the background among the minor aides; and there at the end of the room, almost in the shadow, standing where he had stood so often in the days of his disgrace, Fouché, Minister of Police.

Slowly the procession bore down towards him. But she was conscious that though it moved already in the majesty of an imperial gait, receiving tribute at every step, it did not avoid the appearance of coming as an embassy to that distant figure that awaited it with so much calm—a figure alone no longer, but around which the courtiers swarmed like true believers near the coffin of a Moslem saint.

There were few smiles this time, she noted, even for her mother, none for her husband or herself, not so much as a nod for poor Cambacérès as he hawked his pomposity along; a breathless air of expectation had settled on the room, and the eyes of everyone were on this encounter between two men, the shape of which would show, for days and perhaps for years to come, what kind of obsequiousness would be in fashion—and to whom. Here was an event of supreme importance—the birth of a new hierarchy in the courtiers' heaven—and as the protagonists came together, as the First Consul smiled and nodded and the Minister bowed his emaciated frame, she knew that the poor asteroids would sense at once the power of this new attraction, the orbit they must follow round sun and planet.

The procession was moving on, and she herself was now abreast of the Senator and staring at him like so many others in the room; she did this because she knew that she was personally unimportant to him; he would no more feel her curiosity than he would that of the courtiers who with a touching naïveté pressed around him in a fury to be recognized. Often she had passed him: he had hardly ever spared a glance for her. But this time, as she discovered with a sudden shock, it was different: he was staring back at her, the most peculiar expression in those hooded eyes—why, almost like a gallant who had used her and found her an agreeable, if somewhat unhandy instrument of love.

Quickly she glanced away, shocked by a fancy that must have sprung from her own brain and not from that of Fouché, whom not even his friends accused of gallantry. But as they turned and began the slow progression up the room she was aware that he was looking at her still, paying her the tribute of an amused gratitude that brought the blood rushing to her cheeks, so that from all sides glances turned towards her, hot, admiring ones, and she was back again at Saint-Cloud or Malmaison in the days before her marriage, when everyone had had to take account of her— even Bonaparte, who now stalked towards the doors of the salon, a lonely, unapproachable figure moving through the court. She would see her stepfather. It was her right. He should not treat her as a person of no consequence. But as they reached the corridor and she pressed close to him to catch his eye, she saw him turn with Duroc towards the study, ignoring the sound of violins tuning in the ballroom and the importunities of his wife and sisters, who responded like lovers to a serenade.

In her moment of need there was no help to be got from any of them, even from Josephine, who in the days of Barras had been a force in politics, but was now just good humour and a charming body that could wring a bedroom concession from her husband now and then—a bracelet, the payment of her debts, the dismissal of a too voluptuous and too obliging *fille de chambre*. Her own weapons were the better, she told herself, taking care not to specify, even in her own mind, exactly what they were, but to use them she must reach her stepfather, who, in his sanctum, protected by Duroc and Méneval, was no more accessible than the Minotaur.

Slowly she followed down the passage, hearing the beat of the music from the distant ballroom like a clock ticking off the hours. It was long past midnight: in these March days it would be light soon after six. She told herself that if he did not emerge within the hour she would force her way in to him, knowing, even as the thought arose, that she would never do so, no matter what her heart might will or her mind imagine.

What should she do, then? She began to pace the corridor, the prey of the most agitated thoughts, angry with herself for her cowardice, and with Diane for a perception that was made all the more impertinent by its truth. What had she to do with love? What satisfaction had she received in her life in return for those sentiments that the world wished on her—an assumed guilty feeling for one man, an assumed affection for another that verged on the simple, never mind the innocent? And what obligation did she owe the Vicomte, whose life she had helped to save years before and for whom she had pleaded that very afternoon? He had come to France unknown to her; he had remained in defiance of her advice. For one thing only she did not blame him—the conquest of her maid-of-honour, which her heart, though not her reason, knew was the most blameworthy of all. So much might be forgiven, but she fought with all her strength against the knowledge that in failure she would be responsible for his death. It was unfair, illogical, yet with every minute that passed, with every glance at the door of the First Consul's room, the knowledge grew more certain. A life was in her hands and she was pleading resentments—fine arguments to cover a betrayal.

Far off a clock struck two. She began to walk more quickly, trying to overcome those feelings that kept her from the bold actions of passing the guards at the door and entering the room—not so much fear as the unquestioning obedience of a lifetime. No one had the entrée, not Josephine, not even Talleyrand. Less than an hour had passed. She would wait a little longer, she told herself, for it would take very little time to reach Vincennes, and in the train of that she imagined the young man's reactions when he had the pardon in his hands, recalling herself only by degrees to the remembrance of the First Consul's words that afternoon, his abruptness, his refusal to listen. Feverishly she began to rehearse what she would say, eloquence rising in her at the sight of that door shut against her, never perhaps to be opened the whole night through—and then, as though by magic, a light shone out, there came the sound of voices, and there was Bonaparte, arm-in-arm with Duroc, coming towards her at his brisk gunner's step.

Her heart gave a sudden leap, all her plans and arguments abandoned her, and she shrank back against the wall, a small, dim figure hardly to be distinguished in the shadows between the lamps. He might have passed. But Duroc, in whom the policeman never slept, concerned himself with all those who wandered in the Tuileries by night. "Well, Duroc?" came the First Consul's voice. Less fearful of possible assassination than his aide-de-camp, scenting some adventure, he had followed and now came up behind him. He had done with business, Josephine would be in the ballroom, and he was not unaware that there were in the entourage of his sisters maids-of-honour who had still to make their fortunes—"Eh, Duroc, what have we here?" —for there was in particular a young woman of Pauline's of whom anything, and everything, might be expected. Another step, and that dream faded. "Ah, my dear, it's you!" The eagerness, and at the same time the harshness, had left his voice, and he asked gently: "Why are you not dancing? Why are you all alone?"

Duroc had stepped back from them, and she was able to whisper that she must see him—now, at once. For a moment she thought he would refuse her; a frown appeared between the eyes and he began to tap his nails against his snuffbox; but just as she had made up her mind to some desperate appeal, he took her by the arm and without a word marched her inside the office and shut the door.

"Well?" he demanded. "What is it?" the note of impatience sounding clearly in his voice. He cared more for his stepdaughter than for anyone in the world, but he could not always support these fine emotions; there were times when he felt the need for relaxation, for a woman of the kind that was in Pauline's household, a woman who would be at once eager and submissive, someone understanding and passionate and young.

How different was his stepdaughter, standing now just inside the door and watching him with troubled eyes! "What is it?" he repeated, listening to the distant beat of the music that had passed him by during his conference with Duroc, hearing with irritation her reply: "I've a favour to ask you." Tap, tap went his finger on the lid of the snuffbox. His thoughts had been occupied with a favour he would receive. "Yes," he prompted, "yes, go on." She looked at him piteously, struggling to find words to move him. She could think of no approach but the direct one and faltered out: "Be merciful to that poor man in Vincennes."

He was looking at her in amazement.

"But this is an argument we've had before!"

"Yes."

"I gave you my answer this afternoon. Wasn't it clear?"

"Yes."

"Well then, accept it. Don't trouble me with such things. Don't trouble yourself with them; they don't concern you."

"But they do."

He looked at her. And suddenly his disappointment, his irritation at the meddling of his family in State affairs, even in some strange way his love for her, surged up in him; his face went white and he burst out:

"*You* are asking me this! It's thanks to you and your connection with this man that I've been humiliated; it's thanks to you that I've been held to ransom. Would it surprise you that that rascal Fouché knew where Bellac was arrested; that he was prepared to make it public; that he would have denounced you as the man's mistress and collaborator? And *you* must plead for him!"

He might have looked for many reactions to this onslaught—obedience, tears, or a wave of hysterical grief which he came increasingly to expect of the women who surrounded him: the one thing he had not counted on was the sudden light of an idea giving purpose—bewildering purpose—to that gentle, acquiescent face. He saw it, and his anger rose to greater heights, fanned by the rebelliousness in her that he could sense but could not understand. His voice became coarse and strident as he thrust the compromising images at her:

"What do you expect? Were you brought up in a nunnery? A man is found in your house, and do you imagine that the world, when it's told, won't translate him to your bed?"

"Does Fouché threaten that?"

"He threatened it. Are you a simpleton? He threatened your chastity and, through you, my regime." The tone of the *commerçant* sounded in his voice. "Well, I bought it back for you—with the Ministry of Police."

She was looking at him steadily.

"A high price—higher than I shall ask," she said. At these words, more astonishing than any that his Minister had used, an expression of stupefaction showed in his face. Somehow the humour of it gave her courage, and she added in a tone so firm that it surprised her: "I shall ask only for his life."

"*You* will ask for it!"

"Yes, and you will give it. Or I shall denounce myself."

Silence fell between them. He no longer raved; he had all the virtues of the realist, and disaster always brought out in him a tactical sense that was part of his flesh and blood. To her amazement she saw him smile; he moved towards her and, taking one of her ears between his fingers, he gently pinched it in that gesture of affection which in normal times he reserved for his soldiers, the most biddable of his dupes.

"Ah, you would do that, little one?" he said. She was not moved from her purpose, but continued to look at him with the same determination. "You would ruin yourself?"

"Yes."

"You would ruin me. You know that we stand at the beginning of greater things?"

"I know it."

"Yet you would do all that for this man!" He added, the bitterness creeping back into his voice: "You will tell me he was not your lover. And I shall believe you. I shall sign the pardon. There is really no end to the subtlety of women and the simplicity of men."

# Chapter Thirty-three

OUTSIDE IN THE GREAT SALON THE ball was at its height: the light from the chandeliers shone down on the uniforms of the men, brilliant points of colour against the background of crystal and mirrors and the flowing white dresses of the ladies as they moved in the pattern of the dance. The whole world of the Tuileries was there: the elderly and cynical watching from the walls; fashion more energetically employed, turning its mirror towards its centre where Josephine and the ravishing Caroline and Pauline danced and the First Consul himself, in his gorgeous coat, could be seen marching to the unfamiliar steps with all the suppleness of a Guardsman at Potsdam. Over all rose the pervasive smell of wax and perfume and the throbbing rhythm of the violins that spun this wheel of elegance on its way.

Down near the doors, at the end of the line and far from the elect, Diane was dancing: she had seen Hortense, she knew of the First Consul's clemency, and she found in the surge of the music the response to the overflowing feelings of her heart. Her lover was safe. In a few hours she would see him. The music would play, the candles would gutter in their sockets, and soon the attendants would draw the great curtains and the light of the sun would pour into the room—the day of their reunion. As these thoughts took possession of her she closed her eyes, surrendering herself rapturously to the music that bore her up on a wave of tenderness, forgetful of time and place and remembering only that he was alive, that they loved one another, that she was glad. Dimly, from the world far away, she knew that eyes were watching her, desirous, envious, amused; she saw them as she danced, a whirl of anonymous faces flying past, and one in the distance to which her gaze, attracted by some quality of stillness, returned with every circle of the wheel —the cold, expressionless features of the Minister of Police.

When the music ended he made a faint, almost imperceptible movement of the hand.

She ignored it. She suspected that he was part author of their misfortunes; she feared him as an intriguer; she detested him as a man and even imagined a certain gallantry —so greatly did she misjudge him. The movement was repeated; it was certainly directed at her; she could see it from the corner of her eye; and moving into an alcove by a window, she turned her back on him to watch something a great deal more agreeable—the First Consul regarding, not without trepidation, the jewellery of Josephine, as though he suspected—and rightly—that the bills would be presented in the morning. It was a shock to her when she heard a voice speak at her shoulder:

"Mademoiselle."

She turned. There was Fouché, bowing with that grim suggestion of a skeleton in Court dress.

"Please forgive me." He must have seen that she was preparing to rebuff him, for he said in his most winning voice with a backward glance towards the place-seekers who had surrounded him: "Do me the honour of being a courtier for a little while." She did not respond or seem even to understand, and he explained blandly: "Tolerate my company, at least. You'll find that we have this in common, that tonight we are both restored. Yes, I am restored to office, and you— to happiness."

"I am happy."

"The whole world can see it. Allow me to congratulate you. I know, you see—and I rejoice in it—that the First Consul has pardoned your friend and that the pardon has been sent by courier to Vincennes." He added, looking at her fixedly with his sea-green eyes: "One only wonders when precisely it will get there."

She started back from him with terror in her face.

"You have not asked yourself that?" said the Minister, watching her with an interest that was not without compassion. "It did occur to me as I saw you dance that it was a topic you had overlooked."

He could see that her distrust of him still struggled with her instinct of truth, for she replied:

"Why should I ask it? The pardon was granted."

"Yes, it was granted."

"And it was sent to the château."

"Oh yes, by the official courier."

"There! And do you expect me to believe that he will have taken three hours to reach Vincennes?"

"It's possible," the Minister said.

"No, it is *not* possible. You're choosing to amuse yourself."

"You think so?"

"What else? Why should the courier be late?" A sudden thought struck her and the look of terror returned to her face. "Unless orders were given that he should be."

"Ah, you are acute," said the Minister admiringly.

"You mean that Bonaparte . . . !" The thought was too terrible to be borne and she cried out: "Never! Never! He would never do it!"

"Still more acute. The First Consul has his weaknesses, even his meannesses, but not of that order. I can assure you that he meant the Vicomte to be saved. But consider this. He was in a hurry—some business, some adventure. He signed the pardon. He gave it, for transmission to the courier, to his brother Louis who happened to be by. And Louis, my dear mademoiselle, in his turn gave it—to Morillac."

A terrible cry came from Diane.

The Senator, watching her with the detachment of a man of science, found to his surprise that he had reached out a hand to touch her arm. "Courage, courage! I have depended on you." He added in a rather grumbling tone: "It's like a woman to assume extremes. You rejoice—he is safe. You despair—he is lost. Believe me, truth is never in extremes."

Her face, almost a caricature of the beauty he had seen and admired a few brief moments before, was raised to his.

"You can say that, but you know he's lost. Morillac hates him."

"So I am told," said Fouché drily.

"And you know he will revenge himself and hold the pardon back till after dawn."

"Undoubtedly. So *you* will have to take it."

"What are you saying?"

"That you will take my coach," said the Senator, looking away from her for the first time, for such acts of sentiment affected him with a most profound embarrassment. "You will also take this order to the Commandant, who is an associate of mine. He will release the Vicomte. Oh, don't concern yourself. It is quite legal, for after a suitable interval—say at nine o'clock—the good Morillac is sure to arrive and regularize matters agreeably for us all. No, don't ask questions." He drew back a corner of the curtain. "It's late. You haven't time. Don't ask me why I do this"—for he could see the gratitude in her eyes and wished to spare himself a confession of motives that were far too much like weaknesses. The girl was beautiful, the young man was brave, they had amused him vastly. After all, he thought, as she turned from him with a glance that touched his heart —after all, the Vicomte was a royalist and influential, and one day the Bourbons might return: thus self-interest put its head out and his *amour propre* was saved.

It was all too true, though, that she had little time, for not ten minutes since—over an hour after the event—he had heard of the choice of messenger. She had a chance. The coach was in readiness; the firing squad at the fortress needed light. He drew back the curtain again and peered out through the panes, seeing the moving figures of the dancers and the sparkle of the chandeliers beyond the silhouette of his own body and the hand he had raised to shield his eyes. Pitch darkness still.

But Diane, coming into the courtyard of the Tuileries, could see what he could not—the faint glow on the eastern horizon, that pallor of starlight that precedes dawn, day not so much advancing as night retreating like a servant who knows his place. Within an hour the sun would have risen, coming up with no clouds to hide him directly in her path. Long before then they would be stirring in the castle. She could see the picture in its drab shades of grey—the battlements rising against the sky, the file of soldiers drawn up in the moat on the tufted grass. But except in the east it was still dark—streets, houses, trees, sensed more than seen around her, contrasting with the glittering lights of the palace she had left. Dawn would come slowly. She rememered that other morning when Charles had climbed to her room, the gradual shading of the light from the time of their parting at the window till the rays of the sun had shone on the body of Morillac. It was natural she should think of that and of her enemy, now somewhere in the darkness ahead, a force she had accepted as so much a part of her that it had not been surprise that had moved her at Fouché's words but the breathless recognition of her destiny.

Now under the drive of action her courage was returning. There was such purpose in the drumming sound of hooves, the crack of the driver's whip, the swaying of the great coach as it hastened on its way past the walls of the Louvre, the towers of Notre-Dame, seen dimly rising beyond the river mist, and that bare plot of land, Bastille, only the name remaining as an epitaph to tyranny. Around them was a different Paris from the one she knew—a city of mean streets and houses whose outlines gradually detached themselves from the darkness, the quarter of the Revolution, the faubourg Saint-Antoine. Here it seemed to her that the clatter of their passing redoubled, echoing between the enclosing walls, the crack of the whip was more insistent as the horses began to labour against the camber of the road, and she could only comfort herself with the thought that more than half the distance had been travelled and the night still lay over Paris, a curtain withdrawn with infinite slowness.

Place Saint-Antoine, rue du faubourg Saint-Antoine; ahead lay the eastern outskirts closed by the Barrière de Vincennes; then a belt of forest no wider than the distance between the Tuileries gardens and the Hôtel de Ville; why, the whole journey was no longer than the ride she had made so often with her mistress to Saint-Cloud, the merest step that hardly gave one time to regret the jewels and hair-styles one had chosen for the night.

But morning also was advancing, though she did not recognize it till the carriage slowed down for the barrier, and leaning from the window, she caught a glimpse of walls silhouetted with terrifying clarity against the glow of colour in the east. A gentle light was shining down the rides of the forest as the coach passed the old fortifications of the city and began to move forward beneath the trees, dawn seeming to draw on more quickly in this space open to the sky, though still a laggard behind the sounds of the morning—the movement of small creatures in the undergrowth, the incorrigible bustle of the birds. She could deceive herself no longer, for with every minute the scene through the windows disclosed itself more clearly, colour returning to the world in pastel shades—the gun-metal of trees whose branches raised a tracery as delicate as that of the master of Amboise, the powder-blue of the sky, the undertones of bracken, and the mould of autumn leaves. Ahead of her the road stretched out, grey and ghostly, bordered on the right by a screen of woods; suddenly this drew back towards the south and there ahead, astonishingly close, the walls of the fortress rose in jagged line, the towers touched already by the first faint gilding of the sun.

At that sight her self-control gave way and terror caught her by the throat. Why, it was light! There was light enough to see every detail of the façade and western gate and even the sentry by the barbican, a small, shapeless figure against the towering walls. The coach was slowing; she could hear the sentry's voice raised above the scrabble of hooves and the grating of the brake—"Halt there! Halt! I say." A grumbling, disembodied voice came from above her, and then, distinctly, the reply: "I don't care whose coach. For no one passes."

She peered through the window. There was the man moving towards them past the traces, the musket levelled in the parade of a threat at the coachman on the box. But when she pleaded it was only to meet his invincible good humour —"Don't you worry. It won't be long. It's just some aristo they're shooting." He was alongside now and she could see his pig's eyes smiling their appreciation of the petulance of ladies' ways. "You're best here. You wouldn't like it. They'll have got him in the moat."

No sooner had he spoken than all her fears were gone; she was conscious only of a purpose that left no room for any other feeling in her heart. She did not answer, she did not hesitate, but opening the door on the far side from the sentry, slipped to the ground and began to run towards the *corps de garde*. The voices continued to speak behind her and she was halfway up the ramp before the shot rang out —misread by her for one terrible flash of time, till looking stupidly down at her left hand, she saw the stain of blood.

Men came running. She saw them dimly, then, as the pain eased, with an unnatural, brilliant clarity—the sentry hurrying up the hill, an officer she did not recognize, then Councillor Réal, and behind him, at the far end of the bailey, a squad of soldiers with a bareheaded figure in their midst.

As they came up she held out Fouché's order like a talisman and smiled to herself at its effect, for it seemed to her only the briefest instant before she was in her lover's arms.